Cynthia Harrod-Eagles is the author of the contemporary Bill Slider Mystery series as well as the Morland Dynasty novels. Her passions are music, wine, horses, architecture and the English countryside.

Visit the author's website at www.cynthiaharrodeagles.com

Also in the *Dynasty* series:

The Poison Tree

Cynthia Harrod-Eagles

Sphere

An imprint of
Little, Brown Book Group
100 Victoria Embankment,
London EC4Y 0DY

An Hachette UK Company
www.hachette.co.uk

sphere

SPHERE

First published in Great Britain in 2002 by Little, Brown
This paperback edition published in 2003 by Time Warner Paperbacks
Reprinted 2004
Reprinted by Sphere in 2006, 2010

A CIP catalogue record for this book
is available from the British Library.

ISBN 978-0-7515-1246-5

Typeset in Plantin by Palimpsest Book Production Limited,
Polmont, Sterlingshire
Printed and bound in Great Britain by
Clays Ltd, St Ives plc

Papers used by Sphere are natural, renewable and
recyclable products sourced from well-managed forests and certified
in accordance with the rules of the Forest Stewardship Council.

Mixed Sources
Product group from well-managed
forests and other controlled sources
www.fsc.org Cert no. SGS-COC-004081
© 1996 Forest Stewardship Council
FSC

THE MONKLAND FAMILY

To Hannah with all my love

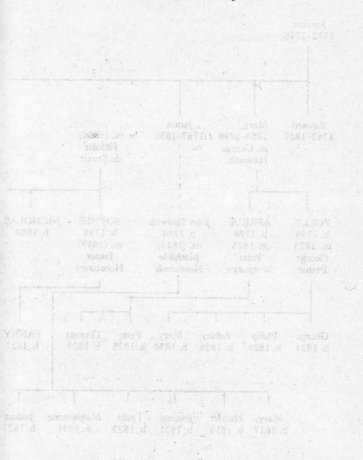

THE MORLAND FAMILY

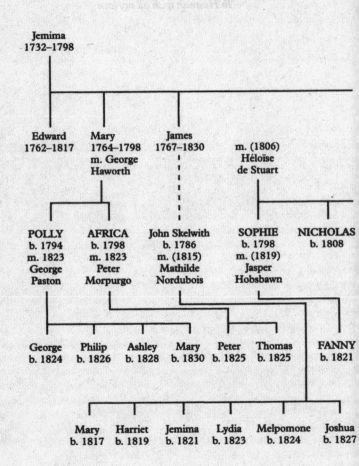

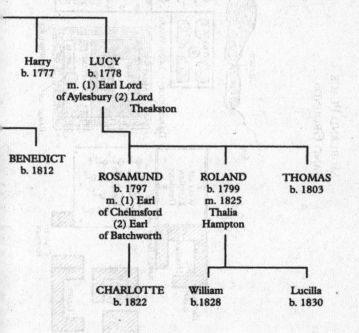

Harry
b. 1777

LUCY
b. 1778
m. (1) Earl Lord
of Aylesbury (2) Lord
Theakston

BENEDICT
b. 1812

ROSAMUND
b. 1797
m. (1) Earl
of Chelmsford
(2) Earl
of Batchworth

ROLAND
b. 1799
m. 1825
Thalia
Hampton

THOMAS
b. 1803

CHARLOTTE
b. 1822

William
b.1828

Lucilla
b. 1830

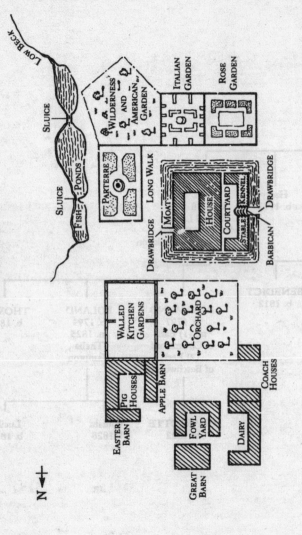

MORLAND PLACE AND GROUNDS

MORLAND PLACE IN 1830
GROUND FLOOR

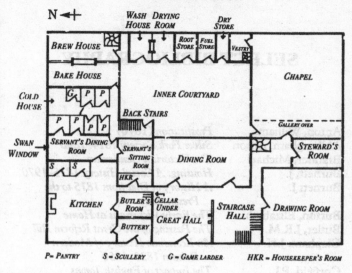

N

WASH HOUSE · DRYING ROOM · DRY STORE

BREW HOUSE

ROOT STORE · FUEL STORE · VESTRY

BAKE HOUSE

CHAPEL

COLD HOUSE

G · P · P

INNER COURTYARD

P · P · P

BACK STAIRS

GALLERY OVER

SWAN WINDOW

SERVANT'S DINING ROOM

SERVANT'S SITTING ROOM

DINING ROOM

STEWARD'S ROOM

HKR

KITCHEN

BUTLER'S ROOM

CELLAR UNDER GREAT HALL

STAIRCASE HALL

DRAWING ROOM

BUTTERY

P = PANTRY   S = SCULLERY   G = GAME LARDER   HKR = HOUSEKEEPER'S ROOM

FIRST FLOOR

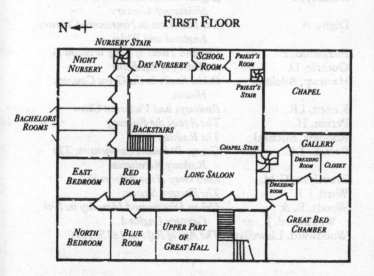

N

NURSERY STAIR

NIGHT NURSERY

DAY NURSERY

SCHOOL ROOM

PRIEST'S ROOM

PRIEST'S STAIR

CHAPEL

BACHELORS ROOMS

BACKSTAIRS

CHAPEL STAIR

GALLERY

DRESSING ROOM · CLOSET

EAST BEDROOM

RED ROOM

LONG SALOON

DRESSING ROOM

NORTH BEDROOM

BLUE ROOM

UPPER PART OF GREAT HALL

GREAT BED CHAMBER

SELECT BIBLIOGRAPHY

Anton, William	*Prostitution* (1870)
Aldburgham, Alison	*Silver Fork Society 1814–1840*
Brander, Michael	*The Victorian Gentleman*
Burnett, J.	*Housing: A Social History 1815–1970*
Burnett J.	*A History of Diet from 1815 to the Present Day*
Burton, Elizabeth	*The Early Victorians at Home*
Butler, J.R.M.	*The Passing of the Great Reform Bill*
Clapham, J.H.	*An Economic History of Modern Britain 1820–1850*
Corfield, P.J.	*The Impact of English Towns*
Dennis, R.	*English Industrial Cities of the Nineteenth Century*
Digby, A.	*The Poor Law in Nineteenth Century England and Wales*
Fitzgerald, P.	*Life and Times of King William IV*
Guthrie, D.	*A History of Medicine*
Hartcup, Adeline	*Below Stairs in the Great Country Houses*
Kellett, J.R.	*Railways and Victorian Cities*
Perkin, H.	*The Age of the Railway*
Robbins, Michael	*The Railway Age*
Rolt, L.T.C.	*George & Robert Stephenson: The Railway Revolution*
Trevelyan, G.M.	*Lord Grey of the Reform Bill*
Ward, J.T.	*The Factory System*
Woods, R. & Woodward, J.	*Urban Disease and Morality in 19th Century England*
Woodward, Llewellyn	*The Age of Reform 1815–1870*

BOOK ONE

The Journey

Even those I loved the best
Are strange – nay, they are stranger than the
rest.

John Clare: *Written in Northampton*
County Asylum

BOOK ONE

CHAPTER ONE

November, 1830

'Do you realise,' Benedict said, lifting himself on one elbow to look down at his mistress, 'that it's exactly two years since we met?'

'Is it so?' said Serena. 'But you shouldn't remind me, my dear. At my age the passing of years is not something to celebrate.'

Benedict sat up, ruffled. 'Oh, you talk such nonsense about your age, as though you were —'

'Past my prayers,' she finished for him. 'But the fact remains that I'm thirty-four and you're eighteen.'

'Nearly nineteen. I'll be nineteen in March.'

'Four whole months away!'

'Three,' he corrected seriously. 'My birthday's on the first of March.'

'Oh, to be young enough to count in months!' she teased. 'I remember when it seemed an eternity between birthdays. Now they come round only too soon.'

'But age doesn't matter,' Benedict said restlessly. He hated it when she distanced herself from him. 'If it mattered, we wouldn't be here together like this, would we?' He took a strand of her luxuriant red-gold hair between his fingers and turned it into a curl. 'With your hair loosened on the pillow like that, you look so beautiful. I swear anyone would think you were nineteen!'

'Foolish beyond permission!' She reached up to tug one of his vigorous dark curls in response. Though he was not exactly handsome, his face had the charm of youth and good humour. Everything about him seemed brimming with health and vigour. He was dark-haired, dark-eyed, brown-skinned as a gypsy from his outdoor life; a strongly-made, rather bull-necked young man, with fine teeth for his boyish smile, and fine, powerful hands that knew a man's business. She found him utterly irresistible. Every time he had come into her shop she had shivered with desire for him, which was why she had engineered the meeting at last, bumping into him in Micklegate and dropping her parcels so that he felt obliged to offer to carry them home for her. After that, the rest was easy. Benedict Morland already had a reputation for liking women.

'Two years,' she mused. 'Two years since I knocked you down in the street by way of beginning our acquaintance.'

'Lord, yes! You made me sit down in a puddle. How wet and cold it was inside my trousers!'

'But I wish you could have seen the expression on your face when I invited you into my house to get dry: propriety was battling with some most improper desires!'

'It was not!' Benedict said indignantly. 'I thought only of you: I was afraid I might compromise you.'

'I'm sure you thought I was a woman of easy virtue.'

'With a butler like Avis standing there holding the door? No-one could be more fearsomely respectable!'

'But my dear, respectable widows do not seduce young gentlemen half their age – particularly on first acquaintance. I must be a *harpy* at least, if not a *painted harlot*.'

His smile disappeared rapidly. 'Has someone said such a thing to you?'

'Young Mrs Cowey whispered the words to Mrs Percy Bolter in the doorway of Hargrove's Library yesterday. But they may have been talking about someone else, after all. It was probably mere coincidence that I was passing them at the time.'

'If anyone speaks ill of you, I'll kill them!' he said fiercely.

'Of course you'd like to,' she said sympathetically, 'and I love you for it, but it wouldn't change the facts.'

'The facts are that I love you and nothing else matters!' He looked down, biting his lip, and she knew what was coming next. 'Oh Serena,' he said passionately, 'why won't you marry

4

me? I've asked you often enough.'

She reached up and cupped his cheek. 'It wouldn't do, my love. I'm too old for you.'

He pulled away angrily. 'Age again! Why must you always go back to that?'

'Because in ten years' time you will be twenty-eight and still young, while I shall be forty-four and old. How would you get rid of me then, when you were tired of me and wanted someone younger?'

'I will never be tired of you,' he declared passionately.

'And never want anyone else?'

'Never, I swear!'

'Don't perjure yourself, my love. Haven't you already been casting eyes at a certain lady's maid from Clifton?'

He blushed too plainly to be able to deny it. 'How did you —? Oh – well, I – but that's nothing! I only *talked* to her. And it isn't love. I really do love you, you know.'

She sat up, drawing her hair round her like a shawl, modestly covering her breasts. They were fair and round and taut, and hiding them in that way had the opposite effect to the one intended on Benedict's attention.

'Bendy, listen to me,' she said. 'You are a young man, and full of the sap of life, and there will be many women before you settle for one and one only. When you do, I hope she will be handsome, accomplished, young, and very rich. By then I expect you will be far away from here, and if you think of me at all, it will be as a distant – and I hope pleasant – memory.'

'But I want to marry *you*,' he protested.

'It's not possible. Quite apart from the difference in our ages, I am not of your station in life. You are a gentleman: your family is one of the oldest and most distinguished in Yorkshire. I am only an artisan's daughter and a tradesman's widow.'

'Oh, that sort of thing's all nonsense! Not of my station? Who cares for that sort of thing nowadays?'

'I never took you for a Jacobin,' she said mildly. 'What would your mother say?'

He blushed. 'It isn't as if I'm the eldest son. Morland Place and everything else will go to Nicky. I shall have nothing.'

'Then how would you support a wife?' she asked gravely.

'Well, I don't think Mama has really thought about what's to be done with me. I ought to have a career, but I have the feeling that she expects me to stay at home and help Nicky with the estate. But if I married you I'd be provided for, and it wouldn't even cost her anything, as it would to send me into one of the professions —' He stopped anxiously as Serena put her hands over her face and made a choking noise; but the look of concern changed to one of annoyance as he realised she was not crying, but laughing. 'Now what have I said to set you off?' he asked indignantly.

'What a picture you paint!' she gasped. 'I am not quite of your order, of course, but I am very, very wealthy!'

'Well – yes, I suppose I did say that,' Bendy stammered, digging an ever deeper hole for himself. 'Not that you aren't of my order, of course, but – well – if I'm not to have a career —'

'Quite a reversal of the usual way of things, don't you think? In my young day, it was portionless girls who were married to rich old men to provide for them.'

He looked at her with dismay, not knowing how to make amends for his clumsiness.

'But Serena –' he began hesitantly, 'there's no denying that it does make a difference, your being wealthy.'

'Yes, it does. My wealth makes me independent. It means that I can do as I please, and go where I please, and even flout the conventions a little. It means I can live alone without having a tiresome lady-companion forever hanging about me – which in turn means that I can have you for my lover, my dear one,' she cupped his cheek, 'as long as we are discreet about it. So let's be grateful for what we have, and not make ourselves ridiculous by striving for more.'

She could see that she hadn't convinced him, and, in a way, she was glad. He was all youthful ardour, all chivalry, and she loved him for it, even though she knew perfectly well that it was not just for her, that he would be the same towards any woman he temporarily loved. Indeed, she loved him because of that very thing. There was something gentle and kindly about him – a lovingness at the bottom of everything he did, which itself attracted love.

'I have been very happy these two years,' she said. 'You

have given me more happiness than I dreamt possible.'

He took her hand and lifted her fingers to his lips. 'Whatever you say,' he vowed with conviction, 'I shall always love you.'

She left it at that, put her arms round his neck, and drew him down into a most satisfactory silence.

The weather had changed while he was in her house. When he emerged into Micklegate the sky had clouded over, the air was bitterly cold, and the numb greyness of the sky promised snow before long. Indeed, as he set off for Morland Place, the first fine flakes were just beginning to drift down. Fand, his dog, ran ahead of him, her head down, intent on getting home, only occasionally glancing back to be sure that he was still close behind. Benedict felt in his pocket for his gloves, then dropped the reins on Beau's neck while he searched two-handed. Beau put an enquiring ear back for a moment, wondering what was happening, then pointed them both homewards again and clopped steadily on. He was not the sort of horse to take advantage of a loose rein, which was one of the reasons Bendy loved him, and did not pine (or at least, not very much) for a younger, faster mount.

Not, of course, that he would have got one if he had pined, he thought. (No, the gloves were not in any of his pockets. He was sure he had put them there this morning. Could he have dropped them somewhere?) One might have thought, now that he was nearly nineteen – a man at least, if still a minor – that he would have been given a proper horse of his own. If Papa hadn't died the matter might have been adjusted by now; but Nicky was in charge of running the estate, and Nicky would not part with so much as a rotten potato if he could help it. He meant to have everything to himself.

Of course, everything really belonged to Mama, hers to bequeath wherever she wished (though there had never been any doubt that she would leave everything to Nicky, the eldest). The difficulty was that since Papa died she had withdrawn more and more into herself, taking no interest in anything but her memories. She worked all day on the History of the French Revolution which she had been writing haphazardly for as long as anyone could remember. She

7

seemed suddenly, for some reason, to be determined to finish it, and she spent her days poring over notes and letters, reading other people's histories, and talking to Father Moineau, their chaplain, about the olden days in France.

Any question put to her about the estate she simply referred to Nicky; Nicky, on the other hand, used her as an excuse to refuse to do anything he didn't want to do – like giving Bendy a horse of his own, for instance. 'It's not for me to make the decision,' Nicky would say smugly. 'You'll have to ask my mother.' When it was a matter of his own comfort, though – like moving his own horses into better and more convenient stables – Nicky gave orders like the Autocrat of Russia, and expected instant obedience.

Benedict checked these thoughts guiltily. Nicky was his brother: it was disloyal, and impious, to think so unkindly. He could be annoying and arrogant, but he was the eldest after all; and since he did not enjoy robust health, every allowance must be made for him. He had always been delicate, and Bendy thought it must be dreadful never to feel really well and full of energy.

In any case, it was just plain wrong to judge other people; and if one once allowed oneself to stray down the path of resentment, there was no knowing what awful things one might find oneself suspecting. Bendy had already had experience of that danger: he had found himself wondering about Nicky's actions on the day their father was killed, and had brought himself to such a pitch of anxiety that he had had to seek advice of their chaplain. Father Moineau had warned him gravely that unfounded suspicion of other people, even if one never voiced it, poisoned everything around one. One must always keep a cheerful mind and a grateful heart, said Father Moineau, and leave judgements to God, whose business they were.

So Benedict reminded himself now, very firmly, that he wanted for nothing; and if his future looked uncertain, still he had a comfortable present. He had his home, enough to eat and to wear, and this good horse to ride. He leaned forward and patted Beau's neck, and the bay replied with a little friendly snort and a slight quickening of pace as they passed under the arch of Micklegate Bar and out of the walled city.

Nicky was his brother, and Bendy was obliged by every commandment of religion and civilisation to love him. And whenever things grew uncomfortable in Nicky's vicinity, Benedict could always go and visit Serena.

She was the widow of William Makepeace, the saddler and harness-maker whose vast shop in Coney Street was such a landmark in York. Her father, a tanner, had no other child, and gave her the education and fortune he would have lavished on a son, with the result that when she was fifteen, she caught the eye of Makepeace, who was then fifty-five.

Though it had been an arranged marriage, it had worked very well. Makepeace was a kind and liberal man, Serena an intelligent and ambitious girl. Under her influence he had wrought a number of improvements to his business, eventually increasing his profits fourfold. He expanded from harness into whips, canes, umbrellas and walking-sticks; valises and trunks; and finally into gentlemen's gloves, boots and shoes. By the time Makepeace died at the age of seventy, his shop had engulfed those to either side, and it was difficult for any gentleman of York or the surrounding country to get through a month without a visit to Makepeace's.

In justice to his partner and helpmeet, and to the surprise of the stiffer elements of society, Makepeace had left his entire fortune to Serena, who had thus found herself, at the age of thirty, both wealthy and independent. She remained in the large old house in Nunnery Lane which had been in the Makepeace family for generations, continued to run the business with success, and two years later had met Benedict.

It had been a dazzling experience for Benedict: she brought him not just physical delights, but companionship, something he had been short of all his life. Nothing in his previous sexual experience – which though wide had been necessarily shallow – had suggested that one might enjoy the company and conversation of the woman one bedded. He had no vocabulary for something so new and all-consuming, except to call it love; and loving her, he wanted to marry her, for his natural instinct was always to serve, protect, and cherish.

Sooner or later, he feared, there would be trouble if they went on as they were. Serena's servants were loyal and discreet, and he tried to be careful, but the time would inevitably come when someone would find out, and inevitably that someone would tell Mama. Bendy quaked at the thought of the storm he would have to face then. Mama would be so shocked, so angry. He knew she would think it a grave sin – well, he supposed it *was* a sin, though it didn't feel like one to him when he was engaged in it. He dreaded exposure, both for Serena's sake – young as he was, he knew the public odium would fall unfairly on her rather than on him – and because he didn't want to upset Mama. She was neither young nor strong any more, and when he thought how distressed she had been by his minor kick-ups, he felt he would rather do anything than risk her finding out about Serena.

He didn't want to give Nicky anything to use against him, either; for loyalty to his brother notwithstanding, Bendy had to admit that Nicky liked making trouble for him. Not that it would matter in the long run – when Nicky finally inherited Morland Place he would turn Bendy out, that was certain. He had hinted as much – more than hinted – on many occasions. But though Bendy knew he would have to leave one day, he didn't want his mother's mind to be poisoned against him. He loved her, and wanted her to love him. It was an uphill struggle: not only did she love Nicky best – which was inevitable – but Bendy seemed naturally to fall into scrapes which made Mama shake her head over him, while Nicky always managed to keep out of trouble.

The snow was falling more thickly now, beginning to gather in a crust on Beau's mane, and muffling his hoof beats. Ahead, Fand was growing harder to see through the murk, and worries over the complicatedness of life sank under a simple desire to be home and out of the cold. Benedict hunched up his shoulders and urged Beau into a faster trot down the darkening road.

The first large, light flakes of snow were falling as Nicholas emerged onto the wooden staircase which led down into Little Helen Yard, and he paused automatically to fasten his greatcoat at the neck and turn up the collar. He was feeling light, almost transparent, with shock, and his fingers fumbled at the buttons. The familiar stream of thought ran through the background of his mind: he had a weak chest, and it would never do to get a cold on it at this season of the year. November was always a tiresome month, with its fogs and chills, and no-one really appreciated how delicate his health was. Even his mother had been known to be unsympathetic, and suggest that he needed fresh air when what was really wanted was a good bright fire and no draughts. Now it was beginning to snow, and he had come to York in his tilbury. If he were to get a wetting on the way home, he would be in bed for a week.

But the habitual trickle of complaint was like the murmur of a distant stream, only half heard and barely regarded. The forefront of his mind was occupied with images and emotions so large and violent they shut out the capacity for rational thought. It was as though the inside of his head was frozen in a silent scream.

He had come in normal spirits to the little apartment for his usual entertainment. There had been the usual small itch of excitement, the little hot trickle of expectation – which sadly these days was often the forerunner to a feeling of anticlimax afterwards. However, he had entered the apartment in all innocence, calling out to Annie as he opened the door ... He shuddered as the ghastly image sprang again before his mind's eye; and he glanced instinctively behind him to make sure the door was shut, half afraid that it would swing open and expose his hideous situation to the public gaze.

The public gaze? Self-preservation rose up hot and strong, thrusting back even horror and distress. He must at all costs prevent anything from being discovered! There was no-one in the yard; but through the gaps between the plank-steps of the wooden staircase he could see the window of the ground-floor apartment. Here lived Clulow, the stained-glass artist, whose bench was set up right against the window to get the light on his work. Nicholas could imagine Clulow now as he had so often seen him, the bald crown of his head gleaming as he bent low over his work, his attention thoroughly absorbed – or so it seemed.

Nicholas had always taken pains to come and go unobserved. He had made sure that Clulow had his head down before he crossed the yard, and had kept his face averted and in the shadow of his hat. He didn't think he had been recognised so far; but this time it mattered so much more if Clulow looked up and saw him. Sooner or later the thing in the upstairs apartment would be discovered, and then questions would be asked of the little, pallid-faced artisan. Nicky could imagine the scene: Clulow before the magistrate, his eyes gloating behind his gold-rimmed spectacles as he identified the gentleman who visited the upstairs tenant . . .

The hideous image, which Nicholas had temporarily blocked from his mind, leapt out violently from his memory. He stood immobile, held rigid by the horror of it as it dangled before him again just as it had when he pushed in through the door half an hour ago. The *thing* – he could hardly think of it as a person – was hanging from the crossbeam in the middle of the room by a rope. It was bloated and black in the face, blotchily swollen in the limbs. The teeth were bared in a ghastly grin, and the tip of a purple tongue stuck through them like a lump of ox liver jammed in a white paling fence.

He did not think he had screamed. He had been too frightened at first to move. He had stood there trembling, unable even to look away as the image was etched ever more deeply into his mind. It was plain that she was dead, and had been dead some time. She must have stood on a stool and kicked it away, but her neck had since stretched grotesquely, so that her feet were now scraping against the floor. One of her shoes had fallen off and he noticed with faint and fainting horror that the yellowish toe of her stocking was neatly darned. It had seemed too human a detail to be borne in that context.

His first impulse, when he was able to think at all, was to call for help. Someone had to do something. He had to get Clulow up here and make him·go for a doctor or a constable or – or *anyone*! His legs, however, scotched these early plans by threatening to collapse under him. He staggered to a chair and sat down, trembling violently; and while he was recovering, second and wiser thoughts came to him.

If he made a public outcry, how would he explain what he was doing here? The minds of the vulgar would instantly fasten on one explanation and one only; and while many a gentleman kept a little lovebird in a secret nest, not every gentleman had a mother like his, a mother of stern moral fibre – and whose entire fortune, moreover, was unentailed. Such a mother might well leave everything away from a son who offended her ideas of propriety, and Nicky would do anything – anything – rather than let Bendy have what was rightfully his!

Furthermore, Nicky's love-nest had some unusual aspects to it which, even if all else were forgiven, would be extremely embarrassing, to say the least, to have to explain. There were the articles in the wall cupboard for one thing: they might cause some searching questions to be asked. And for another, his last visit to Annie had been pretty boisterous, and he was fairly sure the marks he had left would not have disappeared yet. People might even blame him for what she had done to herself – the rope, after all, had been brought there by him, though for quite other purposes.

And then there was the question of what everyone – and in particular his boon companions – would say about him if it came out that his mistress had hanged herself rather than remain in his keeping. He imagined the sneers of Jack Cox, the sniggers of Carlton Husthwaite . . . No, no, his name must not be connected with this business at all! Thank heaven he had not acted on his first impulse and raised the alarm. He must think, *think*.

He thought, staring blankly round the room. All looked as usual. It was a rather bare little room: his allowance was not so generous he could afford to furnish it with any luxury, and he had hardly ever bought Annie presents. In any case, by origin she was nothing but a pauper slut from the workhouse, and however bare the room, it was better than she deserved or could have hoped for. The bareness suited his purposes, anyway: the austerity, almost grimness of the place and the lowness of his companion had been part of the play he made for himself there.

Of late, indeed, she had seemed to be sinking ever lower, practically to the level of a dumb beast. She had never been very clever, but he had begun to wonder if she weren't getting a little touched in her upper works. Just lately she had greeted him when he visited with dull eyes and sullen wordlessness, replying to his comments and questions in grunts, doing what he bid but without even the pretence of willingness. He had been keeping her for three years, but he had begun to think she had outlived her usefulness. He had even planned how he would tell her he no longer required her services and that she must vacate the apartment. But of course, he checked himself, he could never have let her go. She knew his secrets. She might have spoken to others of what they did together, and he could never have allowed her to do that, even if it meant . . .

An eddy of wind spattered snowflakes into his face, bringing him back from the deep cavern of his thoughts. He realised he was still standing at the top of the steps, exposed to the elements and being chilled to the marrow by the icy wind. He must move before he caught his death of cold. He must get away from here before someone came and saw him. It was growing dusk and getting colder all the time, and he fumbled in his pocket for his gloves. His hands were already numb and as he struggled to drag the first one on, the second one slipped from his grasp and fell; he cursed and made a grab for it, and dropped the first glove too, scuffled after them, and saw them tumble through the gap between the steps into the yard below.

Crouching, he peered down and saw them lying on the cobbles just before Clulow's door. Damnation! What the hell was he to do now? To reach them he would have to walk right past Clulow's window, and there was no chance in the world that the artisan would not look up at someone apparently coming to his workshop door. He would just have to abandon them, he thought resignedly. They were an expensive pair his mother had bought for him for his last birthday; but then she had gone on to buy Bendy a pair almost identical for his birthday, which had spoiled the gift as far as Nicky was concerned.

In fact, now he thought of it, that was Bendy's pair anyway! He brightened at the realisation. He had left his own upstairs this morning, and rather than go all the way back for them, he had taken Bendy's out of the pocket of his greatcoat, which had been lying across a chair in the hall. Nicky smiled to himself. He would make good sure to draw Mama's attention to the fact that Bendy had cared so little for her gifts he had already lost the gloves she had bought for him. When the moment arose, Nicky could make good use of that!

So now he pulled his hat firmly down, tucked his stick under his arm and thrust his frozen hands into his pockets, hunching his shoulders so that as much of his face as possible was obscured by his greatcoat collar as he went quickly and quietly down the steps. He could only hope that the dusk and Clulow's devotion to his art would prevent his seeing – or at all events recognising – Nicky as he left.

He hurried across Little Helen Yard and dived into the narrow alley which led into the next court. He had to get to Grape Lane where his horse and tilbury were stabled, but his first aim now was to make sure he did not meet anyone who knew him. If he went through the courts, rather than along the respectable streets, he would be safe, for it was here that the poorest of the poor lived, crammed together in tiny rooms in the rotting carcases of what had once been the large houses of well-to-do tradesmen. The better-off now lived outside the walls in Bootham or Clifton or Fulford, and the indigent had settled like flies in the vacated spaces. Their filth, and that of the animals they kept, was thrown into the street to stand in festering dungheaps and stagnate in black pools. Now Nicholas was glad of the bitter weather, for it had frozen the surface and killed the odour, making the going a little less unpleasant than it would otherwise have been.

There would be no gentleman to recognise him in these blighted alleys. Human creatures there were, but he hardly regarded them even as people; like the disgusting thing that was approaching him now along Mucky-Peg Lane – an old, bent pauper with an almost hairless skull, which seemed horribly smooth in comparison with the creased and tooth-less face. To Nicholas's amazement as much as alarm, the thing did not step aside and press itself against the wall to give him way as it ought. Instead it stopped, swung its head sideways to look at him, and then shuffled forward again with its hand outstretched and cupped like a beggar's. It peered at him out of a small, dark right eye; the left was useless, white and seeping, bulging grotesquely out of the seamed face with the swelling of a massive infection in the eye socket.

With the uncertain light and grim surroundings, it seemed

15

to Nicholas in his shaken state to be part of the ghastliness he had already experienced. It was as if the place were breeding monsters to torment him; as though the hanging horror in the apartment had called to its own kind to emerge from the shadows and avenge it. Nicholas stood still, watching the thing approach, unable to believe until it was almost touching him that it was real.

'Alms, master – for pity –' the thing whined. The cupped, distorted claw, black with a lifetime's dirt, trembled barely an inch from his greatcoat. 'Spare a penny, master. For pity.'

For a moment they faced each other, motionless. Nicky's mouth was dry, and it took him a measurable pause to find enough spittle to croak, 'Get out of my way.'

The creature only turned its head slightly, tilting its good eye up a little to survey Nicholas's face. It made no other movement. 'Master Morland,' it said at last.

Terror swelled up in Nicholas at the sound of his own name coming from that shapeless mouth, as though the avenging God had spoken to him through this grotesque medium. In surging panic he lifted his walking stick and hit the thing as hard as he could on the side of the head. It staggered and cried out, throwing up its arms. He hit it again in the same place, and again, and at last it went down. It fell without a sound, collapsing shapelessly into the filth like a heap of rags.

Shaking with fear and outrage, Nicholas skirted it and ran. It had almost touched him! Was it, even now, rising from the ground behind him and shuffling after him? The feeling of being followed, the sense that there were eyes watching him from every dark window, could not be stifled. Sobbing in panic he stumbled on over the frozen waves of filth until with a violent surge of relief he reached the three-way junction of Mucky-Peg Lane with Swinegate and Back Swinegate.

Grape Lane lay ahead of him, cobbled, civilised, leading to the inn, the stable, his horse, home. He stopped a moment to catch his breath. The snow was definitely falling now, fine, large flakes floating down, twirling slowly out of the iron sky, landing soundlessly on the road, on window-sills, on his shoulders. He suppressed the desire to brush them off wildly. Nothing had followed him out of the darkness. He was safe.

He laughed shakily. The nerves of his hand and arm

rehearsed to themselves the sensation of hitting out at the beggar, and he felt a mixture of fright and excitement at the memory. It had gone down like a sack! Had he killed it? He lifted his walking-stick, ran it cautiously through his hands. Two-thirds of the way down there was a dent in the lacquered wood. A dent! Good God, he must have hit it hard! But he was safe. No-one had seen him. No-one would ever know —

'Nicky!'

He started so violently he bit his tongue and almost dropped the stick. He turned his head and glared like a madman at the huddled shape approaching him, his mind whitening with panic, ready to kill again if he had to. But it was only Harry Anstey, hurrying with his collar turned up and his eyes squinting against the snow which was blowing in his face.

'Hullo, Nicky! Foul weather, ain't it? I wish I'd seen it coming: I'd have brought an umbrella.'

Nicholas scowled in furious reaction, tasting blood in his mouth from his bitten tongue. 'What the devil do you mean, jumping out on me like that? What are you doing here?'

'I'm on my way to the Maccabbees,' Harry said mildly. 'And I didn't jump out on you, anyway, I was just walking along the street. Why were you standing there like a ghost staring at your walking-stick? And what on earth were you doing in Mucky-Peg Lane?'

'I wasn't in Mucky-Peg Lane,' Nicky snapped, too taken aback to think of a more elegant reply. He ought to have asked Harry what business it was of his – mockingly would have been best, but haughtily would have done – but it was too late now.

'Yes you were. I just saw you coming out of it,' Harry said, staring in surprise.

Nicholas flushed dully. 'You mind your own business!' That wasn't elegant either; and it was too late to take that line anyway.

'Certainly, old chap,' Harry said placatingly. 'Anything you say.' He began to turn away.

'No – wait!' Harry stopped and looked at him doubtfully. 'I – I was just taking a short cut,' Nicholas stammered. 'It started to snow, and ... I'm on my way to The Grapes to

17

fetch my horse. Why not come in and have a glass of something with me? They – they do quite decent mulled ale. Come and have a wet.'

Harry shook his head, but the look he gave Nicholas, though wry, was friendly. 'Thanks all the same, but I'd prefer the Maccabbees. I suppose you wouldn't like to join me, to show you forgive me for speaking out of turn?'

Nicholas didn't know what to say. He and Harry had been friends since childhood, had gone to school together and later shared the same tutor. If anyone might without offending ask what he was doing here, it ought to have been Harry. Nicky cleared his throat, 'Look here,' he began in a conciliatory tone, though without any clear idea of where the sentence was going to lead.

But Harry shook his head again. 'No, no, entirely my fault. I apologise.' The snow was beginning to settle on them both, on shoulders and hat brims. Harry glanced up into the whirling downwards mass of it tumbling out of the heavy sky. 'If you're going back to Morland Place, I suppose you'd better get going, hadn't you? This looks as though it's set in; and it's getting dark, too.'

'Yes – of course – I suppose so,' Nicholas muttered awkwardly. 'Well, I'll be off, then.'

He raised his hand in a vague sort of salute, and hurried away from Harry towards The Grapes. He had handled the situation as badly as could be; but perhaps nothing would come of it after all. He was far enough from Little Helen Yard now, and there seemed no reason why Harry, even if he ever came to hear of the death by suicide of a nameless woman of the lower orders, should associate it with Nicky's presence in Mucky-Peg Lane. It would be the damnedest impudence if he did! But that was Harry Anstey all over – impudent, inquisitive, always poking in where he had no right; always in the wrong place at the wrong time. It was the damnedest of bad luck to have bumped into him like that; but then Nicky always had bad luck. If ever a person was plagued by undeserved misfortune, he thought plaintively, it was him! Plagued with ill luck, and surrounded by nothing but selfish people – with his pitiful health it was a wonder he had survived to his present age! Driving home in this snowstorm would probably be the death of him.

The familiar litany of inner complaint re-established itself, pouring its emollient numbness over the wounded parts of his mind. He had managed now entirely to shut off from himself the image of the horror in the apartment – locked it away in a cupboard which housed all the other things he did not dare to remember. The pauper he had already entirely forgotten.

CHAPTER TWO

It wasn't snowing in London. The day had been chilly and misty, and as the hidden sun declined the mist grew thicker and colder. Lord Batchworth was only halfway up Whitehall when he regretted his decision to walk home from the House instead of taking a cabriolet. Normally he would have walked across the Park to get to St James's Square, where he had rented a house, but seeing how thick the fog was, he had changed his mind. He was not of a nervous disposition, but there was so much unemployment and unrest in the country these days that a prudent man did not court danger by leaving the main roads in weather like this.

He walked on up Whitehall to the Charing Cross and turned left along Cockspur Street. To his right, dark and unseen in the fog, was the large site of the disused Royal Mews, which the new King, William IV, had promised to knock down to make space for a public square. King Billy – still in the first six months of his reign – had already had a number of sensible, practical ideas for giving pleasure to his subjects, like making a passage between Waterloo Place and the Park, for instance, and opening the East Terrace at Windsor to the public on Sundays. A public square was much needed in London, for there was really nowhere for large public gatherings. King Billy had had the happy thought of dedicating it to his friend, the Hero of Trafalgar. Batchworth smiled as he remembered his mother-in-law's wrath when she had heard the news. Lady Theakston had always disliked Nelson intensely. The real Hero of Trafalgar, she contended, was Admiral Collingwood: he had done all the work, while Nelson, by contriving to get himself killed, had snatched the glory.

Still, Nelson Square, or Trafalgar Square, or whatever it was to be called, would be a fine addition to the capital when it was finished. The King had promised some kind of grand monument in the centre, and statues and fountains. With the façade of Gibbs' fine church, St Martin's, flanking it on one side, it would begin to look almost like an Italian piazza.

It looked like nothing at all, now: the fog had thickened into a real London Particular. People trod the flagways muffled to the eyebrows, indistinguishable, appearing and disappearing as though they were only fog made solid. Beyond the kerbstones the ghostly horse traffic glided, wheels and hooves muffled by the accumulated mud and manure, the feeble gleam of the coach lamps flickering disembodied like marsh-lights. Now and then a horse coughed hollowly, invisible out there in the river of murk. When one passed close enough to be seen it was a sorry picture, rat-tailed with mud, splashed to the blinkers. November weather was a great leveller: today my lady's peacocky pair would look as draggled as any cab horses.

Batchworth turned up Haymarket to get the benefit of the gas lighting. The lamps, looking like yellow balloons with their fog-haloes, were only dimly visible; but still a number of people had had the clever idea of navigating their way from lamp-post to lamp-post, and curses were fluent as people collided and lost their foothold in the mud. Those shops that had lighted windows had pedestrians clustered about them like great, grey moths stuck to the glass, not so much eager to view the wares as reluctant to pass on into the darkness.

He turned down Charles Street, and here was St James's Square at last, quiet and dark, the garden in the centre invisible, and a number of the houses still closed up, for not everyone came up for the Little Season. He felt his way along the railings, counting the openings, and groped his way to his own front door, glad to be home. The vestibule was lit welcomingly by a large fire and an extravagance of candles, and Raby took his hat, greatcoat, gloves and cane and said, 'Her ladyship is in the drawing-room, my lord. Lord Theakston is with her.'

'Lord Theakston? I wasn't expecting him.'

'He has just this moment stepped round, my lord.'

21

'Have you taken up the sherry?'

'I was about to do so, my lord, when you arrived.'

Batchworth ran up the stairs energetically, glad to be released from the restraint of the fog. He could smell its sulphurous taint clinging to his clothes and hair. The time would come, he thought grimly, when it would come down and simply never lift again, and they would all wither and die like grass under a tarpaulin.

In the drawing-room Rosamund was sitting by a splendid fire before which her stepfather, Lord Theakston, was warming his coat-tails. She lifted a glad smile towards Batchworth as he came in, and said, 'It's too late, Jes. Papa Danby has told me the news.'

'You mean the news that the Government has been defeated?'

Lord Theakston shook hands with him apologetically. 'I had it from Tom immediately after the division, so I came straight here to tell you. I didn't know you were in the House as well.'

'If we hadn't missed each other, we could have shared a cab,' Jes said. He went to catch and kiss his wife's hands. 'So I can't tell you anything?'

'You can tell me everything,' she said. 'Papa Danby's only just got here. He's only had time to tell me the bare fact of the defeat. What was the margin?'

'Twenty-nine votes,' said Batchworth. 'But it was a very trivial issue – took everyone by surprise. Sir Henry Parnell moved an amendment on the Civil List, and suddenly all the opposition forces seemed to come together, without any pre-arrangement – and down went the Government!'

A sudden suspicion crossed Rosamund's mind. 'Which way did Tom vote?' Her younger brother Tom Weston was MP for Winchendon, a seat in the gift of their other brother Lord Aylesbury; but Tom was notoriously independent and unpredictable.

Theakston looked reproachful. 'How can you ask? Winchendon is a Tory seat. How could Tom vote against the Government?'

'I'll wager he did all the same,' Batchworth said. 'Reform isn't a party matter any more. Two years of unrest – three

22

months of riots – we could be on the brink of revolution! We've got to have Reform. Tom knows that. Everyone but Wellington knows it. He's out of touch with the country and he has to go. A lot of Tories must have voted against the Government today, and I wouldn't be at all surprised if Tom were one of them.'

Rosamund frowned. 'But if the defeat was over a trivial issue, as you said, it need not be a resigning matter, surely?'

'*Need* not,' Theakston agreed. 'But when checkmate is inevitable you don't go on playing. War's like chess in many ways, and the Beau was always a good soldier.' He sighed. 'I hadn't time to tell you yet, but he's gone straight off to St James's to tell the King that he's resigning.'

'I didn't know that,' Jes said. 'That was quick work.'

'Oh dear,' said Rosamund, looking uncomfortable. 'I hope Tom didn't have a hand in it after all. The Beau's such a friend of the family, and he's always been so kind to me. Won't he be dreadfully upset?'

'It had to happen sooner or later, m'dear,' her stepfather said kindly. 'Indeed, after that speech a fortnight ago, the wonder is that he's hung on until now.'

'I suppose it was tactless,' Rosamund admitted.

'Tactless?' Jes exclaimed. 'It was a suicide note.'

Wellington's speech in the House on November 2nd had been fiercely anti-Reformist, and even some of his supporters agreed it was ill-judged. For the leader of a country convulsed with civil disorder to deny categorically that he meant to introduce any measure of reform – to declare, indeed, that he would always feel it his duty to resist such measures when they were proposed by others – was unwise, to say the least.

After the speech London had erupted in demonstrations almost amounting to insurrection. The unrest was so bad the Cabinet had felt obliged to cancel a banquet they were giving for the King at the Guildhall a few days later, rather than admit they would have needed a military escort to get them through the streets of the City in one piece. Unpopularity with the Mob did not necessarily spell the death of a ministry, but now that the Lower House had turned against Wellington's so pointedly, it must be the end.

'Ah well,' Rosamund said philosophically, 'after all, Mother

23

says the Beau never really wanted to be Prime Minister.'

'True,' said Lord Theakston. 'He only took it on out of a sense of duty, and he'll be glad to be out of it, so you needn't mourn him.'

'I suppose the King will accept his resignation?' Rosamund asked on a sudden thought.

'The King admires him, but he knows we have to have Reform.'

'Thank God for Billy,' Jes said. 'At least he has an ear for the voice of the people. Our last king would have precipitated a revolution.'

'Mother always used to say that Billy was the best of the princes,' said Rosamund hopefully. 'And Tom says he's a very decent old party, and works tremendously hard.'

'High praise for a prince,' Jes laughed.

The door opened, and Raby entered with the tray of sherry, Madeira, and a basket of Shrewsbury biscuits. When he had withdrawn, Jes served his wife and father-in-law with his own hands.

Lord Theakston went on talking about the new King. 'Taylor says he never leaves things undone at the end of the day as Prinny did. And from my own experience, when anyone comes to him with business, he listens carefully and asks questions until he's sure he understands it properly.'

'As Prinny didn't,' Rosamund smiled. 'Mama says he would never ask a question, for fear of seeming ignorant.'

'I heard that when he died, there were forty thousand documents awaiting the Royal Assent, because he couldn't be bothered to sign them,' said Jes.

'It's true,' Theakston agreed. 'Poor Billy sat up every night for weeks, signing away until they were all done. Taylor said it made his heart ache for the old man, because he has arthritis in his hands and it must have given him great pain.'

'Hard working, sensible, and kind; and he knows we must have Reform,' Jes said. 'We could hardly have done better.'

'Hmm,' said Theakston doubtfully, and sipped his Madeira with the air of one suspending judgement.

Rosamund looked at him questioningly, sifting out the reason for his hesitancy. 'Papa Danby, you're not against Reform are you?'

'Don't like change,' he said. 'You Reformists seem to want to change everything.'

'Only what needs to be changed. You surely can't think our system is perfect?' said Jes.

'It works,' Theakston said succinctly. 'Our country's the envy of the world for stability – and liberality! Meddling always makes things worse. Look at France.'

'Hardly a fair example, sir. And if we hadn't had to spend twenty-five years fighting the French, we'd have had Reform long ago. You've only got to read the Parliamentary reports: Lord Grey was urging it back in the 'eighties.'

'Yes, I remember,' said Lord Theakston. His opinion of Grey was plain in his tone of voice.

'The country's changed since 1789,' Jes went on, warming to his argument. 'The population was only ten million then – now it's sixteen and a half million. And that vast increase is mostly urban – living in towns that were no more than villages before the war. The problems *that* causes are quite new, and we have to have some way of coping with them.'

'Nothin' to do with the Government,' said Theakston. 'Government's business is to raise armies in time of war, and to uphold the law. Individuals must solve their own problems.'

'That may have been the case once, but the problems arising now are beyond the power of an individual to solve. Concerted action is needed, and concerted action must be centrally controlled.'

'Ha!' said Theakston, putting down his glass triumphantly. 'All the more reason not to change our Parliamentary system. It's been arranged so that we can be sure of getting the right people in. Whole point of nomination seats! Pick the right man for the job.'

Batchworth shifted ground. 'What about a case like Old Sarum? It returns two Members on a total of seven votes, and since those votes are attached to empty fields, the actual electorate is one – the landowner. Yet Manchester, with a population of a hundred thousand souls, has no Member at all.'

'There are absurdities, of course,' Theakston said. 'Don't say there ain't. But in the end, I don't see that it matters *how* a Member gets his seat, as long as he's the right man. Tom's a nominee, and you can't say he ain't an ornament to the House!'

'True, but —'

'And besides, a Member can't maintain his independence if he's all the time looking over his shoulder to see how the voters are reacting. What becomes of your Parliamentary integrity if the Members are bein' pushed this way and that by factions and interests?'

Jes grinned disarmingly. 'Ah, there you see through me! I wouldn't be half such an enthusiast for Reform if it weren't that my interest *isn't* being represented! It's always those who don't benefit from a system who perceive its imperfections!'

'Now there's a handsome admission!' said Rosamund. 'Come, Papa Danby, you must give him points for that.'

Theakston smiled at her affectionately. 'Give him best,' he acknowledged. 'I'm not so opposed myself to a modicum of reform, but you know what your mother fears: that if you once start down that road, it will lead in the end to universal suffrage, where every man's vote, however ignorant or misguided or even wicked he is, counts the same as ours. Start meddlin' with the constitution, and before you know where you are you've got a revolution, and we've become a republic.' He glanced at Batchworth. 'Don't want to see your brother-in-law disinherited, do you – to say nothing of yourself?'

'Not in the least, sir. I believe we must have Reform specifically to *avoid* revolution. But I promise I won't ask for universal suffrage. No man of sense could tolerate that!'

'Well, at all events,' Lord Theakston said, stretching out one elegant leg and contemplating the shine on his boot, 'Wellington's gone, and we shall have Grey and the Whigs in now. They've sworn to bring in a Reform Bill, so we shall see what comes of it.'

'You think the King will definitely call Grey?' Jes asked, with slight anxiety.

'Bound to. Goderich is the only alternative, and he's no alternative at all, poor old fellow. So even though Billy don't trust Grey – taint of bein' a Jacobin back in the 'eighties still clings to him —'

'The very whiff of brimstone!' Batchworth laughed. 'Prinny thought he was the Devil incarnate.'

'Billy don't think much differently,' Theakston said. 'But he'll call him to the Palace tomorrow all the same, you mark my words.'

'A Whig government!' Rosamund said wonderingly. 'It hardly seems possible after all these years. Who will Grey bring in with him, I wonder?'

'Palmerston to the Foreign Office, that's for sure,' Batchworth said.

'Pam's an able man,' Theakston admitted.

'And Grey's bound to want Althorp, of course – I don't quite know what he'll do with him, though, because ten to one but Melbourne will get the Home Department. Durham will probably be Privy Seal —'

'Graham to the Admiralty,' Theakston suggested.

'Oh, certainly. The real problem will be, where to put Brougham,' Jes said with a frown. 'I know he'd like to be Master of the Rolls, but that would give him too much influence in the Commons for some people's taste.'

'Why put him anywhere?' Rosamund protested. 'I don't like that man. Mother's right: he's quite mad – and dangerous.'

'Too dangerous to leave out,' Jes said. 'Besides, he has a first-rate brain; and the Mob adore him. The thing is to neutralise him: bring him in, but put him somewhere where he can't cause trouble. Maybe he'd take Lord Chancellor.'

'And what about you, Batchworth?' Theakston asked. 'Are we to hear your name mentioned? Surely Grey won't leave out one of the ablest young men in the Upper House?'

Rosamund looked at her husband quickly. 'Jes, really? Have you expectations?'

'I'm not one of Grey's closest friends, but my experience in the factories *is* thought to be valuable,' he admitted. 'It was hinted – in a very general way – that I might be useful as President of the Board of Trade —'

'Oh Jes!'

'No-one better. Just the thing, my boy!' said Theakston generously.

'It isn't a settled thing yet,' Batchworth protested cautiously.

'Sure it must be,' said Lord Theakston. 'And there's nothing more likely to reconcile her ladyship to a Whig government. With her son-in-law in the Cabinet, you might even get her to see the merit of Reform, given time.'

'That would be a miracle,' Rosamund laughed.

'No, no,' Theakston said seriously. 'Your mother has no political persuasions, you know. It's all a matter of loyalties with her – and families come first. There's you and Batchworth, and probably Tom, on the Reform side already. Only talk Roland over, and she'll have no reason to hold out any longer.'

Lord and Lady Batchworth dined alone that evening. Since they had no company Rosamund had the meal served in the small dining parlour, and ordered it to be laid in the old-fashioned way – *à l'anglais* as it was called nowadays – with all the dishes on the table at once. Once the soup had been removed, she dismissed the servants, saying that they would wait on themselves, and ring when they were ready for the dessert.

'You don't mind, do you?' she asked her husband when they were alone. 'I know it isn't fashionable – Thalia would be horrified —'

Her sister-in-law, Roland's wife, was determined, as far as she could between babies, to make the Aylesburys leaders of Society. In their house in Berkeley Square *service à la français* – where the dishes were dressed and handed round by the servants – was the rule. But already Thalia's fashionableness was being overtaken by a newer style, *service à la russe*, where each dish was dressed in the kitchen and offered simultaneously to every diner from an individual vessel. Since this necessitated having a servant for each person at the table and a vast amount of china, it could only be attained to by the wealthiest; but at a grand dinner the sight of, say, forty liveried servants moving as one, was a wonderful spectacle. Thalia hadn't given a dinner served *à la russe* yet, to Rosamund's knowledge, but it could only be a matter of time. Sometimes she mischievously planned to get in first, just for the fun of stealing Thalia's thunder.

But tonight everything was resolutely English, with a single

28

course and nothing but the sideboard to augment the table.

'Of course I don't mind,' Jes answered. 'It's much nicer to be alone with you. I'm glad you thought of it.'

'I expect Raby will be shocked. He thinks there's a certain grandeur to be expected of an earl. I saw his eyebrows fly up when I sent them all away.'

'Nonsense. Raby doesn't think anything of the sort. He isn't paid to think.'

'You sounded just like my mother then,' Rosamund smiled.

'Thank you. What can I carve for you first? These pheasants look good.'

'Roland sent them up from Wolvercote. The raised pie is veal, by the way, and that made dish is brawn, I think, with truffles.'

They were busy for a while serving each other. Then Rosamund asked, 'Will you really have a seat in the Cabinet? You didn't mention it before.'

'I didn't want to say anything until I was sure – and I'm not sure yet. But would you mind if I did?'

'Mind? Why should I mind? It would be a great honour for you.'

'It would mean spending much more time in Town, especially with the Reform Bill to get through. We'd have to live here more or less permanently while the House was in session.'

'Should I consider that a hardship?'

'You might find yourself becoming a great political hostess.'

'Ah, now I see the objection! But how would the factories fare if you were here for half the year?'

'The factories can get along without me.'

'I never thought to hear you say that.'

He smiled ruefully. 'It's different now I'm the earl. When I was only plain Jesmond Farraline with nothing to do and pockets to let, it filled a void in my life to bring the factories up to their full glory. But now they're running smoothly, and my agent's such a good man I'm hardly needed. I have you, and I have my political career. Those must take precedence.'

'But you won't like to let the factories go entirely. It's a pity Manchester's so far away.'

'The railways are going to change that, my love. In the future, perhaps in as little as ten years from now, I predict it will be possible to travel from Manchester all the way to London by railway, in a matter of hours. Just think of it!'

Rosamund looked up from her plate, and was transfixed by the sight of him sitting across the dining table from her. Every once in a while it astonished her to find herself married to him; astonished her to remember that it was already fourteen, nearly fifteen years since she had first met him that day on the sands at Scarborough. She had thought him the most staggeringly handsome man she had ever seen. How unfair it was, she thought, that a woman's beauty diminished as the years passed while a man's only grew: he was a hundred times more handsome than when she met him – and a thousand times dearer to her, though the glister of his fair hair was now not all gold, and there were fine lines etched about his heavenly blue eyes. But now he was not merely a handsome stranger, he was her dear husband and lover, the person who knew her best in the world. She could lean her soul trustingly against his, and know that just as she was – faulty, weak, unworthy – he wanted her, and would care for her always.

'Expeditious, safe, comfortable, and cheap,' Jes was saying. 'From the heart of one city to the heart of another in a matter of hours! Distances annihilated! People brought together, ideas exchanged ...' He must have realised she had not been listening, for he stopped in mid flow and looked at her quizzically. 'I'm sorry, am I being a bore?'

'You could never be that,' she said, and dragged her mind back to the subject of railways so as to prove to him that he was not being. 'You don't need to convince me of the benefits, you know – just the likelihood. A railway from Manchester to London?'

'Look how successful our own Liverpool and Manchester Railway has been: four hundred and sixty thousand passengers carried in the first year! That's four times as many as the largest number that ever did the journey by coach!'

'Yet it was planned as a goods railway,' Rosamund mused. 'None of you guessed in the beginning that *people* would want to travel on it.'

'True, and the demand for goods carriage is still not great.

We'll be carrying goods from next month, but the advance bookings are most disappointing. Still, I have high hopes of our scheme to carry the mails. I begin to think that passengers and mails will prove to be the natural combination after all.'

'The roads will be deserted,' Rosamund said.

'Yes. The canals may continue to give us competition in the freight trade, but the passenger trade will be all ours. I think we will see that effect repeated wherever a railway is built – and they will be built, Ros! Think of all the millions of people in the country who have never been more than five miles from their birthplace!'

'Why on earth should they want to?'

'Everyone wants to travel,' Jes said firmly. 'Why shouldn't the lower orders do it as well as the wealthy?'

'Very well: why should *you* want them to? Don't tell me – so that your railways will make a great profit and pay out a handsome dividend!'

'Contempt of money is the root of all evil,' he said with a smile.

'I think you have that wrong, my love! But I must say the idea of mobs of labourers moving round the country so freely worries me. Look at all the rick-burning and rioting there's been in the last few months. It would only make it easier for them if they could travel great distances cheaply by railway.'

'But don't you see, those people have no work, and if they could move easily to another part of the country where work was available, they'd have no reason to riot. We can't move industry about the country in search of labour, so we must have the means to take the labour to the work. That's what the railways will do, dearest. That's why it is in the interests of everyone, not just the shareholders, to build them.'

'Very well, I allow you to convince me,' she said. 'And I suppose spending more time in London will allow you to shepherd through lots more Railway Acts?'

'That's what I've come for, of course.'

'I didn't suppose it was for the sake of my wardrobe.'

'Don't think I don't know how much courage this takes for you,' he said, suddenly serious.

'Yes, there's a new spirit of *Adelaidism* abroad in London,' Rosamund said lightly. 'Our new Queen has a very German

31

sense of propriety. I don't think I would be very welcome at St James's, do you?'

Jes knew as well as she did that Queen Adelaide had refused to receive the Duchess of St Albans because she had once been an actress, and Lady Ferrers because she had lived with her husband before she married him. He said, 'I shouldn't think you would want to be. I hear it's deadly dull.'

'It was different when Prinny was King,' she said. 'Being disgraceful was all the fashion.'

'You are not disgraceful. You are a respectable married woman, and a countess into the bargain – my countess, I'll have you remember.'

'How could I forget? But equally, how is the Ton to forget that I am a divorcée?'

'It wasn't by your choice that Marcus cast you off.'

She shrugged. 'All the same, in Manchester I may be accepted – even welcomed – but London Society rates itself more highly. A divorced woman is not considered respectable.'

'Oh, there may be a few high sticklers who'll stand out against us, but we needn't mind them,' he said.

'You have to mind what the Patronesses of Almack's think. They have enormous influence.'

'Why should you care a jot about Almack's?' he said, and abruptly realised where his attempt to comfort her had led them.

'Because I have no daughter to bring out, you mean?' Rosamund said, and looked down at her plate to avoid his eyes. 'Well, you're right of course. What is Almack's to me now?'

Her voice was expressionless, her face remote as a stranger's glimpsed for a moment through a fog on the other side of the road. After a moment he said quietly, 'Don't shut me out. You must know I didn't mean to hurt you.'

'I know,' she said. He thought that that would be all, but after a moment she said, 'She comes with me all the time – the thought of her – like something seen out of the corner of your eye, but when you turn your head it's gone. Do you know that feeling? And you want to weep with frustration because you can't see it, you know you'll never see it.'

He could think of nothing to say to encourage her to speak, and sat in stupid silence; but eventually she went on, 'My daughter will be eight next month.' She looked up. 'Every child of that age I see in the street, I think, "I wonder if my daughter looks like that."'

'I know. I've seen you looking.'

'I ache for her. A piece of me is lost, and I'm not complete without it.'

He only nodded. He wished he could have made her complete. There were times when he fought against a resentment that he was not everything to her, as she was to him. But he was not a woman, and he had never had a child, and he had enough imagination to believe that when you have grown another human being inside your own body, sustained it with your own blood, born it in travail and fed it at your breast, you must feel something for it a man could only guess at.

She went on musing. 'I haven't seen her since she was ten weeks old. And now that Marcus has taken her out of London, I have no hope of ever seeing her again. Oh why did he do that? Why? It was cruel! Even if I couldn't see her, knowing where she was was something.'

It seemed such a very poor something. He wished he knew what to say. As to *why*, she knew why as well as he did: once Marcus was rid of Rosamund, his one desire was to make sure she and Charlotte never saw each other again. Obviously it was becoming too difficult to isolate a lively, growing girl in the centre of London; so he moved the household to some remote spot where they were not known and were not likely to be found.

Jes had done what he could. Enquiries had been made from every source he could think of – lawyers, bankers, estate agents, everyone – but without success. Marcus had covered his tracks well. A wounded fox, Jes thought, is often the most cunning.

At last he said, 'Perhaps it will be better for her in the country – fresh air and wholesome food and so on. And you know Marcus would never let any harm come to her.'

'That's what Sophie said,' Rosamund said bleakly. 'And I

said to her, would you want Fanny to be brought up by someone like Marcus, someone whose mind is as crippled as his body? And with no female influence but his sister – poor Bab, who is almost as deranged as he is?'

'But they are both devoted to her,' he said, and she looked at him, and sighed slowly, as though she had come back from a long distance.

'Yes, I know. I'm sorry. I haven't forgotten our long talk, Jes. If we are to have any kind of happiness together, I must put her out of my mind.'

'Not that precisely,' Jes said. 'You can never forget her, I know, and I wouldn't want you to.'

'But I have to stop brooding about her, or it will poison everything. I must be cheerful and get on with my life as best I can.' She smiled – a little crookedly, but a smile all the same. 'I've a great deal to be grateful for; and if I can't have my own daughter, Sophie will let me spoil hers instead. As you already do.'

'Nonsense! I don't spoil Fanny,' he protested. He saw that she needed respite from her feelings, and was taking it in playfulness, and he followed her in willingly.

'Not spoil her?' Rosamund said sternly. 'Only last week you took her away from her lessons and drove her to the Exchange for absolutely no good reason.'

'I had an excellent reason,' Jes defended himself vigorously. 'I'd seen the most delicious blue velvet muff with white fur trimming which was exactly right for her.'

'So you bought it for her. And for that you took her away from her history lesson – the Kings and Queens of England, I think it was.'

'But my darling wife, just think how much more use it will be for her in ten years time to be able to carry a muff elegantly than to know the dates of Matilda and Stephen and all those tiresome Henrys!'

'Very true,' Rosamund said. 'Though I'm not sure Sophie entirely agreed with your point of view.'

'Oh, Sophie will come round to my way of thinking once she has a son to educate. She'll be only too glad for me to take Fanny away and spare her the expense.'

'Yes, she's quite convinced her new baby's going to be a

34

boy,' Rosamund said, smiling. 'I think she and Jasper have his name, school and future wife all picked out for him already.'

'She's looking so well, too. It must be a nervous time for them, after the previous miscarriages, but I really think it will be all right this time, don't you?'

'What tender concern for my cousin's health! I'm sorry I haven't been a good wife to you. I wish I could have given you a child.'

He flinched at the turn the conversation had taken, but when he looked at her, he saw it was all right. 'You are all the wife I ever wanted,' he said. Then, cautiously, 'You don't mind that I enjoy being with Fanny, do you?'

'Not at all. I'm glad you have the opportunity of vicarious fatherhood, at least.'

'I'd like to know who told you about Fanny's and my trip to the Exchange, though,' he said sternly.

'Sophie did,' Rosamund answered, 'when I called on her in the afternoon to tell her we were going to London. Miss Molton had complained of you to her – said she wasn't sure that you were a very proper influence on her charge.'

Jes laughed. 'I didn't do it to be proper,' he said. 'I did it to be popular!'

CHAPTER THREE

The wind had veered right round in the night to the south-west, melting the snow and bringing the fog to York. It was still cold, but a different sort of cold: raw, damp, and penetrating – 'graveyard weather' they called it.

Just before noon Cedric Laxton, younger son of Sir Percy Laxton, strolled into the outer office of Pobgee and Micklethwaite and found his friend Harry Anstey just emerging from the inner office of Mr Pobgee junior.

'Hullo! What are you doing here?' Laxton cried cheerfully. He was a chronically underemployed young man of just Harry's age – his mother's pet and the despair of his father – who had been put to so many careers and given them up within a matter of weeks that Sir Percy had lately decided it would come cheaper in the long run simply to keep him at home in idleness. At about this time of day young Laxton could usually be found lounging about the city, looking for company and spoiling for a chat.

Harry gestured with the long envelope he was holding. 'Come to collect an affidavit. What are you doing here?'

'Oh, I just wandered in, y'know, on the off-chance. Never know who you'll meet in here,' Laxton said vaguely.

Harry smiled to himself. It was a well-known saying in York that if you waited for long enough in the outer office of Pobgee and Micklethwaite, you would eventually meet everyone you knew. It was not a saying he was encouraged to repeat in the hearing of his own employers, Greaves and Russell of High Ousegate, but one which Ceddie Laxton had evidently taken to heart.

'I say, Harry,' Laxton now added, brightening at the

thought, 'ain't it just about your dinner time? What say we browse together?'

'I have to take this back to the office first,' Harry said.

'Not to worry – I'll walk down with you. Where do you feed these days?'

'The Jolly Bacchus in Micklegate. They have a very good ordinary.'

'Right-ho! That'll do for me,' Laxton said amiably, trotting out onto the street in Harry's wake.

They chatted as they threaded their way through the crowds and traffic of the town – or at least, Laxton chatted and Harry responded with a series of grunts of agreement which were all that was needed to keep his companion happy while he concentrated on not getting run over. They had just reached the door of the offices of Greaves and Russell when something in the soothing flow of trivia caught Harry's attention.

'. . . this business in Mucky-Peg Lane. Can't think why the Guv'nor's so exercised over it, except that —'

'Mucky-Peg Lane? What business is that?'

'What I was just telling you, old fellow,' Laxton said. 'Weren't you listening?'

'You know I never really listen to you, Ceddie. Tell me again.'

'Well, old boy,' Laxton said, quite unoffended, 'the Guv-'nor's quite up in the air about it, and I can't think why, except that there seems to be a gentleman involved, if you can believe what the lower orders say, which I hardly ever do, because it seems to me they tell the most frightful bouncers without even blinking. But Havergill says —'

'Havergill? What has Dr Havergill got to do with it? Look here,' Harry went on quickly, realising this was not the best way of getting sense out of his friend, 'I think you'd better tell me the whole story. Just let me deliver this affy to Mr Greaves, and we'll go and find a quiet place to talk.'

'Right-ho,' said Laxton, taking up a Pisa-like stance against one of the doric pillars that flanked the office doorway. 'Can't say I felt much outrage about it myself, but the Guv'nor seems to think it's important.'

★

In a corner booth in the coffee room of The Jolly Bacchus, with a laden table before them, Harry gently eased the details out of his friend.

'One of the constables – Hecky, d'you know him?' said Laxton through a mouthful of beef and mustard.

'He comes in to ours sometimes. Rough and ready sort,' Harry nodded.

'Aren't they all? Well, he came to see my Pa – Pa being one of the magistrates – to say that some old pauper had died up at the County Hospital. Havergill said that he'd been sick of an infection for weeks, but it wasn't the infection that killed him. Apparently, the woman who brought him in told some strange story about him being knocked down and left for dead by a gentleman.'

'And when was this?' Harry asked, with a horrid cold feeling creeping up his back.

'Tuesday, in the late afternoon. According to Hecky, the woman said she'd been standing in a doorway and saw it all. The gentleman was walking down the middle of the lane, and the old man approached him to beg. They both stopped, and then the gentleman whacked the old man on the head with his cane several times. The old man fell down and the gentleman ran away.'

'Did she recognise the gentleman?'

Laxton shook his head. 'He was wearing a greatcoat with the collar turned up and a tall hat pulled well down, so there wasn't much of his face to be seen. And it was dusk, and in that dark street —'

'Quite,' Harry said. He didn't know whether to feel relieved or disappointed. But what was he thinking? *Nicky?* His friend Nicholas Morland of Morland Place? He would never do anything violent, or cowardly. Yet the image was there in his mind, of Nicky coming out of Mucky-Peg Lane, and standing staring at his stick as though in a dream. And he had behaved so strangely when Harry spoke to him . . .

Laxton, spooning potatoes onto his plate, was still talking. 'I couldn't see why the Guv'nor was getting so excited – I mean, you can't believe a word these people say, can you? And it was only some old good-for-nothing beggar who was going to die anyway. But Pa seems to think it's a stain on every gentleman's honour for something like this to happen – if it did happen – and besides, with all the riots and rick-burning and what-not down south, I think he's afraid the lower orders may start a riot here if they think one of 'em can be done away with and nothing said.'

'Oh, surely not?' said Harry, taken aback. 'Our people in York aren't like that.'

Laxton shrugged. 'You never know with the lower orders these days, with all this agitation over one thing and another – political unions and radical newspapers and whatnot. But I don't suppose there's a word of truth in the story anyway. I say, old fellow, you ain't eating. Try some of this beef – I must say the grub here isn't half bad. Jolly sort of place, ain't it?'

'Very jolly,' Harry said rather blankly.

'Shall we have the pudding, or the cheese? Or what d'you say to both? Hey waiter —!'

Anstey House, a large, rambling and inconvenient mansion on the Lendal, was a family home in the old style, seething with generations of resident Ansteys and visiting cousins. The present head of the house was Jack, third Baron Anstey, who had spent his whole life at sea and returned to the family home only on the death of his father three years ago. Alfred, the second son, was an MP, unmarried, and lived at home when Parliament was not in session. The family fortune was in coal, and the family business was in the capable hands of the third son, Benjamin, who lived at Anstey House with his wife and four children. Harry, the fourth son, was also unmarried, and there were three unmarried sisters at home. A married sister, Mrs John Shawe, was a frequent and protracted visitor with her three children, and recently the household had been swelled by the permanent addition of elderly widowed Aunt Celia, who had returned to save her purse and to have someone on whom to inflict the sour disposition which had hurried her husband to his grave.

At the present the distaff side of the family was seething with excitement over the forthcoming marriage of one of the sisters-at-home, and when Harry arrived the Great Hall – the hub of the Anstey universe – was a babel of women, children, silk samples and guest lists. Harry, who was an affectionate brother and enjoyed a little cheerful racket, would normally have joined in with relish, but today he only exchanged brief greetings with everyone, ruffled a few children's heads in passing, and headed for the peace of the library. In its severely masculine spaces he expected to find the solitude to think over his worry, but instead he found his brother Jack installed in a chair by the fire.

'Hullo! Escaped the riot?' Jack asked, looking up as Harry hesitated. 'Come and join me. I came in here to do a bit of thinking, but I'm not sure I'm getting anywhere.'

Harry took the settle on the opposite side of the fire, and was just wondering if he could possibly confide his problem and ask Jack's advice when Jack got in first.

'Look here,' he said, leaning forward and clasping his hands between his knees, 'I wonder if I might confide in you?'

'Of course,' Harry said at once. 'What is it?'

'It's a matter that's been brought to me, and I don't know whether I ought to do anything about it.' He smiled nervously. 'If I were still on board my ship I'd know exactly where I stood, but things are so much more complicated ashore.'

'Yes, they are,' Harry agreed feelingly.

'Well, look, I've had a visit from a man called Clulow – d'you happen to know him? No? He's an artisan, respectable from anything I know, has a little place in a yard near St Helen's Square, makes up stained glass pieces in the workshop in front and lives in the back. Unmarried. Regular in his attendances. Rather strait-laced sort of fellow, as he comes across – bald head, gold-rimmed spectacles, neat as a pin.'

Harry nodded encouragement.

'Well now, upstairs from his place is a separate dwelling with an outside staircase which comes down in front of his workshop. So naturally he notices the comings and goings to a certain extent – though he says he keeps himself to himself and doesn't poke into other people's business. All the same, he couldn't help knowing that there was a single young woman living there, and that she had regular visits from a gentleman. Just the one gentleman, so he concluded she was in keeping.'

'Yes,' said Harry.

Jack nodded. 'Nothing in that, of course. It happens. None of his business, he thought. But yesterday he realised that he hadn't seen the girl for some time, or heard her moving about, and he wondered if she was all right. So he went up the steps in a neighbourly way and knocked at the door – got no reply – found the door wasn't locked and went in.' Here Jack paused to take out his handkerchief, wiped it across his brow, and then blew his nose briskly. 'He found the girl there,' he went on soberly, 'dead. It seems she'd hanged herself.'

'Good God! How shocking!'

Jack nodded. 'Worse, perhaps, because she'd obviously been dead some time – several days at least. Clulow felt upset, naturally enough, that the poor creature had been so friendless she'd taken her own life, and no-one had even discovered it. He sent a boy for the constable, and the body was taken away, and that was the end of it as far as Clulow was concerned.'

'But —'

'Yes, of course, you've come to it. And so did Clulow after an hour or two. Who was her gentleman keeper, and why didn't he know how distressed she was – distressed enough to commit such a horrible crime? The last time Clulow saw him was Tuesday afternoon. He's sure he hasn't been back since then, because he's been keeping a lookout for him, for the reason that the gentleman dropped his gloves outside Clulow's door on Tuesday, and Clulow wanted to give them back to him.'

'He doesn't know the gentleman's identity?'

'No. Never spoken to him, and taken care not to be looking up when he went past his window. And the gentleman took care to keep himself muffled up, so evidently he didn't want to be recognised. The thing is – the point that worried Clulow so much when he got to thinking about it – that if the girl had been dead several days when he found her on Wednesday, she must have been already dead when the gentleman last visited on Tuesday.'

Harry was silent.

'The gentleman always visited on a Tuesday and a Friday,' Jack went on reluctantly. 'And he didn't visit today – as if he knew there was no point.'

41

'So what is Clulow suggesting? Not that there's a crime involved, surely?'

'Only the girl's: suicide's a crime, don't forget. So if the gentleman knew she was dead, he ought to have reported it to the authorities. Clulow doesn't know if he should take the matter any further. It can't help the girl any, and he doesn't want to make trouble for the gentleman, but —'

'But how can he, if he doesn't know who the gentleman is?'

'Well, there are the gloves, you see – expensive ones.' Jack reached behind him. 'Handmade, very fine – rather distinctive. He thought probably the maker would remember who he had made them for, if he were asked. The question is, *should* anyone ask? That's the problem Clulow brought to me, and I must say it's left me in a quandary.'

He turned the gloves over in his hands. They were made of fine leather, of an unusual light colour, and were finished with a lining of black fur which was turned back into a cuff. 'They come from Makepeace's – says so on the inside. The question is —'

'Jack?' Harry was staring at the gloves with a feeling of confusion and dread. He had seen them many times before.

His brother looked up. 'I say, old chap, what's wrong?' he asked in concern. 'You look rather odd. Do you feel all right?'

'No need to trouble Makepeace's. I know whose they are.'

In the end Harry went to Morland Place alone. Jack had felt very firmly that there was nothing further to be done.

'It's rather shocking, I suppose, that he didn't report the poor girl's suicide to the magistrate, but it's a minor matter really, and doesn't harm anyone. And if he's taken such pains to keep the whole thing quiet all along ... It would be very embarrassing for him if it were to come out – and Lady Morland is so very strict about those things, and her health hasn't been of the strongest since her husband died ... No, I can understand it. I suppose he felt that nothing could bring the girl back, and that there was no point in upsetting his mother and sacrificing his credit ...'

Harry argued, but Jack stood firm. 'It isn't what I like – I should be sorry to know any of my brothers had behaved so – but it's not my business to go confronting people with their own secrets. The Morlands are one of our oldest and most respected families, and they would have every right to be deeply offended at such impertinent speculation on our part. Besides, we don't know that it *was* Nicholas – the gloves may have come there some other way – or they may not even be his gloves. No, Harry! I'm sorry. We don't know the whole story – and I for one don't want to know it.'

Harry sat in silent thought for a few moments. 'It's no use, Jack,' he said at last. 'I can't leave it at that. Nicky's my oldest friend, and I can't bear a shadow of suspicion to hang over him in my mind. Ten to one but there's a simple explanation, but I must find out how his gloves came there. Will you let me have them? I'll take them to him and ask him straight out, have it all open and frank between us.'

Jack shrugged and handed them over. 'Do as you please about it,' he said. 'but don't bring my name into it. I think you're wrong, much better to leave well alone – but I see you're determined.'

'Thanks,' Harry said, standing up. 'I'll let you know what comes of it.'

'No, don't,' said Jack. 'It isn't my business, and I mean to put it out of my mind. That's what I shall tell Clulow, too.'

When Harry, looking unnaturally grave, said he had something of a delicate and private nature to discuss, Nicholas suggested that they remove to the steward's room, where they could be sure of privacy. This gave him time to think and to compose himself. Harry was his oldest friend – they had known each other from earliest childhood – and such an approach was so out of character that it must bode no good. Harry must be going to ask impertinent questions about his presence in Mucky-Peg Lane, he thought. With anyone else he might stand on his dignity and simply refuse to answer, but with Harry that might be dangerous. He would hear everything in silence, he decided, declining to say anything at all until he knew exactly what it was Harry suspected. If the worst came to the worst he would simply deny everything. Harry could have no proof, or he'd have come before now –

43

and there was nothing to prove anyway, he reminded himself hastily, as his mind drifted dangerously towards things he had forced himself to forget. He must remember he had done no wrong.

So in the steward's room Nicholas sat behind the desk, leaning back in the chair, his mouth resting on his steepled fingers – which had the advantage of enabling him to keep half his face hidden. Harry, sitting very upright in the chair on the other side, plainly much embarrassed, retailed what Clulow had said about the girl and her gentleman caller. He didn't look directly at Nicholas as he spoke, for every moment he grew more embarrassed, feeling it was outrageous that he should be here at all, implicitly asking Nicky to defend himself. Nicky listened, his eyes fixed on Harry, his mind white with panic at what might be the dénouement of the narrative, unable to think of a single thing to say. This was not what he had expected. Damn Clulow! Damn all busybodies!

Harry came to the end of his speech. He laid the gloves on the desk before him, and said, 'These are the gloves – and Nicky, I know they're yours, because I've seen you wearing them a hundred times. And I know you were in York that day, because I saw you – you remember – and you looked upset. Now I know you may say it's none of my business, but we've been friends so long I thought you would not mind if I came to you, because I can't bear to have the slightest suspicion hang over you. I know you can explain it all to me. Pray – pray tell me what happened that day and make me easy again.'

Having stopped speaking, Harry looked at last at Nicholas, hoping that there would be an instant *éclaircissement* offered him, the simple explanation for everything which had not yet occurred to him. When nothing followed but silence, he feared the worst – that Nicholas was horribly offended, and that a painful and embarrassing scene was about to erupt which would leave Harry feeling like the worst beast in nature.

In fact, the silence did betoken enlightenment, but on Nicky's side. He had just had a wonderful idea – so wonderful that it illuminated his entire mind and made him wonder why on earth he hadn't thought of it before. Everything fell into place complete and perfect – the whole plan – the answer to all his problems. All he had to do was to carry it off; and as the silence extended he worked under his concealing fingers to assemble exactly the right expression of gravity, regret, shame, and stern adherence to painful duty.

When at last he put down his hands and spoke, his mouth did tremble with nervousness, but it imparted to his voice a slight quaver which, as he heard at once, was very affecting.

'Let me see the gloves.' Harry pushed them across the desk, and Nicky took them up and pretended to examine them. Then he sighed and put them down. 'I thought so. I didn't really need to look at them, but I hoped there might be some mistake. These are not my gloves, Harry.' He met Harry's eyes steadily. 'They come from Makepeace's, as you see from the label. There was a very fine piece of leather of an unusual colour, just enough to make two pairs of gloves, and my mother bought them for Bendy and me. Bendy, unfortunately, is careless with his possessions. He was in York on Tuesday, and he admitted when he came home that he had lost his gloves, though he couldn't say where. Mine are still upstairs in my room – I can have them fetched, if you'd like to see them.'

Harry was stricken with embarrassment. 'No – no, of course, I don't want to.'

'In any case, there are very slight differences between the two pairs. The cuffs on mine fold down – these, as you see, are stitched. And there is a mark on the right thumb of mine where —'

'Please, Nicky, there's no need to say any more. I'm so sorry I brought it up; but I knew there had to be a simple explanation, and —'

'An explanation there is, but I'm afraid it's not simple. What you've told me is very painful, but I'm afraid it doesn't come as a complete surprise to me. You see, I've known for some time about Bendy's – mistress.'

Harry began to speak, but Nicky continued, mournful as a graveyard. 'Her name is – perhaps I should say was – Annie. I don't know that she ever had another. Bendy and I knew her from childhood. She was an orphan, taken from the workhouse by one of our tenant farmers, Pike by name. He farms

Eastfield – a most respectable man. Perhaps you know him? He'll confirm what I say, at any rate. He employed Annie about the house and farmyard, until Benedict debauched her.'

'Please, you don't need to —'

'Let me tell you the rest,' Nicky begged. 'I've carried the burden alone for so long, and now you know so much, you may as well know it all. I believe the girl wasn't to blame – indeed, she tried to break the unlawful relationship by running away from Eastfield to York, but Bendy found her again and, by what means I don't know, persuaded her to go into his keeping. After that, he visited her regularly, but over the years his tastes changed. He —' He put his hands over his face for a moment and shuddered. 'He told me about it one day – about the vile unnatural lusts he sated on that poor girl. No wonder she was driven in the end to take her own life! She did not deserve such a fate. If only I had intervened sooner!'

'It's not your fault,' Harry protested automatically. 'No-one could possibly blame you. But – but Bendy? I can't believe it. He's so young – and such a nice, friendly sort of fellow —'

Nicholas looked grave. 'If you knew him better you wouldn't find it hard to believe. The image he presents to the world is very different from the reality. His vices are so many – his drunkenness, his violence, his debaucheries —' Another shudder. 'I keep it from our mother; shield him as far as possible from exposure, for her sake. Perhaps I shouldn't have done so. If he had been exposed sooner, perhaps this poor girl wouldn't have been driven to the extreme.'

Harry sat in stunned silence. It was so hard to believe of Bendy – and yet, what had he been suspecting of Nicky? He didn't quite know; but not this, not such a catalogue of depravity and callousness. Bendy was a little wild, perhaps – Harry had encountered the fringes of some of his kick-ups, but they had been no more than the high-spirited larks of youth. Or so it had seemed. Well, after all, he had seen little of Bendy since he had stopped coming to Morland Place for lessons, and a person could change a great deal in seven years – particularly when they were the years of change from boyhood to manhood. Bendy had always been solitary, going off on his own for long periods. Harry had to admit he didn't really know him.

There was one more thing he had to ask. 'Nicky, what *were* you doing in Mucky-Peg Lane that afternoon? Was it something to do with – with this business of Bendy's?'

'In a way,' Nicky said slowly, thinking hard. 'I – I was just going back to fetch my horse from the Grapes, when I saw him coming out of Mucky-Peg Lane. Seeing him there I guessed where he must have been – I knew he kept his wretched mistress somewhere in that vicinity – and I thought it would be a good moment to tackle him on the subject, try to make him see the error of his ways. But when I spoke to him he became violently angry, told me to mind my own business, and hit out at me with his cane. Fortunately I caught the blow with my own —'

'Yes, I saw you staring at it.'

'Left quite a dent,' Nicky said with a rueful smile. 'Anyway, he ran off – I don't know where – and then you came along. I was so shaken I'm afraid I spoke rather roughly to you.'

'No matter. Please, I understand,' Harry said vaguely. Was it Benedict, then, who struck the pauper down? Or some other gentleman? Would it not be a coincidence that there should be yet another gentleman in those back lanes? But there was no proof. No proof of any sort.

Nicholas was watching him from under his eyelids. Now for the dénouement. He sighed heavily and said, 'His sins have been great, Harry, but still he's my brother. I don't want him to be exposed. Who else knows about this?'

'No-one,' Harry said. He hesitated, wondering whether to tell Nicky about the pauper; but he had no proof it was Benedict – and no proof but a beggar-woman's word that the attack had been unprovoked, or that there had been an attack at all. The old man might have fallen and broken his head on a wall or kerbstone. Better not to say anything. Yet if Bendy were of a violent disposition —

Nicky fixed his eyes on Harry pleadingly. 'Need he be exposed? Need our family be brought to public shame? I think of my mother chiefly. She—' a broken note crept into his voice, 'she has not been well since Papa was killed in that dreadful accident. She isn't strong, and I'm afraid another shock —'

47

'Good God, no!' Harry said quickly. 'I would not for the world – it isn't for me to say anything to anyone. I only came here – you must understand – when I saw the gloves I thought were yours – and Clulow said the girl must have been dead already when —'

'I understand,' Nicholas said, lowering his eyelids to hide the gleam of hatred in his eyes. *I will never forgive you, Harry Anstey, for suspecting me of – of I don't know what.* 'I don't blame you in the least. But it needn't go any further, need it?'

'Not from my tongue,' Harry said. 'But Nicky, have you thought – if he really is as depraved and violent as you say, what might he not do next? You may be in danger yourself —'

'No,' Nicholas said. 'I shall be safe enough. But you're right – I can't put anyone else at risk, particularly not my mother. Even the slightest hint of what his true nature is might kill her. Bendy must be sent away. It's time and past time that he was put to an occupation – in fact, it's my belief that he would not be half so much trouble if he had something to do to occupy his time.'

'Do you think so?'

'I know so. And I know just how to handle it. I shall say you have been here to warn me that you have heard, through your employment, that there may be a prosecution against him for failing to report the death. I shall tell him that I will persuade the magistrates to let it drop, provided that he goes away from Morland Place. I will arrange for him to join some profession or trade – something that will give him the means to support himself honestly, if he applies himself.'

'But what will your mother think about that?' Harry asked doubtfully.

'He shall tell mother that it is his wish to go. That may upset her a little, but not nearly so much as knowing what he really is. All I need, Harry, is your promise that you will never tell anyone – and particularly not my mother – anything about this business.'

'It seems to be the best solution,' Harry said after a moment. 'If it's what you want, I will go along with it. But must he be banished for ever? Surely your mother —'

'Oh no,' Nicky said generously, 'only until he has proved he can behave in a civilised manner. I'm confident that if he has some hard, honest work to do, he will settle down. He has had rather too much the power of doing as he pleases these past few years. And after all,' he shrugged, and his eyes grew cold, 'if he does not change his ways, he will certainly end on the gallows in a very short time – that, or they will lock him up in bedlam. Either way, his account will be settled.'

'Yes,' said Harry uneasily. His mind was reeling from the shocks it had received in the past few hours, and he was longing now for solitude to compose himself. He stood up to take his leave. 'When will you – confront Bendy?'

'At once,' said Nicky, and sighed. 'There can be no delay in a matter like this. The sooner he is gone the better.'

'I shall be glad,' Harry confessed, 'not to have to meet him again, knowing what I know.' He looked at his friend with pity. 'How much worse for you, old fellow,' he said gently. 'I am so very sorry, Nicky! You must feel it dreadfully.'

Nicky nodded sadly, looking down at the desk. 'I shall feel it every day of my life. But I must do my duty, to Morland Place and the family, and to my mother. She must be protected at all costs. And we can hope, can't we,' raising his eyes to Harry's face, 'that Bendy will change – that the shock of being discovered will make him mend his ways.'

'Yes,' said Harry. 'Yes, I'm sure it will. I can't believe he is so very bad – not having been brought up here, and by the same good Father Moineau as us.'

'I hope you're right,' Nicky said. 'The sad fact of the matter, though, is that Father Moineau didn't beat Bendy enough. Papa often commented on it, and now I'm afraid he's been proved to have been right.'

Benedict faced his brother white-faced, feeling physically sick with the mixture of shock and anger which had raged through him while Nicholas spoke.

'You can't believe such a thing of me! You can't!'

'I have all the proof I need,' said Nicholas calmly.

'It isn't proof! How can you think it? I know you've always hated me, but —'

'Hated you? What nonsense! You're my brother. Hate the sin but love the sinner, isn't that what we're taught? Your sins

49

have found you out, that's all – and hateful they are indeed! Not only to debauch that girl, inflict your horrible depravities on her, driving her to her death, and leave her poor body without reporting it to anyone – but then to kill a harmless old beggar in cold blood —'

'But I didn't! It's not true! It wasn't me!'

'You may splutter all you like, but the fact is that you're caught, and you know it! Farmer Pike has confirmed that you debauched the wretched girl, Annie. Can you deny she was your – your mistress, for want of a better word?'

'No – no, I can't, but —'

'And everyone knows that those are your gloves. Look at them, if you like. Mine have a small stain on the right thumb, as you know, and the cuffs are different. There's no doubt about it. Can you explain how they came to be outside the poor girl's apartment?'

Benedict stared at the gloves, feeling dazed by the rapidity of events. 'I lost them somewhere. I don't know where. When I was coming home from York on Tuesday I felt in my pockets for them, but they were gone.'

'Ah, you admit you were in York on Tuesday, then?' Nicky said quickly.

'Of course I was! But I was —' He stopped.

'Yes? You were where, brother? Where did you spend your time in York that day? Produce your witness, if you please.'

Bendy hesitated, looking at Nicky with troubled eyes. Whatever the cost to himself, he could not expose Serena. He could not throw her to the jackal gossips, to be torn to shreds; could not allow their love to be dragged through the mud and made tawdry. And some deep instinct, born of the experience of being Nicky's brother all these years, told him he must not put Serena into Nicky's power.

'I can't say,' he muttered at last.

'Well then, you can't expect anyone to believe you,' Nicholas said triumphantly. 'The evidence is clear. The man who drove that poor girl to her death is the man who killed the beggar; and that man is you. You are guilty, guilty, guilty.'

'No!' Bendy cried in frustration. 'It isn't true. No-one could believe I would do such a thing —'

'Harry Anstey believes, with no trouble at all, and he knows you pretty well,' Nicholas cut in.

'But you – what about you? You know me, brother. Can you believe I would do such a thing?'

'I wish I need not,' Nicky said, strong but sad, 'but what choice have I? The evidence all points to you, and you cannot explain yourself to my satisfaction. The magistrates believe you guilty, and if I do not hold them off, they will go to our mother. Would you like to try if she will believe? We can go together now and tell her – if that's what you want.'

Bendy shook his head. He thought of his mother, frail, withdrawn, grieving for their father. The shock would be appalling, whether she believed it or not – and how could she not believe, when Nicky, her beloved firstborn, told her it was so? Between the two of them, she would have to take Nicky's word over Bendy's, and the struggle might break her heart. He loved her too much to put her to the pain. 'I don't want our mother to know,' he said.

'I'm glad of that,' Nicky said. 'My only concern is to keep it from her. That is all I care about. It would break her heart to know what a monster her son has become.'

'What do you mean to do, then?' Bendy asked blankly. He felt as though he were trapped in a dream and unable to wake up.

'I will take care of everything, and make sure Mama never knows about any of this, provided you agree to go away,' Nicky said.

'Go away?'

'You must leave Morland Place. I have persuaded the magistrates not to make charges against you, provided you go away from this district and do not show yourself here again. They do not wish to destroy our family and break our mother's heart. But you must go at once, otherwise I cannot promise your secret will be kept.'

'But where can I go?'

'I've thought about that. There must be a plausible reason for your going. I don't want Mama to grieve for you. She must think you've gone of your own accord.' Bendy stared uncomprehendingly, and Nicky smiled suddenly. He was enjoying himself immensely. 'You've always been mad for the railways, haven't you? And I've often heard you say to Father

51

Moineau that you wish you could have become an engineer. Well, your ambition is about to be realised! You will write our mother a note to say that you have gone to Northumberland to seek out Mr Stephenson, to ask him to take you on as an apprentice. You will say your heart is not in helping me run the estate, and that you mean to stay away until you have learned enough to be able to earn your living honestly amongst the railway undertakers. You hope she will not blame you, but as you fear she might try to prevent you, you are giving yourself the necessary pain of leaving without saying goodbye.'

'No – please —!'

'That way she might think you ungrateful or undutiful,' Nicholas continued implacably, 'but she will not worry about you, or try to bring you back.'

'When – when shall I return?'

'If you prove yourself honest and diligent, and conduct yourself like a gentleman, after a few years it may be possible to persuade the magistrates to allow you to return. I cannot tell.'

'But my mother —'

'When you are settled somewhere, you may send a letter telling her you are well and happy; but nothing more. Remember I shall make a point of examining her letters before she sees them, and anything I don't care for will not reach her. At all costs she must not be upset.'

Benedict bent his head, unable to think of anything to say.

'You had better go immediately, before dinner,' Nicky went on. 'Otherwise you will have to meet Mama again, and I don't wish her to be exposed to you any more. Take with you only what you can carry in a small valise – anything larger may cause comment. Say nothing to anyone. Be sure no-one sees you packing. When it is dark you can slip out the back way and walk across the fields. Here is a purse – enough money for your coach fare and your immediate necessities. If you are careful, it should be enough to keep you for several months.'

'Thank you,' Bendy said dazedly. 'You are – most kind.'

'I am doing it for our mother's sake, not yours. If I were you, I should mend my ways – or at least learn to be more discreet, when you get to your new home. You need not, of course, go to Northumberland. That is merely what you will tell Mama. For my part, I would do anything rather than further the cause of those vile railways.'

In the shock and bewilderment of what was happening to him, Benedict saw the railway idea as the one gleam of comfort. 'I will go to Northumberland,' he said.

'You may suit yourself,' Nicky said with an indifferent shrug.

It was only when Benedict was actually at the nursery-stair door and about to open it that he realised Fand was with him. She had been his father's bitch, but she had come to his knee when Papa died, and had been called his ever since. After having lost one master, she didn't like to be separated from her second even for a short time. If he left her behind at any time, she greeted him on his return with wild joy, as though reprieved from death; but usually she managed to slip out with him.

Benedict stopped and looked down at her. 'Not this time,' he said softly. She swung her tail slowly at the sound of his voice. He flung out a stern hand. 'No, Fand. Go back!'

She gazed up at him earnestly with her wolf-yellow eyes, trying to express her willingness to go with him wherever it was, even though there was a warm fire back in the house, and it was snowing outside. Benedict put down his bag, hunkered down, and caught her muzzle in his hand. 'Listen, fool! You can't come with me.' She swung her tail harder, lashing it heedlessly against the wall. 'I've got a long walk ahead of me, and an uncertain destination. I can't take you, foolish one.' Fand wriggled in ecstasy, trying to get her muzzle free so that she could lick his face, and suddenly he laughed, though he felt much closer to crying. He released her and stood up. 'On your own head be it, then,' he said. 'No complaints from you later about cold or hunger or sore paws.'

Fand capered joyfully, butting his hands with her muzzle, and he was glad for once that hounds of the Morland breed did not bark. He picked up the bag, unlatched the door, and stepped out into the white world, and she shouldered past him gladly, to make sure she would not be left behind, and ran forward, taking foolish bites at the strange falling white stuff.

The snow would hide their footprints, Benedict thought. He resented being forced to leave his home like a thief in the night, without being able to say goodbye – to Mama, to Father Moineau, to the servants, to dear old Beau. But he would have had to leave some time. He had always known that Nicky would drive him out one day. He only had not expected it to be so soon – and not like this!

What was the truth about those gloves? They were his all right – there was no doubt about that – and he had lost them, but how had they got to the place where they had been found? The suspicion had crossed his mind just once that what he had been accused of was in fact Nicky's crime, and that he was saving himself by blaming Bendy. It was a hideous thing to think about one's own brother, and he banished it fiercely from his mind. He must put the suspicion from him and never think it again. Above all Mama must be protected. It would break her heart if Nicky told what he had threatened to tell, and if this was the only way to save her from that, he must do it.

He hunched his shoulders against the whirling snow, and set off across the fields he knew so well. Fand, puzzled but philosophical, tucked herself in behind him and kept her head down. Why her god wished to go walking in this weather instead of toasting his feet on the fender she didn't know, but she would follow him until she dropped, rather than be left behind. The snow crusted on her harsh coat until she was almost invisible from above. It filled their footprints as they went, as though the elements wished to obliterate even the memory of them.

CHAPTER FOUR

When Fenby, the butler at Hobsbawn House in Manchester, opened the door to his master on Christmas Eve, he saw that it had started snowing again – that soft, wet, tiresome snow that settled only long enough to make a gentleman's coat wet and stain his boots, without giving the ladies anything pretty to look at the next day.

Jasper Hobsbawn met his servant's eyes as he stepped into the hall, and smiled ruefully. 'Yes, I know, I shouldn't have walked! But I didn't know how long I would be, and I don't like to keep the horses waiting in this weather.'

'Just as you say, sir,' Fenby said, looking gloomily at his boots. Jasper took off his hat and gloves, and Fenby surreptitiously wiped the crown of the hat on his sleeve before putting them down on the hall table. He didn't want troublesome watermarks to have to remove. In his opinion no gentleman ought ever to walk, and it was the coachman's business to worry about the horses, not the master's. But Mr Hobsbawn wasn't nearly particular enough about appearances. He removed his master's coat and shook it with an air of delicate reproof. 'Mr Henry Droylsden is here, sir.'

'Is he indeed? Excellent,' Jasper said, heading for the stairs. Droylsden was the son of a local banker who had been bankrupted in the crash of Christmas 1825. Henry, with his brother Percy and his wife, had set up house in an economical way, with their parents as lodgers sharing the bills. Percy was now undergoing the novel experience of working for his living as a clerk in one of the new joint-stock banks which had recently been set up; Henry, much less reluctantly, had found work with the *Manchester Observer*, which made him both an

55

amusing companion and a useful friend to Jasper.

'Will Mr Droylsden be staying to dinner, sir?' Fenby enquired of his master's departing back. Jasper realised that was meant as a pointed reminder that he was already late and that it lacked only half an hour to dinner. It was a wonderful thing, he thought, to be wealthy enough to have servants, but they were a dreadful restriction on one's freedom.

'Oh, Lord! I expect so.' The Droylsdens' budget was such that an invitation to eat at someone else's table was rarely refused. 'Mrs Hobsbawn will talk to you about that,' he added, escaping upstairs.

As he approached the drawing-room he heard the sound of music and smiled to himself; opening the door quietly he was able to view the scene for a moment without disturbing it. Henry Droylsden – no mean musician, whose talent with the fiddle had made him a popular guest in lighter-hearted days – was seated at the pianoforte playing the accompaniment, while nine-year-old Fanny stood beside him, heels together and hands behind her back, singing 'The Ash Grove'. Fanny's fair hair was arranged in ringlets which were held back by a blue ribbon the same colour as her eyes, and one long curl was disposed to droop becomingly over her shoulder. She looked like an angel, Jasper thought, and sang pretty much as well as one.

Fanny's mother was sitting in the fireside chair, her hands clasped together in pride, her whole admiring attention given to Fanny; but Fanny's eyes were fixed on Mr Henry Droylsden, and when he glanced up at her every few notes, as an accompanist should, her long eyelashes fluttered down and brushed her rose-petal cheeks. Jasper chuckled silently to himself. Fanny was not strictly speaking a beauty, but she already had all the wiles of a coquette, and it seemed doubtful that any male creature would ever be heartless enough to resist her.

The last note was sung, Droylsden played a rippling arpeggio with several unnecessary flourishes, and Fanny sank in a balletic curtsey to him, holding out her skirts to either side and pointing her leading toe daintily.

'Well done, darling!' Sophie cried, applauding.

Jasper joined in. 'Yes, bravo my little nightingale!' he

laughed. 'A heart-rending performance.'

Fanny rose. 'Papa!' she cried, and rushed across the room to him with flattering eagerness. 'How late you are! Is it still snowing? Will everything be white when I wake up?'

'It is snowing, but I don't think it will settle,' Jasper said, returning her embraces. She smelled innocent as fresh laundry, sweet as pot-pourri. 'It's not the right sort of snow. Isn't it past time you were in bed, my love?'

She lowered her eyelashes beguilingly at him. 'Mama said I might wait for you. I was *so* worried when you didn't come home.'

'So you were keeping everyone's worries at bay by entertaining them,' Jasper suggested. 'How philanthropic of you.'

Fanny didn't know what philanthropic meant, but she could tell from the way Mr Droylsden laughed that she was being roasted. She pouted a little. 'I want to go toboganing with you tomorrow,' she complained. 'You *said* we could.'

'Much as I would wish to be able to pluck the stars out of the sky for you, Fanny Hobsbawn,' Jasper said, 'I'm afraid I cannot control the weather.' His hand still fastened in Fanny's, he walked over to his wife and stooped to kiss her. 'Well, Mrs Hobsbawn?'

Sophie looked up into his eyes and exchanged assurances with him. 'Very well, thank you.'

'How has young Master Hobsbawn behaved himself today?'

She coloured. 'Jasper, we have company,' she murmured protestingly.

Jasper straightened up and grinned at Droylsden. 'Oh, Henry counts as family. Anyone who has been flirted with by Fanny must count as family.'

'Either that,' Droylsden said agreeably, 'or she will have to marry me to save my reputation.'

Fanny was still catching up. 'Papa, who is young Master Hobsbawn?' she asked suspiciously.

Droylsden laughed, Sophie blushed deeper, but Jasper said airily, 'Oh, did I say Master? I meant Miss, of course. How has Miss Hobsbawn behaved herself today? Have you been good, Fanny?'

'I am always good,' she replied with certitude.

'Of course. Foolish of me to ask,' he said, pulling the bell.

'And now it really is time for you to go to bed.' He forestalled her mutinous look by bowing to her and saying, 'I am very glad you waited up for me, Miss Hobsbawn. May I have the honour of breakfasting with you tomorrow morning?'

She took the cue and curtseyed in reply, and the door opened and the nursery maid, Janet, appeared. 'Miss Hobsbawn wishes to retire, Janet,' said Jasper grandly.

Fanny said her goodnights and retired with reasonably good grace, pausing in the doorway to announce superbly, by way of a parting shot, '*And* I know who Master Hobsbawn is, but I'm too p'lite to mention it in company.' The door closed behind her.

'Jasper, you are shamed!' Droylsden declared.

'She's a minx,' Jasper agreed, laughing.

'You spoil her,' Sophie said, a little discomfited.

'Who has a better right?' Jasper said lightly. 'I collect you are thinking of Lord Batchworth; but he's a mere pretender. Would you have me yield my place to some Johnny-come-lately, however nobly born?'

Droylsden stood up and closed the piano lid. 'You will have to give up your place one day, and I don't think you'll like it whenever it happens,' he said shrewdly. 'What will you do when the beaux start to dangle after her in earnest?'

'Keep guard with a shotgun,' Jasper said. 'But I think I may still have five years left to me on the throne, so let me enjoy them! Sophie, Fenby was asking whether Henry is staying to dinner. Should you give instructions?'

'Yes, of course,' Sophie said. 'Henry, you'll stay, I hope?'

'Thank you,' said Droylsden. 'If you don't mind my not being dressed?'

'Of course not. We are quite informal.' Sophie looked at Jasper. 'Have you a great deal to discuss? Should we put dinner back?'

'No, no, I don't want to put myself further in Fenby's bad books. We'll talk afterwards, if that's agreeable to you, Henry?'

'You shouldn't let your servants bully you,' Droylsden grinned. 'My father used to make a point of inconveniencing them severely at least once a week, just to remind them who was master.'

'But Fenby already knows perfectly well who is master,' Jasper said. 'If I didn't have the mills to play tyrant in, I should have no self-regard at all.'

Sophie, who was six months pregnant, retired to bed immediately the cloth was drawn. 'I have to be very careful,' she apologised obliquely to Droylsden.

She had had two miscarriages in the past, and had not expected to conceive again, so her and Jasper's hopes were very much bound up in the present situation. Droylsden knew as much as he needed to of this history from his sister-in-law Agnes, whose own sister Prudence was not only Sophie's particular friend but also the wife of her physician. Henry did not embarrass Sophie by any further comment or enquiry, but when she had left the room, he said to Jasper, 'Mrs Hobsbawn is looking very well. I hope all is going smoothly this time?'

'It seems so,' Jasper said cautiously. 'As she said, we are being very careful. She wanted very much to go to Morland Place for Christmas, but Hastings said a long journey by carriage at this time of year would be dangerous. Of course, Hastings says she must not be upset or made anxious, either. It's a difficult business, balancing the one against the other.'

Droylsden nodded sympathetically. 'But it will be worth all the trouble when you have a son to follow you at the mills,' he suggested.

'I don't know,' Jasper frowned. 'I had sooner not put Sophie through it. Of course, I shall be glad once the baby's here and it's all over, but I'd have been happy enough to settle for Fanny and no more.'

'Fanny's an original,' Droylsden agreed. 'I'm only sorry I'm a good twenty years too old for her, or I'd be one of the puppies making a nuisance of myself outside your window in five or six years' time.'

'You'd have to get past Batchworth first,' Jasper said. He stood up. 'I know that you like to blow a cloud after your dinner, so I told Fenby to light a fire in the business-room. Shall we retire there?'

'Very decent of you, Jasper,' Droylsden said, 'but if you don't mean to indulge yourself —'

'Oh, I don't do it very often because Sophie doesn't like it, but I think I may join you tonight,' Jasper said. 'Tonight I just have a fancy for a good cigar.' He picked up a branch of candles from the table and led the way downstairs and across the hall to old Mr Hobsbawn's business-room, which, now that Jasper conducted all his business from the mill, did service as the smoking-room when one was required. The fire had burned up nicely, and the decanter and glasses set on a low table beside the box of cigars were sparkling in the firelight.

'I say, this is something like!' Droylsden said. 'I'm never allowed a fire in the smoking-room at home. A sort of punishment, I suppose, for indulging in the filthy habit! Papa don't, and Percy is terribly disapproving, so he sets aside the smallest room with the illest grace. Oddly enough, Mama and Agnes don't seem to mind nearly as much, though of course since no-one would ever smoke in their presence, I suppose it don't affect them much.'

'The smoking-room at Batchworth House is like that,' Jasper said. 'Icy cold, and no furniture but two hard chairs and a fire-bucket! But at Morland Place one has to go outside in the garden, whatever the weather, so you should think yourself lucky!' He opened the armoire in the corner and took out his smoking-jacket and cap, and a spare set kept there for the guest who did not come prepared. When they had changed, Jasper hung up their ordinary jackets in the cupboard, and they made themselves comfortable by the fire and lit up.

'So, how did the meeting of the Improvement Commissioners go today?' Droylsden asked, blowing his cloud towards the glowing fire. 'I suppose there was the usual *tracasserie* from the opposition?'

Jasper frowned. 'Yes, though it's nowhere near as bad as it used to be under the old system – well, you remember.'

'I do indeed,' said Droylsden, who had been a commissioner himself at one time, before his father's bankruptcy.

'At least now that we have elected commissioners, we can make sure only the right people get onto the board. But still the radicals seem to object to everything we try to do.'

'What was it this time?'

60

'Oh, a committee representing the ratepayers, objecting to the cost of cleaning Market Street. They said that it wasn't their horses that fouled the road but the carters', and they didn't see why they should pay for the manure to be taken away. And when Audenshaw explained to them very kindly that the sale of the manure would more than defray the cost of collecting it, they wanted to know why their own manure wasn't being collected from outside their houses and the profit put back into their own pockets.'

Droylsden laughed. 'A truly flexible attitude of mind!'

But Jasper was not amused. 'Not so much flexible as contorted!' He sighed and shook his head. 'When we want to put up street names and number the houses, they accuse us of trying to institute a police state. When we plan to widen a road, they object to the compulsory purchase of some dilapidated ruin that would have fallen down before long anyway.'

'I know, I know. They want things done, but don't want anyone to have the power to do them! And if you do manage to achieve something, someone always knows how it could have been done far better, and for no expense at all! You could resign, you know.'

'Yes, but there's so much that needs doing. The condition of the poor in the worst areas, especially the filthiness of the streets and the lack of a decent water-supply, are things I can't turn my back on. I don't suppose you'd remember the cholera epidemic of '06 – perhaps you were too young – but I tell you unless we do something about those conditions, Manchester will see another epidemic one of these summers.'

'You may be right,' Droylsden said. 'The smell in some of those courts and alleys off the main streets is intolerable.'

'Yes, and in the miasma lurks the infection! That's where our plague will come from; and this time it will be much worse, because the overcrowding is so much more severe.' He drew on his cigar to calm himself. 'It's so hard to get anything done.'

'People are astonishingly resistant to whatever is good for them,' Droylsden agreed. 'You must look for your reward in heaven, I fear.'

61

Jasper smiled ruefully. 'I'm sorry to bore you with my complaints. You wanted to talk to me about something in particular?'

'Yes, but it is apropos of what we've been discussing.' Droylsden leaned forward. 'I have had word, through a roundabout route, of a more than usually well-organised protest against your scheme for widening Exchange Street.'

Jasper looked surprised. 'But surely everyone must agree on the necessity? It is a main thoroughfare – everyone in Manchester passes through it practically every day, and the nuisance, especially to the ladies, of the narrow flagways and the accumulation of dirt —'

'Yes, yes, old fellow. I know all about that, and I know it's your hobby horse. What's more to the point is that some other people know how dear it is to your heart, and that's where the trouble may lie.'

'What can you mean?'

'There is opposition to your scheme.' Droylsden counted off on his fingers. 'There are the usual complaints that it's unnecessary: "I never walk there myself, you know!"; and the ratepayers' objections to the cost: "If it were my own street it would be different. Let those who live there pay for it." Then there are the anti-Jacobins, who believe that every change of any sort must inevitably lead us helter-skelter down the road to disorder, degeneracy, and thence via the universal franchise to revolution. You've heard 'em —'

'"Remember Peterloo!"' Jasper supplied. 'Yes, but —'

'And *then* there is a rather odd and sinister collection of people who claim to be representing the occupants of Elias Buildings – one of the tenements which would have to be pulled down to make way for the scheme.'

'But those rooms are occupied by the poorest sort of Irish immigrants. They don't have employment, and I very much doubt if any of them pays a penny in rent. Who on earth would want to represent them?' Jasper asked, puzzled.

'There's the worrying part,' said Droylsden. 'I discovered today that one of the leaders of this strange group is that Irish weaver who tried to organise a strike at your mills last year.'

'Good God! You don't mean Maloney? How did you find that out?'

'Oh, working on the *Observer* I get to hear things,' Droylsden said lightly. 'When I was in the Pack Horse the other day —'

'You frequent that place?'

'Only in the line of duty, old chap! I hear things in there that I wouldn't discover in a year of hanging about the Red Lion or the King's Arms. As I was saying, I was in there the other day, and an informant of mine told me that Maloney and his friends had been overheard swearing revenge on you for breaking their strike and starving them out. They are very anxious to start up a Trade Union in this town, and people like you stand in their way.'

Jasper was angry. 'There's no need for associations of that sort: I will take care of my own employees, without asking permission of some outsider who knows nothing of my dispositions. They're only interested in their own power, anyway, people like Maloney! He never had any real interest in the welfare of my mill hands. Self-aggrandisement was his sole aim, and he meant to achieve it by stirring up trouble amongst my people.'

'I dare say you're right,' Droylsden said mildly. 'I'm just telling you what I heard. But Maloney and his friends are not the only members of this Elias Buildings committee who have a personal spite against you. There's another element just as sinister.'

'And what's that?'

'I learnt – to my considerable surprise – that Elias Buildings recently changed hands; for a very low price, understandably, but still it seemed odd that anyone would want to buy a building under threat of demolition. Unless, of course, they wished to have a legitimate right to protest against the project, to delay, even to defeat it. I decided to find out who was the eager purchaser, and just today my informant told me that it was bought by one Martin Duxbury —'

'Martin Duxbury?' Jasper wrinkled his brow. 'Who on earth is he?'

'He's a chapman – dealer in odds and ends – unsavoury reputation. One or two short periods in the County Gaol for this and that. But he's a small player on a larger stage, Jasper. He is acting on behalf of a former bankrupt who, naturally enough, wishes to remain in the background. *He* is the someone who really wants to scupper your project. The someone who has a long grudge against you, and wishes you ill. Do I need to name him to you?'

'You can't mean – Olmondroyd?'

'The same.'

'But he went away from Manchester back in '25, when he had to sell his new mill and everything else at a loss.'

'Well, he's come back,' Droylsden said, 'and apparently he has acquired enough money in some way to be able to employ Duxbury, and to keep one or two others like Maloney sitting around his fire.' Henry paused, surveying his friend's face. 'Now you see why I'm worried. The combination of Olmondroyd and Maloney is a powerful blend of spite and unscrupulousness. They are going to try to make trouble for you. I only hope they don't find a way.'

'I don't see what they can do to harm me,' Jasper said slowly, 'but at all events, Sophie mustn't learn of this. She mustn't be alarmed.'

Droylsden spread his hands. 'No reason for the moment why she should know. But what do you mean to do about it?'

'I don't see that there's anything I can do, unless they do something in breach of the law. If they make their objections to the Exchange Street scheme in form, we will deal with them in form. In the end, it will be for the commission as a whole to decide. It isn't a matter in which I personally have the final say – as they must very well know.'

Droylsden shook his head. 'I admire your courage, Jasper. But I think you should be on your guard. Neither of them has any scruples, as far as I can see, when it comes to getting his own way. Indeed, I doubt whether Olmondroyd is wholly rational; and Maloney commands a considerable following amongst those who are not averse to a little violence from time to time. Well, you already know what he is capable of. The attack on your mills last year —'

Jasper nodded gravely, his mind busy. 'I'll double the watch for the next few weeks. I have good men there – they were tested during the strike. If there should be any attempt, they'll fight it off all right. Olmondroyd still believes I had a hand in burning down his first mill,' he added, meeting Droylsden's eyes. 'I suppose he may try to retaliate in the same manner.'

'Double the watch on your mills, day and night,' Droylsden agreed, and added reluctantly, 'And on your house, Jasper.'

Jasper was shocked. 'Surely you don't think —?'

'No, of course not, old fellow. But these are not men like us. I wish you would take every precaution – for Sophie's sake, and Fanny's, if not your own. And I'll keep my ear to the ground. If anything is planned, I ought to have advance warning of it.'

The two men sat talking so late that the rather meagre supply of coals left them was used up and the fire burned low. It was the creeping coldness of the room which roused them from their deep conversation, and Droylsden was just stretching himself and murmuring that he ought to be thinking of going when there was a tap on the door and Fenby appeared, looking a little ruffled and more than a little put out.

'I beg your pardon, sir, but there is a person at the door who insists on seeing you.'

'A person? At this time of night?' Jasper exclaimed, and then, seeing Droylsden's reaction out of the corner of his eye he thought of the dangers of Maloney and Olmondroyd. 'What sort of a person, Fenby? Do you know him? Out with it, man! Don't be coy with me.'

'I have never seen the person before sir,' Fenby said in offended tones. 'He has the appearance of a gentleman who has been travelling for some considerable time, sir, without the benefit of suitable accommodation. And he is accompanied by a large dog.'

Droylsden was amused by the butler's circumlocutions. 'I think he means it's a gypsy, Jasper,' he grinned.

'The gentleman *claims* to be madam's brother, sir,' Fenby said witheringly.

'Good God!' Jasper said, much astonished. 'Well, bring him in here, then, Fenby.'

The butler bowed slightly and went away, to return a moment later to announce, with an air of almost violently disassociating himself from the matter, 'Mr Morland, sir.'

Jasper was on his feet. 'Bendy! It is you! What on earth are you doing here?' He eyed his visitor's coat and boots and said quickly, 'Come to the fire. You look perished – and that poor dog, too. Is it still snowing? Fenby, have some more coals sent in at once! Have you eaten? No? Fenby, some cold meat and bread and a bottle of sherry as well, as quick as you can – and a plate of scraps for the dog.'

The butler departed with a mortified air. Benedict stood gratefully before the poor fire and accepted the last of the brandy which Henry Droylsden had silently poured for him, while Fand crouched shivering at his feet.

'Thanks,' Bendy said, and took a swallow. 'I'm sorry to come so late, Jasper, but I didn't want to run the risk of upsetting Sophie. You'll know best how to break it to her.'

'Break what to her? Is it bad news? Your mother —?'

'No, Mama's well enough. But I'm afraid I'm in disgrace.'

'Shall I go?' Droylsden asked discreetly.

'Lord, no, not on my account. I've nothing to be ashamed of, but I know Sophie mustn't be frightened, in her condition, so I thought I'd better wait until she'd gone to bed. I thought I might have left it too late when your man was so tardy coming to the door, and that you'd all retired. But I'd seen you go in, Droylsden, and hadn't seen you come out again. Began to think I must have missed you, though, or that you'd slipped out another way.'

'You've been waiting outside all evening?' Jasper asked. 'You must be frozen to the marrow. Where is that man – ah!' The door opened and Fenby came in with a tray, followed by a sleepy-looking footman with his coat awry, bearing a welcome scuttleful of coals.

When they were alone, and the fire – after some brisk work with the bellows – was burning up again, Jasper handed Bendy a plate and glass and said, 'Well now, in your own time, perhaps you'll tell us what's happened?'

Between mouthfuls, and without going into detail, Bendy told the tale of his accusation and banishment. 'I swear to you I'm innocent of everything I'm charged with,' he said at last. 'I was – well, I was with someone the whole of the time who could attest to that, but I can't – I mustn't —' He blushed. 'It is a lady, you see, and I couldn't possibly name her to save my own skin.'

Henry looked away to conceal a smile, but Jasper said

gravely, 'No, I see that, old fellow. A gentleman couldn't.'

'So I couldn't see any way out but to do as Nicky said. To fight it would have meant mother knowing about it, and that was the one thing I agreed with Nicky about – that she must not be upset.'

Jasper looked grave and cast a doubtful glance at Henry, but the latter shook his head minutely, and said to Benedict, 'Once mud has been thrown, there will always be a little that sticks. I don't think I would have acted as patiently as you did, but I do see you were in a predicament.'

Bendy looked grateful. 'Well, that's what I thought. And then when I thought about it more calmly, it seemed like a God-sent opportunity for me to do what I had always wanted to do anyway. I must have a career of some sort, you know, some way to provide for myself, but Mama would never consider it. She thought I would just live at Morland Place for ever and be Nicky's second-in-command, but Nicky wouldn't like that even if it would satisfy me, which it wouldn't. So after all I'm off to seek my fortune.' He glanced from one to the other and smiled ruefully. 'Well, perhaps I won't make a fortune, but at least I hope to be able to support myself honestly and with dignity.'

'But where have you been for the last month?' Jasper asked. 'And what brings you here?'

Bendy took a draught of sherry and shifted his steaming legs more comfortably before the fire. 'I took the stage-coach to Newcastle at first. Oh Lord, that stage! It was so cold and slow and uncomfortable, and poor Fand kept crying and pawing at my leg, trying to persuade me to go back. But I was determined by then to present myself to Mr Stephenson and ask to be taken on as an apprentice engineer. I know I haven't been trained, but I've always been nutty on engines and particularly locomotives, so I've read everything I could lay my hands on about them, and about railways. I'm well educated and I'm quick to learn, too – and after all, it's a new science, isn't it? They must all be learning as they go along. I thought it was worth a try, at all events.'

'And what did Mr Stephenson say?' Droylsden asked.

Bendy made a face. 'He wasn't there. I suppose I ought to have known, but he lives in Liverpool now, because of the

Liverpool and Manchester Railway. I've travelled on it now,' he added, brightening. 'Once each way. The stage brought me to Manchester, and I rode on the railway out to Liverpool to see Mr Stephenson, and back again today. What a wonder it is! So smooth – so fast – it's like flying! And the noise and the smells and the air rushing past one's face – oh heaven! And on the journey back I got into conversation with the driver, and well, the upshot was that he allowed me to ride on the engine with him. To see it all at close range! It gave me one or two ideas about how it might be improved – however,' he contained his enthusiasm with difficulty, 'I won't bore you with them.'

'Did you see Mr Stephenson in Liverpool?' Jasper asked.

'Oh! Yes! Did I not mention?'

'No, you missed it out quite neatly,' Henry said.

Bendy smiled. 'Well, I found his house in Upper Parliament Street easily enough. Quite a little house, nothing grand about it at all. And Mr Stephenson was kindness itself to me. I introduced myself and told him I'd gone up to Northumberland to see him, and he and his wife invited me to dinner in the most generous way! We soon got talking about engines and such like – you can imagine —'

'Oh yes,' Droylsden said hastily. 'I can imagine.'

'Engineering is a *lingua franca* between enthusiasts,' Bendy said with a grin. 'But the long and short of it is that he took a liking to me, and thought I could be of some use to him. So I am off to Leicestershire. They are all moving there – Mr Stephenson and Mr Robert and Joseph Sandars and some others – to be near the new project.'

'And what project is that?' Jasper asked obediently.

'There's to be a new railway, a mineral line from Swannington to Leicester. The idea was put up by a colliery owner, William Stenson, together with John Ellis, who's a local landowner, because they have no water transport in West Leicestershire to move their coal about, and of course the roads are impossible. The two gentlemen asked Mr Stephenson and Mr Robert to survey the route, and so they went down there and looked it over and agreed that a railway could be built, and now an undertaking company has been set up to do it.'

'And you are to work on it?'

'Yes, but there's more than just a railway at stake,' he went on eagerly. 'The coalfield there is being worked only very shallowly at the moment, and Mr Robert is convinced that if deep shafts can be sunk, they would find rich seams and it would become tremendously profitable. The local men don't believe deep mining is possible because of the nature of the ground, but the Stephensons do; so they are moving – goods, chattels and households – down to Snibston to undertake it. It will be a massive work – together with the new railway – and a lot of engineers will be needed. Mr Stephenson is going to take me on as an apprentice.'

'How – er – splendid,' Droylsden said.

Benedict seemed to think it was. 'He's given me a letter of introduction to Mr Ellis so that I can start straight away. It won't pay much, of course – at least, not at first – but the experience will be invaluable. I shall be able to go anywhere with the skills I shall learn there. And think of it,' he said with a blissful smile, 'working with railways and locomotives all day and every day!'

'If it's what you want, I am glad for you,' Jasper said.

At that moment the door opened again, and Fenby entered to enquire, in a voice so devoid of expression it was plain that he was furious, whether 'Mr Morland' would require a bed made up.

'Good idea,' Jasper said, which was not at all what Fenby hoped to hear. Jasper looked at Benedict. 'You'll stay, won't you? There's no point in going back to your inn now.'

Benedict smiled ruefully. 'Well, to tell the truth, I hadn't got as far as planning where I would spend the night. I've had to save money where I could, so I've been sleeping on the road quite often. All this travel – even on stage-coaches – works out rather expensive.'

Jasper noted the condition of Bendy's clothes and thought that he probably hadn't slept in a bed very often since he left Morland Place. 'Then you'll stay here, of course. Why not stay for a few days? I dare say you need feeding up. And it's Christmas Day tomorrow, or had you forgotten?'

'I had, actually,' Bendy said. 'Thank you, I'd love to stay – but what about Sophie? I don't want to upset her.'

'It would upset her to know she had missed you altogether. Don't worry, I'll think of some gentle way to explain to her why you left home. And to tell you the truth,' Jasper added, 'I think it would do her a lot of good to have you here. She's been fretting about not being able to go to Morland Place for Christmas – now you can bring Morland Place to her.'

'So will that be one extra bed, sir,' Fenby put in at that moment, 'or two?'

'Lord, I had better be on my way back to mine,' Droylsden said, getting to his feet. 'Look at the time!'

'One extra bed, Fenby,' Jasper translated. 'And see it's well warmed. You needn't wait – Mr Droylsden will see himself out.'

The butler withdrew, and Henry Droylsden burst out laughing. 'Well done, Jasper! That's inconveniencing your servants on a grand scale – my father would be proud of you!' He offered his hand to Benedict. 'In case I don't see you before you leave for Leicestershire, good luck with your new life,' he said.

'Thank you. When I've done with the coal mine, I shall come back and revolutionise your factory engines!'

'Not mine, my dear boy,' Droylsden said. 'I'm strictly a man of letters.' He turned to Jasper. 'Thank you for your hospitality. I will see you again soon. Remember what I said.'

'How could I forget?' said Jasper.

Nicholas was very particular about the cut of his coats, and was so long in the tailor's that his groom, Ferrars, had been outside leading the horses up and down for almost half an hour by the time he finally emerged. It hesitated on the tip of his tongue to toss a casual apology, but he thought better of it. One should never appear to consider menials, he thought: one should appear to be above noticing them at all. He walked over to Checkmate and automatically felt the girth before taking hold of the stirrup to mount.

'Hello, Nicky!'

He put his foot down again and turned to see Harry Anstey standing on the footway just behind him.

'How is everything with you?' Harry asked pleasantly.

'Pretty well,' he said shortly.

'Are you spending all of Christmas at Morland Place?'

'Yes, of course. Can't leave Mama alone – Sophie doesn't come this year. She's increasing.'

'Yes, so I heard. I'm very pleased for her.'

'But I'm going to Leicestershire to hunt for a couple of weeks after Christmas. My friend Winchmore, you know: his father, Lord Hazelmere, usually takes a box for the season.' The words sounded sweet in his own ears, and put Nicky in an unexpectedly benevolent mood. 'You must come out and dine with us one day before I go.'

'Yes – thank you – I should be delighted,' Harry said awkwardly. 'Er – have you heard from Bendy?'

Nicky frowned. 'Not a word. You know that he left home quite suddenly and went off to seek his fortune?' he said loudly, in case any of the passers-by were listening. 'Went without even saying goodbye – just left a note for my mother. Thoughtless as always!'

Harry stepped closer. 'No, really though, Nicky – have you heard? He is all right, I hope?' he asked quietly.

'Why should you care what becomes of him? You of all people know what he's really like,' Nicky snapped.

Harry looked troubled. 'Yes – yes, I suppose so. But I must say I never was more shocked, or more surprised. I would never have thought he would turn out so bad. I really liked him, you know. Well, he was like a younger brother to me. And when I think of that trip we all made together to Northumberland to look at the railways —'

'I never understood what you saw in them; and you can see now what a corrupting influence they've been, can't you?' Nicky interrupted harshly. 'Well, he will have all the railways he wants now. I always said they were the Devil's work, and to the Devil his own.'

Harry blinked a little at the turn the conversation had taken; but reflecting that Nicky must be even more deeply shocked than he was to have discovered Bendy's failings, he said nothing further, only gave his friend a brief, sympathetic grasp of the hand, bid him farewell, and walked on.

Nicky mounted his horse with a sense of inner satisfaction. One of the many pleasant things about having got rid of Bendy was that it had provided the means of turning Harry against him. Harry was supposed to be *his* friend, but there had been time in the past when he had found Harry dangerously prone to like Benedict too much. They both had a love of railways and engines and suchlike, and Nicky had often felt left out by their common enthusiasm. There would be no more of that now! A good thought of his, to link Bendy's crimes with his railway mania. It would prevent Harry from bringing up the subject again in his presence.

He rode to the silent accompaniment of his thoughts until they turned off the road and onto the track, when he was surprised by Ferrars' addressing him.

'Do I anticipate correctly, sir, that you will be taking me with you to Leicestershire when you go to stay with Lord Hazelmere?'

'You'll be told when the times comes,' Nicky answered shortly. The impudence of the man! As if a gentleman would discuss his plans with his servants! He looked at him briefly and with disfavour: Ferrars was an undersized man with bad teeth and a bad complexion and thinning, carroty hair. He was an excellent groom, but Nicky – though he was not consciously aware of it – had chosen him at least as much for his unprepossessing appearance as for his skill with horses. It was good to have someone on whom one could look down so thoroughly.

Ferrars kept his eyes to the fore, as he should, but he dared to speak again: 'When going into such company, sir, a gentleman usually takes a manservant with him, to take care of his clothes and so on. I think Lord Hazelmere would expect it. Mr Morland of Morland Place ought not to have to make do with the services of a borrowed footman.'

Nicholas stared at him in astonishment. 'What the deuce do you mean by talking to me in that fashion? Do you think I don't know better than you what's done and what's not done?'

'Oh no sir, of course not,' Ferrars said obsequiously; yet at the same moment he looked round at his master, and though he did not quite meet Nicky's eyes, there was something disquieting about the look. 'I merely thought, sir, that if you would care to take me with you as your personal attendant, I would be more than happy to serve in that capacity, as well as ride your second mount in the hunt. One of the other grooms – Grice is the best of them, sir – could come along to do the menial work of the stables.'

Nicholas was staring at him open-mouthed with astonishment, and now Ferrars did actually meet his eyes, though in a fleeting manner, as though such contact was unnatural to him.

'It would be by way of a promotion for me, of course – a little more comfort, a little more respect in the servants' hall, a little more money. It's what I've been looking forward to for some time now, and I think I've deserved it, don't you, sir?'

'You – you – have you lost your senses, man?' Nicholas gobbled, outraged.

'Not at all. There's nothing wrong with my senses. Sight, hearing, wits, memory – they all work very well. I do know how to hold my tongue, though, and that's very much to your advantage, isn't it?'

A coldness crept along Nicky's spine. 'What are you talking about?'

Ferrars didn't quite smile, in something the same way as a crocodile doesn't. 'A man who knows as much as I do about your private life, sir, had better be discreet, don't you think? What an unlucky thing it would be for anyone but you and me to know the truth about Annie, wouldn't it?'

Nicholas felt a sweat break out under his armpits. 'What – what do you mean? Annie? Who – you mean my brother's mistress?'

'No sir, I mean the girl you kept in your secret love-nest in Little Helen Yard – that Annie. Such curious antics you got up to with her, sir, didn't you? Curious – and dangerous, I'd say.'

Nicky felt his stomach churning. His hands were sweating inside his gloves, too. He must have eaten something that disagreed with him. He hoped he was going to be able to get home in time. 'I – I don't know what you're talking about,' he said faintly. 'Dammit, I don't feel well.'

'It's a wonder there wasn't a nasty accident, the things you got up to with her,' Ferrars went on inexorably, looking straight ahead of him again. 'In fact – wait a minute – is my memory playing tricks on me after all, or *was* there an

73

accident? Yes, I remember now – a very distressing accident, wasn't it, sir, which would have been very difficult for you to have to explain away?'

Nicky felt faint with fear. The thing he had blotted out from his memory was lurking near the surface, and he didn't want it to break through. He couldn't bear it. He felt sick, his bowels griped, and he gripped the reins so tightly that Checkmate jerked his head back and snorted in annoyance. Nicky tried to find his voice, tried to be masterful and turn the tide of talk away, but all he could manage was a feeble 'What —?'

'Fortunately for you, sir, you had a friend to tidy up after you, make everything look all right – or as all right as it could look, given the circumstances. Didn't you guess, sir? You were lucky – a friend to cover up for you, and a brother to take the blame. Well now, you can't really thank the brother for his part since he's gone missing, but you can show a bit of gratitude to the friend, can't you? That would be the gentlemanly thing to do.'

'You – you —' Nicholas gasped. 'You can't blackmail me! No-one would believe you! You can't prove anything! Leave me alone, I tell you, or I'll —'

'Come now, Mr Morland,' Ferrars said broadly, 'we don't want any of that talk. Blackmail? Whoever mentioned such a horrid word? As for proving and believing – well, I don't think you want to put that to the test, now do you? Mr Benedict has gone, and that's that. Best to let sleeping dogs lie.'

'But you – I don't understand,' Nicky said faintly. 'What do you want?'

'Want, sir? I don't want anything – except to serve you, of course. Serving you is such a pleasure to me, I wouldn't give up my place for a fortune, that I wouldn't. It just seemed to me, sir, that a gentleman of your standing ought not to go to Leicestershire without a personal attendant. If it would be agreeable to you, sir, I'd be happy to step up for the occasion.'

Nicky bent in half, crouching over the saddle. 'I think I'm going to be sick,' he moaned. His inward discomfort was so acute, it had blotted out all the horrible memories. He couldn't even remember what it was he had been talking

74

about. All he knew was that he must get home before anything happened. He kicked Checkmate clumsily into a trot, clutching his stomach with one arm, holding the reins one-handed. 'Oh God,' he moaned again. 'I'm ill. I feel so ill.'

'Of course you do, sir,' Ferrars said, pushing his horse on to keep up. 'I understand. But don't worry – I'll take care of you. I'll always take care of you, Mr Morland.'

CHAPTER FIVE

In February 1831 a small family party was held in Lucy, Lady Theakston's house in Upper Grosvenor Street to celebrate Lord Theakston's birthday. Rosamund and Jes were present, Roland and Thalia, and Tom Weston.

'Though what there is to celebrate in being another year older is more than I can tell,' Lord Theakston said cheerfully.

'The years pass for all of us,' Lucy pointed out, in one of her literal moods, 'and since there's nothing to be done to stop it, I suppose we might as well celebrate it.'

'You put us all to shame anyway, Papa Danby,' Rosamund said. 'You never seem to look a day older.'

'That's the effect of candlelight,' Theakston said modestly. 'I shouldn't look half so good in Roland's dining-room.'

'Under his deplorable gas-chandelier, you mean?' said Rosamund. 'You really shouldn't have done it, Roly. Gaslight is all very well for factories, but to put it into a dining-room —'

'It's absolutely the go,' said Thalia indignantly. 'And ours is the first house in Berkeley Square to have it. It shows off one's diamonds wonderfully.'

'But it's ruinous to complexions,' Rosamund returned. 'It makes everyone look green and ghastly – as if they've just been dug up.'

'Ros, please!' Roland protested, with a glance at his wife. Thalia was increasing again – their third baby was due in June – and he was endlessly protective of her.

'I hear there's talk of putting gas lighting into Buckingham House,' Batchworth said.

'Queen Adelaide's idea, I suppose,' Lucy remarked

witheringly. 'But I don't suppose they'll ever hold court there anyway. Billy much prefers St James's.'

'You were at St James's yesterday for the Queen's birthday, weren't you, ma'am?' Thalia asked. 'Did you see the little Princess – Princess Victoria? Mary Petersfield said she would be going to her first Drawing Room yesterday. I wondered what you'd think of her.'

'Yes, I saw her,' Lucy said. 'A short, fair child. Rather common-looking, but pretty-behaved. The Duchess of Kent may be a dreadful woman, but she has taught her daughter nice manners.'

'You only dislike the Duchess because she's a Whig, Mama,' Tom said provokingly.

'Nonsense,' Lucy rose to the bait. 'I have many friends who are Whigs. They can be perfectly sensible people.'

'Why, thank you, ma'am,' Jes murmured.

'I dislike the Duchess because she has some very wrong and vulgar notions,' Lucy went on. 'It's disgraceful that the Heiress Presumptive of England should be under the influence of a man like John Conroy. The child mixes with no-one but *his* relatives: the Duchess even tries to turn her against the King and Queen, who have always been so kind to her.'

'But the fault's not all on the Duchess's side, surely ma'am?' Thalia said. 'After all, the King did send Lord Grey to tell her the Princess's name must be changed, just because she's named after her mother.'

'All Grey said,' Tom corrected, 'was that as the Princess may be Queen of England one day she ought to have an English name, like Charlotte, or Elizabeth.'

'I think Victoria's a perfectly good name for a queen,' Thalia objected. 'It's noble-sounding and – and sort of Roman. We like Roman-sounding names, don't we, Roland?'

'Eh?' said his lordship, who had stopped listening several sentences ago in favour of fiddling with his watch. 'Talking of Grey, were you? Yes, he seems a decent fellow – except for the bee in his bonnet about Reform.'

'I thought I'd reconciled you to the necessity by now,' Tom said, accepting the change of subject.

Batchworth joined in. 'I think it's unlikely the Reform Bill, when it's finally presented, will change anything very much.

Something purely anodyne is all we'll get, I'm afraid.'

'I wonder,' Tom said thoughtfully. 'Lord Durham's had the drawing-up of it, and he's quite a radical in his way. And he's had Lord John Russell at his elbow all the time. Russell won't be happy with a half-measure.'

'Do you know what's going to be in the Bill, then?' Roland asked his brother with interest.

'Lord, no!' Tom said. 'I'm nothing but a lowly member of the Lower House. Only the inner circle knows that; and they're all being monstrously discreet, ain't they, sir?' he added with a grin at Lord Theakston. 'Grey took the proposals to the King in Brighton on January the thirtieth, and not a word has anyone heard since as to what the King agreed to.'

'Too important to be gossiped about,' Theakston said. 'Russell presents it to the House on March the first. We'll all find out then.'

'You can't fox me, Papa Danby,' Rosamund said affectionately. 'You know all about it, don't you? The King wouldn't keep you in ignorance – he'd need to ask your advice about it.'

'If he knows, he hasn't told me,' Lucy said. 'Your step-papa is as tight as an oyster.'

Theakston protested. 'All the King told me was that there was nothing about secret ballot or universal suffrage in it. He said that once he was sure of that, he was willing to go along with it.'

'It must be milk-and-water stuff then,' Jes said. 'I've heard Brougham say he wants five boroughs disenfranchised, and he's the most extreme member of the Cabinet. Half a dozen is the most we can expect. A dozen would be wonderful indeed!'

'Oh come,' Roland protested. 'I'd have to vote against it if it were a dozen.'

'Oh Roly!' Tom said despairingly.

'Damn it, no, reason in all things, Tommy! Four would be enough for you, Batchworth, wouldn't it? I'd say yes to four all right. Then your precious Manchester and Birmingham could have two seats each, and we could settle down again and forget all about this nonsense.'

Jes laughed. 'I'd compound for four rather than nothing.'

'But I'm sure Tom must really know what's in the Bill,' Roland insisted. 'He's such a pet of King Billy's. 'Fess up, old fellow!'

'I deny everything,' Tom laughed. 'The King just likes to talk to me about his life at sea. Of course the only time I've ever been on the sea was when we crossed the Channel on our Grand Tour, Roly; but he seems to think I know all about the inside of a king's ship. I don't like to disillusion him, so I draw largely on my imagination and Southey's *Nelson*, and we get along famously.'

Since Tom had bachelor rooms in Ryder Street, Rosamund and Jes took him home in their carriage on their way to St James's Square.

'A pleasant evening,' Jes commented as the chaise rattled round the corner of Grosvenor Square. 'I think everyone enjoyed it, don't you?'

'Papa Danby did, that's the most important thing,' Rosamund said. 'He is the nicest, kindest person I know. You're lucky to have him for a father, Tom.'

'Don't I know it?' Tom said into the darkness. 'What did you think of Roly's waistcoat? He's such a tulip! I couldn't help wondering what Mr Brummell would have said if he could have seen it.'

'Were you thinking of Mr Brummell too?' said Rosamund. 'It does seem so long ago that he ruled us all with a lift of his eyebrows – like another world. I don't suppose he'd recognise London now,' she went on. 'Could we ever have been so frivolous as to worry about the cut of a coat or the right way to handle a snuff-box? I can't believe we never noticed how serious life really is.'

'I'm sorry to say that's just the sign of your age,' Tom said. 'We younger folk still contrive to have a little fun.'

'I don't believe *you* do,' she said. 'You haven't it in you to be frivolous.'

'Why ma'am, what do you think I get up to in my hours of leisure?' Tom laughed.

'I haven't an idea. You're such a perfectly finished person, Tommy – like an alabaster statue of a Greek God.'

'Thank you! I shall be sure to tell my tailor that – he believes he created me himself.'

'What I mean is that I can't imagine you having normal feelings and desires like the rest of us. I can't imagine you doing anything so untidy as falling in love with an ordinary woman.'

'Thank you again! But if I do, my dear sister, she will be the first to know.'

'Oh, don't be miffed. I only want you to be happy.'

'There's no doubt that Roland is happy,' Tom said, turning the talk away from himself. 'Don't he just love being a husband and father!'

'Yes, and Thalia has settled down much better than I thought she would. She was such a minx, but she's the perfect little countess now – and a surprisingly attached mother.'

Tom assented briefly.

'She dotes on little William, but I can't blame her for her partiality,' Rosamund said. 'He really is such a nice child. He reminds me of you when you were a little boy, Tom, and used to follow Mother around like her shadow.'

'Does he indeed? Well, here we are,' Tom said as the carriage stopped at the corner of St James's Street and Little Ryder Street. 'Thank you for bringing me home.'

'I'll see you at the club tomorrow, as we agreed,' Batchworth said as Tom descended into the dark street. He lifted a hand in salute and walked away, and the carriage jerked and moved on.

'Did you think he was rather subdued?' Rosamund asked.

'Tom? No, not particularly,' Jes said. 'I think perhaps he's not much interested in talk of children.'

'No, I suppose not,' Rosamund said. 'It's a great pity he doesn't find himself some nice, good-natured girl to marry. I don't like to think of him living alone in rooms for ever.'

'Not a natural bachelor? But I thought you considered him a universe unto himself.'

'That doesn't mean that I approve of it. No-one ought to be independent of all human contact. Anyway, he may seem so, but I don't believe he really is like that, inwardly. He was brought out of the nursery too young, that's what it was: going into Society with Mother when he was barely out of frocks.'

80

'I think he can manage his own life, my love,' Jes said. 'He's a sensible man.'

'Too sensible, that's just my complaint,' Rosamund said. She hesitated, and then added, 'What did you think of Mother's looks? It struck me that she didn't look quite well this evening.'

'I see what it is,' Jes said kindly, 'you haven't enough to worry about, so you're busy manufacturing things. The truth of the matter, my darling, is that everyone looks pale in London at this time of year. If I were not mad in love with you, I'd have said you did, too.'

'Thalia didn't. Thalia looked radiant.'

'Thalia always looks radiant.'

'And I don't?' she said, pretending offence; but as the carriage lurched a little on taking the corner into Pall Mall, he felt her hand creep into his, and he closed his fingers round hers warmly.

They passed the closed and shuttered façade of Chelmsford House, lit only by the gas-lamp in the street, and she thought briefly of her married life there, of Charlotte's birth, of the little girl playing in the high-walled gardens behind the house where Rosamund had liked to sit under the cherry trees. Even when she didn't consciously think of her, there was a constant undercurrent of awareness at the back of her mind, as though a ghost tugged at her sleeve with transparent fingers, trying in vain to make her look round.

Would that change, she wondered when . . .? Or perhaps, given her past history, she ought to say if . . .? She had not meant to say anything yet, but suddenly she felt she could not withhold it any longer. There was something about Tom which always made her feel uncomfortably disconnected from the world. Jes's body was warm beside her in the darkness of the carriage, and she needed to feel his mind lying equally close up against hers.

She said, 'I think it's possible that I did look pale this evening. I didn't mention it before, but several times today I've felt rather queasy; and when we went upstairs before dinner, I suddenly felt quite faint and had to sit down on the bed for a moment. It passed off almost at once, and fortunately no-one else noticed —'

'Fortunately? Why didn't you say something? Do you feel all right now?'

'Oh yes. It was only a momentary thing.'

'But you're not given to swooning,' he pointed out. He sounded anxious.

She began again, hesitantly. 'Not usually. But haven't you noticed anything lately – about – about my health?'

'No,' he said contritely. 'I thought you were well; just as usual, you know. I've been so wrapped up in my own damnable interests, I *assumed* you were. I'm so sorry, darling. But if you've been feeling unwell, why didn't you say so at once? We must consult a physician. Your health is very dear to me, you know.'

'I know. But the first time I was sick I thought it was just something I'd eaten. And then when I began to worry that perhaps something was wrong, I said nothing because —' She pressed his hand tighter. 'It's very foolish, but I was afraid. I didn't want to admit I might be ill, in case that made it true.'

'Darling!'

'I know it was stupid of me. I tried to seem just as usual so as not to worry you. But of course there was one thing I couldn't keep from Moss. I shouldn't have thought I'd be able to keep it from you either, but I suppose you have too much on your mind to remember the date.'

'The date? What has —?' He stopped, straining to see her through the darkness of the carriage. The rumble of the wheels transmitted through the fabric was like a breathless silence, like the sound of one's own heartbeat in the depth of the night – only half heard, somehow frightening. 'Ros, you don't mean —?' He sounded afraid.

They turned into St James's Square, and her body swayed lightly against his for a moment before she straightened again.

'I didn't mean to tell you just yet, unless you guessed,' she went on, and her voice was high with some emotion – joy or fear? Probably both. 'But I don't want to keep it to myself any more. I need to have you know. I can't bear the waiting all alone.'

'Ros – my love —'

'Moss thinks – she is almost sure – that I am with child,' she

82

said. She heard the words hit the silence like stones in a pond, as if they had not come from her; and she felt a crazy, superstitious terror that by saying them she had altered something, set something in motion that she could not call back, and whose effect she could not guess at. Like a boulder rolling down a hill, it would gain pace, unstoppable, until —

Why did he not speak? In the absence of his voice, she could only blunder on. 'I dare not believe it yet. I'm afraid to believe it. But if you remember it was the twenty-third of December, just before Christmas, when I —'

'Oh God!' Jes said at last. As an ejaculation it was hardly satisfactory: it might have represented any emotion at all; but he had her hand in both of his now and she could feel what he felt. The carriage was drawing up in front of their house. What a time to tell him! he thought. They would have no more privacy now until they were in bed together. 'Ros, my darling,' he said urgently. 'I will take care of you! Whatever you want you shall have – only name it. If you want to go back to Lancashire —'

'No,' she said, laughing with relief. 'How absurd you are! Whatever will happen, will happen, no matter where I am. I only needed to know that you would be waiting with me. I need your support.'

'You have it. Whatever happens, I am with you.'

'I know. I love you, Jes.'

'I love you too.'

The door was opened, and the steps were being let down. In their last moment of privacy, as he rose, stooping, to climb past her and down, he heard her say softly, 'Won't Sophie be surprised?'

Tom's rooms in Ryder Street were modest, like most bachelor sets, but they were comfortable. Though he engaged in a full social round, his expenses were not great: he had no establishment to maintain; he did not keep a carriage in Town, nor a string of hunters out of it; he was no gamester; and though – contrary to what Rosamund seemed to suppose – he had a normal appetite for female company, he did not have the expense of a regular companion. On the whole he preferred older women, and three discreet married ladies very willingly provided all he needed. Indeed, the liaisons were so discreet that each of the ladies thought she was the only one, while his sister evidently believed he lived in celibacy.

It was fortunate that he was not extravagant, for his income was as modest as his rooms: his natural father Captain Weston's fortune was just enough to keep him respectably. He liked to eat and drink well, and his food and his clothes constituted most of his expense; but Lord Theakston, whose fortune he would eventually inherit, frequently paid his tailor's bill for him, while his mother bought all his wine, and his brother Roland sent him parcels of game from Wolvercote. All in all, he lived comfortably; and though he had one other, secret drain on his income, he managed to accommodate it without too much anguish.

When his man, Billington, opened the door to him that evening with an urgent and significant look, he knew that his secret expense had come to the fore again.

'Is he here?'

'Yes, sir, in the drawing-room.' Billington gestured slightly with his head. 'He has been waiting for some hours, sir, so I took the liberty of providing him with a light repast – bread and cheese and a tankard of ale.'

'The deuce you did,' Tom said, surprised.

'I beg your pardon, sir, but he seemed considerably excited, and I thought if I sent him off to the ale-house for an hour or two —'

'Yes, I see. You did quite right,' Tom said. Knowledge was power: best keep the man sweet.

'Thank you, sir,' said Billington, and led the way through the small vestibule to the drawing-room. Sharrick had made himself comfortable, dragging the most commodious chair up to the fire and depositing his large booted feet in the hearth. The air was blue with the fumes from his short clay pipe, and a tray bearing an empty jug and tankard and a plate of crumbs bore witness to his enjoyment of the 'light repast'.

He was not a good-looking man: short, thickset, and swart, with greasy hair straggling out from under a greasy hat which he had not found it necessary to remove when he came indoors. His clothes were undistinguished and mud-coloured, his boots built for endurance rather than elegance, and his appearance was further marred by his severely pocked skin, and a deficiency in the matter of fingers to his left hand. His eyes, however, were dark and shrewd and quick, and his mouth, set amid a badger stubble of grey and white, was firm.

He had had a chequered career, beginning as a parish constable of a village in Hertfordshire, until the onset of war had seemed to offer a more varied life and he took the shilling. He had fought right through to Waterloo and emerged remarkably unscathed: it was not the French who had maimed him. On his discharge he had returned to something like his former trade by enlisting as a Bow Street Runner. One day he had been sent out from Bow Street to arrest a murderer who had gone to ground in Hatfield, but the murderer had proved unwilling to be taken and put up a spirited defence with an axe, in the course of which Sharrick had got his man and lost two fingers.

In 1829 The Metropolitan Police Act had set up a paid and professional constabulary for London under the direction of the Home Department, and Sharrick, in common with many of the Runners, had applied at Scotland Yard for the new job. But despite his experience it was considered that his age – he was then fifty-seven – and his appearance were against him, and he was turned down. Undeterred, he had remained a free-lance, hiring himself out to private persons as an investigation agent, and to the Home Department as a bounty-paid law enforcer and thief taker.

He had been recommended to Tom by Sir Robert Peel – then the Home Secretary – to whom he had applied for advice.

'He looks rather an ugly customer,' Peel had said, 'but that's part and parcel of the trade. It means he goes unnoticed amongst the lower orders, and particularly amongst the criminal classes, where he gathers most of his information.'

'Is he honest, sir?' Tom asked.

Peel hesitated. 'I wouldn't like to guarantee any of the Runners one hundred per cent in all circumstances, but you may trust him in so far as the job in hand goes, and that's what matters. Sharrick has undertaken many commissions for me, and I've been satisfied with him. The reason that I recommend him particularly is that he enjoys his work, which makes him stick to it to the end – and I imagine this will be a long-drawn-out investigation?'

'I imagine so,' Tom agreed.

That had been eight months ago, and there had been times since when Tom had wondered what madness it was that had made him undertake to pay Sharrick seven shillings a day (which was nearly as much as he paid Billington) to comb the home counties in what seemed the increasingly wild hope that he would be able to find where Marcus had hidden himself with Rosamund's daughter. If he did not find them in the home counties, the search would have to be widened into shires where Sharrick's encyclopaedic knowledge was lacking, and the chances of success would diminish sharply.

Not that they were very good to begin with. Searching for a needle in a haystack sometimes seemed the more hopeful enterprise; but then Rosamund was his sister, and since no-one else had thought of a plan of action, it seemed to be up to him.

But as he approached Sharrick through the haze, he began to feel that slight tingling sensation in the fingertips that he got when an outsider he had backed came in at a hundred to one. Sharrick's expression was different. Usually he looked something between sullen and remote; today he had an air of suppressed excitement.

'Well?' Tom asked, standing before him. 'You have news for me?'

Sharrick heaved himself belatedly to his feet and brushed his knuckle over his forehead – as near as he could bring himself to doffing his hat. A natural iconoclast, he did not care to truckle to 'the nobs' as he thought of them, but he harboured a reluctant liking for Tom Weston. He was something of an outsider, like Sharrick himself, and yet managed to live on the inside, which Sharrick never had. Tom was like the cat, which makes use of man's house and fire without ever becoming domesticated, and Sharrick admired that.

Moreover, Tom cared enough about his sister to want to

find her little daughter for her; was willing to pay Sharrick the first sum of asking, and had the courage to go on paying it even when there were no visible results. In other circumstances such compliance might have signalled 'softness', and marked the compliant one out as ripe for plucking; but only a zany would have thought Tom Weston soft. So Sharrick had been giving of his very best, searching minutely and in a wide arc, following false trails and cold trails and even the faintest suggestion of a scent, and conscientiously getting drunk only once a week, which he considered both a prophylactic precaution, and every man's right under God.

'Yes, I have news,' he said tersely. 'The best. I reckon I've found her.'

'Thank God!' Tom said. 'Sit down and tell me everything. No, Billington, I want you to hear too. Make yourself comfortable, man.'

Billington, whose stoniest glare had failed to prise Sharrick's hat from his head, made himself comfortable by standing up straight as a wand by the door with his hands folded before him. Sharrick resumed his fireside chair, and Tom drew another out to face him and sat down.

'Where is she?' he asked.

'The gennleman what I've been a-looking for has taken the lease of a house in a village called Kenton, in the county of Middlesex. Do you know the place, Captain?'

'No, I don't, I'm afraid. I'm not much acquainted with Middlesex.'

Sharrick nodded. 'Nobs ginerally ain't,' he observed. 'Middlesex is all hay fields; humbug country as far as hunting goes, and the roads the worst in the country. Why our gennleman chose Kenton I don't know. It's a poorish sort of a place, not much more'n a hamlet, and nothing to recommend it – except that it's only four or five miles from Harrow-on-the-Hill. Did he go to Harrow School, as it may be?'

Tom shook his head. 'Private tutor at home,' he said economically. 'This village – or hamlet – which direction out of Harrow?'

'Atween there and Watling Street. You know The Stag at Redhill, on Watling Street just south of Edgware?'

'I've changed horses there,' Tom said.

'Well, there's a lane that comes out just opposite The Stag, which is the lane that goes through Kenton to Harrow-on-the-Hill – and a sorrier, windinger, muddier, sheep-trod of a lane you wouldn't hope to get stuck in, I give you my word! As to Kenton itself – eight houses and a blacksmith's, that's the sum of it. You're out of it afore you've well noticed you're in it.'

Tom frowned at this description. 'Are you sure it's the man you've been looking for?'

'Yessir, sure as a gun. It's Lord C, all right. Goes under the name of Meldon —'

'That's possible,' Tom nodded. 'Baron Meldon was Lord Chelmsford's cadet title.'

'Issat so? Well, *Mr* Meldon, as he calls hisself, lives in a stone house at the end of a lane what runs off the main street just beside the blacksmith's. Called Draycott House. Household consists of Mr Meldon, his sister, the little girl, a sour-faced old cat of a lady's maid name of Hendorp, valet, footman, boy, two maids, cook and kitchenmaid. Mr Meldon is badly lame and the valet – name of Fadden, white haired, elderly cove, but uncommon spry of his age – nursemaids him and ginerally acts the steward, paying the bills and ordering the necessaries and so on. All but the lady's maid and valet are local people, hired when the house was taken. This Fadden come down ahead of the family to choose 'em.'

'Cautious,' Tom said.

'I believe you,' Sharrick agreed. 'The little girl is aged nine years, commonly supposed in the village to be the sister's daughter – subjeck of an indiscretion, if you take my meaning, Captain – which is why the family chooses to ruralise; that and the gennleman's game leg.' He nodded significantly to Tom. 'It serves its purpose as a story. Mr M – or if I'm not mistaken, more like this Fadden, which is a downy bird and up to all the rigs or I don't know a flash when I see one! – he's done well to let the village people make up their own reason for it, rather than spin 'em one. Folk are always better willing to believe tales they've made up their-selves.'

Tom passed over this remarkable insight into human

88

nature and asked pointedly, 'But have you seen her? Actually seen her yourself?'

Sharrick sighed. 'Twasn't easy. She's kept pretty close, and the Hendorp creetur is as sharp as a packetful o' pins. But this Draycott House has a large walled garden where the little girl plays – overgrown and neglected, lots o' shrubbery and well screened with trees.'

'Probably why it was chosen.'

'I believe you! Well, there's an old oak tree grows close to the wall at one place, and I've climbed up it and caught a glimpse of her playing there, but that's as close as I could get. I didn't try to speak to her, them not being your instructions, and also for fear of frightening her. This ain't a face to bring on sweet dreams in a little 'un,' he added frankly, inserting his pipe in it as though it might as well be useful if it couldn't be decorative.

Tom was silent a moment, having formed, while Sharrick talked, an uncomfortable mental picture of a grim stone house with a grim, wintry garden, and a small, pale child wandering listlessly about under the cold eye of a hatchet-faced female.

'Does she have companions of her own age?'

'Not of any age. Not allowed. The maids talk in the village, and they think it's a crying shame to shut her up so close.'

'But is she well? Did she appear healthy? Do they say in the village that she is healthy?'

'Doctor's never been next or nigh the house since they moved there, so I was told. She looks bonny enough from a distance, Captain. More than that I can't tell.' There was a pause. 'So what do you want me to do now? Do you want me to call off, or go on a-watching of 'em?'

'Go on watching, for the time being, if you please. Is there some excuse by which you can establish yourself in the village?'

'I can think of something. You want me to get meself a slum there?'

'If you can without arousing suspicion. I want you to try and gain the confidence of one of the servants; find out everything you can about the child and how she's treated. Also the gentleman's plans: what does he mean to do with her in the end? Does he intend ever to come back to Town?'

'I can do that,' Sharrick said. 'Same rates as before?'

'Yes. And you'll report to me once a week as before? In writing, to this direction. And if anything urgent should come up —'

'I come straight here in person.' Sharrick coughed discreetly. 'There was mention of a certain sum by way of a bounty, or reward, so to speak, if I was to find the party.'

'Yes, of course,' Tom said. 'I haven't the sum about me this minute, but I shall go to the bank in the morning, and if you call again tomorrow at noon you shall have it. I am grateful to you.'

'A job's a job,' Sharrick said evenly. 'It ain't no favour either way.' He heaved himself to his feet, and with a civil nod to Tom followed Billington out.

Tom sat by the fire, staring into the flames and thinking over what Sharrick had told him. He felt elated that the quarry had been run to earth at last, and yet he wasn't sure where the information left him. What should he do now? His natural first instinct was to rush straight round to St James's Square, late as it was, and tell Rosamund all; but the image kept coming back to him of the little girl playing all alone in the tangled garden, the pale prisoner, helpless in her captivity. If the thought of it upset him so much, then how much more would it upset Rosamund?

He needed to know more before he spoke. His sister grieved because she did not know where her child was; but would knowing the mere fact of the location help her? She would ask questions – Tom could anticipate the flood – and if he had no answers to any of them, she might fall prey to the urge to go and see for herself, which would be disastrous.

He must wait for Sharrick to establish himself and winkle out some more information; but the thought of that made him feel restless. How long would it take: days? Weeks? Perhaps even months?

Billington came back into the room, breaking his thoughts. 'Was there anything else, sir? Shall I bring your supper?'

'Yes. No, wait – your advice, Billington.'

'If I can help in any way, sir —'

'I was thinking that before I tell Lady Rosamund what

90

we've heard today, I ought perhaps to go and see for myself, with my own eyes, the place the child is being kept in. What do you say to that?'

Billington regarded his master thoughtfully, sifting the words for a clue to his state of mind. 'I am not, of course, acquainted with her ladyship, sir,' he said at last, 'but it does seem to me that she might well have more questions than you are at present able to answer.'

'Just my thought,' Tom said eagerly, and Billington breathed a sigh of relief at having guessed correctly. 'I think when Sharrick calls tomorrow for his money, I tell him I'm going back with him, and have him show me the house and the village. At least then I'll be able to describe them to her ladyship.'

'Quite so, sir.'

'Good. I'm glad you agree with me. Thank you, Billington.'

Billington bowed and prepared to retreat.

'One other thing. Sharrick – do you think he can be trusted to keep his mouth shut?'

'I think he's straight, sir,' Billington said. 'It strikes me that it's his pride to do his job and be paid for it. If he was to blab, he'd be letting himself down rather than you, if you'll pardon me, sir.'

'I understand you. Very well, Billington. I'll have supper now.'

Billington bowed again and went away, and Tom resumed his silent contemplation of the fire.

CHAPTER SIX

Aunt's bedchamber on the north side of the house was a dark room, dark and red and brown: a sombre place, not a place for laughter. Not that Charlotte laughed in Aunt's presence. She couldn't remember ever having done so. Sometimes she laughed with Papa, but with Aunt she did not even smile, for in her presence she was always being reminded of duty, and of how easy it was to fall into error, and of the awful consequences of doing so.

Charlotte did not often enter Aunt's bedchamber, but she was summoned there today because Aunt's cold had got so much worse that she was not able to rise from her bed this morning. Miss Hendorp conveyed the information and the summons to Charlotte, and managed also to convey that the worsening of the cold was somehow Charlotte's fault. Miss Hendorp did not like Charlotte, as Charlotte was well aware. She had seen Miss Hendorp in whispered conversation with Papa's manservant, Fadden, and noted the hard, sidelong glances towards her that accompanied the whispers.

Charlotte thought that Miss Hendorp blamed her for the fact that they had moved from the big house in London into the country. Miss Hendorp did not like the country: she thought it was unhealthy. As she led Charlotte along the passage to Aunt's room she was grumbling, 'Though I'm sure it's no wonder that madam should have taken to her bed, living in a place like this. All those damp fields all around – and this house is not what she's accustomed to, either. What her poor mother would say if she were alive today —!'

Charlotte bowed her head meekly under the rebuke. She didn't understand it, but she knew it was a rebuke all the same. Whenever Miss Hendorp mentioned Aunt's mother she gave Charlotte her most bitter, blaming look, though Charlotte knew she had not even been born when her grandmother died, so she didn't see how she could have done anything to upset her.

But life was full of unexplained things, and Charlotte, who loved to know and understand, had learnt that there were questions she must not ask, on pain of her elders' displeasure. She must not ask, for instance, why they had suddenly left the house where she had been born to come and live here. She must not enquire why Papa was referred to as Mr Meldon, or why Miss Hendorp now called Aunt *madam* instead of *my lady*. She must not ask why they had not brought their old familiar servants with them, but hired new ones. She must not ask if they would ever go back home – and especially, she must remember not to talk about it as 'home'.

Miss Hendorp was holding open the door to Aunt's bedroom now, and saying forbiddingly, 'Well, Miss Charlotte, in you go – and mind not to upset her. She's not at all well.'

Charlotte advanced across the dark red carpet, aware of a variety of pungent odours: wintergreen and cinnamon, and apple wood on the fire were the pleasant ones; the choking sweetness of the burning pastilles and a sharp, rank smell of sick humanity were definitely unpleasant. Aunt Bab, with a brown shawl round her shoulders, was propped on the pillows in the big mahogany bed with its heavy maroon draperies. Aunt was very fond of brown and maroon, and even crimson if it were a brownish sort of crimson.

'Here's Miss Charlotte, madam,' said Miss Hendorp.

Aunt Bab turned her head wearily on the pillow. Her face was very pale – not white like the pillows, Charlotte thought, but a waxy, slightly yellow sort of white, like the white part of a Stilton cheese. Her pale eyes looked strangely shiny, like the glass eyes of a stuffed animal, and when she spoke, her voice was faint and hoarse.

'Come here, child,' she said. Charlotte advanced to the bedside and arranged herself as she had been taught, heels together, toes out, shoulders back, hands clasped in front. Usually she got some part of it wrong, but today Aunt only glanced at her before turning her head away again.

'Have you read your scripture for the day?' she asked.

'Yes, Aunt,' Charlotte said doubtfully. She had read it, but it had not made much sense to her, and it was very difficult to learn something if you didn't understand it.

'What was it? Remind me.'

'The First Book of Samuel, Chapter Three,' Charlotte said, glad to be able to be certain about something. 'Do you wish to hear me now?' she asked reluctantly.

But Aunt made a weary movement of her head. 'No, not now,' she said faintly. 'It is time for your walk. You must cultivate regular habits: the same task at the same time every day. That way you will always be usefully occupied, and there will be no moment left when temptation may find you idle and turn you from the path of righteousness.'

'Yes, Aunt,' Charlotte said. She had heard that speech many times before, and knew it by heart. Next would come the bit about Charlotte being particularly vulnerable to the wiles of the Dark Gentleman, who would lay traps in her path which she must be extra vigilant to avoid. Regularity, usefulness, obedience: they must be her watchwords. She would have liked to know – had so often wondered – why she was more likely to fall into error than other people, but Aunt would never tell her, would only shake her head with a sad and significant look, and sometimes a sigh.

But this time Aunt said, 'Go along, then. Think about the chapter you read yesterday in *Exemplary Lives and Joyful Deaths* as you walk, so that your mind may be exercised as well as your body.'

'Yes, Aunt,' Charlotte said again, and obedient to the heat of Miss Hendorp's glare on the back of her neck, she curtseyed and left.

Miss Hendorp followed her out, and in the corridor said sharply, 'Madam is far too ill to be left alone. I must stay with her, but I've told Ada to walk with you. She will report to me if you dawdle or slouch or do anything unladylike that madam would not approve of.'

Charlotte lowered her eyes meekly, but she could not help a reprehensible surge of happiness. There was, she noted, a definite hint of nasalness in Miss Hendorp's voice, so that 'madam' came out more like 'badab'. Was it possible that Miss Hendorp was catching Aunt's cold? The thought of her taking to her bed was blissfully gratifying. Miss Hendorp was a Good Person, and undoubtedly much beloved of God, but Charlotte didn't like her, and she couldn't help feeling that Providence was taking a hand in things as a special act of kindness towards Charlotte herself. She walked away sedately, but as soon as she was out of the abigail's sight, she ran down the stairs into the sunlit regions below with a lifting of her heart.

Charlotte knew a lot about Providence from Mrs Angus, the cook. She wasn't encouraged to chat to the servants, but Aunt felt it was important that she should know something of domestic economy, against the day when she would command a household of her own. And so once a week she went down to the kitchen and Mrs Angus taught her about baking and preserving and salting, butter- and cheese-making, laundering and ironing, the care of household linen, the keeping of ducks and chickens, how to clean pewter and silver, tapestries and carpets, chandeliers and fine china, and what kind of cats made the best mousers.

Mrs Angus, wonderfully, knew all about everything. She had worked in great houses all her life, beginning as a scullery maid when she was only eight years old, and working her way upwards through all the ranks of service until she was housekeeper to a lord who lived in a castle. She said of herself, quite frankly, that she was not a first-rate cook, and she admitted a personal prejudice against females being cooks at all; but her heart would no longer stand the strain of the great positions she had been used to fill, and the quiet life at Draycott House suited her in what she called the Evening of Life. And, she added equally frankly, she was a quite good enough cook for *this* household, where food seemed to be looked upon as a necessity rather than a pleasure, and even her relatively modest culinary skills were not stretched.

Mrs Angus did not, of course, talk like that when Aunt or Miss Hendorp were present. Then she maintained a respectful and subdued mien, and said 'Yes, ma'am,' and 'No, ma'am,' and very little else. But though one or other of them always brought Charlotte down for her lesson, they did not remain in the kitchen during it, so the weekly visit to the kitchen had become Charlotte's favourite time, and she looked forward to it almost as if it were a magic trip to another land.

The kitchen was always warm (unlike any other part of the house except Papa's room) because the fire and the big stove were never allowed to go out. It always smelled of good things (roasting meat and baking cakes, cinnamon and nutmeg and thyme and rosemary) while the rest of the house smelled of dryness and coldness and medicine and Being Good.

Mrs Angus, when 'madam' and 'the old hen' were not present, was kind and chatty and gave Charlotte delicious things to eat. She never mentioned the word 'duty', and was never cross or disapproving. Philly, the kitchenmaid, who 'had a slate missing off her roof' according to Mrs Angus, was flatteringly admiring of Charlotte, and often said very droll things without really understanding them. And there was Sampson, the big black kitchen cat, who sat on top of the coolest part of the stove, and would, when the mood was on him, consent to play with the end of a piece of string twiddled by Charlotte.

The maids, Ada (the pretty one) and Feena (who had a squint), would sometimes come in from their work for a moment, just for the sake of talking to Charlotte. The kitchen boy, who spent his entire life in the scullery cleaning boots and knives, would pop his head round the door to stare at her, and when she spoke to him would turn scarlet, giggle, and pop it back again. Even the footman, Colin, contrived to pass through at some time during her hour, or tapped at the window on his way to the woodshed to wave to her.

From the beginning Charlotte had understood – without Mrs Angus's ever having to explain it – that the real nature of her kitchen life must be kept secret from Them. They (by which was meant Papa and Aunt, Miss Hendorp and Fadden) would not have approved of any part of it. In fact, if They even found out that Charlotte looked forward to those visits as to the hope of Heaven, it would all have been stopped on the instant, and probably Mrs Angus and Philly and the others would have been sent away.

So she had learned to live a secret life within her life. With

Them she was quiet and dutiful and obedient, did her lessons and said her prayers, and never spoke until she was spoken to. But for one hour a week in the kitchen under the benign warmth of approval she opened up like a flower: she smiled and chatted and sat with her elbows on the table and ate cinnamon biscuits and played with Sampson and listened to stories.

Mrs Angus knew wonderful stories, and they were not about good children who died noble, selfless deaths and went to Heaven, or bad children who died as a result of their wickedness and went the other way (good or bad, it seemed, death came and got you, and only the subsequent route varied). Mrs Angus's stories were about kings and witches and adventurous soldiers, talking animals, mermaids, giants, and princesses languishing under enchantments. Charlotte thought sometimes that it was rather as though she were under a spell which only broke when she passed through the kitchen door: in the rest of the house, she felt as though she lived inside an invisible cage of ice.

It was from Mrs Angus that Charlotte learned about Providence, the god of the kitchen, who seemed very much more like a proper god to Charlotte than the one Aunt taught her about. Providence was arbitrary and unfair, but that, as Charlotte could see for herself, might work for one as well as against one: good things and bad tumbled out indiscriminately from his pockets, and one might be showered by the one as easily as the other. Providence, for instance, had carried off Mrs Angus's husband, which was sad; but had also seen to it that Colin was passing by the stream when a farmer was about to drown a sackful of kittens, which was how they had got Sampson.

Aunt's God, though, kept careful score of one's wrong-doings and punished every little thing, but only promised to reward one for good deeds in Heaven, which was pretty much the same thing as saying 'never' as far as Charlotte could see. So she was quite sure that it was Providence who had arranged things that day by keeping Aunt and Miss Hendorp penned up in Aunt's room. Best of all, Fadden had gone in to Harrow on business for Papa and would be away all day. All round the house Charlotte could sense little spurts of holiday excitement about his absence, like wraiths of steam escaping a tight-lidded pot.

Ada, who was waiting for her in the hall to help her put on her outdoor things, smiled as she came running down the stairs and said, 'There now, miss, I think the sun's coming out for your walk – though putting you out whatever the weather, just as if you were a cat instead of a Christian, I can't understand and never could.'

'Fresh air and exercise are important,' Charlotte said. 'Aunt says everyone should be out of doors for a full hour every day.'

Ada sniffed, unconvinced. 'Hold your head up, Miss Charlotte, while I tie your ribbons.'

'Ada, you believe in Providence, don't you?' Charlotte asked.

'Of course I do,' Ada said. 'Why, what a funny question.'

'I was just thinking, you see, that though Aunt must be very uncomfortable with her cold and sore throat, she will like being able to stay in bed, having her meals on a tray instead of having to eat with me and tell me off about things. And being ill does mean she can have a fire in her bedroom, and be warm and comfortable without upsetting God.'

Ada stared at her. 'What a funny little thing you are, Miss Charlotte! Upsetting God indeed! Don't you worry about madam. She'll be better by and by.'

'I know,' Charlotte said. 'I was just thinking, you see, that Providence is very clever at working things out so that everyone has something to be glad about.'

'That's why He's called Providence, Miss Charlotte,' said Ada, feeling a little out of her theological depth. 'There you are now, miss. Mind you keep that muffler round your throat. We don't want you coming down with the cold next.' She propelled Charlotte gently towards the door.

'Aren't you coming out into the garden with me?' Charlotte asked.

'I am not,' Ada said firmly. 'I've enough to do with sick people in the house as well as my own work, and master to fetch and carry for, Mr Fadden being out all day. Besides, fresh air may be all very well for gentlefolk, but it doesn't do a bit of good to people of my sort. You wouldn't catch anyone in my family walking about a garden in February, I can tell you!'

'I'm to go out on my own, then?' The idea seemed charming, but Charlotte added anxiously, 'You won't get into trouble?'

'Not unless you tell, Miss Charlotte. You can't see the garden from your aunt's window,' Ada said. 'Off you go now, miss. I'll call you in when you've had your hour.'

'I wish I had a little dog to play with,' Charlotte said as Ada opened the door on the grey day and the wintry garden.

'Why, so do I, miss,' Ada agreed. 'And I could get you one easy as easy from my brother Bob, who has a nice little terrier bitch which pupped at Christmas. But your aunt would never allow it.'

'I know,' Charlotte said. 'I just wished, that's all.'

She didn't mind being sent out into the garden alone. It was rather an adventure. Normally she went out with her aunt, and they walked sedately round the paths for an hour while Charlotte recited lists of things – Kings and Queens, capital cities, dates of important battles, metals and semi-metals, the principal rivers of Russia, the Roman emperors and their dates. Or, if Aunt were in a melancholy mood, she improved the hour with a lecture on virtue and obedience and the frightful penalties involved in abandoning either.

But today, with no-one to watch her or forbid her, Charlotte could wander where she liked, and indulge her imagination – which, because of her solitary and restricted life, had developed into a powerful organ. She could pretend she was a soldier of fortune in a foreign land, exploring a wilderness where no man had trodden before. There might be wild beasts living in the shrubbery (which was dense enough to do service as a jungle); or there might be elves in the tree trunks, a witch in the potting shed. Beyond the lawn and the paths and the dull, formal flower-beds the garden was quite interesting. Right down at the bottom beyond the shrubbery there was a rough area where the gardener kept the compost heap and the pile of logs drying out for fires. The wall there was ivy-covered and rather crumbling, and there were nettles and brambles and other wild things that would not have been allowed in the garden proper.

For a while she wandered there, enjoying peopling this wilderness from imagination; so she was much more interested than startled, and not at all afraid, when she saw the man up in the tree. It was the big oak tree which she could see from her bedroom window at the top of the house. There was a fork just above the height of the wall which she had noticed many a time, and the man had done what she had often imagined doing – he had climbed up and was sitting in the fork, looking quite comfortable, as though it were a drawing-room sofa.

The really interesting thing was that he was a grown-up man, not a boy; and that he was dressed like a gentleman, in a dark brown felt greatcoat and a grey beaver hat (which meant he blended in rather nicely with the tree. She wondered if he had chosen them for that reason). Charlotte had never heard of a gentleman climbing a tree. She was fairly sure that it was an unusual thing for one to do.

'Hullo,' she said as she arrived just beneath him. 'Why are you up there?'

He looked down. 'Because I like being up here.'

He took off his hat. Charlotte saw he had smooth light brown hair and a nice face and warm brown eyes under fine, arched eyebrows. She liked him immediately, and thought his explanation perfectly reasonable.

'Don't you like climbing trees?' he asked her.

'I don't know. I've never tried it,' she said.

'You should,' he said gravely.

'I wouldn't be allowed to,' she said simply. 'I didn't know grown-ups climbed trees.'

'I don't think they do, usually. That's one of the disadvantages of being a grown-up – one of the many.'

She glanced at his boots and legs, dangling down towards her. 'Won't you get into trouble? You've scraped your boot caps and there's moss on your trousers.'

'Ah, that's one of the benefits of being a grown up – one of the few. If I make a mess of my clothes, there's no-one but my manservant to care, and he can't tell me off because I pay his wages.' He smiled suddenly, and she thought he had the best smile she had ever seen. It made her feel as if all sorts of things were possible. She felt as if she had known him all her life.

'What's your name?' she asked.

'Thomas. What's yours?'

'Charlotte.'

He nodded approvingly. 'How do you do, Charlotte?' he said. 'Do you live here with your mother and father?'

'I live here with Papa and my aunt. My mother died when I was born.' This didn't sound exciting enough to engage the interest of a tree-climbing gentleman, so she added, 'We used to live in London, only just down the road from St James's Palace, where the King lives. But then last year we left and came here.'

'Why did you leave?'

Charlotte frowned a little and chewed her lip. 'I think it was my fault,' she said. 'You see, I had a friend called Mr McIver. He was the gardener, and we used to talk and talk and have such nice times. And one day Fadden – he's my father's man – found me talking to him, and the very next day Mr McIver was sent away. And not long after that Papa told me we were going to live in the country. No-one ever said, but I think they didn't like me having Mr McIver for a friend, and that's why we shall never go home – back to London, I mean.'

She looked up at him anxiously, but Thomas seemed to take this guilty revelation in his stride. 'Did you like London?'

'Oh yes. I liked it better than here. It was my home, you see – and we had a much bigger garden there, and I was allowed to play in it on my own. Here I have to walk with Aunt, or sometimes Miss Hendorp, and recite things. I'm not allowed to play in the garden, or come out alone.'

'It sounds dull,' Thomas said sympathetically. 'But you're alone now, aren't you?'

'Aunt has a cold, and Miss Hendorp is sitting with her. And the maids don't like fresh air. But I'm not supposed to be here on my own. You won't tell, will you?'

'Of course not. And you won't tell about me being up here, will you? I don't think your aunt would approve.'

'She doesn't approve of anything,' Charlotte sighed. 'I won't tell – of course I won't. I'm good at keeping secrets. Last year a blackbird made a nest in the ivy outside my bedroom window, and I didn't tell anyone. If I'd told, Aunt would have made the gardener get rid of it. She doesn't like nests in the ivy because she thinks they make a mess on the path.'

'Sometimes it can be very important to keep something secret,' he said.

Charlotte nodded agreement. 'I didn't even tell Mrs Angus. I thought if I didn't tell anyone at all, I'd be sure it would be safe. The blackbird laid three eggs,' she added impressively.

'Did they hatch?'

'Yes. And they all grew up and flew away. Do you live in the village?'

'No, I live in London; not far from the King, either – in Ryder Street.'

'Yes, I know it!' Charlotte said excitedly. 'It's quite near our house! Sometimes – years ago – when Papa took me out in the carriage, we used to drive past Ryder Street.' She sighed. 'I liked going out in the carriage, seeing all the people and the horses and carts and everything. London was much busier than here.'

'Do you go out in the carriage here?'

'Only to church on Sunday. That's nice, but not as exciting as London. And I'm never allowed to talk to anyone, even at church.'

'Don't you have any friends?'

She hesitated. 'Only Mrs Angus. But you won't tell?'

'Of course not. Who's Mrs Angus?'

'She's the cook. I'm not supposed to talk to the servants – well, not to chat, anyway.' Eagerly, she told him about Mrs Angus and the kitchen lessons.

When she paused, Thomas looked sad for a moment. 'We all find the modicum to survive,' he said mysteriously, and for an anxious moment she thought perhaps he disapproved. But then he smiled and said, 'Mrs Angus sounds nice.'

'She is. She tells me wonderful stories – not about people being good and dying, like in Janeway's *Exemplary Lives*, or Watts' *Divine and Moral Songs*, which is what Aunt makes me read, but stories about giants and dragons and magic animals.'

'They're the best sort,' Thomas agreed. 'Especially the animals.'

'Mrs Angus has a cat called Sampson that I play with. I wish I had a dog, though. Have you got a dog?'

'No.'

'I'd have a dog if I were grown-up,' she said in mild reproach.

'It does seem a waste, now you come to mention it,' Thomas agreed. 'My father used to have a cat. He was a sea-captain, and it went with him on all his voyages.'

'What sort of cat?'

'Ginger. Called Jeffrey.'

'Does he still have it?'

'He's dead now. They both are.'

'Oh, that's a pity!'

'Isn't it? You without a mother and me without a father.'

'Did you go to sea with your father?'

'I'm afraid not. But I have a cousin called Africa, who's named after a ship. She was born on it, and grew up on it and sailed all over the world. All the sailors were her friends.'

'Didn't her mother mind?' Charlotte asked wistfully. It sounded a wonderful life.

'Her mother died when she was born —'

'Just like me,' she said eagerly.

'A little like you,' he agreed. 'So she lived on the ship with her father, and learned to run up and down the rigging and dance hornpipes like the sailors. One of them made her a toy Noah's Ark with all the animals carved out of wood and ivory. She has it still – her own little boys play with it.'

Charlotte gazed up at him, enchanted, seeing it all in her mind's eye. 'I wish I could meet her,' she said.

'I wish you could too. She's the dearest person.' A movement caught his eye and he looked up, away down the garden. 'I think someone's coming looking for you. Pretty and blonde, in a maid's cap and a grey cloak.'

'That's Ada.' Charlotte's face fell. 'I suppose I'd better go. I'm supposed to stay on the path.'

'And I'd better go before anyone sees me.'

'Will I ever see you again?' Charlotte asked wistfully. 'I'd like you to tell me some more about your Cousin Africa.'

'It will be difficult, if they never let you go anywhere alone,' he mused. 'But I promise you we will meet again one day. I don't know exactly when or how; but I shall never be far away, even if you can't see me.'

'But if I can't see you, we shan't be able to talk to each other.'

'We'll imagine it. I'll imagine I'm talking to you, and you imagine you're talking to me. That way when we meet again we'll feel like old friends. Can you manage that?'

'I think so. I've never tried it before, but I'm good at imagining.'

Ada's voice was heard, calling for Charlotte.

'Here she comes,' Thomas said. 'I'm off.'

Charlotte looked away for a moment, towards the sounds of Ada approaching; and when she turned back to say goodbye, the man in the tree had gone. She hadn't even heard him jump down.

'Miss Charlotte! Come out of there! You know you're meant to stay on the paths. You naughty girl, just look at your boots!' Ada cried breathlessly from the other side of the thicket through which she could see Charlotte but not reach her.

'Coming, Ada.' It was just as well that he had gone when he did, or Ada might have seen him. She went back the way she had come and joined Ada, to receive a mild shake by way of reproof.

'You gave me such a fright, when I looked out and couldn't see you. What were you doing in the bushes?'

'Nothing,' Charlotte said, and added more inventively, 'I thought I saw a bird.'

'Walking about in the shrubbery like that, it's not ladylike,' Ada said. 'What would your aunt say?' Then, perhaps realising what her aunt would say, she added more kindly, 'Did you find the bird?'

'No. It had gone when I got there.'

'I expect you imagined it,' Ada said.

Did I? Charlotte wondered as she walked meekly beside the maid back towards the house. *Did I imagine him?* On the face of it, that seemed more likely than that there should be a strange gentleman up a tree at the bottom of the garden. Or perhaps he was some kind of spirit or magic person. That was better: that would explain why he had said he would always be near, even if she couldn't see him. He was a fairy prince; a friend with magic powers – her secret, invisible friend. She rather liked the idea of that. If she couldn't have a dog, it was the next best thing.

'You're very quiet, Miss Charlotte,' Ada said, breaking into her reverie.

'Oh, I was just thinking,' Charlotte said.

Ada glanced at her curiously. 'Lord, what a one you are for thinking! It would give me the headache, all the thinking you do. No wonder you look so dowly sometimes. But I tell you what, miss – here's a treat: you are to have your dinner in the kitchen with us just for today. Your aunt says so.'

'Oh Ada!'

'Yes, miss.' Ada's eyes were twinkling. 'Mrs Angus is to see to it that you sit up straight and don't lean your elbows on the table and chew every mouthful one hundred times. And she's to see you don't speak with your mouth full, and if there is any conversation in between, it is to be on improving subjects. Mrs Angus is to take note of what's said and report afterwards to Miss Hendorp.'

'I'll be as improved as you like! Dinner in the kitchen!' Charlotte laughed with pleasure; and even as she did, Ada reflected on how rarely she had ever heard that particular sound.

The Wheatsheaf was the village inn, and stood next to the blacksmith's forge for the convenience of travellers unlucky enough to have cast a shoe when they were just too far out of Harrow-on-the-Hill to turn back. Apart from such victims of mishap, the inn catered only for local people, mostly labourers and lower servants. The taproom was low-ceiling and dingy, the two bedchambers available for let so cramped and primitive that it was fortunate they were rarely put into use; but the fact that some of the wilder pupils from the great school at Harrow sometimes came out this way to polish up their adolescent misdeeds meant that The Wheatsheaf did have a coffee room, albeit small and dark, and that the fire was kept alight in it.

Here Tom met Sharrick over a large jug of mulled ale, which he pronounced, with surprise, to be 'None too bad at all. I've had worse more often than I've had better. Try some. It will warm you up.'

'No, thank you,' Sharrick said neutrally. 'A boy's drink, that. They make it up for the Harrovians.'

Tom laughed. 'I feel like a boy today. Climbing trees has taken twenty years off me! Oh, don't look at me like that! You remind me of my old tutor at Eton. What will you have, man?'

'Two of Scotch cold, sir, is what keeps me warm, thank'ee. But if there's to be any more of this sort o' work —'

Tom shook his head. 'I don't quite see how there can be. I have seen her, Sharrick! Seen her *and* spoken to her, but that was simply the most tremendous piece of luck! I happened to choose today to climb your tree, and today it happened that she was allowed out in the garden alone because all her gaolers are sick a-bed. But it isn't likely the circumstance will be repeated, and I can't sit up a tree for the rest of my life hoping for it.'

'No more can't I,' Sharrick said dourly. 'This place is too small for a stranger to go unnoticed. Already they're beginning to ask what I'm hanging about for. If there's any more of it, word will get back to that Fadden, and he'll tell his master double quick. And then —'

'Then they will take fright and up-sticks, and we'll have the finding of her all over again.'

'Right,' Sharrick said, seeming glad that he had grasped that much, at least.

'No, we must be grateful for what we have, which is to know where she is, and that she is alive and well. Oh, but she is a wonderful child! Not pretty, exactly, but with such an interesting face, so full of expression, and a such quick mind. We had the most absorbing conversation. She's remarkably sweet-tempered, too. How she has grown up so well in such a household I can't imagine! I wouldn't even say she is unhappy – would you?'

'That's not in my competence to say,' Sharrick said, disapproving of these flights. 'If we might discuss —'

'Children are so adaptable,' Tom went on. 'I remember my

106

own childhood was not so very conventional; and my brother was positively persecuted! But we grew up like other boys, and found the modicum to keep our flames flickering on. It's a wonder.' He eyed his companion with amusement, and consented to return to business. 'Well, Sharrick, what do you propose?'

'I will have to find some other way to keep an eye on her. And you must not come here again.'

'You are in the right. But here is our way: a female called Mrs Angus, cook to the household, has befriended the child. She lives in, but presumably she has a day off, so she must emerge sometimes.'

Sharrick looked doubtful. 'A female cook – elderly, unmarried – I know that class o' female. Tongues run on wheels. You don't want to be trusting one o' that sort.'

'Ah, but this one has a kind heart, my man, and understands the situation. She has already warned the child against letting any of the family – particularly the valet – know about their friendship; and the child understands that too, you may be assured. She has a strong sense of what is needed for her own survival. I think you should cultivate friendship with the cook, Sharrick. I much mistake if she is not our natural ally.'

Tom arrived back in Town just about dusk, feeling properly elated, and looking forward to taking his tidings to his sister. He not only knew where the child was, but he had seen her and spoken to her, and was in a position to assure Rosamund that, whatever the spiritual privations of her home, she was healthy and contented, and growing up in a way that promised everything good. So much, he thought, would ease Rosamund's mind; and with the hope of further bulletins from time to time, might help to fill the gap the loss of Charlotte had made in her life.

He left his horse at the mews, and walked round to Ryder Street to change his clothes, for he could hardly present himself at St James's Square in this tousled condition. But as he approached the door of his lodgings he saw the familiar form of Lord Batchworth just coming out.

'Ah, there you are!' Batchworth greeted him cheerfully. 'Where the deuce have you been? Your man had a sudden fit of discretion and would only say that you were out and that he didn't know when you'd be back.'

'I have been on a secret mission,' Tom said with a grin. 'I was just going to change my clothes and come and find you. I have things to tell you.'

Batchworth returned the grin even more broadly. 'And I have things to tell you – the very best of news! – though we must beg you to keep it to yourself for the time being. We're so happy we can hardly believe it, and of course it's early days yet, but Rosamund wanted you to know – you and her mother and Lord Theakston. I suppose you can guess what it is? She's gone to see her mother, but I had to come and find you, because if I don't have another sensible man to help me celebrate the news I think I shall go distracted. Listen to me – I'm babbling like a lunatic as it is! Tom, my dear brother, wish me joy – wish us both joy!'

Tom stared, his thoughts churning. 'You mean – you and Rosamund – you think she's —'

'Yes!' Batchworth's illuminated face was enough to vouch for it. 'In September, as near as we can tell – the end of September or the beginning of October. Now, is that not worth drinking a bumper to?'

Tom smiled slowly. 'As many as you like – only let me change my clothes first.'

'Oh the deuce with your clothes! They're well enough. Come along, old fellow, and let me babble in comfort.' He put an arm round Tom's shoulders and turned him from his door. 'The thing is, I mustn't babble at home. Because she has had miscarriages before, Rosamund must be kept as quiet as possible until it's all over – no excitement and no upsets – so I shall have to be a monument of calm all the time I'm with her. If I don't boil over now, I shall never have the chance, so take pity on me. You can tell me your news by and by, when I've done with mine.'

'My news?' Tom said. No excitements and no upsets? He walked with his brother-in-law down towards St James's Street and the clubs. 'Oh, it wasn't anything important. I'll tell you some time. But go on about my sister now – how is she really? When did you find out? I can't tell you how pleased I am for you both. You'll be hoping for a boy, of course . . .'

Charlotte's time for visiting her father was six o'clock, just before her supper and his dinner. She was brought to the door of his room by Ada, tapped upon it, and was admitted by Fadden, who had just brought his master the single glass of sherry he allowed him. It was dark by six o'clock, of course, and the curtains had been drawn against the winter night. The fire was bright, the room warm, and there was a profusion of candles which made the red carpet and wall-paper glow and all the silver and glass in the room wink merrily.

Papa was in his chair drawn up to the fire, his bad leg supported on a foot stool, the small table pulled up to his elbow with his glass upon it, together with a small dish of walnuts, of which he was very fond. He turned his head painfully as Charlotte came in, and held out his hand to her.

'Come and kiss me, chicken.'

She ran to him, caught hold of his hand, and resting her other hand carefully on the chair-arm to support herself leaned over to kiss his offered cheek. She knew from the way he sat that his bones were hurting tonight, which meant she must be careful not to touch him or brush against him.

'Is it bad, Papa?' she asked carefully as she straightened.

'It's this wretched weather,' he said by way of answer. 'I wish it were summer all year round.' He put her back from him. 'Let me look at you. Stand up straight. What have you got on?'

She stood back, holding out her skirts to either side. 'My blue, Papa. You always liked it best.'

'It never used to be so short on you, I'm sure. I think you're growing again.'

He looked at her with the painful mixture of love and regret she always roused in him. She had a long face, a little bony now that she had grown out of her baby chubbiness and was beginning to shoot up; not a pretty face, precisely, but full of a luminous charm and life that made it better than pretty. Her hair had been flaxen when she was very small, but it had darkened year by year to a barley-gold shade; and her bright eyes were sea-coloured, changing between blue and green and grey according to some internal rule of her own, as if they reflected a sky none but she could see.

He loved her consumingly, and was afraid of her; afraid of what she might make him feel. She might stop loving him, turn against him, leave him. Of all things, he was afraid of losing her, his caged songbird: that was why he kept her so close, and tried to make sure she would never learn that she could fly.

'Only taller, Papa,' she said, anxious to please. 'Just a little. It still does up.'

'You should have a new one. I shall ask your aunt to order some material and she and Miss Hendorp can cut it out.'

'Aunt is in bed with a cold, Papa,' Charlotte reminded him carefully.

'Yellow, I think. I should like to see you in something primrose – or jonquil – something to remind me of the spring.' He looked automatically towards the window. 'I long for the sun, for spring. Sometimes I feel as though it will never come. It's as if the winter comes out of me and kills everything it touches.'

The last words were almost inaudible, and she saw he had drifted away, forgetting she was there, so she remained silent, watching him. Her pity for his crippled state combined with the images of yellow he had put in her mind made her suddenly think of a caged canary. Aunt had had one once, hung up in the window in her sitting-room in the other house. She remembered its shape against the light, and how it would fluff itself out at night, and how it sang and sang when the sun shone as though filled with gladness. But it had not liked the move to Kenton, or its new position at the window of Aunt's bedchamber, where the sun never shone. Gradually it stopped singing, and pined, and died.

Charlotte stared at her father with wide, anxious eyes. No, no, it was silly to think like that. Papa was no canary. But he was caged, her mind argued back. Not a caged bird, but more like a caged bear, large and grey, helpless in the ruin of its strength, the more pathetic in its helplessness than a small, weak creature could ever be. He stared past her at the curtained window, gone away into his memories, and she wondered what it was he saw. The house was unusually silent, and she felt very alone, and cold despite the fire. She wished he would come back, but was afraid of his wrath if she called him. Yet she could not prevent herself from speaking.

'What will become of me?'

She said it so quietly that he might easily not have heard her; but she saw his eyes change their focus from the curtains to her face.

'What do you mean?' he asked, and his voice was flat – she thought with anger.

She did not dare ask the worst question – *what will become of me if you die?* She said instead, 'What will happen to me when I grow up?'

He stared for a long moment, and she waited for his hard expression to dissolve into anger. But at last he said, almost as if bewildered, 'What should happen to you? You will stay here with me, of course. You were not thinking of leaving me, I suppose?'

'Oh no, Papa. Of course not.' It seemed a strange question – where could she go? 'I just thought – well —' She could not finish the question.

'Everything I have is yours,' he said. 'You should know that. You will stay here with me for ever and ever – safe with Papa. Papa will take care of you, my dove. You needn't be afraid.'

'No, Papa. I'm not afraid,' she said. As long as he didn't pine away and die, like the canary, she was not afraid. She would have a new yellow dress, she thought a little confusedly, and that would make him feel better. Papa would take care of her; but she must take care of Papa. She must never do anything to upset him. Suddenly she felt guilty about her kitchen visits, which she had to keep secret from him because she knew he would not approve. It was wrong of her to do things Papa wouldn't like. She ought to tell him at once, confess all, be punished, and then never sin again.

For a moment the urge to confess was so strong that she was actually forming the opening words in her head ready to blurt them out. But for no reason she could think of she suddenly saw in her mind's eye the image of the man in the tree; and in her mind he shook his head at her, and raised his finger to his lips. *We all find the modicum to survive*, she heard him say. She didn't know what that meant, but she knew it

111

was important. She felt strongly that he didn't want her to tell Papa; that if she told Papa, he would disappear for ever, and she didn't want never to see him again. Remember the blackbird's nest; she told herself. Sometimes it can be very important to keep something secret.

'That's my good girl,' Papa said, and the tight, hard look went out of his face. 'What did you do today?'

'I read my scripture, wrote out my collect, walked in the garden – and then after dinner I read to Aunt for an hour,' she said, hurrying past the garden part.

'What did you read?'

'From Foxe's *Book of Martyrs*.'

Papa made a funny face. 'Was that a wise choice for an invalid, I wonder?'

'It was what she wanted,' Charlotte said anxiously. 'I wanted to go on with *Pilgrim's Progress*, but Aunt said it was too heating to the imagination.'

'Oh,' said Marcus, rather blankly. He couldn't think of anything very heating about that particular work. Perhaps Bab was more ill than he had thought. 'Did you do your practice today? I thought I heard you downstairs.'

'Yes, Papa.'

'What were you playing at the end? It sounded familiar.'

She hung her head. 'I learned a new song from the book – "Drink to me only with thine Eyes" – but Aunt says I mustn't play it again because it isn't suitable for a young girl.'

Suddenly he smiled. 'Nonsense! I remember your aunt learning it when she was no older than you. Our mother taught it to her, so it must be all right, mustn't it? I shall tell her so when I see her next; when she's out of bed and well again – it wouldn't do to upset her now. Sing it for me now, sweetheart. And next time I come downstairs you shall play and sing it.'

So Charlotte stood before him, folded her hands together, and sang the old song in a small, sweet, tuneful voice; while Marcus waved one finger gently to the music, and the glowing fire and candles laid moving and unsubstantial bars of shadow about them.

CHAPTER SEVEN

On the 1st of March 1831 Lord John Russell stood before the House of Commons to read out the terms of the Reform Bill. It was not quite a complete house. Amongst both Tories and Radicals there were those who expected a very mild and anodyne measure which would hardly be worth their while attending to debate: the merest court-plaster of a reform to stick over the nation's wound until it healed.

Still, it was crowded. Tom found himself sitting between Alfred Anstey and Sir John Fitzwalter, the member for one of the Cornish seats – a very fat, red-faced man who was already sweating in the close confines of the benches, exuding a miasma of starch and fine port, and whose hot, damp thigh Tom could seem to find no way of escaping with his own.

'Splendid stuff, ain't it?' Anstey said to Tom when Russell paused after the preamble to turn a page. 'I have it on good authority,' he added confidentially, 'that there are to be a dozen seats disenfranchised!'

'A dozen? Surely not,' Tom said mildly.

'Aye, aye, my man tells me it will be so. Grey means to do the thing properly once and for all, you see.'

'Bah!' said Fitzwalter loudly, overhearing him. 'Never heard such a lot of nonsense! Grey should be horsewhipped. All you damned Radicals should be horsewhipped.'

'No, no, sir, we must have a modicum of change,' Anstey explained kindly across Tom's intervening body. 'The people demand it. Yield them a little, and they will be quiet and content again.'

'The people? Damn the people! The people should be horsewhipped!' Fitzwalter snorted. 'That's what I'd do with those who make damned impudent demands – flog 'em. Twenty lashes a man and they'd be quiet and content again, I promise you!'

Anstey plainly meant to debate this energetic view, but Russell was ready and people were looking round impatiently for silence. Tom shushed him sternly and he subsided and fixed his gaze on Lord John with the smug, anticipatory look of one who alone among the rank and file knew what was in store.

'Schedule A,' Russell said. 'Boroughs of less than two thousand inhabitants, to be disenfranchised.' And he began to read out the names.

The first six were received in silence. At the seventh, someone said audibly, 'There's to be a dozen after all,' and Anstey elbowed Tom and nodded complacently. Tom ignored him, trying to concentrate on the names.

The tenth name was that of Fitzwalter's seat. He gasped and half rose, spluttering and crimson with fury. 'Shame!' he shouted. 'Shame, sir! It is piracy, plain and simple! I will not have it, sir!' Someone shouted something in reply which Tom did not catch, but which must have been ribald, for it occasioned some rather coarse laughter.

'Order!' said the Speaker. 'Kindly sit down, Sir John. It is not your time to speak.'

Fitzwalter subsided, and dragged a handkerchief out of his sleeve to mop his face, muttering to himself angrily.

Russell, who had waited patiently for silence, resumed. The twelfth name was read out; and then a thirteenth. There was a stir from the proximity of the member whose constituency it was, and someone sitting next to him said in a penetrating voice, 'Thirteenth? I say, that's dashed unlucky, Jack!' There was laughter in the House: the sort of laughter that comes with the release of tension, when danger has threatened and then has passed over.

'Order! Order!' the Speaker shouted.

Russell surveyed the House with his calm, dark eyes; his wide, thick-lipped mouth always looked as though it were secretly smiling. He waited for silence, and then resumed. Now there was great tension as everyone told off the numbers inside his head, waiting to know the total. Fourteen. Fifteen. Sixteen.

'By God, there's going to be two dozen at least!' Anstey whispered excitedly. 'Grey's a magician!'

Seventeen. Eighteen. Someone laughed nervously and was immediately shushed by his neighbours. Nineteen. The list went on. It passed twenty-four, and there was a surge of hostile muttering which died down again. It passed thirty, and now there was a stupefied silence. *Thirty-one*? Was it possible? Was he really going on? *Thirty-two*?

'This is insanity, sir!' someone shouted. 'This is the purest fantasy!'

'Order!'

Behind Tom someone said to his neighbour, 'He can't do this, you know. These boroughs *belong* to us! We paid good money for 'em. He can't just take 'em away.'

'He must be drunk,' the neighbour replied in a hopeless sort of voice.

'Drunk or mad.'

'*Order!*'

And the relentless voice went on; name after name was read out, some to protest, some to ironic laughter, some to a deathly silence. The list went on beyond amazement, beyond ridicule, beyond even disbelief. No-one had any longer any idea of the tally. The names ceased to have any meaning, except to each member concerned; to the rest they became a mere incantation, a series of senseless syllables falling into numbness.

At last the list was ended. 'A total of sixty boroughs,' Russell concluded, 'returning one hundred and nineteen members.'

'Sixty? This is outrageous!' someone shouted, and a buzz of comment burst forth, mostly angry, some – from the Radicals – excited. Tom felt dazed, and beside him Alfred Anstey was for once reduced to speechlessness. On his other side Fitzwalter awoke from the doze into which he had fallen for the last dozen names, and added his voice to the protests. 'This is a disgrace to our Constitution sir, and an insult to the House! We will not have it! You shall have your answer, sir!'

Russell remained standing foursquare, his papers in one hand and the other tucked under the tails of his coat, looking calmly to this side and that while the comments fell around him as harmlessly as raindrops falling into a lake, waiting to continue. He looked utterly imperturbable. At last silence fell and he said, 'There is more yet, gentlemen.'

Someone laughed nervously. On the opposition front bench Peel and Herries exchanged a look, and Peel shook his head doubtfully. Hardinge had his chin sunk on his chest and his eyes closed, as though he had escaped into the refuge of sleep.

'I come now to Schedule B —' said Russell.

'Be damned to your alphabet!' someone shouted wearily, and there was a sharp explosion of laughter.

'Schedule B,' Russell repeated, unmoved. 'Boroughs of between two and four thousand inhabitants which are to lose one member each.' The relentless list of names began again, and was listened to in silence. 'A total of forty-seven boroughs; and in addition, the combined borough of Weymouth and Melcombe Regis is to lose two of its four seats. Taking Schedules A and B together, it is proposed to eliminate a total of one hundred and sixty-eight seats.'

That was the point at which Tom began to laugh, though silently, simply to himself. He thought of all the talk he had heard, and even joined in with, over whether it would be four, or six, or as many as a dozen seats involved. But *one hundred and sixty-eight*! Oh, it was priceless! Durham and Russell and Grey had tricked them all finely. And, by God, what courage the King had shewn to agree to it all! Courage, yes, and discretion – for Grey had gone down to Brighton on the 30th of January to explain to King William what he proposed, and it was now the 1st of March; yet in that time not one single word of what the Bill contained had leaked out.

A thoroughly decent old cove, our King, Tom thought to himself. A sea-officer at heart, who knows that secret orders must remain secret. Thank God for him!

The meeting in the Town Hall in Manchester had been going on for two hours and the atmosphere was growing heated in both senses. Mr Cuffington was on his feet again, his eyebrows and whiskers bristling aggressively. Since he was a short and sandy man, he looked increasingly like an irate terrier.

'In 1817, as I don't need to remind you, gentlemen, the Commissioners built a gas works out of public money, and they have since prevented any private company from laying down any further gas mains. In my opinion that was a false step – I may say, gentlemen, a catastrophic step – in political economy!'

Someone in the auditorium groaned loudly: 'political economy' was one of Cuffington's favourite phrases, and few there were – numbering not even Cuffington himself amongst them – who knew what he meant by it. On the platform the chairman, Sir John Whitworth, tried to stem the flood.

'If we could keep to the matter under discussion, Mr Cuffington —!'

'This is apropos, sir, very much apropos, the matter in hand!' Cuffington countered fiercely. He looked round, gathering his audience. 'I say to you all that when we consented to the gas works scheme, we converted our Commissioners at a stroke into dealers and chapmen! We secured to them, gentlemen, the exclusive sale of their wares – and at such a price, be it large or small, as they might deem reasonable and proper!'

Old Mr Chadwick Arnold, who was very probably drunk, stood up at that point and said loudly, 'I would like to associate myself, sir, with the sentiments of the last speaker,' and sat down again rather abruptly.

From the back of the hall, where some of the less urbane elements had gathered, there was rude laughter, and someone shouted, 'Get out of it, you old fool!'

'Mr Cuffington, we are not discussing the gas works,' Sir John said desperately. Amongst his fellow Commissioners on the platform, Mr Ferriar, the physician, was quietly paring his nails, Jasper Hobsbawn was scribbling furiously on a piece of paper, and Mr Whetlore, the attorney, was chatting quietly to Mr Worsley, who had his arms folded and his chin sunk on his chest, and was nodding away like a mandarin.

'But *I am* discussing the gas works, sir,' Mr Cuffington retorted, plainly enjoying himself enormously, 'and I say again, sir, that it is very much apropos to the issue in hand. You may ask me why, sir —'

'Why?' bellowed the wit at the back of the hall, and there

was prolonged shushing like the escape of steam from a headed-up engine.

'You may ask, and I will tell you!' Cuffington repeated, increasing his volume in response. 'I say we secured to the Commissioners the power to set the price of the gas either high or low as they thought fit. And how have they set it? They have set it *high*!' he bellowed, reaching the crescendo of his speech. 'As high as heaven itself! We are being shorn like sheep, gentlemen, and for what purpose? In order to create such a profit on the sale of gas as they can spend on their pet schemes for town improvements! Is this, I ask you, the way to foster political economy?'

There were many raucous shouts of 'Yes!' and 'No!', and one of 'Hot chestnuts!' from the back of the hall. Mr Chadwick Arnold rose swaying to his feet again and said loudly, 'I wish to associate myself with the shentiments of the last shpeaker!'

'We are not discussing the gas works, but the water supply,' Sir John said, pitching his voice up over the laughter. 'Has anyone anything to say on the subject of the water supply? Yes, Mr Allenby?'

Allenby, a substantial citizen in the corn-chandling way stood up and said, 'I would just like to say, Sir John and gentlemen, that Mr Hobsbawn has spoken feelingly about the need for stand-pipes in order to clean the streets, and I have nothing against clean streets in principle – indeed, it may be a good idea at last, and certainly in the summer some parts of our town are not very pleasant to walk about —'

A very coarse remark indeed was made at the back of the hall, but fortunately it was *sotto voce*, so that only those immediately to hand understood it.

Mr Allenby paused a moment with an enquiring look, and then went on. 'Well, sir, all I have to say is that stand-pipes may be a very good idea, but I don't see why in order to have them the Commissioners need to be buying up all the water companies – and with our money, too.'

This seemed a popular view: applause laced with loud cheering broke out all round the hall, and through it Mr Cuffington rose again like an obstinate boil on the public neck.

'That is my point! That is exactly my point, sir! Mr Allenby has made my point! I say the Commissioners have become so fond of their new role as dealers and chapmen that they cannot refrain from buying up companies! The proposal to buy the water companies is a move to increase the Commissioners' own powers – their considerable, undemocratic powers – into a complete tyranny over the rate-paying citizens of this town, in a manner which is incompatible with the principles of free competition and political economy!'

'I wish to ashoshiate myshelf—'

'Gentlemen, gentlemen, we must have order!'

When the noise subsided a little, Mr Audenshaw, a millmaster, stood up and said reasonably, 'Why cannot the private water companies put up stand-pipes? Surely that is their business.'

Sir John, with relief at the sound of a sensible question, turned to Jasper and said, 'Mr Hobsbawn, will you answer?'

Jasper spoke. 'The private companies could put up stand-pipes, Mr Audenshaw, but they will not, for the obvious reason that no-one would be paying them for the work or the water, so there would be no profit to them. A private company must make a profit. And in my view it is not sensible for us, on the rate-payers' behalf, to pay the water company to install the pipes and then pay them for the water, without having control over the supply.'

A thin, shabby-looking man at the back of the hall stood up and said, 'I don't see why we want the streets washed. We do very well as we are. And what would become of sweeping boys and sweeping men? Is it the Commissioners' business to put honest folk out of the way of earning their living? If sweeping boys turn to pick-pockets, it will be the Commissioners' fault.'

Another man, portly and prosperous, rose to say, 'If the streets were washed they would be always damp, and it is a well-known fact, sir, that dampness causes disease. It would make the whole town sickly.'

This also seemed a popular view, and a buzz of discussion broke out as individual stories of fatal illnesses caused by dampness were retailed to sympathetic listeners.

Jasper spoke again. 'The fact of the matter,' he said bluntly,

119

'is that the worst epidemic diseases, as Dr Ferriar will confirm, are caused by atmospheric impurities – the miasma created by dirty streets, poor drainage, and impure water. We cannot clean the streets without water, we cannot have water without stand-pipes, and we cannot have stand-pipes unless we control the water companies. And if we do not embrace cleanliness in this town, we shall have another outbreak of fever before we are much older.'

The portly man began to mottle with annoyance at being contradicted. 'We have not had an outbreak of fever in this town since the year six, sir! And the fever only affects the lower orders in any case. It is nothing to do with us. Why should rate-payers have their money squandered by the Commission to provide washing-water to Irish beggars?'

A storm of applause greeted this down-the-road speech, and the portly man sat, beaming to left and right like an opera-singer. As the applause died down the sound was clearly heard of Mr Chadwick Arnold snoring. A neighbour kindly nudged him and he half-woke, said 'Beaver hats, eh?' and relapsed into sleep again, but quietly now.

Mr Webb, a mill-master, stood up. 'I would like to say, Sir John, that we have not enough water to put out fires in this town. Last year there was a fire at my mill, and when the fire-engine came they had to take water from the river in buckets because there was not enough in the pipes and barrels.'

Mr Cuffington was on his feet again explosively. 'And there's another disgrace, sir! Why should the Commissioners provide the town with fire-engines, at such enormous cost to the rate-payers? If the town kept no engines, private fire-offices would provide them, and the free competition between the fire-offices would be such that the town would be better served – and at no expense to us!'

Applause and cheers greeted these words, and someone at the back of the hall shouted 'Cuffington for Mayor!'

A swarthy man in a regrettable waistcoat stood up on the crest of the wave and shouted, 'Is there to be no end of these cursed improvements? Is there to be no limit to the Commissioners' powers? Are we Frenchmen, to be ruled by these dictators, with their police spies and their house-numbering and their infernal compulsory purchasing?'

A shouted 'No!' of increasing volume followed each of these propositions.

'Now they want to widen Exchange Street!' the man went on, gathering his audience with sweeping gestures. 'They will force honest property owners to sell their houses against their will, and pull them down to replace them by new ones, built by their friends!' He flung out an arm, and a rigid, accusing forefinger pointed at Jasper. 'Mr Hobsbawn there is in the pocket of a speculative builder called Skelwith, who is making his fortune out of changing the face of this town. And Skelwith is not even a Manchester man – he comes from across the Pennines!'

A communal groan and shouts of 'Shame!' greeted this awful revelation.

'The Exchange Street scheme was put up in the first place by Mr Hobsbawn – ask him why!' The audience roared. 'Ask him why he is so anxious to keep the fire-engines in the Commissioners' control! Ask him what he knows about the fire at Olmondroyd's Mill!'

Several members of the committee were on their feet now, shouting back, and Sir John was desperately trying to regain order, but in vain. The audience was baying for blood, and the swarthy man was urging them on like dogs in a rat-pit.

'Are we free men? Do we bow the knee to oppressors? Did we fight Boney abroad only to accept tyranny at home?'

The meeting was now so completely out of hand that Sir John formally closed it, though no-one could have heard him do so. But his actions were clear enough: he collected his papers together, pushed back his chair and moved away from the table, plainly intending to leave the platform, and the other members of the committee began to follow suit. The only exit was down the steps into the auditorium and out with the rest of the crowd, and though some people in the body of the hall were leaving, or trying to leave, it would be no easy matter for any commissioner to force his way through.

'You had better linger until the crowd's thinner,' Worsley said to Jasper, leaning over so that he could hear him. 'They look ready to tear you to pieces down there.'

Ferriar joined them. 'The usual ignorance and intolerance,' he said. 'The greatest deficiency of the democratic

121

system is that one has to listen to so many uninformed views.'

Jasper managed a shaky smile. 'One good thing about our friend Mr Cuffington is that he's clearing a space in the middle of the hall. I think he's still expounding political economy, and it's driving people away in droves.'

Henry Droylsden had wriggled his way to the front of the crowd and now mounted the platform and limped across to stand in front of Jasper. 'What a zoo!' he exclaimed. He leaned down. 'Do you know who that last speaker was, Jasper? The one who whipped them all up?'

'I don't recollect seeing him before, but he seemed to have a spleen against me.'

Henry nodded. 'That was Martin Duxbury.'

'Ah, I see. The conspiracy you warned me about?'

'The same. That's why he brought up the Olmondroyd theme again, though I think everyone was making so much noise by then few people will have heard him, or at least they won't have taken in what he said.'

Ferrar called Jasper's attention. 'Mr Worsley agrees with me, Hobsbawn, that it might be better to put aside the Exchange Street scheme for the moment. The water issue is much more important, and there is nothing to be gained from confusing them in people's minds.'

'It wasn't I who did the confusing,' Jasper said, a little resentfully.

'Nevertheless,' Ferrar said, 'we can't allow any stain of disrepute to jeopardise the water-supply issue. I think it would be best all round, Hobsbawn, if you were to withdraw it at the next meeting.'

Jasper closed his lips tightly and nodded, more in acknowledgement than agreement, and Ferrar moved away. The crowd out in the auditorium was lessening, and the movement was generally towards the doors, though here and there a knot of fierce debate was still clogging the flow, with that extraordinary propensity of people to stop and talk just where they will be most in the way.

'I think it's probably safe to leave now,' Droylsden said to Jasper. 'But I'll stick with you for the time being, old chap, just in case. Is your carriage coming for you?'

122

'No, I was going to walk – or get a cabriolet.'

'We'll take a cab. I'll see you home, and then it can take me on to mine.'

Jasper stared. 'You don't really think —'

'Temperatures are a little raised, that's all,' Droylsden said comfortingly. 'People sometimes behave rashly when they're excited.'

At Hobsbawn House Sophie, having heard Fanny sing her new song – 'Sweeter Thy Face Than Phoebus' Smile' – three times, and played several games of cribbage with her, finally convinced her that she was not to be allowed to wait up for Papa tonight, and despatched her upstairs to bed, with the rather shameful bribe of a currant tart for her supper.

Sophie adored her child, but she was glad when the door closed behind her, for Fanny's liveliness and chatter could be wearing, and this evening they had given her the headache. Yet hardly had the longed-for silence settled over the drawing-room than it began to oppress Sophie. She felt restless and nervous, and walked about the room, unable to settle to her work or a book. Sitting was, in any case, not very comfortable at this stage of her pregnancy, and she could neither work nor read in a reclining position on the sofa. Her back ached and her ankles were swollen, and though she was deeply thankful that she had carried her baby safely this time, after all the mishaps, she wished fervently that it was all over.

There were another three weeks to go, if Dr Hastings had calculated correctly, but Sophie felt sometimes as though she could not bear another three hours. She wished the baby were here already, safe and sound. She wished Jasper were here. He had asked her several times if she minded his going to the meeting this evening, and of course she had said no, because she knew how important it was to him; but the truth of the matter was that she did mind. She wanted him here with her. It was selfish, she knew, but there it was.

She wished it were not so still in the house. The tick of the clock seemed too loud, the quiet beyond the drawing-room unnatural and somehow threatening, as though it were lying in wait, listening to her. The servants were moving about somewhere in their normal way, and her ears were straining after every distant creak of a floorboard or click of a closing door. Sometimes she thought she heard voices, and they were thin and spectral-sounding, and it was impossible to tell where they were or how far away. Once there seemed a footfall in the room above her, and her irritated nerves reminded her that that was the bedchamber where the last châtelaine of Hobsbawn House – her father's first wife Mary Ann – had died.

Annoyed with herself, she walked across to the piano and sat down, putting her hands on the keys, meaning to break up the stillness with a tune; but when she touched a key the note sounded too loud, and it made her afraid. She sang the few words of Fanny's song in a wavering voice, and then stopped. The silence lying just beyond the door had lifted its head, listening, and she did not want to disturb it. She must wait quietly for Jasper to come and rescue her.

Jasper, her love – her parfit gentil knight – who rescued her from all dragons! Folding her hands patiently in her lap, she stared ahead of her, and suddenly remembered the day of the 'Peterloo' riot, when Jasper and Jesmond Farraline – as he then was – had gone out to the meeting on St Peter's Field, and she and Rosamund had waited in this very room for their return. Oh, that was a dreadful day! Remembering the baby, she turned her thoughts away from it, trying to think instead of beautiful, peaceful things. Dr Hastings had recommended – earlier in the pregnancy when she went out more – that she spend as much time as possible looking at pictures of beautiful children, or even beautiful men and women, to influence the growing infant in her womb and ensure that it, too, would be beautiful. And if she could not find lovely things to look at, he said, she should think lovely thoughts.

Sophie had told Dr Hastings that she had no need to go far for a beautiful child to look at, and he had laughed and said she could not do better than produce a second child as lovely as her first. Sweet, pretty Fanny! Named after Sophie's dead sister, to please Sophie's Papa. Poor Papa, who died almost a year ago – broke his neck in a horse-race, oh shocking! Her eyes filled with tears at the thought. A year ago he had been alive and well and – oh, how she wished he could have been here to see her new baby!

Maman would not be here for the birth either. She had written to say she did not feel well enough to make the journey. But Maman was never ill! It was only since Papa died ... Sophie wondered tremulously whether perhaps Maman was going to die too, and leave her entirely parentless. Then she realised that she was thinking all the wrong things for the baby, and the tears overflowed and she had to press her hands to her mouth to catch back a sob.

She got up and walked about, telling herself firmly to stop being foolish. It was nothing but her condition: Dr Hastings had told her that ladies often became watering-pots at this stage of pregnancy, and that it was nothing to worry about, though any tendency towards morbid fancies was to be discouraged. Uncomfortable or not, she had better ring for a reading-candle and occupy her mind sensibly with a book, rather than mope and spout in this ridiculous way.

And then she heard the sound of horse's hooves outside, and her heart lifted gladly. It must be Jasper! Oh let it be Jasper! How late he was, she thought, hurrying to the window and drawing the fold of the heavy curtain aside. The candles reflecting in the black glass meant she could not see down into the street properly, so she stepped close to the window and let the curtain fall behind her, and the scene jumped into view, lit by the torches to either side of the door, and the coach-lamps of the cabriolet which had just drawn up outside the gate.

The door opened, and a man stepped down, turning back to say something to someone within before closing the carriage door again. The driver shook the reins and the horse moved off, and Jasper – for of course she knew at the first glimpse of his emerging foot that it was Jasper – turned towards the house.

It was easy enough for Henry Droylsden to talk of taking a cab, but quite another matter to achieve it. The crowd outside the town hall was dispersing by the time he and Jasper came out, and many of those still gathered were waiting for their own carriages – there was a queue stretching far down the road of private vehicles creeping forward in line one by one to collect their masters. But a good many others were also hoping to hire a cab, and the jarveys were only too willing to be hired, if only they could get close enough to the entrance. They dashed up on the outside of the private carriages, at considerable risk of locked wheels and splintered shafts, and the arm-waving gentlemen struggled through the gap between the mud-caked rear wheels of one vehicle and the high-fed horses of another to gain their prize and the leisure, once inside, to assess the damage to their polished boots.

It was a case where the battle was to the strong, and Droylsden was too lame and Jasper too diffident to be able to secure a cabriolet until almost everyone else was suited and those who were walking had strolled away. Droylsden gave the direction and they climbed in.

'Soon be home now,' Droylsden said, settling back against the squabs. 'That was as unpleasant a meeting as I ever hope to attend. I say, what do you think to Ferriar turning against you like that?'

'Oh, he isn't a bad chap,' Jasper said, 'only very single-minded.'

'That's the pot calling the kettle black, if you like!'

'Nonsense,' Jasper smiled unwillingly. 'I have a great many strings to my bow; Ferriar is naturally more interested in preventing another outbreak of the plague.'

Droylsden grinned. 'I should like to associate myself with the sentiments of the last speaker,' he said. 'No plague sounds like an excellent programme to me. Shall you call off the widening of Exchange Street, then?'

Jasper frowned. 'And own myself beaten by this – conspiracy? That man Duxbury was deliberately inciting the meeting to opposition.'

'Yes, but didn't he do it well? This is no common order of opposition you are facing, Jasper. I wish you would think better of it.'

'They will have to learn that I have no common order of determination. What kind of world would we live in if honest men allowed themselves to be bullied out of what they knew was right? We have to stand by our principles. The widening of Exchange Street is a necessary thing, and unless it is voted down by due process, I shall not give it up.'

'I thought you would say that,' Droylsden sighed. 'You are

a stubborn creature sometimes.'

'I wouldn't be where I am today if I hadn't been. And you're no weakling either, Henry, so you can stop playing Devil's advocate!'

Henry laughed. 'You mistake me! I meant every word. But here we are at Hobsbawn House, safe and sound. Poor Sophie will be thinking you have fallen by the wayside.'

The cab stopped, and Jasper got down, leaning in again to say, 'Thanks for all your good advice, Henry. Will you come to supper tomorrow? Sophie likes to have company.'

'Gladly,' Droylsden said.

'Bring your fiddle, if you will, and we'll have a musical evening.' He closed the door, the driver shook his reins, and the cabriolet moved off with a loud rumbling of iron-shod wheels on cobbles.

Jasper turned towards the house, glancing up as he did at a tiny chink of light at the drawing-room window. The servants would not have closed the curtains so clumsily; Sophie must have been looking out for him, anxious because he was late – she was nervous and fretful at the end of her pregnancy, and he felt a twinge of conscience for having left her alone again for a whole evening. He ought to —

Then the world erupted into violence. The safe familiarity of his own front yard gaped like the mouth of hell and he tumbled through into chaos, as out of the laurels which grew to either side of the gate-posts two men sprang on him. They were large dark shapes, muffled up, with hats pulled down and scarves wound about the lower part of their faces, and they came out of the shadows as if the shadows themselves had taken menacing life. The first hit Jasper full in the face with his fist, and a searing bolt of pain shot through him from his nose, making his eyes flood with tears, so that he could not see nor speak, only gasp.

There was no time to cry out. The second blow had hit him in the stomach, making him double forward with the sickening sensation of suffocation as he was forced to breathe out again when he was desperate to breathe in. He was hit again on the side of the head, this time with a heavy stick, and he fell to his knees, and then over onto his side as they belaboured him with fists and sticks and boots. He was helpless to resist or call for help; he could only try to curl himself up into a ball to protect his most vulnerable parts.

But the blows continued to land on his head, arms, shins, back, until he was one throbbing mass of pain. Surely someone must come to help him? he thought dimly. The servants should have been watching for him – should have opened the door when the cab drew up. He felt his consciousness slipping, and tried desperately to drag it back. He must hold on until help came.

Then there was a stunning blow to his spine, a brilliant, splintering pain like lightning that arched him open like a hedgehog uncurling; followed inside his body by a terrifying silence. He stared up for a moment at the dark shape of his assailant against the starless sky and heard – or thought he heard – a gutteral voice with an Irish accent: 'There's for you, bastard Hobsbawn!' But even as he heard it, it was fading, and the rushing black silence was sweeping over him like the sea. *No-one came*, was his last, despairing thought as he went under.

128

BOOK TWO

The Struggle

O for a beaker of the warm South,
Full of the true, the blushful Hippocrene,
With beaded bubbles winking at the brim,
And purple-stained mouth,
That I might drink and leave the world unseen.

John Keats: *Ode to a Nightingale*

BOOK TWO

The Struggle

O for a beaker of the warm South,
Full of the true, the blushful Hippocrene,
With beaded bubbles winking at the brim,
And purple-stained mouth;
That I might drink and leave the world unseen

John Keats, Ode to a Nightingale.

CHAPTER EIGHT

Sophie was conscious before she opened her eyes, and conscious of a deep reluctance to re-enter the world. Where she had been was nothingness; beyond her eyelids everything was pain. A wild beast was eating her alive, trying to tear her body apart. It was the beast that had been lying beyond the door! That's what she had been afraid of: she had cried out and woken it, and it had burst in and seized her.

She let out a sob and opened her eyes, and through the laudanum-fog of her dreams she saw the beast crouched over her, big and black and horrible, with gleaming eyes. She tried to struggle and cry, but could only writhe weakly and make an inarticulate sound.

'It is I, Mrs Hobsbawn,' said the Beast in a deep voice, cunningly disguised as human: devil, shape-changer, subtlest of evils. 'It is I, Dr Hastings.'

'No,' she protested, and her voice sounded slow and strange, as if she were forty fathoms deep.

'It's Dr Hastings. You know me now, don't you? You must try to help me. The baby is coming—'

She heard no more, turning her head weakly on the pillow, tasting a salt droplet running into her mouth – a tear or a bead of sweat? She could not tell. The voice boomed and faded on the edge of her consciousness like the swell and suck of the sea. The pain tore through her again, but its teeth were strangely blunted. It was like, she thought vaguely, drifting away from herself, like the sensation of playing the piano with gloves on. It would kill her just the same, the beast, but she hardly cared about it. Something was stopping her caring, stopping her caring, stopping her thinking, and she knew that

131

was a good thing. She was going to die, and that was a good thing too. She couldn't remember why just at the moment, but she knew it was right and comfortable that she shouldn't live any more.

Her second waking was slower still, and far more painful. She opened her eyes unwillingly to the knowledge that she really was awake this time, and that the rest had been drug-induced fantasies. Above her was the underside of the tester of her own bed, before her the shape of her own body under the bedclothes. It looked strange, the shape of her body. What was different about it? Why – yes – that was it – it was too flat! She sent her senses exploring the flatness and found a desperate ache and an emptiness where there had been life.

'Oh God, what's happened?' she croaked. There was a movement beside her, a rustling of a woman's clothes, and then a strong hand turned her face gently, and a cloth soaked in lavender-water touched her forehead coolly. When the hands retreated, Sophie looked up into the plain, kind, good face they belonged to. It was watching her carefully.

'Well, who am I?'

'Prudence,' Sophie whispered. Prudence Pendlebury that was – Sophie's friend – now Dr Hastings' wife. Kind Prudence, who worked beside him amongst the poor sick of the town.

Prudence smiled. 'Your throat is dry,' she said. 'It's the effect of the laudanum. We had to give you quite a lot to keep you still. But I have some barley water here —'

She rose and leaned over Sophie, lifting her head and holding a glass to her lips, and held her until she had sipped enough. Then she laid Sophie down again, resumed her seat, and took Sophie's hand in both of hers.

'Well then?' she said gently. 'You have things you want to ask me.'

Sophie frowned. 'What's happened? Am I sick?'

'Don't you remember?'

'No. Not really. It's all so confused. I remember a man in black —'

'Edwin. My husband. Dr Hastings.'

'I thought he was a wild beast,' Sophie murmured.

132

'He will be flattered.'

'He was tearing my—' Sophie's eyes widened as she remember. 'The baby! What's happened to the baby?'

'Hush, my dear! Lie still, or you'll hurt yourself. You are very bruised, and have a great many sutures.'

'I had the baby, didn't I?'

'Yes, love. You had the baby,' Prudence said, stroking Sophie's hand, and the gentleness of the voice told its story. Sophie's eyes filled with tears.

'It died? The baby died?'

'It was a very difficult presentation. A breech birth. You know what that is, don't you? They are always dangerous, but in this case the cord was round the baby's neck, choking it. Edwin and the midwife did everything they could to revive it, but it was no good.'

'No. Oh no.' It was hard, so hard, to believe it. It couldn't be true. To have carried the baby safely to the end, only to lose it by such an accident. Her eyes begged her friend to tell her something different.

But all Pru said was, 'Oh Sophie, I'm sorry.'

'Was it a boy?' Sophie whispered.

Pru nodded, and Sophie closed her eyes a moment against the vast well of sorrow she had discovered, black and cold and sinking for ever inside her. Jasper, she whispered inwardly, I failed you. I let your son die. I'm so sorry.

'Where's Jasper?' she whispered after a while. 'I want to see him.' She needed to see his face, feel his hands on her, making it all right, attaching her to life again. She wanted Jasper with a huge and lonely longing like a child's in the night for its mother. Pru had not answered her. She opened her eyes. 'Where's Jasper?' she said again. 'Is he at home?'

'My dear,' Pru began, and then seemed confused, unable to speak.

Fear crept up from some dark, hidden place in Sophie's mind, from the place of beast-dreams and the fog of evil in which she had struggled. 'What is it, Oh, tell me! Something terrible has happened.'

Pru opened her mouth, but could find no words. She gripped Sophie's hand tightly, her face working with some strong emotion.

'Jasper —' Sophie said again; and then her mind gaped and the images poured in like an unstoppable flood. For she had seen it! Seen it all from the window, like watching a hideous play in the theatre of Hell, scenes acted out before her and etched onto her mind in lines of fire. How could she have forgotten? Now the images ripped at her again, of Jasper coming in at the gate, the two dark shapes springing on him, beating him to his knees, while she screamed and beat against the window-pane, helpless and frantic. And then the black shapes had run away, leaving Jasper lying on the stones of the yard, and the servants had come running out from the house – too late! A thousand, million years too late! Their whole lives too late! And Jasper —

Sophie had turned, frantic to get to him, but the curtain was in her way, the curtain she had pulled closed behind her like a silly child playing a game of hide-and-seek. She couldn't get past it, couldn't find the opening, struggled with it in increasing terror; found a gap at last only to have the heavy material tangle with her long skirt, holding her back – surely with some fiendish intelligence? She remembered grabbing it in both hands, screaming with frustration and terror, and yanking at it with mad strength. She had felt the muscles of her back wrench, felt the stab of pain deep inside her where the baby was, felt the sudden soft, rushing yieldingness of the draperies, and then – nothing!

'Jasper!' she cried out against the memories. 'Where is he? What's happened? Tell me!'

Pru pressed her hand. 'Try to be calm, Sophie, please try to be calm. I'll tell you everything, but lie still, breathe deeply and slowly.' She looked into the frantic face and could only go on. 'Jasper was attacked at the gates by two men – you saw that?' Nod. 'We thought you must have, from your position by the window. By the time the servants got to him, the assailants had run off. They brought Jasper inside, and one of the footmen came to fetch Edwin. When I heard what had happened, I came too. The house was in a dreadful turmoil, because when Fenby ran to fetch you, he found that you had pulled the curtain and the rail down on top of you and knocked yourself unconscious. And by the time Edwin and I arrived, you were in labour. You don't remember any of that?'

'No. I saw Jasper fall, and then – I got tangled in the curtain. That's all I remember.'

'Yes, I understand. Well, Edwin couldn't attend to Jasper and to you at the same time so he sent for Halsey. He was the nearest, and he's a good man.'

Yes,' Sophie whispered. Her lips felt numb. 'He came when Jes was wounded in the Peterloo riot.'

Pru nodded. 'He's a good man,' she said again. 'He attended Jasper.' She had reached the point where she wished to stop and go away and never have to say the words. 'Jasper was unconscious, but alive. Halsey thought at first the damage was superficial – broken ribs and contusions – and he was most worried about the head wounds. But he found —' she wet her lips. 'He found that one of the blows had broken his back. There was nothing he could do then.'

Sophie began to moan. It was odd, because she heard it but didn't seem to be able to stop it.

'He couldn't have felt anything, Sophie. He didn't suffer any more,' Pru said desperately. 'He regained consciousness for a few moments, but I don't think he knew where he was. He – he died the next day. By that time you were out of labour, but you were still very weak, and we were worried for your reason. You kept screaming and struggling and trying to get out of bed. Edwin had to give you laudanum. I've been with your all the time ever since —'

But Sophie's moans, growing louder, now fastened themselves together and left her rigid open throat in a terrible, desperate appeal, like the cry of an animal. 'Mm – mm – *Maman*!'

Prudence jumped to her feet to take hold of the threshing figure, and the door opened and a frightened maid ran in.

'Go and get Dr Hastings. *Quickly*!'

The maid turned and ran, and Prudence held on, tears of shock and pain running down her cheeks, while Sophie cried out again and again in desperate, wordless grief.

At his mother's house in Upper Grosvenor Street, Tom found not only Lord Batchworth, whom he was expecting to meet, but his friend Peter Morpurgo, who was the husband of his Cousin Africa. Morpurgo had been a sea-officer who, as a midshipman, had served under Africa's father George Haworth. Morpurgo had risen to post rank, but had given up his successful career when he married Africa. He and Africa now ran a riding school to teach equitation to the rich and fashionable, and were, in addition, proud parents of two hopeful sons, twin boys of almost six years old.

Tom found Morpurgo ensconced in the best seat and being treated with all graciousness by Lady Theakston, who had a soft spot for sea-officers.

'Hullo, Peter! What are you doing here?'

'Demanding ransom for my wife,' Batchworth said.

Murpurgo smiled. 'I was charged, since I was passing this way, to explain that Rosamund is at our house and will be a little delayed. Africa's dragooned her into helping with a difficult horse. Just supervising, I hasten to add – her life is in no danger, Batchworth, I assure you!'

'I never supposed it was,' Jes said languidly. 'But that's more than one can say for the horse!'

'Scandalous! What a calumny on my sister,' Tom laughed. 'How is Africa?' he added to Morpurgo.

'Just as usual – which is to say positively riotous with health,' Peter said cheerfully. 'Her sole worry at the moment is that neither of the boys shews any interest in ships or the sea, which strikes her as unnatural in a member of the male sex. She does her best to encourage a better state of mind by taking them down every Sunday to sail boats on the pond in the Park, but the villainous children will insist on preferring horses!'

'You must take them to Brighton in the summer,' Tom said. 'Make them walk to the end of the Chain Pier and look at the waves. That will convince them. Take them out on a tuppenny row-boat.'

'Not I, by God!' Peter laughed. 'I was always sick in little boats. A man o'war's one thing, or even a good-sized frigate, but —!'

'Have you foolish children nothing more important to talk about than boats?' Lucy interrupted. 'Here's the most outrageous Bill ever presented to Parliament —'

'Oh, but I wish you could have been there, Mama, to see the faces!' Tom said. 'Even some of the Radicals looked pale.

Grey has pretty well wiped everyone's eye. No-one was expecting anything so far-reaching: it's left the radicals with nothing to complain about, and the diehards with nothing to do but splutter!'

'Peel should have refused to debate anything so preposterous,' Lucy said. 'He should have divided at once and defeated the Whigs there and then.'

'A quick division would have killed the Bill, certainly; but what then?' Tom said. 'We must have reform, Mama. I thought I had convinced you of that.'

'A moderate measure, perhaps. But not this! Surely, Tom you won't vote for it?' Lucy said anxiously.

'I'm not sure,' Tom said. 'It surprised me as much as anyone, but I begin to think it may not have gone too far after all. What did you think, Batchworth? It gives you your seats for Manchester, so I suppose you must be happy.'

Jes, leaning comfortably against the chimneypiece, gazed thoughtfully at the toe of the boot which was resting on the fender. 'Yes, of course I'm happy with that. But I'm afraid Russell was more concerned in ending the abuses of the nomination system than in giving power to the new interest.'

'What new interest?' Morpurgo asked. 'You mean the factory owners?'

'Careful how you speak of them, Peter: he's one himself, you know,' Tom warned.

'Not just factory owners,' Batchworth said, 'but all those concerned with industry and commerce – yourself included, Morpurgo.'

Peter put his hands up in alarm. 'Oh, don't bring me into it! I'm just a simple sailor, as our dear old King Tarry Breeks always says! I know nothing of politics.'

'Nonsense,' Jes said, a little put out. 'You are a rational man. You must have a view.'

'My view,' Morpurgo said rather apologetically, 'is that it all worked perfectly well before, so why do we have to change it?'

'Just what Mama says,' Tom laughed. 'How did the last *Quarterly Review* put it? "There is no more Tory and Whig, but rather the conservative versus the subversive principle". You're a natural conservative, Peter!'

'If that's the case, Grey is a natural conservative too,' Batchworth said. 'I was happy enough with the list of seats to be eliminated, but it's the redistribution that worries me.'

'Two seats each for Manchester and Birmingham, five other large towns, and four districts of London; one each for twenty smaller towns – all previously unrepresented,' Tom said. 'If that's not giving power to your new interest, I don't know what you want!'

'But look how many new seats go to the counties,' Jes said. 'Twenty-six counties have their representation doubled. Yorkshire, which already has four seats, gets two more. It's all calculated to preserve the aristocratic share; the great landlords are to maintain their influence over the House after all.'

'Well, what would you have?' Lucy broke in indignantly. 'The House full of shopkeepers and pedlars? Who should represent the country but those who own the land?'

'Oh ma'am,' Jes laughed ruefully, 'that is the whole debate!'

The door opened at that moment to admit Lord Theakston.

'Well, this is pleasant,' he said. He kissed his wife and smiled round the company. 'All here? Batchworth – Peter my boy. Tom – what did you think of that bombshell of Grey's, hey? The King is as nervous as a green girl. Terrified of a clash between Whigs and Tories; even more so of a clash between Commons and Peers. He wants nothing more than for everything to be left as it is, but he's too much of an officer to think he can baulk the issue.'

'I was thinking myself in the House, sir, that he has shewn great courage – and discretion,' said Tom.

Theakston smiled. 'Yes, and that's one in the eye for all those critics who think Billy can't hold his tongue! *And* those who think he's completely under his wife's thumb: he said he'd support the measure, and as Holland says, once he gives his word, he sticks to it like a barnacle.'

Tom grinned. 'Ever since William came to the throne, sir, I've noticed your vocabulary is more and more laced with sea-going imagery. Don't you think, Peter, my father is becoming a veritable Old Salt?'

'Is the King really for this Bill?' Lucy asked her husband,

cutting through the nonsense. 'I find it hard to believe he knew about it beforehand.'

'Oh, he knew all right, and agreed with it. He's worried about the changes to the franchise, though.'

'They aren't so very great, sir,' Batchworth said. 'Just a few small categories added.'

'Any kind of tinkering with the suffrage sets a dangerous precedent, Billy thinks – and I agree with him.'

'Surely not, sir,' Batchworth said. 'Grey firmly believes the lower orders will accept this as the final settlement —'

'Grey has it wrong,' Theakston said, more downrightly than he usually spoke. 'All he's done is to bring out the difference between the voting and the voteless classes. Once let people think that balance can be altered, and they'll never stop demanding alteration. You know where that leads.'

'Universal franchise?' Lucy said in horror. 'The King fears it will lead to that and still supports the Bill?'

Theakston shrugged. 'Billy believes Government's business is to govern, and his is to support them – as long as Parliament does.'

'Very much to the point, sir,' Tom said. 'Grey's majority in the Commons is flimsy at best: it'll never survive this debate. In the end he must ask for a dissolution and a new general election.'

'Well, he won't get it,' Theakston said. 'Billy has told him quite categorically that he won't order a dissolution. He will help the Government in any way he can, but with the country in a state of turmoil, he will not sanction an election. And when you remember the trouble we had last time,' he added, 'you must admit he's right.'

'Quite right. There are always shocking breaches of the peace during general elections,' Lucy agreed.

'But what is Grey to do, if he isn't allowed to go to the country?' Jes asked.

'He'll never get the Bill past the Tories as it stands,' Tom added.

Theakston shrugged. 'He'll either have to persuade the House, or alter the Bill. Nothing else to be done.' He looked round him. 'Rosamund not here?' I thought we were to see you both.'

'My wife has borrowed her, but she will be here soon,' Murpurgo said, getting to his feet. 'And I am reminded that I must be on my way. I have business at Tatt's. Will you excuse me, ma'am?'

Lucy rang the bell. 'You and Africa must come and dine with us,' she said. 'We don't see half enough of you.'

'Thank you, ma'am,' Peter smiled. 'We'll dine with the greatest of pleasure, if you will excuse us from political talk. The ins and outs of this Reform Bill are far beyond my grasp.'

'I'm sure we shall not be short of things to say,' Lucy said kindly. 'When you dine with us, we'll have naval talk.'

'Quite right,' Theakston said innocently. 'We're all sea-dogs now. In fact, I'm thinkin' of growing my pigtail – might start a new fashion.'

There was a flurry of activity as Hicks arrived in answer to the summons to shew Peter out, but also to announce Rosamund and deliver to her ladyship a letter which had just that moment come up from the post office. Hellos and goodbyes were said, Morpurgo took his departure, Rosamund kissed everyone, pulled off her gloves and dropped gracefully onto a sofa, saying, 'Africa has the patience of a saint! How she manages the riding school with all its unpromising pupils, her two little boys – who are as naughty as they can hold together! – and still find time to school her horses I don't understand.'

'What was wrong with the horse?' Tom asked.

'She's trying to break it to carry a lady, but whenever she puts the side-saddle on it, it will only *go* sideways, which is not at all the idea. Just like a great brown crab! She had it standing in the corner of the ménage, and she wanted me to take the lunge rein while she got up. Her idea was that if it had the wall on its right and behind it, and me with the lunge and whip on its left, there was only one direction it could go, which was forwards.'

'And did it?' her husband asked, amused.

'Not at all,' Rosamund grinned. 'It found another direction she hadn't thought about: as soon as she put her heel to its side, it went straight up in the air and tipped her off.'

'I hope she wasn't hurt?' Tom said.

'Lord, no! Why should she be? Only after the fourth

tumble she decided they'd both had enough and put the animal away. Then we went into the house to have a dish of tea, just as her boys arrived back from their lessons, full of bounce and bobbance and both talking at once. I think the horse was less tiring!'

All three men had been listening to her with amusement, but Lucy had stepped to one side to read the letter Hicks had brought up. Now Lord Theakston looked towards his wife, and seeing her expression moved quickly towards her.

'My love, what is it?'

'Oh Danby —' She reached for his hand and gripped it while she finished reading to the bottom of the page.

'Mother, what is it? Who is it from?'

'You've turned quite pale,' Theakston said. 'You'd better sit down. Tom, pour your mother a glass of wine. Sit here, my love. No, no, don't try to speak yet. There's no hurry.' Tom brought the wine and Lucy, sitting on the sofa beside Rosamund, sipped it gratefully.

'Thank you, I am better now,' she said at last in her normal voice, handing the glass back. She looked from one face to another. 'It's from Manchester.'

'From Sophie?' Rosamund asked. She glanced at her husband with quick apprehension. The baby was due at any time – surely she could not have miscarried at this late hour? 'Not bad news, Mama?'

'It isn't from Sophie, but about her.' The hand that held the letter trembled, and she crushed it down in her lap. Jes moved behind the sofa and laid his hand on his wife's shoulder, steadyingly. 'From her friend Mrs Hastings. Something quite dreadful has happened.'

'I must go to her,' Rosamund said to Jes when they reached home.

'But my dear,' Jes began doubtfully, thinking of the effects of a long coach journey, 'surely her mother will be with her soon.'

She turned her head to look at him, knowing exactly what he was thinking. 'I must, Jes. If the cases were reversed, she would come to me. If I travel slowly and stop frequently I shall be all right. The roads are good: I can still make good time.'

'I'll come with you,' Jes decided.

Her face lit. 'Would you?'

'I can't let you go alone. Suppose an axle broke, or the weather changed for the worse? And Fanny will want me. I must see that my little Fanny is all right.'

'We ought to leave first thing in the morning. I don't think we should delay.'

'We won't,' Jes said, knowing it would agitate her more to be prevented than to hurry. 'We can set off at first light and make the first stage with our own horses.'

Rosamund stared sightlessly ahead. 'I can't seem to take it in. To be attacked and killed like that on his own threshold! And Prudence said they don't even know who the villains were.'

'That's something I may be able to help with. I don't suppose Mrs Hastings will have been able to spare the time.'

'Poor Sophie, what will become of her now?'

'She's well provided for. All the wealth in the case was hers.'

'That's not what I meant.'

'I know,' Jes said.

'I hope her mother is with her by now. Oh poor Aunt Héloïse! And so soon after my uncle's death, too! Oh Jes, why do so many bad things seem to be happening?'

He stepped close and took her in his arms to comfort her. 'Good things happen too, you know. Remember that.'

'I can't,' she said in a small voice. 'I'm too afraid to think about it.'

That all was not well at Hobsbawn House was evident from the fact that the door was opened not by the butler but by Lord Batchworth's own man, Sopwith. He had travelled with Rosamund's maid, Moss, and the luggage, and by making fewer stops on the way had been able to arrive before them, which seemed to have been just as well.

'This is very handy of you, Sopwith,' Jes said as he stepped over the threshold. 'What's to do?'

'We're rather at sixes and sevens here, my lord,' Sopwith said in a low voice. 'The late Mr Hobsbawn's butler was very devoted to his master and has been – er – seeking consolation, my lord, in the bottle.'

'Are there no other menservants?' Rosamund demanded. 'I seem to remember a decentish-looking fellow opening the door to me last time I was here.'

'The senior footman left, my lady, saying that it was not what he was accustomed to; and the lower footman is not what *you* are accustomed to, my lady, if you'll forgive me. I've set him to cleaning the silver, which is all he's fit for in my opinion.'

'Very well,' Jes said, 'you seem to be making yourself indispensable, as usual. I shall need you myself, however, so you had better send over to Batchworth House and ask Raby to send one of our footmen to help out for the time being, until things are more settled.'

'Very good, my lord.'

'Where is everyone, Sopwith?' Rosamund asked, giving him her gloves and muff.

'Mrs Hobsbawn is in her bedchamber, my lady: I understand she has not yet been well enough to rise from her bed. Mrs Hastings is with her; and Miss Hobsbawn is in the nursery with her governess.'

'Is Lady Morland not here?'

'I understand she has not arrived, my lady, nor sent word. Mrs Hastings has sent off a second letter, fearing the first might have gone astray.'

Rosamund and Jes exchanged a look. 'I had better go straight to Sophie,' Rosamund said.

'I'll go and see how Fanny is, then,' Jes replied, and they mounted the stairs together. Rosamund turned off at the first floor and scratched softly at the door to Sophie's room. After a moment it was opened by a woman with a plain, careworn face, dressed in a neat and expensive gown of grey merino. She put her finger to her lips.

'She's asleep – don't disturb her,' she whispered. 'Come in, Lady Batchworth. I'm so glad to see you.'

'Mrs Hastings,' Rosamund said, stepping into the bedchamber. A good fire was burning and the curtains were drawn half across the windows, giving a nursery cosiness to the room. It smelled of pot-pourri with a faint and acrid undertone of medicine, and was quiet except for the soft rapid ticking of the French clock on the chimneypiece.

'You've been with Sophie all the time?' Rosamund went on.

'I haven't been able to leave her. She's in a pitiable state, as you can imagine. Edwin – my husband – sent a nurse to help me, but though she is useful in fetching and carrying, Sophie won't be left with her.'

'Then I shall be glad to be able to share the burden with you,' Rosamund said. 'You must be tired to death.'

Prudence smiled wanly. 'It isn't so bad. She has been sleeping a good deal – and then I can sleep too. Edwin gives her laudanum —'

'I thought I could smell it,' Rosamund said. She repressed a shudder. The smell reminded her of the terrible time just after Marcus's 'accident'. 'Is she hysterical?'

'At times. She's been very uncomfortable, too, from the effects of the birth – it was a painful delivery – but most of all at the moment she's upset that her mother doesn't come to her. She called for her from the beginning, poor soul —'

'Pru?' A faint voice from the bed. 'Where are you?'

'She's woken,' Pru whispered, and hurried over to the bedside. Rosamund followed slowly. 'Here I am, Sophie dear,' she heard Pru say. 'And I've brought a visitor for you. Someone who will do you a great deal of good, I'm sure.'

'Maman?' Rosamund winced at the pathetic eagerness of that cry.

'No, love, not your Mama. But someone very dear to you.' Prudence looked up and nodded to Rosamund, and she walked round the end of the bed and into Sophie's sight, and tried to smile. Sophie had never been pretty, and the ravages of laudanum and weeping had made her look old and drawn. Her eyes were dull and shadowed, her mouth set thin with pain. She looked ten years older than Rosamund.

'Sophie, dearest,' Rosamund said, and her voice sounded very peculiar. She tried again. 'I came as soon as I heard. Oh my poor Sophie!'

The face lit with eagerness, the thin arms were outstretched. 'Oh Ros!'

Rosamund took her cousin in her arms. She felt thin and hot through her night-gown, and smelled of milk and blood and sickness and the sour odour of hair too long unwashed. The smells seemed to transmit to Rosamund the full

144

enormity of what had happened to Sophie: to the agony of losing a longed-for child had been added the desperate grief of losing an adored husband – the husband she depended on utterly for everything in life. And to that intolerable burden of pain had been added yet more – the horror of the manner of Jasper's death. Rosamund could only begin to imagine what that must be like. Had Marcus been killed instead of wounded in his duel —? But then, she did not suppose she had ever felt about Marcus the way Sophie felt about Jasper. How could she bear it? How could she continue to live under such desperate blows?

'You'll stay, won't you?' Sophie said against Rosamund's ear. 'You won't go away?'

'Of course I'll stay, love – for as long as you want. Jes is here, too. He'll come and see you by and by, when you're ready. He'll have to go back to London in a few days, but I shall stay here until you're better.'

The tense body had relaxed a little as she spoke, and now she put Sophie back from her gently, keeping hold of her hands as Sophie lay back against the pillows and looked at her wanly.

'It's been so terrible. Like a horrible dream I can't wake up from,' she said. 'Sometimes I don't know if I'm awake or asleep, but either is equally horrible.'

'That's the laudanum, I expect,' Rosamund said.

Sophie nodded, her eyes going to Prudence. 'Pru's been so wonderful. She's stayed with me all the time. But I don't know how long it is,' she added, her eyes widening. 'Is it days or weeks since – since —'

'Hush, darling, don't think about it. Not until you're stronger,' Rosamund said, pressing her hands.

Sophie looked at her again. 'I lost the baby, you know.'

'Yes, I know.'

'It was a boy. The son Jasper wanted. But it died. I couldn't even – even do that for him —' She began to cry again, tears rolling from her eyes with frightening ease, and Rosamund felt her own throat tighten in response. 'Oh Ros, how do I bear it? It hurts so much!'

'I know.'

'Yes, you know. You lost Charlotte —'

145

'Not the same,' Rosamund managed to say. She was struggling not to cry, thinking it wouldn't help.

The tears were flowing fast now. 'Oh Ros, what shall I do?' The helpless appeal – hopeless, too, since it expected no answer – broke Rosamund's control. Since she couldn't speak, she gathered Sophie to her again like a child, and they cried together.

In the schoolroom, Jes was faced with a figure just as hard to bear: a small, bewildered child dressed all in unnatural black, her golden ringlets bright as true specie against the black ribbons that held them back. She was sitting on a hard schoolroom chair at one side of a plain deal table, studying a book, her short legs dangling clear of the floor, while on the other side sat Miss Molton, plain as bread and neat as a pin, her grey stuff dress unornamented, her close-braided hair innocent of the least suspicion of a curl.

Miss Molton, seeing his movement out of the corner of her eye, looked up, and then Fanny looked up too. Her face lit like a candle, and she flung herself without a sound from her chair and across the room, catching Jes around the waist so tightly that it was a moment before he could release himself even to pick her up. He didn't think Miss Molton would approve of such familiarity with her charge, but for once he didn't care. He held Fanny close against him, and swallowed very hard against the constriction in his throat. Over her shoulder, Jes saw Miss Molton turning away from them, applying the corner of her handkerchief to her eye.

When at last he set Fanny down again she slid her hand into his and dragged him away to sit with her on the old sofa.

'When did you come? I didn't know you were coming.'

'We've just this minute arrived. I came straight up to see you.'

'Is Cousin Rosamund here too?'

'Yes; she's gone to see your mama.'

'Mama is ill in bed. The baby died again, and it makes Mama ill – like the time at Grandmama's. Are you going away soon?'

There was no missing the anxiety of the question. 'Not immediately,' Jes said, feeling treacherous. The pale, solemn

146

face was turned up to his searchingly. Suddenly Fanny's ordered world had become hard to understand, and people she had trusted had begun to do inexplicable things. 'I shall stay for a few days,' Jes went on, 'but then I shall have to go back to London. But Cousin Rosamund will stay.'

'Couldn't she go to London, and you stay?' Fanny asked wistfully.

'I'm afraid not. There is important business I must attend to.'

Fanny but her lip. 'Business like Papa's?'

'No, another kind of business.'

Across the room Miss Molton sat at the table, twisting her handkerchief slowly round and round in her fingers as she watched them. Jes felt a warmth of liking for her for the first time: it was quite obvious that she loved her charge.

'Papa went out on business and he didn't come back,' Fanny said, watching Jes's face for reaction, for help with the understanding. 'He's never coming back again. Miss Molton says he's gone to Heaven.'

Jes nodded. 'That's right.'

'It was my birthday yesterday. I always have a birthday treat. He must come for that.'

'Fanny, your papa is dead. Don't you understand what that means?' Jes said gently.

She didn't answer. 'You've come for my birthday, haven't you? All the way from London?'

'Yes, love. But your papa can't come back. He's dead, Fanny.'

She stared at him a moment longer, and then lowered her gaze, drawing a sigh that seemed to come from the bottom of her soul. Jes waited, holding the small, damp hand and waiting for the next agonising question. At last Fanny said in a small voice, 'I suppose Papa will be with the baby, then.' And in an even smaller voice. 'It's not fair.'

In bed that night, Rosamund lay on her side, facing her husband, her hands folded round one of his while his other hand stroked her head soothingly.

'I think this has been the longest day of my life,' she said into the silence of their thoughts. 'I feel exhausted.'

'Me too,' Jes said. 'Imagine how Prudence feels.'

'She's been wonderful. And Miss Molton. Poor little Fanny, Jes! We must try to do something for her – something to make up for her birthday being missed.'

'I'll take her out for a drive tomorrow, if the weather's fine.'

'Yes, she'd like that. And we could let her have dinner with us, for a treat – if we have it early.'

'That will please her,' Jes agreed. 'Talking of children, how are you feeling? No ill effects?'

'None at all. The roads were so good and the carriage so well sprung. Oh but Jes, how will I ever be able to tell Sophie?'

He moved his hand from her hair to her cheek. 'My love,' he said, 'you'll just tell her.'

'It will break her heart.'

'No it won't. She loves you, so she'll be glad for you.'

'Then that will break mine.'

'Life goes on, my darling. There's no stopping it. Sophie will see that for herself by and by. Fanny will make sure of that.'

'Yes.' A pause. 'Don't you think there's something odd about Aunt Héloïse not coming? I thought she'd have been here by now.'

'The letter must have gone astray. Don't tease yourself. There's enough trouble here without that.'

'I suppose so.' She was silent for a moment. Then, 'Who was that strange little man you interviewed this afternoon?'

'One of the foremen from Hobsbawn Mills – Blake's his name. He was desperate for orders. He's a good man, but he doesn't know what to do, and they have work piling up. That's the trouble with Jasper having taken such an active hand in the business. He gave all the orders, and they can't go on without him.'

'Well, you can be useful there, at least.'

'Yes. Prudence almost begged me to sort matters out – they've been bothering her with questions every day, as well as everything else she's had to deal with.'

'Isn't there anyone who can take over?'

'I shall go in tomorrow morning and see how things stand.

If necessary I can send my manager over from Ordsall to take charge temporarily, until a permanent man can be found – though I would sooner not burden him unless I have to. I suppose Sophie will want to hand over to a manager in the long run. She will hardly run things herself.'

'Hardly. And there's no-one else now to do it for her.'

'It's a damnable thing,' he agreed elliptically. 'And there are enquiries I must put in hand with the magistrates and the constables. I don't believe that no-one in the whole of Manchester knows anything about this business.'

'It won't bring him back to find out who killed him.'

'No. But we can't just let it go without trying to bring the murderers to justice, can we? If it were you in Sophie's position, you would want to know, at least?'

'Oh don't!' she said, shuddering.

'Well, but I must try at least to get things started before I leave for London,' he said gently.

'Oh dear, I was forgetting for a moment that you aren't staying with me. Fanny won't like it when you go away. And I shall positively hate it! I wish you didn't have to go.'

'I wish I didn't, too. I hate to be apart from you. You're everything in life to me, don't you know that?'

She lifted his hand to her lips and then her cheek. 'Oh Jes,' she said very quietly, 'I keep thinking —'

'Don't,' he said.

'How could I bear it if I lost you?'

He gathered her tightly against him. 'You won't lose me. I'll never leave you. Never!'

She pressed herself against him, nudging herself as close as it was possible to be to every part of him, her face against his neck, his arms round her, keeping her. Safe. 'There are patterns, aren't there?' she said after a while. 'You see them sometimes – an order to things.'

'Yes. I suppose so,' he said. He kissed her brow, staring into the darkness beyond her.

'I don't know if it makes me feel better or worse, to think there's order and reason. A guiding principle. I think perhaps it makes me feel nervous.'

'I love you,' he said after a moment, as if it were an answer.

'I love you, too,' she said; and it seemed to have been.

CHAPTER NINE

The cockpit just off Walmgate in York looked from the outside like an artisan's workshop, which was what it had started life as. Inside there had been a large single room which went right up to the roof, except for a gallery along one side which had given access to the gantry of a large lifting apparatus. All the machinery had been removed now, as had some of the floorboards, to reveal the shallow cellar below. Here a circular barricade had been set up to make the cocking arena itself, in the centre of which was the stage, built up a little from the ground and with the mark painted boldly in the middle.

On the ground floor tiers of benches had been set up around the arena for the gentleman spectators, while the lesser sort stood up in the gallery. The setters-on had access to the stage from the cellar, which was reached by an open wooden staircase to the side of the main room. Behind the main room was a smaller room which had once housed the furnace, and was now a small kitchen from which refreshments were served to the gentlemen fanciers. The whole was lit by a gigantic chandelier of rather crude manufacture, which was rumoured to have been the last honest article made there before the artisan went out of business. If its quality were anything to go by, it was probably also the reason he went out of business.

Take it all in all, Nicholas thought, it was the neatest, tightest place you could wish for. It was his groom, Ferrars, who had introduced him to cocking. Ferrars came originally from Kent, where it was a very popular pastime, and had acted as cocker to a previous employer. Nicholas had not seen much in it at first, but the excitement of the fights had gradually communicated itself to him. Then he discovered that Ferrars had the knowledge and skills to produce a winning cock, and realising how much money a win could put into his pocket as an owner, he became a convert to the sport.

Today was a big day for Nicholas, for there was an important match at the cockpit with large prizes: the York Gentlemen (a group of enthusiasts of which Nicholas and his friend Carlton Husthwaite were members) against the York Officers (an extempore alliance of military men from Fulford Barracks) for a thousand guineas the side plus fifty on each bout. In addition there was bound to be heavy betting on the side, and Nicholas had a blue-black which Ferrars assured him was in the peak of its trim and must win against any match. Since Nicholas's pockets had been irritatingly light these weeks past, he was both excited and nervous when he arrived at the cockpit.

He and Husthwaite were accompanied by Jack Cox, the black sheep of York's leading family of drapers, who would bet on anything as long as he had money in his pockets, and for as long afterwards as he could find anyone green enough to accept his vowels; and Felix Thirlby, a gentleman's son rather younger than the other three, who was trying to make a career for himself as a rake, admired them tremendously and did his best to emulate them. Husthwaite, when he was sober, apostrophised him as a tiresome halfling and occasionally in a fit of guilt tried to dissuade him from the worst of their excesses; but Thirlby had a large allowance from his papa always burning a hole in his pocket, and the other two could see no reason why he shouldn't throw it their way if he wanted to.

So the four arrived together at half past five, knocked at the door, were scrutinised through the hatch, and admitted into the cockpit. It was stifling inside, the atmosphere already foul from the candles of the chandelier, the cigars of the gentlemen and the pipes of the lower orders; and thick with the smells of humanity, hot wax, sawdust, and chicken dung. The noise of conversation was interspersed with the hoarse cries of cockerels and bursts of harsh laughter from the rougher element. Thirlby shivered a little with excitement.

Jack Cox caught his arm and said, 'Come, Thirbly, we'll leave the sportsmen to see the weigh-in. You and I must find ourselves a good place. We'll see some blood by and by. Is your purse to hand?'

'Yes,' said Thirbly, patting his pocket. 'But you must advise me how to bet. I don't know one cock from another.'

'Who does?' Cox shrugged. 'Leave that to the experts! You and I bet on the odds, cully, just the same as at the races.' He felt in his pocket for his flask. 'Let's have a wet to begin with, to get us in the mood.'

In the owners' corner, Nicholas found Ferrars waiting, having already weighted in his cock.

'My man ain't here yet,' Husthwaite said, looking round. 'If he's late I'll break his neck for him. Let's have a look at your blue-black, Morland.'

Nicholas nodded to Ferrars, who took the bag from the cocker and drew out the cock.

'He turned the scale at four pounds two ounces, sir.'

'That's the heaviest he's been,' Nicholas said enthusiastically. 'What do you think of him, Husthwaite?'

'Strong-looking bird; good girth,' Husthwaite said conservatively.

'Look at his spurs,' Nicholas said, taking the praise impatiently into his own hands. 'You'll never see longer or sharper; and see how well they hook inwards.' The cock, as if it knew they were talking about it, flicked its head to the side and stared at them with one wicked black eye. Its blue-black feathers were as glossy as shot silk, its comb deeply scarlet. 'He's a beauty,' Nicholas concluded proudly. 'Who's his match, Ferrars?'

'Captain Mattock's grey. Beamy legs and a sharp heel – it'll be a close 'un, sir.'

'But we'll win?' Nicholas said anxiously. Fifty guineas would be more than welcome to him at the moment; plus his share of the side if the Gentlemen beat the Officers.

'I think we have the preference,' Ferrars said unemphatically. His eyes flickered past Nicholas's shoulder, and Nicky turned to see Captain Mattock standing there with one of his cronies. From the flush of Mattock's face, which clashed rather with his scarlet, it seemed that he had been drinking heavily before he arrived.

'I see we're matched, Morland,' he said, leaning on the shoulder of the fair-haired young ensign beside him. 'Or rather, we are ill-matched! My grey will show up your dunghill crow in an instant.'

'I think not,' Nicholas said tautly. 'We've got the girth of you, Mattock. We'll see you off.'

'Girth ain't everything,' Mattock said, breathing heavily. 'Everyone knows blacks are shy. You can't beat a grey for bottom, and that's where we'll finish you.'

'Are you saying my bird's a skirter?' Nicholas demanded.

'I'll put money on it,' Mattock grinned. 'What d'you say, Morland? A little wager on the side, just between you and me? Or don't you have faith in your scrawny little capon?'

'Capon, is it?' Nicholas growled. 'I'll see you eat your words, Captain Mattock. How much?'

'What say we make it interesting? A hundred pounds that my bird sends yours to grass.'

At this Mattock's companion stirred. 'I say, Roger, not a hundred,' he protested weakly. He seemed rather the drunker of the two, for his blue eyes, very bloodshot, kept trying to wander from each other in different directions.

Mattock took hold of his ear and twisted it with a peculiar mixture of affection and malice. 'Hush, Boy! Do you think I don't know the strength of my own cock?' For some reason this made the fair young man laugh, and Mattock looked at Nicholas with sudden geniality. 'What do you say, Morland?'

Nicholas hesitated, aware that he hadn't a hundred pounds to meet the bet if he lost. Ferrars was looking forbidding, probably aware of the same thing, and Husthwaite murmured, 'No need to go overboard, Morland. Plenty of time to place wagers. See how the early fights go.'

'No, no, if you're going to cry craven the bet's off,' Mattock said broadly. 'It's now or never. A hundred pounds on the side; or do you own mine's the better bird?'

Nicholas felt himself driven. 'Make it guineas,' he heard himself say, somewhat to his own dismay.

'That's the dandy,' Mattock grinned, holding out his hand. Nicholas grasped it briefly. 'Boy here will hold the stakes.

He's perfectly trustworthy with money, having so much himself he can't possibly want more. Wouldn't trust him in any other way, however — would I, Boy?'

The young man grinned. 'Be foolish to,' he slurred.

You'll have to take my note-of-hand,' Nicholas said curtly. 'I haven't enough about me.'

Mattock's eyes gleamed with some secret pleasure. 'Why, Morland, do you think I don't trust you? We are all gentlemen, I hope. I don't need your vowel for such a paltry sum. I'll see you on the benches – and may the better man win!'

He and his companion moved away, conversing in low voices and with evident amusement; and Husthwaite was plainly about to remonstrate with Nicky, but at that moment his man arrived with his own bird, a Sussex red, and his attention was distracted.

Nicholas took the opportunity to say quietly to Ferrars, 'We will win, won't we? You said we had the preference.'

'When a match is that close, sir, it can be a matter of luck,' Ferrars said unhelpfully. 'But you must do as you think fit.'

Cold comfort, Nicholas thought. A few minutes later he and Husthwaite pushed through the crowds in search of their companions, some liquid encouragement and the most favourable odds on the first fight. There was nothing for it now, Nicholas thought philosophically. He could not back down from the wager without making a fool of himself. If he lost, he would have to find the money somewhere.

The first fight soon took him out of himself: a blow-for-blow battle between two small but vicious reds which lasted only five minutes before the victor was crowing over the bleeding body of the loser. It was a point to the Gentlemen, which reassured Nicholas; and since Thirlby had, by sheer luck, bet heavily on the winner, he was very excited by the result and insisted that he would buy them all a champagne supper afterwards, a suggestion that only Husthwaite resisted.

The second fight, between a black gallo and a grey-black mottle, was better matched and lasted fifteen minutes, leaving the Officers' winning bird so badly mauled that it seemed probable it would be in the pot by the morning. The finish was frenzied, and Nicholas came to himself as the winner was taken off to find his throat sore with yelling and his hands damp with sweat. Thirlby was so excited he had lost his voice entirely, and Husthwaite and Cox were passing a flask back and forth between them, their faces flushed and their eyes bright with bloodlust.

'Great sport, eh, Morland?' Husthwaite said, offering the flask to him. 'It's your bird next, ain't it? By God, if it's anything as good a fight as the last, we'll see the blood fly. We'll be flecked to the eyebrows by the end!'

Nicholas thought of the hundred guineas and felt suddenly much too sober. He took the flask and upended it, and felt the brandy run down his throat and drop a ball of fire in his stomach. Better! He handed the flask back, and smiled stiffly in reply to Thirlby's rather inane grin. Perhaps Thirlby would lend him the money, he thought hopefully.

Ferrars was down at the stage with the blue-black between his hands; a tough-looking setter-on appeared opposite him with the big grey. The referee raised his hand and the noise in the cockpit sank for a moment almost to silence. Nicholas for some reason looked away from the stage for a moment and saw Mattock almost opposite him, staring at him with a broad grin. He tore his eyes away and watched the birds, going through their preliminaries. Then suddenly they struck together, the noise in the cockpit erupted, and Nicholas forgot everything else. There was now nothing outside that small area where the two desperate birds tore and slashed at each other, sending feathers flying and flecking the front-row spectators with blood. The shouts around him had become a solid wall of noise in which no word could be differentiated. Nicholas knew himself to be shouting, but could not hear his own voice, only feel it tearing out of his throat as he urged his blue-black on to murder. When the two birds went down, their spurs fast in each other and there was a pause, he had no idea how long the fight had been going on.

The setters-on went in to release the spurs and freed the birds again to face each other.

'Mattock's grey's had enough,' Husthwaite said in Nicholas's ear. 'He's dazed, d'you see? By God it's been a good bout! Let's see your black finish him off now!'

But Nicholas could see his own bird was shaken. Both were bleeding from a number of wounds, and the black's comb was torn. The cocks eyed each other and threatened, but neither wanted to close with the other again. The comments of the spectators became raucous, and when the timekeeper shouted the count there was a huge cheer and some less than polite suggestions as the setters-on stepped in to secure their birds and take them to the mark to set them beak-to-beak with each other. Released, the cocks flew at each other again with a flurry of ugly blows. When they broke, the black's comb was hanging down over one eye, and Nicholas felt his heart sink. It must be all over. He had lost. The grey threw its head back and crowed; but as soon as its head came down, the black struck a single lightning blow, stabbing the grey in the eye. The grey reeled over, fluttered a little, and lay still.

Howls of joy erupted from the Gentlemen and their supporters, and Nicholas, dazed, felt his back being pounded, and heard Husthwaite screaming congratulations in his ear. The blue-black was crowing its victory; Ferrars was stepping into the ring to secure it; the grey was lying on the stage just below him, a circle of red in its grey head where its eye had been, its wing-tips still twitching with the memory of its departed life. A damp and icy hand came down over Nicholas's, and he looked round to see Thirlby, green-white in the face, staring at the grey cock's ruin with his nostrils dilating.

'Oh God,' he said in a wavering voice, 'I think I'm going to be —' He shut his mouth tightly on the end of the sentence.

Nicholas, perfectly sure that he was indeed going to be, said, 'For God's sake, man, not in here! Oh Lord, come on, I'll get you outside. Keep your mouth shut and don't think of anything.'

He grabbed Thirlby's arm and shoved him through the crowd towards the door, just managing to get him outside before his self-control lost the battle and he threw up with the dog-like simplicity of the very young and the very drunk.

'Damned young fool,' Nicholas said disagreeably, and was preparing to leave him to his fate when the door opened again and Mattock came out.

'Trying to tip me the double eh, Morland?' he said genially.

'I've heard of men running away in defeat, but fleeing from a victory's new to me!'

'Oh – no – not at all. I was just – that is, young Thirlby's not quite the thing —' Nicholas stammered.

'Ah, I see. Noble of you to take the trouble – but don't you find the infantry palls after a while? I've just managed to shrug Boy off. Why don't you do the same with this green – *le mot juste*, wouldn't you say? – this green lad, and we'll go and find some more adult entertainment. Cocking's all very well, but one can have enough of it quite quickly, if one is not either hopelessly stupid or incorrigibly young.'

'Don't you want to see the result of the match?' Nicholas asked nervously. Mattock was so world-weary and sophisticated that he made Nicky feel as much Mattock's inferior as Thirlby was his. He wanted to impress him as a down-the-road man – or at least wanted not to make Mattock think he was a provincial noddy. He had thought himself quite daring for frequenting cock-fights. Now he felt like a raw curate.

'Do you?' Mattock asked, raising an eyebrow. 'In my experience one cock-fight is much like another. After two or three, my blood is sufficiently up to take the rest on trust.'

'There's a thousand guineas on it,' Nicholas said, trying to sound casual.

'It will be won or lost just the same whether we're there or not,' Mattock said. 'I have a hundred guineas here for you – got it from Boy just before I brushed him off. Now my idea was that we should go off somewhere and celebrate your handsome win. You might buy me dinner, you know, out of gratitude.'

'Gratitude?' Nicholas asked, a little dazed.

'Certainly,' Mattock said with a grin. 'If I had not provoked you to wager, these hundred guineas would still be languishing in Boy's pocket! I'm sure we can make better use of them than he would.' He glanced at Thirlby. 'Your little friend seems to have finished vomiting. You had better decide quickly or you'll find yourself having to take him home to his mother.'

There was no question about it. Nicholas recognised the beckoning of new experience – felt himself being tugged towards a world of sophistication he had only fingered the hem of until now.

'Let's be off, then,' he said, trying to sound bold and carefree.

Mattock gave him that humorously malicious look. 'Good man. Come then, let's away and find a neat supper somewhere, and a decent claret – a great deal of decent claret.' He tucked his arm through Nicholas's and led him away. 'And afterwards,' he said in a low, thrilling voice, 'I think we might visit a certain very sophisticated house in Straker's Passage, where the most arcane pleasures are to be purchased for ready money.'

'Oh, really?' Nicholas said, and to his embarrassed ears his voice came out several pitches too high, and with a shameful wobble in the middle. Arcane pleasures? What on earth could they be? He did not dare ask, but he was breathless with a mixture of fear and excitement.

'Yes, really,' Mattock chuckled. 'And ready money we have in plenty, my dear Morland, thanks to Boy and your blue-black, so let us indulge ourselves.'

Felix Thirlby, leaning against the wall and wiping his mouth with his handkerchief, goggled stupidly at Nicky walking away down the alley. Either it was the poor light or the excess of brandy, but it looked remarkably as though he had two heads and four legs.

It was late when Nicholas got back to Morland Place, and by then he felt as though he had travelled to the end of the universe and back. He had left home that morning a mere tyro of pleasure – almost an innocent child. Now he had plumbed the depths of sophistication; now he knew everything. The experiences of the day, and the substances still circulating in his blood, combined to make him feel both huge and insubstantial. He was a colossus of sin, a giant amongst men of the world, with a weight of weary cynicism resting on his shoulders which must mark him out from amongst his peers. He half expected the earth to shrink humbly from him as he passed over it. Would the very walls of Morland Place bow to him in acknowledgement as his shadow touched them?

But the house looked the same as he rode into the yard, jumped down from his horse and thrust the reins into

Ferrars' hands, avoiding his curious – was it even accusatory – eyes, for he had left him at the cockpit last night without a word. He trod up the steps and in through the great door which stood ajar for him – and was astonished to see a corded trunk standing in the hall. For an instant he thought he must have been found out, and was about to be cast out into the night by an outraged parent, and his soul shrivelled; but at a second glance he realised that the trunk was his mother's.

The second thought that followed the second glance was that he had been found out and that she was leaving him for ever, and he was still wondering whether he would be glad or sorry about that when one of the footmen, Thomas, came into the hall, and stopped guiltily on seeing him.

'Ah, Thomas! What's going on? Is my mother going somewhere?'

'Oh sir,' Thomas said nervously, 'it was a letter, sir, for her ladyship, sir, which coom from Manchester this afternoon. Her ladyship was in a rare taking, sir, and th' long and short is she's oop and off tomorrow morning to Mrs Hobsbawn's bedside, sir.'

Nicky stepped closer, narrowing his eyes. 'A letter – for her ladyship – from Manchester?' he repeated menacingly.

'Aye, sir,' Thomas said, flinching back a step.

'And you gave it to her? I thought I told you to give all letters to me.'

'Aye, sir, but —'

'Correct me if I'm wrong, but I thought I gave you specific orders to bring all the letters to me, no matter who they were addressed to, and no matter where they came from.'

'Aye, sir, you did, but —'

'When I give orders,' Nicky said, his voice rising a pitch in fury, 'I expect them to be obeyed! Why the devil do you think I gave you the job of fetching the letters from the post office?'

'Yes, why did you, Nicky?' came a quiet voice from behind him, startling him so much that he jumped and jerked his head round all in the same movement. It was his mother, standing there in the shadows of the chapel passage which led away from the corner of the hall.

'M-M-Mama!'

'I should like a word with you, Nicholas, if you please,' she said gravely, turning away.

'Oh! Yes – but – I must go and change my coat first,' he stammered, to gain time.

'At once, if you please,' she said without emphasis, and without pausing; and he had no alternative but to follow her, down the passage and into the steward's room. It must be trouble, he thought, or she would simply have waited to talk to him in the drawing-room – but what sort of trouble? His mind swivelled back to the establishment in Straker's Passage – had someone seen him go in and reported it to Mama? Or had that damned bill of his from the Maccabbees followed him home? If that was it, damn it, he would see somebody suffer for it. He'd cancel his membership, and be damned to them! Never, he asserted self-pityingly, had anyone been so abominably plagued with troubles as he was. And where the devil was his mother going?

In the steward's room his mother stopped and turned to face him.

'Sit down, Nicky. I have something to say to you.'

'I'm quite comfortable standing, thank you,' he began.

'*Sit down.*'

He sat, and tried to look unconcerned, arranged his coat-tails behind him and crossed and uncrossed his legs. 'Are you going somewhere, Mama?' he asked casually. 'The box in the hall —'

'Nicky, I have received a letter today,' she interrupted. She looked at him searchingly. 'From your Cousin Rosamund, in Manchester.'

'Oh,' he said. He cleared his throat, and changed the inflexion. 'Oh?'

Something in that single syllable seemed to have conveyed a message to her. In an instant, frighteningly, she seemed to age, and his love and need for her reasserted themselves suddenly and so violently that he shivered. He wanted to catch the moment back and tear it up, to go back to where they were just before it – and further still. He wanted to be a child again, so that she could be young, as she was then. He didn't want his mother to be old, to have the shadow of death in her eyes. He didn't want her to leave him.

He said none of these things. It was she who spoke next.

'You know what has happened to Sophie, then. You know, and you didn't tell me.'

'Know? How could I know. What has happened to Sophie? I haven't heard anything.' It was not convincing.

'Nicky, don't,' she said. Were there tears in her eyes, or was it the reflection of the candles? He pulled his lip in under his teeth to stop it trembling. 'Please. Rosamund and her husband are at Hobsbawn House, taking care of things. My poor Sophie —' Her mouth tightened with vicarious pain. 'There were two letters sent to me from Manchester, from Mrs Hastings. What did you do with them?'

'I don't know anything about any letters,' he began, but she interrupted him.

'Rosamund thought they must have gone astray, but they didn't, did they? From what I have just overheard, you have ordered all the letters to come to you first. You intercepted the two from Manchester, didn't you? Kept them from me. What did you do with them?'

He so badly didn't want to answer that question that his jaws clamped themselves together. It took him a very long while to squeeze out even the two inadequate words: 'Burnt them.'

She seemed to wither. Oh Mama, when did you become a little, old woman? My Mama can't be old, she can't! *Not fair!*

'Nicky, why? *Nom de Dieu!* To keep me from her at such a time – your own sister! Why did you do it?'

'It was to protect you,' he said. His lips felt numb. 'I didn't want you to be upset —'

'*Upset?*'

'You haven't been well,' he said sullenly. 'I didn't think it would be good for you to go all that way, at this time of year, when the roads are so bad. You know you're not strong.'

'But Nicky, you would have had to tell me sooner or later. How could you think – what did you mean to —?' She shook her head helplessly. 'I don't understand you. What could you gain by it?'

'Gain by it?' he repeated numbly. He met her eyes, and was frightened by their remoteness. 'I told you, it was to protect you, that's all. You do believe me, don't you? What other

161

reason could I possibly have?' he demanded passionately. 'It wasn't to keep you from Sophie – how could it be? I love my sister. I was only thinking about you, about your good. I swear it! I didn't think there was anything you could do, and I thought it might make you ill to know about it. I'd have told you in the end – of course I would – but when you were stronger. I didn't see what good it would do to upset you now.'

It didn't seem to be working. She was still looking at him as though she did not know him. He jumped up wildly, flung himself down before her and clasped her hand – her thin, cold hand – and cradled it against his cheek.

She did not stroke his head as she had always done, but she did not pull away, either. After a moment she said, 'How many others?'

'What?' The question took him by surprise.

'How many other letters of mine have you burnt?'

'None, I swear it!' he cried passionately. 'How could you think it? Only those two – only to save you pain.' Still no reaction. 'Mama, it's your Nicky,' he cried, tugging at her hand. 'Your Nicky loves you! You must believe me!'

'Oh Nicky!' Now at last her hand came down onto his head, and he felt the caressing movement. His heart lurched with relief. 'Oh Nicky, I'm sorry. I didn't mean to doubt you. I know you love me, my dearest child. I didn't mean to give you pain. Of course you acted with the best intentions. It was just that I couldn't help wondering that I have not heard word from Bendy in all this time. When I am working on my book, I do not notice always the time pass, and then suddenly I realise how much has passed. It is four months, nearly five, since Bendy went away. I thought he would have written by now to say where he is, that he is safe and well.'

Nicholas raised his head. 'No, Mama. He hasn't written,' he said. 'I'm afraid my brother – well, he isn't worthy of your love. He went away without saying goodbye, and he hasn't even bothered to write to ease your anxiety about his safety. He's never loved you as I do – cared about you – worried about you —' He pressed the hand again to his cheek, and felt his tears wet it, and was for a moment amazed and impressed at the depths of his own feelings.

162

After a moment she said, 'Get up now, my dear. You must not kneel like that, in a draught.' She withdrew her hand and he scrambled to his feet and stood before her, her dutiful son. 'Well, I must go to Sophie – my poor child,' she said. 'I would have gone at once, but I could not leave until I had seen you. I shall go first thing tomorrow morning.'

'Yes Mama, of course. I wish I might come with you, but I must stay here and take care of everything.'

'I know I can trust you,' she said. 'I do not know how long I will be away. I shall stay as long as Sophie needs me.'

'Yes, of course. You must do whatever needs to be done. Don't feel you must hurry back. Everything will be taken care of here,' he said earnestly.

'There is one more thing – will you send word to Mathilde, telling her what has happened? I have not had time to write a note.'

'Of course, Mama.'

'Thank you. I must go now and finish my preparations.' She walked towards the door, and then turned back, hesitantly, looking at him questioningly – almost shyly. 'Please remember that I am still mistress of Morland Place, *mon fils.* Your turn is not yet,' she said very gently.

He lowered his eyes, the conflicting emotions raging inside him making it impossible for him to speak. *It will be mine when you're dead,* he thought fiercely; and even as he thought it, *Mama, love me, you must love me! Mama, don't die!* He felt sometimes as though he were inhabited by demons; and sometimes as though the demons were the real him, that only they had any virtue.

It was late on the second day after leaving Morland Place that Héloïse reached Hobsbawn House. The recent mild, wet weather meant that the roads had been bad and the travelling slow: the carriage was so muddied that the coat of arms on the panel was completely obscured; the weary horses were mired to the collar. Stepping down from the coach stiff and cold, her bones aching from the long sitting and the jolting over ruts, and feeling every one of her fifty-three years, Héloïse acknowledged the justice of Nicky's fears for her.

The door of the house stood hospitably open, and the

yellow light streamed out kindly, speaking of bright fires, warm water, hot food, soft beds. The figure of the butler, Fenby, was in the doorway waiting to receive her, yet weary as she was she would have given anything to be able to get back into the carriage and drive away. She felt old and tired and sad: not strong enough to bear her child's agony.

Duty moved her feet forward and up the steps; duty and love, which with her were much the same thing. Fenby murmured a welcome and stepped aside for her as she entered the hall. Lady Batchworth was there, looking every inch a countess, and handsome, her full-skirted dress of purple-black satin elegantly unadorned, the low shawl-cut bodice and short, puffed sleeves revealing the whiteness of her bosom, neck and arms. Her red-gold hair was dressed high with a diamond comb, and a gold filagree necklace glittered at the base of her throat. But then she put out her arms and ran across the hall, and she was just Rosamund – dear Rosamund, Sophie's best friend.

'Oh Aunt, I'm so glad you've come!' They embraced, and Rosamund helped her off with her mantle, and untied her bonnet-strings with her own hands. 'How tired you must be – and cold. Your poor hands are like ice. Come up to the fire! Will you have some tea, or a glass of wine?'

'No, I must go first to Sophie,' Héloïse said decisively. 'How is my poor child?'

'She will be better the moment she sees you,' Rosamund said as they mounted the stairs. 'Her body is mending, but her mind will take longer. We tried not to alarm her, but she knew by the very fact that you did not come that you must be ill. I hope you are quite well again: we all worried about you.'

It was not for anyone else to know what Nicholas had done, not even Rosamund. 'Yes, I am well,' she said.

They reached Sophie's room. The fire was bright, the candles lit, a screen arranged to keep the glare from the bed. Moss was sitting at the bedside, and stood as the figures appeared in the doorway.

'She's asleep, my lady,' Moss whispered, encompassing them both in the address.

They crossed to the bed, and Héloïse looked down at the thin cheek, the shadows like bruises below the closed eyes, the mouth troubled even in sleep. She looked up at Rosamund. 'I will sit with her now, until she wakes,' she said. Rosamund hesitated, feeling she ought to protest; but Héloïse still had the authority of age and custom over her. She nodded, and drew Moss away.

Héloïse took her place beside the bed, feeling her bones protest at the hardness of the chair, feeling the inner tug of weariness, as though her soul were a kite on a windy day, anxious to get away from the restraint of her body and sail off into the upper air. But it was not her time yet, she knew that. There were still things for her to do, trials and labours God had set out for her as her portion, before she could lay life aside and go home to Him. She would not know what they were until they came; and she knew she would never understand His purposes in choosing them. But it was not for her to understand, only to trust and obey; and the depth of her trust was reflected in her prayer as she watched Sophie sleep. She prayed not *God, take my child's burden from her*, but *God, give my child strength to bear it*.

In a little while Sophie stirred and woke. Her heavy lids lifted, she looked for a moment uncomprehendingly at her mother, and then realisation dawned.

'Maman,' she whispered.

'Yes, my Sophie, I'm here.'

Sophie freed her hand from the bedclothes and Héloïse took it and held it, and there seemed nothing more to be said just then.

CHAPTER TEN

The Reform Bill was put to the vote in the Commons on March the 22nd, after an all-night sitting of the largest house in living memory. Finally at three o'clock in the morning Duncannon read out the numbers: the Bill had passed for second reading by a single vote. The chamber exploded in a triumphant cheer; and as the word was passed back through the lobby, another cheer answered it like a ghostly echo, from the crowds thronging the passages and stairs, who had waited all night to know the result.

Lord Batchworth wrote about it in one of his regular letters to Rosamund in Manchester.

'There was a huge crowd waiting outside the Palace, all shouting and waving their hats. I beckoned up a cabriolet to take me home, and before I could say a word, the driver demanded of me, was the Bill carried? I said yes, by one vote, and he took off his hat and said with profound feeling, "Thank God for it, sir!" That gives you an idea of the strength of opinion amongst the ordinary people over this business. I dare not think what might have happened had the vote gone the other way.

'Your stepfather tells me that King Billy was greatly relieved, for had the Bill gone down he would either have had to accept a Tory ministry or agree to a dissolution, and he still has the gravest fears of what public disorders would attend a General Election.

'But however gratifying the result (they say it was the Irish members who swayed the vote our way) it was only the first skirmish. The committee stage opens in three weeks' time, on

April the eighteenth, and I fear the Bill is bound to be hacked to pieces.'

Jes's fears were not unfounded. On the first day of the committee stage, General Gascoyne moved an amendment: that the overall number of Members for England and Wales should not be reduced. After some debate the amendment was adopted by eight votes. It was not a crucial alteration to the Bill, but word soon spread that the Government was regarding this as a decisive defeat.

'Well, my boy,' Lord Theakston said to Jes when they met at White's the following evening, 'I was talking to the Beau half an hour since. He's confident Grey will resign. What's your view?'

'I tend to agree with Lord Wellington, sir. Grey is so positive that no concessions will ever satisfy the High Tories, that at the end of the day the choice is either resignation or dissolution – and I understand the King's views on another General Election are unchanged.'

'Certainly if the King refuses to order the dissolution, he'll have no choice but to accept Grey's resignation and call in the Tories,' said Lord Theakston thoughtfully.

'I can't suppose he'll feel much reluctance about letting Grey go,' Jes said. 'And after all, whoever's in the Cabinet, there'll have to be some measure of reform – public opinion will see to that. It's only a question of how much reform, isn't it? Even Lord Wellington must see that; and a moderate measure put up by the Tories would be sure to go through.'

'Especially if there's compensation provided for the owners of the seats that are abolished,' Theakston added drily.

'Ah, you heard about that suggestion?' Jes smiled. 'Extraordinary how one is besieged every day by Tory Members pledging their support to a compensation scheme. I never knew so many men eager to get out of Parliament!'

'All the same,' Theakston said seriously, 'I think you've all miscalculated: I don't believe Bill will let the Whigs go. He's determined to see this Bill go through, you know.'

Jes raised a protesting eyebrow. 'I know he feels *some* measure of reform is necessary, but you can't mean he's personally committed to this particular Bill?'

'What you haven't taken into account,' Theakston said mildly, setting down his glass, 'is that the King views his duties as sovereign quite separately from his own personal wishes. He's pledged himself to see Grey and the Cabinet have fair play, and he won't go back on that, whatever it takes.'

'But in that case,' Jes said with a puzzled frown, 'why does he let everyone think he won't grant them the dissolution they want?'

'Because he wants them to work out a compromise that's acceptable to the Tories, of course,' Theakston said simply. 'But if they can't come to an agreement with the Tories in a day or two, he'll dissolve Parliament all right, you'll see.'

Two days later, Lord Theakston's assessment of the situation was proved right. The King wrote to Lord Grey to say he would agree to dissolve Parliament, but that, assuming the Whigs returned after the election with an enhanced majority, they must modify, the Bill so as to conciliate its opponents – though without changing it in any essential principle.

Knowing the mood of the country was behind them, and expecting nothing but good from a General Election, the Whigs were jubilant and called down blessings on the King's head. The High Tories, by contrast, were plunged in gloom as they saw their chance of scuppering Grey's Reform Bill and particular fulminated that there had been no King so misguided or so devoted to his own destruction since Charles I gave all his rights away.

But the troubles were not over. Lord Theakston was with the King at St James's Palace the next day when Grey and Brougham arrived hot-foot from Westminster requesting urgent audience. Lord Grey, tall, gaunt, aesthetic-looking, appeared as agitated as was possible for him. Brougham, dark and ugly as a gargoyle, was almost hopping up and down in his anxiety.

'Your Majesty,' said Grey, 'something of the utmost urgency has arisen! Lord Wharncliffe has announced his intention of introducing a motion into the Upper House today against dissolving Parliament.'

'Eh? What?' said the King, startled. 'What do you say?'

Grey repeated it. 'And I'm sure I don't need to remind Your Majesty that since there is at all times a natural Tory majority in the Upper House, the motion has every likelihood of being passed!'

Brougham joined in. 'The rift between the two Houses would then be made apparent, sir, to all eyes; publicly exposed in the most undesirable way —'

The King's light blue eyes were bulging dangerously. 'God damn it!' he roared, cutting Brougham off. 'What is Wharncliffe about? Damn his eyes! Damn his head! Who taught him to interfere with the Royal Prerogative? If I choose to dissolve Parliament, damn it, I will dissolve it! I'll not be gainsaid, no, not by a thousand Lord Wharncliffes!'

'We may be thankful, Your Majesty, that there is only one,' Lord Theakston said gently.

'Aye, aye, you're right, Theakston! One is too many, damn his eyes!' the King rumbled. 'I cannot have my two Houses set against each other. The Lords and the Commons in conflict is what I have always most dreaded, since the beginning of this Reform business! I warned you about that, did I not, Grey? And what the devil's to be done about it now? You're m'Prime Minister – advise me, damn it!'

'I can see but one solution, Your Majesty,' Lord Grey said. 'If you would proceed to the House without delay and at once prorogue Parliament, it would put an end to all dissent.'

'Go now, myself?' You mean leave at once?'

'Yes, Your Majesty. There is no time to lose.'

'The Duke of Richmond has pledged to try to delay matters, sir,' Brougham added. 'He is bringing up points of order to prevent the debate from starting, but he cannot hold it off for ever, and once Wharncliffe's motion is actually put to the vote —'

'It seems there is no choice, Your Majesty,' Lord Theakston said.

'Aye, man, you're right. I must go at once and teach these mutinous dogs to mind me! The rope's end is what I'd give 'em, if I could! But I must not stand here talking – I must be off.'

'If your Majesty would but command the state coach,' Brougham said eagerly, 'I have already given the order for an escort of the Horse Guards, which should be here at any moment.'

'Oh, you have, have you?' the King said, raising his eyebrows at this freedom.

Brougham looked a little conscious. 'Merely to facilitate what I anticipated would be Your Majesty's immediate wish to lose no time —'

'Aye, well, that's right, I suppose. No time to stand upon ceremony, Theakston – no, I shall want you. It had better be Durham: trot off, there's a good fellow, and pass the word to the Master of Horse to fetch up the state coach at once.'

Durham left them in haste. Lord Grey said, 'If I may, sir, I would like to take this opportunity to express the gratitude which Your Majesty's Cabinet owes to you for the utmost confidence and kindness with which you have always treated us.'

'Well, well,' the King said gruffly, 'I gave you my word to support you, sir, and I hope I know what is due from one gentleman to another. I shall do my part – but after the election, mind, you shall do yours, d'ye hear me? Conciliation, my lord, that's what we must seek. The common ground between yourselves and the Tories over this Reform Bill! There must be enough common ground somewhere for men of good will and good sense to stand upon together.'

'Indeed, Your Majesty,' Grey murmured. 'I pray we may find it.'

'Oh, prayer's all right – I have nothing against that. Use it m'self sometimes. But you'll use your wits and your best endeavours too.'

Grey bowed.

'You do your part, and I will back you whatever you decide on. But no secret ballot – now mark me! I won't have that put in the Bill! It's un-English, dammit! A free and manly avowal of opinion is what has always distinguished the people of England. We ain't sneaking foreigners, creeping about in the dark to stick a knife in a man's back whom we wouldn't dare to face in honest daylight! No man shall put his mark in secret to anything he's ashamed to own publicly, not in this country, not while I'm King!'

'The secret ballot is not a measure we have ever contemplated, Your Majesty,' Grey said soothingly.

'Glad to hear it. Now where the devil is Albemarle got to with that damned coach?'

'I think I hear them coming now, Your Majesty,' said Theakston.

Lord Durham came in with the Master of Horse behind him. Albemarle was considerably fluttered. He made an incoherent apology about having still been at breakfast when Durham summoned him, and drew out his handkerchief to dab at his lips, as if he feared some indefensible egg might still adhere to them. Then he went on to say that he deeply regretted it was not possible to have the state coach made ready at such short notice.

The King's face, always healthily pink, suffused with growing rage. 'Impossible? What the devil d'you mean, impossible?'

Albemarle blinked nervously and his hands clung to each other for comfort. 'It is a matter of the deepest regret to me to be obliged to say so, Your Majesty, but proper notice is needed to prepare the coach and the greys in a manner suited to Your Majesty's dignity. The plaiting of the horses' manes alone cannot be done properly in less than an hour, to say nothing of —'

'Plaiting?' the King roared. 'God damn it, man, this is an emergency, not a damned review! We're teetering on the brink of a revolution and you stand there talking fustian to me about plaiting? If you cannot have the coach here in five minutes I'll go Westminster in a damned hackney cab!'

'Bravo, sir!' someone said in a strange, hollow voice. 'Well said, Your Majesty!'

The King looked around, his eyes bulging. 'Was that you, Theakston? Good God, what's amiss with your voice, man?'

Lord Theakston kept his countenance and said gravely, 'The voice seemed to come from behind the arras, sir.'

'Eh? What? Oh, yes,' the King said with some relief, 'that must be the Bow Street officer. There's always one on duty somewhere about me, in case of assassins, y'know!' He raised his voice and pitched it at the arras. 'Is that you, Townshend? On guard, are you?'

'Yes, sir. I am here to see that Your Majesty has fair play,'

171

the tapestry replied warmly. 'And I must say, I think Your Majesty is damned right!'

'Now that,' Lord Theakston remarked softly, as though to himself, 'is true sovereignty, when even the furniture agrees with one.'

The Upper House was in uproar. Lord Batchworth had never seen such scenes. The Duke of Richmond was still on his feet, arguing points of order of increasing pointlessness, but he no longer held the floor alone. Lord Mansfield was bellowing like a Smithfield porter and hurling insults at the Government, aspersing their intellect, personal habits, appearance, and probable ancestry going back several generations. Lord Londonderry, feeling that words alone did not bring the point home forcefully enough, was lashing out in all directions with a horse-whip, while several of his colleagues clung on to his coat tails to try to keep him from actual murder. Lord Carlisle was trying to convince Lord Greyshott that a vote against the dissolution was a vote against civilisation itself, but since they were separated by the width of the floor the argument was having to be held at roaring-pitch. So, indeed, was every other conversation in the chamber; and the Lord Chancellor, having temporarily abandoned hope of regaining order, was talking earnestly to Lord Melbourne with the aid of large hand gestures.

The noise was such that when the King and his train at last entered the robing-room, the hubbub could be heard quite clearly.

'What the deuce is that shocking row?' he asked, startled. 'What the devil's going on?'

Brougham could not resist. 'If it please Your Majesty,' he said straight-faced, '*that* is the Lords debating.'

Lord Theakston had a coughing fit, and the King looked at him suspiciously. 'Well, well, no time to waste,' he said. 'Theakston, stop blowing like a porpoise, man, and hand me my robes. Hastings, have you the crown there?'

Lord Theakston, stepping forward with the mantle, murmured quietly in the King's ear, 'Strictly speaking, Your Majesty, as you haven't actually been crowned yet, you ought not to wear the crown.'

172

'Oh, deuce fly away with you!' the King said impatiently. 'How d'ye think I shall quiet *that* bear-garden without sporting my colours? Never mind precedent! Give me the crown, Hastings! No, no, I shall put it on for myself, thank'ee, since the Archbishop ain't here! There now,' he said, turning to Grey as he pulled the crown firmly down onto his brows, 'take up the sword of state, my lord, and let's give 'em a broadside. The coronation is over.'

The King looked grimly purposeful, but as they formed up the procession he found time to murmur to Lord Theakston, 'We shall have to pad this blessed thing for the real coronation, however. With my coconut of a head, it don't fit me above tolerably, and it won't do to have it tumbling off on the day, and rolling about the cathedral with a dozen scrambling after it like dockside urchins!'

The doors were opened and the noise rushed in like water; and then died rapidly away as the procession moved forward. The King, suddenly dignified, entered the chamber of the Lords, with Grey at his shoulder holding the sword of state like a grim executioner, and marched with firm step to take the throne and prorogue his first Parliament.

Nicholas had been sitting most of the afternoon in the same corner of the Maccabbees, and by the time he saw Captain Mattock come in he was halfway down the second bottle of claret and feeling extremely sorry for himself. He waved a limp, pale hand to catch Mattock's attention, but the captain had already had Nicholas pointed out to him by a helpful waiter and came strolling over, looking as full-bodied and powerful in his regimentals as Nicholas was blanched and stringless, dwarfed by the wing-backed chair he was drooping in like a rather sorry leek.

Mattock stood over Nicholas, looking down with that dark gleam of amusement in his eyes which always made Nicholas feel cloddish and juvenile.

'Oh gad, Nicky, have you been sousing all day?' he asked pleasantly. 'What a bore you are! If I'd known, I'd have gone with Mab and Sooty after all. They're off to dine at The Black Bull. Do you know it? It's the most deliciously low alehouse out at Osbaldwick, where they serve tripe, and pigs' trotters, and eels stewed in the most extraordinary green liquor: viscous, you know, with gobbets of fat floating about on the top —'

'For God's sake, Roger!' Nicky muttered, turning a shade paler. He threw off another half glass, and then wished he hadn't.

'What's the matter, halfling? Feeling frail?' Mattock asked largely. He sat down on the edge of the chair next to Nicholas, flicked his coat-tails free and stretched out one handsomely booted, well-calfed leg. Everything about him suggested ease and self-confidence, and contrasting Mattock with himself, Nicky felt close to crying.

'The rules of engagement are the same in all pleasures, my lad,' Mattock went on. 'Play and play! If you can't take your drink like a man, don't take it at all; or at least – since it would be a damned dull life without wine, such as I wouldn't wish on anyone – take it in private. The sight of you spreading over that chair like a puddle of misery is not edifying.'

Nicholas muttered something unintelligible, and Mattock continued, 'What did you want to speak to me about, anyway? It doesn't look as though you were going to ask me to dine with you.'

'Eh? Oh, yes, later if you like,' Nicholas said distractedly. 'Not that I feel up to it, but a man must eat, I suppose. The thing is, Roger, I'm in the most damnable fix.'

'The usual thing, I suppose? Pockets to let, and some contemptible squeak-beef of a tradesman threatening to set the bailiffs onto you?'

'No, it's not that,' Nicholas said. 'It's nothing to do with money. It's something much worse.' he shivered and hunched down in his chair, groping blindly for the bottle.

Mattock gently moved it out of his reach and said, 'No, dammit, not before you send for another glass! If I have to listen to your ill-luck story I must have a little fortification. Here, you, Hobson – bring me a glass, will you!' He held the bottle up the light and added, 'And bring another bottle while you're at it. Put it to Mr Morland's account.' He turned back to Nicholas. 'All right. young 'un,' he said, not without sympathy, 'begin. What's happened to put you in such a quake?'

Nicholas raised sodden but frightened eyes to Mattock's face. 'Something dreadful! I'm ill, Roger. I think I'm dying,' he said in a low, tremulous voice.

'What?' Mattock exploded into hearty laughter, which was not at all the reaction Nicholas felt he deserved. He scowled peevishly.

'No, dammit, it's no laughing matter! I'm ill, I tell you! It's – it's damned serious.'

'Well, what are you telling me for, you fool? I'm not a physician. Go and see the sawbones if you're ill – or if you think it's too late for that, seek out the clergyman of your choice, and pick out a handsome grave plot for yourself.'

Nicholas bit back a retort as the waiter arrived with the clean glass and third bottle. When he had departed, Nicholas hissed fiercely, 'Why the deuce do you laugh at a fellow? I'm telling you I'm ill, and I don't know what the devil to do about it! I come to you for advice and all you can do is sit there cackling like a damned hen!'

'I beg your pardon,' Mattock said, straightening his face, 'but really, you don't look like a dying man to me – no more than usual, at any rate. You always were a pasty, pale-green sort of fellow. Why don't you consult your physician, for God's sake?'

'I can't, dammit! Don't you think I've thought of that? But it's a matter of – it's too—' He gained a slight degree of colour at that point. 'Well, it's personal, that's all.'

'Personal?' Mattock asked, gently malicious.

'Private. A matter of the greatest delicacy. Surely you must know what I mean?' Nicholas tried to convey deep meaning with his eyes, but wasn't sure he was succeeding. It was hard to tell with Mattock. 'It's not the sort of thing I can ask the physician about, who's known me since the cradle and treats all the family. His wife visits my mother, dammit. I mean, not that she would ever – oh, hell and damnation!' He spread his hands in a mixture of pathos and exasperation. 'I'm sick! I have symptoms of a most private nature, and I don't know what to do.'

Mattock sipped his wine appreciatively. 'Well I must say,' he said, 'if I understand you rightly, I call it the outside of enough to suppose *I* would know anything about your beastly condition. What the deuce do you mean by suggesting it?'

'I didn't mean that I thought you would have – of course not! Only you're a man of experience, that's all,' Nicholas stammered. 'You know all sorts of things – and after all,' with a little spurt of weak indignation, 'it was you who introduced me to that damned place in Straker's Passage —'

'What makes you think that damned place, as you so delicately put it, has anything to do with your ailment?' Mattock enquired with a lift of the eyebrows.

'Well, hasn't it? I made sure it must, seeing that it's —' Nicholas looked at him pathetically. 'I mean. I can't think of any other reason. Don't you think it's that? If it's not, then what the deuce is happening to me? I'm scared, Roger. Is it – does it – am I going to die?'

Mattock let him suffer a while longer, while he sipped the wine thoughtfully. Then he put down the glass and looked at Nicholas with a broad grin. 'Let us be frank about this – oh, not too frank, I hasten to add,' as Nicholas drew a confidential breath. 'We can understand each other without resorting to coarseness, I hope. I collect you have some reason to suppose all is not well in the, er, realms of pleasure?'

'Yes,' Nicholas said eagerly. 'You see when I —'

'Thank you! I've no desire to hear the symptoms. Well, my dear boy, it would seem that you have caught a cold.'

'Oh God, don't torment me! What is it?'

'Drawing on my military experience as a leader and confidant of men, I'd say it was a contagious disease associated with moments of joy.'

'But is it – is it bad?'

'I'm sorry to say that I've heard the cure is most tedious and sometimes painful.' Mattock said. 'But a cure there is. You won't die. It almost seems,' he added thoughtfully, 'as though it's intended as a sort of divine tax on pleasure.'

'What must I do, then?'

'Go and see a physician, of course. He'll tell you all about it. If you don't care to consult your family friend – and I quite see that it might be embarrassing – I suggest you speak to Havergill at the Dispensary. He's a man of the world. I don't suppose you can show him anything he hasn't seen before.'

'Have you – is he the one you —?'

'Dear Nicky, I should be very sorry to have to call you out, for it would certainly go ill with you if I did, but I shall have to do so if you suggest again that I might ever have found myself in your predicament! And now, shall we change the subject? I think you were about to invite me to dine with you, were you not?'

Nicholas stood up, not without difficulty. 'I'm sorry, but I don't think I could. Not feeling quite the thing. I'm afraid I shall have to leave you. Order anything you like, charge it to my account, only pray – pray excuse me!'

Mattock watched him stumble away, and then moved himself into the vacated armchair, picked up the newspaper, and refilled his glass. 'And he hadn't even had one glass out of the new bottle, poor chap,' he murmured to himself. 'What a pity!'

Sitting alone in the drawing-room after dinner the following evening, Nicholas reflected on his situation. The only good thing about it was that with his mother still away, he had no need to dissemble or make cheerful conversation. But that was cool, if not cold comfort. It seemed to him that he was the most unlucky, put-upon person in the world. No sooner did he find an agreeable new friend who introduced him to agreeable new sensations, than it all turned sour and he – he, mark you and not the new friend! – was singled out for a most hideous and unjust retribution.

Havergill had not been unkind. When Nicholas had finally plucked up the courage to seek him out at his office at the hospital, the doctor had been matter-of-fact, briskly practical, as though he were being consulted over a cold in the head or a cut finger. When Nicholas had stammeringly begged him to keep his confidence, he had raised an eyebrow as if it were the most ordinary request in the world, hardly worth the trouble of mentioning.

Yet Nicholas felt that he must have seen into the inmost corners of his being, taken in at a glance all his blackest secrets. The doctor must hate him, despise him; and Nicky's imagination offered him a ghastly picture of Havergill at his club, telling all his censorious friends exactly what Nicholas

Morland of Morland Place had consulted him about. The family's man of business, Pobgee, was a close friend of Havergill; he'd be bound to tell him, and *he'd* tell Mama. Bayliss, the newspaper proprietor, was another of Havergill's intimates. A cold sweat broke out under Nicky's armpits as he imagined the story prominent on the social page with his identity only thinly disguised by initials.

He groaned and drained his glass, and doing both simultaneously brought on a coughing fit. His life was over, he thought, mopping his eyes and catching at his breath. He would never be able to go into company again. He would never be able to have any fun ever again. And the very last straw was that this damned bottle was empty, which meant he'd have to get out of this chair and walk across to the other side of the company to ring for another. Life was so harsh!

But at that moment the door opened and Ferrars came in. Nicholas looked up in irritation, but his brow cleared when he saw the bottle on the tray which Ferrars was carrying.

'I thought you might need this, sir,' he said. 'I noticed earlier that the bottle was not more than half full.'

Nicholas sat up straighter, and studied his servant's expression suspiciously. He wasn't sure if Ferrars was being kind, or insolently suggesting his master was a sot. It wasn't *his* business to check the level in bottles; but there was no doubt that the brandy was badly wanted just then.

'Put it down there' he said brusquely. Ferrars bowed and obeyed, placing it within Nicholas's reach. 'I may or I may not have some later,' Nicky said loftily. 'You needn't have brought it – I could have rung if and when I wanted it.'

'It occurred to me, sir,' Ferrars said softly, 'that tonight you must be in need of the solace a fine brandy can bring.'

'Solace?' Nicky scowled.

Ferrars bowed again, with his most insinuating smile. 'After your visit this afternoon, which must have been most unpleasant for you, sir, I thought —'

'You think a damned sight too much,' Nicky snapped. 'And if you think I will brook insolence from a damned —'

'From your personal attendant, sir, who has your best interests at heart,' Ferrars said smoothly. 'It would be very injurious to your dignity as heir to Morland Place if the nature of your unfortunate malady were to get about.'

Nicky took a breath to express his outrage, choked himself on it, and fell back in his chair, spluttering. Ferrars took the opportunity to pour another measure of brandy into the glass and administer it to his master with an air of tender concern which rendered Nicky even more furious.

'Don't try to speak, sir,' Ferrars said gently. 'Your secret is safe with me, as I'm sure I don't need to remind you. I'm accustomed to keeping secrets – especially your secrets, sir. As deep as a well, is Edgar Ferrars. You've nothing to fear.'

Nicholas managed to gulp down some brandy, and pushing his manservant away said. 'What do you want?'

'Only to help you, sir,' Ferrars said, looking surprised. 'I mentioned your unfortunate situation for no other reason. You are thinking that nothing will ever be the same again, now aren't you, sir? But there are lots of other pleasures to be had, and I can put you in the way of them, sir – pleasures that won't put you at risk of this happening again.'

'Really?' Nicholas said, forgetting in the interest of the idea to be lofty.

'Trust me, sir. When you're well again, I will seek them out for you. You'll see. There's nothing that can't be had for money – and the Master of Morland Place won't lack for that.'

'Ha! But I'm not Master of Morland Place,' Nicky said.

'You will be, sir – and there are plenty who will lend you any amount you want on the strength of that. I can put you in their way, too, sir, if you like. No need to be short of the ready. It isn't what I like to see in my master, sir, if you'll forgive me. A gentleman ought to be seen to be flush, so he can behave generous to his friends. It hurts his standing otherwise.'

Nicholas was thoughtful. To borrow money against his ultimate inheritance of Morland Place seemed like an excellent idea. Money would give standing – and, to an extent, independence of his mother's approval. The allowance she gave him had never been adequate, and he hated having to ask her for more, because she always wanted to know what he spent it on.

'It sounds like a good idea,' he said. 'As long as everything does come to me in the end.'

Ferrars nodded. 'It's bound to, sir, don't you think? Now that Mr Benedict's gone – and as long as we make sure he never comes back.'

'From his letters, it doesn't sound as though he means to,' Nicky said.

'Quite so, sir – but would it not be a good idea to make sure he can't? Perhaps it's time one of his letters reached his mother.'

'But, for God's sake, man,' Nicky exploded, 'I've been going to endless trouble to make sure they don't!'

'Quite so, sir, I was thinking of a special letter from him – one that puts him beyond his mother's forgiveness.'

'And how would you propose making him write anything like that?' Nicky said impatiently.

Ferrars smiled. 'There's no need to be troubling Mr Benedict, sir. You have enough examples of his handwriting in your possession, and I have no little skill at copying. I'm sure I can concoct something that will convince her ladyship.'

'You can forge his handwriting?' Nicholas said, open-mouthed with admiration.

'I can do it so that even *he* would believe he'd written it.'

'Ferrars, you're a marvel!' Nicholas said after a moment. 'There's a rise in salary for you in this, if you can do it.'

'Thank you, sir,' Ferrars said modestly. 'My only wish is to serve you; but you were always the most generous of masters.'

The proroguing of Parliament at least allowed Lord Batchworth to return to Manchester and be with his wife again. In between catching up with his own business, he continued to oversee matters at Hobsbawn Mills. The foreman, Blake, was a good man, and managed the day-to-day running very well, but Jasper's method of business was to take such personal control of everything that there was still a need of someone to give overall guidance. Finding the right man was the difficulty.

Jes was sitting at Jasper's desk in Number Two Mill one day

when there was a tap at the door. It opened to admit a slender man in a good but by no means new coat, his hat in his hand; a rather pale-faced man whose straight, dark hair had slipped forward over his brow like the forelock of a pony. He pushed it back with an automatic gesture as he crossed towards Jes, smiling in a friendly way. He limped slightly as he walked.

'Lord Batchworth – I hope you don't mind being disturbed?'

'Not at all. You come very opportunely: I was just beginning to think about breaking off. How do you do, Mr Droylsden? Won't you sit down?'

Henry sat. 'I understood from Agnes – my sister-in-law – that you were sorting out Jasper's business affairs. I came to see if I could help in any way.'

'Very good of you,' Jes said.

'Is it a muddle?'

'No, it isn't that. Jasper was a good manager. The difficulty will be finding someone to take his place.'

'No-one can do that,' Henry said, and then burst out, 'It was a rotten business! God, if I hadn't been in such a hurry to drive off! If I'd waited just a moment or two more, I could have gone to help him – and the cab driver, too! But I thought having dropped him at his gate that he'd be safe. It never occurred to me that a man might be attacked on his own carriage-sweep!'

'I'm sure no-one blames you in the least,' Jes said, rather taken aback.

'I blame myself,' Henry said bitterly. 'Tell me, how is Sophie? I know from Prudence that her health is mending slowly, but how is her mind?'

'It's only two months – one mustn't expect too much. Of course, now that her mother is with her, she bears up better. But why don't you pay her a visit? I'm sure it would do her nothing but good, and I know she was always fond of you.'

'Good of you to say so,' Henry said shortly. 'But I wonder if she will still be fond of me when she knows how I failed her – and him. God, I can't believe it, even now! What a hideous thing to happen.'

Jes eyed him curiously. 'Do I understand you were afraid of something like this happening?'

'An attack on Jasper, yes – but I didn't think it would end in murder.'

'I think you'd better tell me about it,' Jes said. 'One moment —' He got up and went across to the cupboard in the corner and brought out a decanter of sherry and two glasses. 'My own thought,' he said. 'Jasper was too industrious to indulge himself in the office, but I must say I feel the need of a little fortification from time to time. You'll join me?'

'Thank you.' Henry received the glass and sipped appreciatively. 'By God, that's good! From your own cellar?'

'From Hobsbawn House, in fact. Old Mr Hobsbawn – Jasper's cousin – laid down some excellent wines during the war and didn't get round to drinking the tithe of it. It all came to Sophie with the house.'

'I suppose you must know how things are left? Knowing Jasper, he would not have been careless about such things as Wills?'

'Oh, we found his Will in the safe at Hobsbawn House, and in fact there's a copy in the safe here and another with the attorney. He was very careful. But the house and all the contents belonged to Sophie anyway, and he only had a life interest in the mills. On his death that passes to Sophie. It was all in the marriage settlement, so there's no difficulty about it.'

'I'm glad of that, at any rate.'

'Now then, tell me about your fears for Jasper's safety,' Jes said, settling himself comfortably with his glass.

Henry told the story, about the Exchange Street scheme and the opposition to it, and about Olmondroyd and Duxbury and Maloney.

Jes listened in grave silence, and at the end of it emptied his glass, refilled both, and said, 'So you think that Jasper's assailants were in the pay of Olmondroyd? Or do you think Olmondroyd himself carried out the attack?'

No, not him. I don't think Duxbury would risk soiling his hands either – he's just an agent of Olmondroyd, and he's never been in trouble for anything like that. Maloney, now, that's another matter. He's violent and dangerous, and quite mad enough to do it. My money's on him and a crony of his called Ballater – especially as they've both gone missing from

182

their lodgings since that day. Perhaps the more interesting question, though, is whether Olmondroyd knew anything about it.'

'Have you told anyone else what you've just told me?' Jes asked.

'I did tell Sir John Whitworth, but he doesn't believe there's anything anyone can do. There is no evidence at all against anyone – no clue to follow through the labyrinth. He has said that if Maloney or Ballater reappear, he will arrest them and question them, but that's all he can promise. As to Olmondroyd, he says there's nothing to suggest he is involved in any way, and I'm afraid he's right.' He sighed. 'I'd give a monkey to be able to bring Jasper's murderers to book – assuming, of course, that I had one to give,' he added wryly. 'But my pockets are to let. I expect you know my circumstances.'

'Yes,' said Lord Batchworth thoughtfully. 'Look here, a plan is forming itself in my head which might benefit us both.'

'Yes, sir?'

Jes thought a moment longer, and then said, 'I expect you know that I am very much concerned with the passage of the Reform Bill through Parliament?' Henry nodded. 'When the House reconvenes, I shall have to go back to London and spend much of my time there. We will have a lot to do, trying to persuade the Tories to support the Bill. It will probably be a matter of speaking to every one of them individually.'

'And will you succeed at last?'

'If we don't, we shall have riots up and down the country such as we haven't seen since the year nineteen.' Unconsciously he touched the scar on his cheek. 'But the point is this: since I shall be away from Manchester, I shan't be able keep directing the business here at the mills, and it becomes more essential than ever to find a manager to take Jasper's place. It occurs to me that, if you would agree to it, you might be the ideal person for the job.'

'Me?' Henry ejaculated.

'Please, don't be offended – let me explain.'

'Good God. I'm not offended. But I know nothing about cotton mills.'

'You don't need to. All Jasper's people are very good, and they understand the day-to-day running. Everything runs very smoothly. All that's needed is someone to co-ordinate their efforts. Now you may not know anything about cotton, but you understand business, and you understand how to handle employees. Above all, you're a gentleman, and someone known to and trusted by Sophie. I want to leave her in safe hands, and I can't think of any safer than yours.'

'Kind of you, sir,' Henry muttered, embarrassed. 'But Sophie may not agree.'

'Humbug! You know she will. She will be glad not to have to deal with a stranger at this period of her life. Think of the distress you will be saving her, man.'

'If you put it like that —' Henry said with a faint smile.

'I do. But look here, also: as manager of Hobsbawn mills, commanding decent income and a respectable position, you'll naturally mingle with other managers and mill-masters. You'll have access to those who know Olmondroyd – perhaps to Olmondroyd himself. You'll be in the very best position to hear if anything if every said that might implicate him in this business.'

'It is possible,' Henry said. 'And if I did hear anything —'

'We will know what to do with it.' Jes met his eyes gravely. 'This business of Jasper's death is utterly damnable, and the only thing one can hope for is the opportunity to put a rope round the necks of the men responsible.'

'I'm with you there,' Henry said.

'Then you'll take the manager's position?'

'If Sophie wishes me to, I will,' he said, and added, 'I'm very grateful to you.'

'You'll be doing us all a kindness,' Jes said politely.

Jes told Rosamund about it that evening while she was dressing for dinner.

'He's a good man,' Rosamund said. 'I always thought it was a great pity he should be circumstanced as he is; but as Sophie's manager, he will be respectable and useful.'

'It will be to Sophie's advantage too,' Jes pointed out. 'She will have someone she knows she can trust to act as go-between for her with the mills.'

184

'Yes, and spending so much time together —' Rosamund began, and broke off.

'Yes, my love?' Jes encouraged.

'Oh, nothing,' she said. She smiled a little secret smile which he pretended not to see. 'Do you really think he may find out who murdered poor Jasper?'

'If anyone can, he will. But I don't think we should talk to Sophie about that.'

'Of course not,' Rosamund said. 'I wish I might talk to Sophie about anything at the moment. Every topic seems forbidden, and when I don't talk at all there's nothing to distract her from thinking and thinking over what happened.'

'Have you told her about your expectations?'

'Not yet. I haven't dared.'

'Perhaps you should. It would give her something else to think about.'

'I couldn't. I would seem too cruel. And besides,' she turned to look at him. 'I feel absurdly nervous and superstitious about it. I'm afraid if I tell anyone something will go wrong.'

He put his hand on her shoulder, and she covered it with hers. 'Don't be afraid. All will be well.'

Her eyes crinkled in a smile. 'It's foolish, but I always feel better just for hearing you say that – as if you have power to make things come out right.' He kissed the hand that lay on his. 'You'll have to go back to London, of course, after the election. I wish you didn't have to.'

'You could come with me.'

'I don't feel I ought to leave Sophie.'

'I know. Well, God forbid I should try to come between you and your duty. As long as you take care of yourself as well as her.'

She looked up at him seriously. 'I will. I'll take care of both of us. There's too much at stake for me to dare to be careless.'

He nodded, but felt too nervous to say anything. The idea that she was carrying his child seemed too extraordinary, too exotic. It made him afraid, as though they had dared too much. His classical education had taught him what happened to the hero who provoked the gods in that way: his hubris was all too prone to be punished by the gods' taking away everything from him, and leaving him with less than he started with.

He nodded, but felt too nervous to say anything. The idea that she was carrying his child seemed too astonishing, too exotic, it made him afraid, as though they had dared too much. His classical education had taught him what happened to the hero who provoked the gods in that way: his hubris was bringing her the occasional little present of a drop of gin, or a couple of rabbits once of the men had given him.

CHAPTER ELEVEN

On the railway works only one Sunday in three was designated a knock-off Sunday, and since the works must be supervised by an engineer at all times, and since the Sunday supervision naturally fell to the most junior engineers, Benedict was not able to keep up his church observances as he felt his mother would have wished.

It was all the more annoying, therefore, that when knock-off Sunday came around, he should be disturbed just as he was putting on his hat to go to morning service. His landlady came up the stairs to his room and tapped upon the door.

'Mr Morland?'

'Yes, Mrs Brooksby?' He opened it. 'I was just going out.'

'Oh, Mr Morland, I'm sorry to disturb you, but there's a boy downstairs asking for you.'

'A boy?'

'Asking for you most particular. One of the lads from the works – you know, a navvy boy.'

'Which one?' Benedict asked, frowning. Perhaps because he was more approachable than some of the other engineers, or perhaps simply because he was amongst them more often, the navvies often brought their problems to him, but he really didn't want to be bothered this morning.

Seeing his frown, Mrs Brooksby grew apologetic. She didn't want to upset him, for Mr Morland was a good lodger, not only prompt to pay his bill – which some gentlemen could be very difficult about, sticking up their noses in a grand way and getting angry if a person pressed, just as if a person didn't have the butcher and the coalman to pay himself, and no putting *them* off! – but generous too about extras, and even bringing her the occasional little present of a drop of gin, or a couple of rabbits one of the men had given him.

'If I was to die for it I can't tell one from another, Mr Morland, dirty little infidels that they are. I would have sent him away with a flea in his ear, only he does seem really put about, and crying fit to stop his eyes out, such as a mother's heart finds it hard to ignore, Mr Morland, I promise you – to say nothing of rousing the neighbourhood. That Mrs Pike next door was looking out just now – pretending to see if it was raining, the artful creature – so if you could p'raps just come down and send him away yourself sir —'

'Yes, all right Mrs Brooksby, I'll come,' Benedict said shortly, taking up his hat, stick, and prayer-book in the hope that it would be a short diversion and that he could go on to church after all. At the bottom of the stairs the lower servant, Fib, stood in the passage before the open front door wiping her hands mechanically over and over on her apron and staring open-mouthed at the boy on the doorstep, who was weeping for her entertainment and knuckling the tears from his eyes and nose with a fist as black as it was bony.

Mrs Brooksby made short work of the servant. 'Don't stand there gawping, Fib, when you've work to do! Get on and clear the breakfast dishes. Haven't you ever seen a navvy-boy before?'

That he was a navvy-boy was evident from his clothes – moleskin trousers, canvas shirt and red handkerchief tied about his neck – but Benedict knew him anyway. He was one of the tip-drivers, a boy of about fourteen known for reasons about which even he was vague as Dandy Dick. Benedict had noticed him in the first place because, although his appearance was as unprepossessing as any of the boys, he had an air of quiet dignity about him – which might perhaps have been what gave rise to his nickname. Once he got to know him a little better, Benedict had come quite to like him, for he had an enquiring mind. When he was supervising the works, he would try to find time to stop for a word or two with the boy, sometimes walking with him as he led his horse back from the tip, and was amused by the questions Dandy asked in his quest for self-improvement – varying from how a horse-gin worked to what made the sun come up in the morning.

Now, however, Benedict was not disposed to be amused. 'Now then, Dandy,' he said briskly, 'I can't have you coming bothering me here just whenever you please – and especially not on a Sunday. Take yourself off at once.'

The boy, however, didn't stir, looking up at Benedict with a desperation which overrode even his ingrained obedience.

'Oh, please sir, will you come?' he gasped, even reaching out a hand to Bendy, and though he didn't quite have the nerve to pull at Benedict's sleeve, the gesture was unmistakable.

Mrs Brooksby was outraged. 'The sauce of it! Be off with you, you nasty dirty urchin, and don't come knocking at my clean door again with your nasty dirty face.'

The boy backed a pace, but fixed his pleading eyes on Benedict, and Benedict began to feel that there must be some extraordinary reason for such unusual effrontery. 'What is it, Dandy? What's the matter?'

'Oh sir, please —' He glanced quickly at Mrs Brooksby. 'I can't tell, only to *you*,' he said in a penetrating whisper.

Benedict sighed, and turning to the landlady said, 'I'll deal with it now, Mrs Brooksby, thank you. Don't you trouble yourself.'

Mrs Brooksby, not sure whether to bridle with offence or be grateful, took herself away with the parting shot: 'He means trouble, the scurvy brat, that I *can* tell you, and you mark my words!'

Benedict turned sternly to the boy. 'Now then, Dandy, out with it. And make it sharp. If I find you've been cutting a wheedle —'

The hand came out again. 'Oh no, sir, *please*, sir! But I couldn't say in front of *her*. It's my sister, sir. She's desperate sick, sir, and please will you come?'

'Sick?'

'Sick as a horse, sir.' He bit his lip in his anxiety and fidgeted from one foot to the other.

'But what d'you suppose I could do?' Benedict said, beginning to feel badgered. 'I'm not a physician.'

'No, sir, only she's awful bad-off, and I s'picion she's going to die, and if you could bring your prayer-book and say something good over her —' The tears rolled freely again.

189

'Een-eye Peg says if you die without a prayer said over you, you go to the Bad Place. Oh sir, I don't want my sister to go there!'

Een-eye Peg was the old woman who cooked, made the beds, and washed and mended the clothes for the men in the shanty in which Dandy currently lived. She was a villainous-looking and usually drunken crone with a foul tongue and an even fouler fund of stories not fit for human ears, least of all a child's; but Benedict had learned by now what a hellish life these women led, and tried to suspend judgement on her. Her masters treated her considerably worse than their dogs, abusing and beating her quite often simply for amusement.

'She won't go to Hell,' Benedict said to the boy. 'Peg's not telling you true. In any case, it's a priest you want, not me. You should ask the parson up at the church.' But even as he said it, he knew it was a stupid thing to suggest.

'He wouldn't come,' Dandy said simply. 'He hates us navvies. He says we're a scourge and a plague.'

Benedict knew this was true; but what decided him was that the desperate look in Dandy's eyes had died, to be replaced by dull hopelessness. The boy thought that Benedict would not come, that his sister would go to Hell, that he had failed; and Benedict knew what it was to be a child and to feel helpless. In an instant – which he equally instantly regretted – he gave up the idea of going to church that day, of having a restful afternoon reading and a leisurely dinner, and pledged himself instead to a long walk over rough fields to whatever distressing sight would await him at the shanties.

'All right, Dandy, I'll come and do what I can.'

The dirty, unprepossessing face was radiant with hope again. 'Thank you, sir,' he said fervently. 'Oh please, will you come now?'

'Yes, yes, right away,' Benedict said. 'Just let me fetch my dog from the back and we'll be off.' He might as well give Fand a walk, so that the morning should not be entirely wasted. It also occurred to him that if he was going up to the shanties he might be glad of her protection. Many – perhaps most – of the navvies liked to spend knock-off Sunday getting drunk, and when they were drunk there was nothing they liked better than a brawl.

He went round the side of the house to the back yard, where Fand was tethered (Mrs Brooksby, amongst the numerous prejudices common to her sort, would not allow animals in the house), accepted her enormous, silent gratitude at the unexpected release from boredom, and with his prayer-book in his pocket and his dog running joyfully nose-down ahead of him, started off down the village street with his incongruous companion.

Benedict had been once to the shanty where Dandy lived. It was a large one, and comfortable of its sort: rectangular, built partly of wood, partly of piled sods, and roofed with tarpaulin stretched over timber, with a tiled area around the chimney. The door was halfway along one of the long sides, and to either side of it was a window, glazed but not made to open.

Twenty men lived here. One end of the hut was the sleeping-place, the walls fitted with bunks from floor to ceiling, and when Bendy had gone there on a previous knock-off Sunday, there had been a number of men sprawled out on the bunks either asleep or drunk. Many of them kept dogs – terriers and lurchers for poaching and fighting dogs for status – and they shared their masters' bunks with them. One man, though evidently dead drunk and insensible, had curled himself carefully round a whippet bitch suckling a very new litter of whelps, and was sleeping in the little space she had left him.

In the centre of the shanty, suspended from the highest point of the roof with ropes, was a huge wooden crate which Dandy had told him was the 'brat-cage': reached by a ladder which was put up at night, it was where Dandy and the other two boys in the shanty slept.

The other end of the hut was the kitchen and living area: a fireplace in the centre of the short wall with a brick chimney, and next to it a large copper with a fire under it; a large wooden table, and wooden benches against the walls; three barrels of beer just under the window, with locks on the taps whose keys were in Een-eye Peg's keeping; a double row of wooden cupboards against another wall, one for each man, in which to keep his personal belongings.

When Bendy had visited, Een-eye Peg had been cooking

191

the men's dinners in the copper. Whatever each gave her to cook for him – potatoes and cabbage, pudding, a bit of bacon, butcher's meat if the man were flush, poached game or rabbits if he were cunning – she would put in a net and suspend in the water by a string, each string being attached to a stick which was marked with notches to identify the owner. Otherwise, as Een-eye had told Bendy frankly, she might get them mixed up and then 'Ah s'd get me head brokken for it, twinty times ower.' That was how she had lost her eye, he learnt. In her inexperienced youth she had given one navvy's bit of beef to someone else by mistake, and he had hit her in the face with a three-legged stool to teach her to be more careful in future.

Thinking about the shanty as he strode across the fields, with Dandy Dick scampering and hopping along just ahead of him in his anxiety, Benedict wondered where the boy's sister slept. The men in that particular shanty were all unmarried – which was to say they did not have a regular woman with whom they lived. Een-eye did the housework for them, and if they wanted a woman and were lucky enough to find one willing, they brought her in just for the occasion, or had her out in the fields where there was more privacy. He couldn't think how Dandy's sister fitted into this arrangement. Perhaps she belonged to a man from another shanty.

'I never heard you tell of a sister before,' he said. 'Is she wife to one of the men?'

The boy turned his head in alarm, and paused to let Benedict catch up with him, looking up at him anxiously.

'No sir, no sir. She not stopping in our shant. Nobody knows about her. You won't tell, will you, sir? She's hidden in a place I'll take you to. But if the men was to find out about her —' He bit his lips at the horrible thought.

Benedict could complete the sentence for himself. 'Of course I won't say anything. But tell me about her. How does she come to be here?'

Bit by bit Dandy extruded the story. His widowed mother had remarried, and he had run away from home to join the navvies to get away from his stepfather, who had beaten him and threatened to send him to the mills. Benedict considered what Dandy had run from and to, and could see little

192

difference. The work here was just as hard and considerably more dangerous than factory work. Perhaps working out of doors might be more pleasant, at least in the warmer months; but the navvies must clout and even beat the boy pretty often, through perhaps less purposefully than a stepfather would.

But probably Dandy had not considered what lay ahead when he ran, only what he was escaping from, and he had evidently thought the mills the worst fate that could befall him. He had told no-one where he was going except his sister – two years older than him and closest to him in the family. She had begged him not to go, and asked him what he thought would become of her if he left her, and Dandy had suggested that she should come with him. But she was more afraid of the unknown than he, and had refused.

But two days ago she had turned up, waiting for him hidden in the bushes near the shanty, and calling to him softly as he went past on his way home. She had run away like him, she said, because the stepfather had begun mistreating her when Dandy left, and she could stand no more. Dandy had seen at once that she was feverish and ill, but he could not take her to his shanty. In the first place, he was the lowest of the low there, only one grade above Een-eye Peg in the eyes of the men, and his rights in the shanty were limited to eating and sleeping, provided it didn't discommode anyone else. And in the second place, young as he was, he knew better than to introduce his sister amongst the navvies, which would have been like introducing a lamb to a pack of hungry wolves.

'She's not that sort of girl sir,' he assured Bendy earnestly. 'So I hid her, and took along a bit of my own supper, which was taters, and I hoped she'd get better, but she's getting worse, and I think she's dying now. There wasn't nobody I could tell, to ask what to do, except on'y you, sir. Cos if she must die, she ought not to go to the Bad Place, for she's done nothing wrong, on'y run away like I done.'

He had begun crying again, and Benedict saw that he must be very fond of his sister, as well as very frightened. He laid a comforting hand on the boy's shoulder. The boy flinched and looked up, automatically expecting a blow. Benedict removed his hand, and said, 'We'll do what we can. And if she is dying, I promise you she won't to go to Hell. I have my prayer-book here, and I'll say what's proper.'

The boy gave him a watery smile, and then bent his head and trudged on. Before they reached the shanties the track passed through a small wood. With a glance at Benedict, the boy turned off the path and led the way through the trees, and eventually they came out on the hillside above the works. Fand, approving heartily of this Sunday walk, ran out and coursed back and forth with her nose to the short, rabbit-bitten grass, snuffling down the glorious smells. Dandy, having peered cautiously this way and that to see that there were no men about, led Benedict towards what looked like some kind of outcrop, or perhaps a place where there had been a landslip, just below the crest of the hill.

'I fun' this one day when I come up after rabbits,' Dandy said. 'There used to be a navvy – Hermit Jack, he was called – what wouldn't live with the other men. He would be alone, so he built himself a shant up here, in the hillside. But he was kilt on the workings last year, so it's empty now.'

Benedict saw now what it was. He had not seen turf huts like this before, but he had heard of them from the gangers, many of whom had lived in such shelters on other workings. It was simply a burrow dug out of the hillside, the front extended with timbers which had been covered with turfs to make them weatherproof. The earth which had been dug out was piled up against the timbers on the outside and the grass had grown over it, so now the whole thing blended in with the natural hillside.

'I'd best go in first and warn her,' Dandy said apologetically. Benedict nodded and stopped where he was, a few yards off, calling Fand to him and catching hold of her collar. The boy ducked into the turf hut, and a moment later came out and beckoned him forward. The wooden door stood open, so Benedict stooped and went in. Inside the burrow was about ten feet long by six wide and about six feet high. It was quite empty of furnishings – just bare walls and a bare floor, no chimney or ventilation: Hermit Jack must have done his cooking on a fire outside the door, he supposed. It was occupied now by a bundle of clothing lying on a heap of dead bracken, which he could only just see in the dim light. As the light was further obscured by his own shadow, he squatted down next to the bundle, and in a moment was able to discern that it had propped itself up on one elbow and was looking at him. Fand thrust a motherly nose past him under his arm and the figure flinched a little in surprise.

'It's all right, she won't hurt you.' Benedict pushed Fand back and went on. 'How are you feeling? Your brother brought me to you. He says you are unwell.'

'Oh master, Diccon shouldn't have troubled you,' she whispered.

'It's no trouble. I want to help you,' Benedict said gently. He could see well enough now to determine a small, rather pointed white face, a tangle of dark hair, and dark eyes which at present were marked with shadows of sickness. 'You look feverish,' he said, and reaching out slowly, so as not to frighten her, laid a hand over her forehead. It was stinging hot, and she was trembling with fever. 'Can you tell me what's happened to you?' he asked.

She did not answer for a moment; then she whispered. 'I cannot. I'm 'shamed.'

'Please,' Benedict said. 'I will help you, but you must trust me.' She was silent. Fand pushed past him again and sniffed at the girl, and then licked once at her face and pressed up against her, lashing her tail in approval. The girl caressed Fand's head feebly, and Benedict said, 'Tell me what ails you.'

Another silence, and then she whispered, 'Make Diccon go outside then, sir.'

Benedict turned to where Dandy was hovering in the doorway. 'Is she going to die?' he asked anxiously, in a hoarse undertone.

'I don't think so,' Bendy said. 'She wants to talk to me alone, Dandy. Will you wait outside?' The boy hesitated. 'Come, I shan't hurt her.'

'I know that, sir,' Dandy said quickly; and to his sister, 'Mr Morland's a right 'un, Liza. If anyone can help us, he can.'

The boy departed. Liza drew breath to say something and at once was racked by a coughing-fit. When it was over, Benedict, cursing himself for not having brought anything with him, not even a drop of brandy, took off his coat and put

195

it round her shoulders. Then he said, 'Lie down. Don't tire yourself. Just tell me when you're ready.'

She obeyed him, and after a moment, staring blankly towards the opening and the daylight, told him the horribly commonplace story in a flat, matter-of-fact tone. It must have happened to many girls whose mothers remarried when their daughters were of an age to be interesting, but Bendy heard it with a sense of shock. At the end of her recital he was so consumed with anger on her behalf that he could not immediately speak. After a moment she said with a broken cadence of sorrow, 'Now you'll blame me, sir, but it was not my fault, 'deed it was not.'

'I know that, poor girl,' Benedict said. 'Good God, I don't blame you! I don't know what else you could have done.' He paused a moment, and then asked diffidently, 'What happened to the baby?'

'I buried it,' was the stark whisper. 'In a hole amongst some tree-roots, in the wood where I was hid. I scraped some earth over it and covered it with leaves. It was the best I could do.'

'Yes,' said Benedict, much shaken.

After a pause she went on, 'I was glad it was born dead, when I thought how it came to be. But now —' Benedict saw a glint of tears on the white face. 'I think I'm very sick. Am I to die too, master? Diccon thinks I am. Maybe it's best.'

'I don't think so,' Benedict said, far more certainly than he felt. Childbirth was women's work, and he knew nothing about it, but it seemed to him that for a young girl to give birth all alone, with no midwife or other woman to attend her, and then to spend several nights sleeping on the cold earth, must endanger her life. What the devil he was to do with her he did not know, but one thing was certain: he could not leave her here. If he did, she certainly would die.

'Do you think you can walk?' he asked. 'I must get you to a warm place where you can be looked after.'

She nodded doubtfully, but when she tried to raise herself she hadn't the strength. Probably she hadn't eaten for days, either, Benedict thought – apart from Dandy's potatoes.

'I shall have to carry you, then,' he said. She protested a little, but he said, 'You can't stay here. There is nothing else for it.'

Her hand came out of the darkness – as cold as her forehead was hot – and gripped his wrist with the strength of fear. 'You won't send me back?' she whispered.

'To your stepfather? To the brute who did this to you? No, by God!' Benedict said vehemently. 'I swear he shan't come near you.'

She continued to look at him apprehensively, and he saw that life had not taught her to trust a man's word, which hardly surprised him. Oaths would not do it, only experience, he thought, and decided to save his breath. He had no idea what he would do with her, where he could find a safe place for her, but for a moment it was essential to get her to civilisation – warmth, food, and a doctor's care. Beyond that he could not look. If she survived, that would be time enough to worry about her future. She was obviously very weak and feverish, and Dandy Dick's assessment might yet turn out to be the right one.

It was one thing to speak gallantly about carrying her, but Benedict soon discovered that even a small and famished woman is tremendous weight over rough fields. Fand ran around him, muzzle up, puzzled, and Dandy hovered anxiously, desperate to help. At last Benedict stumbled over a tussock and ended on his knees, and when he found himself quite unable, for the moment, to rise again, the boy intervened.

'Liza, you're too heavy for Mr Morland to carry. T'ain't fitting besides. If I was to help you, don't you think you could walk a bit?'

'Yes, I can walk,' she said. 'Put me down, master, pray.'

Benedict was doubtful, but it was found that with him and Dandy on either side of her to support her, she was able to put one foot in front of the other, and though their progress was painfully slow it was at least constant. In this way they descended the hill, skirted the wood, and made their way into the village. It was fortunate that most of the population was at church, but they still attracted a number of amazed stares. It was only when they arrived at the door of Benedict's lodging that he realised he had come here instinctively, without really considering what he was to say to Mrs Brooksby.

It turned out to be more a case of what she would say to him. Fib opened the door and let out a scream at the sight of the three of them which made Fand flatten her ears and lift her lips threateningly, and brought Mrs Brooksby hurrying from the kitchen. When she realised that Benedict proposed bringing the draggled creature in she barred his way and scolded him like a cut-purse.

'Bring that dirty slut into my clean house? You must have lost your senses! Who knows where she's been or what she might have? Riddled with God-knows-what: invite the plague in, I might as well!' Fand was sniffing at her, and she thrust the dog away with a sharp cry of disgust. 'Get away, dog! I will not be put upon, Mr Morland, so don't think it! I wonder you should abuse a decent female so – and when I've done everything to make you comfortable here, just as if I was your own mother. To bring a creature like that into my front hall, to say nothing of the boy – oh, take her away, you nasty brat! Dirtying my doorstep! Sister, indeed! Be off with you, or I'll call the constable!' She grew lachrymose. 'I never should have had anything to do with railway folk, and that's the truth of it! Mrs Pike said I should regret it, but I did think an engineer would be a gentleman at least, though I see was sorely mistaken in you, Mr Morland, indeed I was!'

With that she began loudly weeping, covering her face with her apron; but when Benedict began to plead she dropped the apron instantly and glared at him with a dry and angry eye. 'I won't hear another word, Mr Morland. Sick, indeed! And why should I bring sickness into my house, pray? Let her go back to her own people, if she has, which I doubt, unless they're gypsies. Thieves most like, as well, spying on decent folk's houses to see what they can steal. What's to become to her? Why should I care – or you either? The likes of her knows where to go at a pinch, I dare say. Send her away this instant – and take that dog out of my house or I shall have the vapours!'

'Mrs Brooksby, the girl is not suffering from a disease. Please listen to me! She is cold and famished, which has made her feverish. She must have a bed and something to eat soon or she will die. I cannot send her back to her people for she would die before she got there, and in any case it's they who have brought her to this pass.'

'Well I'm not having her die in my house. The idea!'

'She won't die, if only you let me put her to bed. Come, please, we can't stand here in the hall arguing over her. Look how pale and faint she is, poor child.'

'Poor child? That one's more than a child, as you would know if you weren't so milky,' she snapped, but the realisation of Benedict's milkiness seemed to reassure her a little; as perhaps did her own assessment of the girl, which was that she was not as bad as first looked. 'Besides, I have no room for her,' she said, not realising that by changing her argument she was signalling capitulation.

'Oh, but she can have my bed,' Benedict said, eager only to end the argument. 'I can sleep in the hayloft or – or anywhere.'

'Hayloft, nonsense! And what about my clean sheets? Look at the state of her!'

'I will pay for the washing, of course; and I will give you extra for any trouble you are put to,' Benedict said quickly. The mention of money seemed to soften the landlady's resolve. Benedict went on hopefully, 'It really is tremendously good of you, ma'am. And I will get the apothecary in at once to reassure you that there is nothing about her you need fear. Let me carry her upstairs now.'

But Mrs Brooksby eyed Liza shrewdly and said, 'No, she can walk, if Fib and me helps her. Betty,' to the upper servant, who was hovering in the kitchen doorway, 'put on a can of water to boil and bring it up as soon as it's hot, and those old sheets I put by for mending. Fib, get your shoulder under her arm the other side, that's right.'

'What can I do?' Benedict asked anxiously.

'Nothing for the moment. Just get rid of that dirty boy off my doorstep and come inside and shut the door. I don't want every neighbour peering in. I'll put her in your bed for now, but she can't stay, that's for certain sure.' She took Liza's other side and started up the stairs, grumbling. 'Fleas, I make no doubt, if it isn't lice – and I don't know what besides. Hold her up, Fib, I can't do everything myself.'

Benedict turned to Dandy, who was looking very glum. 'Don't worry. Your sister will come to no harm, I promise you. That one's bark is worse than her bite. You'd better go now, or it will make her mad. I'll tell you tomorrow how your sister goes on.'

Benedict counted the coins into Dr Hubert's hand, wishing he were so well-breeched as to be able to part from them without pain. He noticed, and then mentally rebuked himself for noticing, that the doctor's palm crooked quite naturally to receive them, like a practised beggar. The fact was that it annoyed him that Dr Hubert would not yield up any information about Liza until he had been paid. *She* might have the appearance of a pauper, but Benedict was used to receiving the respect due to a gentleman, and it annoyed him not to be trusted.

'I think that is correct, is it not?' he said with the last coin, allowing himself a hint of irony.

Hubert was unaffected. He transferred the coins carefully to his purse and put the purse into his bag before he spoke. 'Quite correct. And now, as to the young – the young *person*. I think I may say she has come to no permanent harm, despite the, er, unusual nature of her experiences. She has a robust constitution and is, as yet, too young to have impaired it by the excesses common to those of her stamp. It is the case,' he added oracularly, 'that where there is no congenital weakness in the system, females of the lower orders, like animals, give birth more easily than ladies of refinement.'

Though Benedict had not the knowledge to fault the content of the doctor's speech, there was something about his tone which made his hackles rise; but he forced himself to speak calmly and politely. 'You say no permanent harm has been done, sir?'

'She has lost a great deal of blood, and is weak from inanition, and there is a certain lassitude which is the result of the recent irritation of the nerves. We must not suppose,' he said with a slight smile, 'that because the lower orders lack sensibility, they are incapable of suffering from anxiety.'

'No, sir,' Benedict said.

'However, I am confident that the fever has no putrid tendency, which of course was my principal concern. I have bled her —'

'Bled her? But I thought you said she's lost a great deal of blood?'

Hubert raised a supercilious eyebrow. 'My dear Mr Morland, bleeding is indicated in all cases of fever. You must not presume to instruct me in my own craft.'

'No, sir. I beg your pardon. Pray continue.'

'Thank you. I have bled her, and I recommend a low diet for the next week, bread and milk, gruel, light broths and so forth. No meat, or anything of a heating nature, and if there should be any recurrence of the feverish symptoms, you must send for me at once, for it could herald the onset of childbed fever, which as I think you must be aware is always fatal. But if there is no relapse, I think she may rise from her bed in a fortnight, and you will find in a month she is her usual self again – whatever that may be.'

'A month?' Benedict muttered in dismay. And in bed for a fortnight? Mrs Brooksby would never stand for that. What on earth was he to do with the girl?

Hubert was watching his face, and said now with sternness which did not quite mask a certain relief, 'It brings me to the point, Mr Morland, of your own conduct in this matter. You may think it is none of my business —' Benedict took a breath but Hubert gave him no chance to answer what was not intended as a question '– but I reprehend very strongly your bringing the girl here. As I have said, I find no putrid tendency, nor anything of a contagious nature, but you were not to know that, sir, when you introduced this – this *person* into the household of a decent, God-fearing woman.'

'But she —'

'Mrs Brooksby is a most respected member of our village community. Her husband was a valuable patient of mine for many years through his last illness – indeed, I was privileged to attend his death-bed, and he made an excellent end, most affecting and uplifting. And into the household of this – if I may put it so – this Roman matron, you, sir, thrust a – a – well, I will not soil my tongue with the word which best describes her; but how any *gentleman*, whatever his relationship with the creature, could so take advantage of a helpless widow as to expose her, not only to the filth and infections which must hang about persons of that stamp, but to the evil miasma of moral degradation which rises from her very pores —'

'Dr Hubert!' Benedict said forcefully, desperate to stop him before he worked himself into an apoplexy of salacious rage. 'You are under a misapprehension, sir – several misapprehensions. In the first place I have no relationship with the girl. Her brother begged me to help her because he had no-one else to turn to, and I should have thought it behoves every Christian to succour the suffering —'

'Not,' Hubert interrupted, breathing hard, 'when they have brought suffering upon themselves through their own moral turpitude! When a girl so young falls thus into error, it must betray a nature so lost to all decency that —'

'Your other misapprehension, sir, is that the girl is morally corrupt,' Benedict interrupted angrily. 'She did not choose her condition: it was forced upon her in the most abominable way!'

'As she told you, no doubt,' the doctor sneered. 'You are too trusting, Mr Morland.'

'You are not trusting enough, Dr Hubert!'

'You are insolent, sir! How dare you speak to me so? Did your parents teach you no respect for your elders?'

Benedict breathed hard. 'I beg your pardon. I did not mean to be disrespectful, but you seem too ready to believe ill of her without reason.'

'I have every reason,' Hubert returned. 'Not only does her own plight condemn her; it is enough that she is one of *them*. The navvies!' He rolled his eyes up to heaven. 'Is there to be no end to the evil we suffer because of them? We have had no moment's peace since they came among us.'

Benedict did not want to get into that argument. It was true that the navvies were a rough, uncultured, ungodly lot; that they poached whenever and wherever they could, and stole too, and left behind unpaid debts; and that when they went on their 'randies' – drunken sprees – they could be very troublesome, fighting, damaging property, and debauching servant girls. But it was also true that when they were in the district they were unjustly blamed for everything that was broken or went missing, and that the residents were inclined to tar them all with the same brush, without discrimination, or even evidence.

He said quietly, 'Is she well enough to receive a visit from me, sir? I must discuss her future with her. I do not know what is to be done with her, but she must not be sent back to those who abused her so shamefully.'

Dr Hubert sniffed. 'It will do no harm for you to speak to her. She is weak, but not confused. But I must tell you, Mr Morland – indeed, Mrs Brooksby has asked me to tell you – that she cannot stay here. It is unthinkable that Mrs Brooksby should be burdened with the care of such a person, and subjected to the talk it would give rise to in the neighbourhood. You must remove her.'

'But where?' Benedict said helplessly.

'That is for you to determine,' Hubert said with relish. 'I fear you should have thought about that before you interfered in the case.'

At the top of the stairs Benedict found Mrs Brooksby hovering, torn between a sense of her own grievance and a desire not to offend a paying lodger.

'Doctor says there's nothing wrong with her, Mr Morland – nothing catching, at any rate.'

'Yes,' Benedict said. He knew he must conciliate her, for he certainly needed her help, so he added, 'It is good of you to allow her to use my room, Mrs Brooksby. It was a very Christian thing to do.'

'Well, now, Mr Morland, as to that, she can't stay there. I can't go taking in all the scaff and raff just because they're unfortunate, or where would it end? And what would the neighbours say? I've got my good name to think of.' She was working herself up nicely now. 'I mean to say, there she is using up one of my best rooms, a girl that should never be allowed amongst decent people! And there's you sleeping in the attic, which when all's said and done is two rooms and two people's meals and washing, to say nothing —'

'I have assured you I will pay you for everything,' Benedict said loudly, to stop her. 'I do not wish you to be out of pocket.'

'Yes, well, even so – it isn't the money, you see.'

'It isn't?' Benedict tried not to be sarcastic and didn't quite succeed.

She eyed him like an angry hen. 'No, it isn't. I'm sorry, Mr Morland, because I'm sure you meant well – though anyone with an ounce of sense would have known better than to interfere, and if you'd come to me first and asked I'd have told you so! But when you come bringing the likes of her into my house without a by-your-leave, a dirty, godless, gypsy trollop, and no better than she should be – well, I won't have her here, and that's all there is to it!'

'I see,' Benedict said.

His forbearance seemed to give her pause. She looked at him defiantly. 'She can stay one more night, but tomorrow you take her out of here, and that's my final word.'

Benedict could think of no way of opening his lips without saying something unforgivable, so he kept them closed, nodded to her, and went to his room. He scratched on the door and went in, and Liza turned her head on the pillows and looked towards him apprehensively. He smiled reassuringly, but she did not respond.

'How are you feeling now?' he asked.

'Much better, thank you, only so very tired,' she said.

'That's natural enough, after all you've been through. But the doctor says there's nothing seriously wrong, and that you'll soon be feeling quite well again.'

She looked at him bleakly. 'You've been having a set-to about me, haven't you? I heard angry voices. You shouldn't have brought me here.'

'No, I should have left you to die out on the hillside, of course,' he said genially.

She didn't smile. 'You've been very kind. And the lady that owns the house has, too. But she don't want me here. I don't blame her.'

'Don't you?'

'No, sir. I'm a vagrant now,' she said simply. 'A fallen woman. Decent folk don't have to do with the likes of me.'

'What happened was not your fault,' Benedict said, but she only shook her head a little, staring blankly into the middle distance.

She really was looking much better, he thought, now the feverishness had left her – only thin and pale, with shadows of weariness under her eyes. She had cleaned up very well, too.

Her hair, brushed free of tangles, was thick and dark brown and vigorously curling, her face, washed clean, was remarkably pretty – or so it seemed to him. She had a small, straight nose and a pointed chin, and her eyes were set a little on the slant. He had thought they were dark, but in daylight he could see that they were hazel, almost a golden brown. He thought she had rather the look of a fox-kitten, and he wished he could see her in her normal health and spirits. He wanted to see her laugh.

First, though, he must be practical. 'At any rate, you're right that Mrs Brooksby doesn't want you to stay here. We must decide where you are to go.' She looked at him with swift alarm, and he said, 'I've promised you you shan't go back to your stepfather; but is there no other relative – an aunt or uncle, grandparents maybe?'

She shook her head. 'If there had been, I'd have run away long since. My grandparents are dead, and I never had an aunt or uncle. I had an older brother, but he went away when Mother remarried and I don't know where he is now; and then there's just the three little ones left at home.'

'You must be worried about them,' Bendy said.

'They won't come to no harm: they're my stepfather's own children. It was only Diccon and me he hated.'

'Does Diccon know – what your stepfather did to you?'

'I just said he mistreated me. I don't want Diccon to know, please, sir. Poor boy, he's changed so much since he joined the navvies. He used to be such a merry child, always full of fun.'

'He ought to go to school. He has an enquiring mind.'

'Mother couldn't afford to send him, after Father died. We all had to work at whatever we could. Mother and me took in washing.' She stopped abruptly. He could see speaking tired her, and he reverted to the point.

'So there's no-one you could go to? No friend of your father's or mother's?'

She shook her head, and when he did not immediately go on, she said in a small, frightened voice, 'Must it be the workhouse?'

'No,' he said quickly. 'I won't let it come to that. I'll find somewhere safe for you until you are well again, and then —'
Words came easily enough, but a feeling of helplessness was

overcoming him. 'Perhaps I could find you a place as a servant somewhere. To a nice lady who would treat you kindly.'

'Not round these parts you couldn't,' she said baldly. 'They'll all know what I am – *she'll* see to that,' with a glance towards the door. 'No decent lady'll take me in after this.'

He clenched his fists. 'It's so unfair!' The words burst out of him. 'Condemned for something you didn't do. I know what that's like. I was driven out of my home by a false accusation.'

'What did they say you'd done?' she asked with interest.

'I was accused of murder,' he said. 'I'll tell you all about it some time.' Then he added with a faint smile, 'I didn't do it, though.'

'No,' she said seriously. 'I would never have thought you did.'

206

CHAPTER TWELVE

There were two inns in the village: The First and Last, at the far end, which was hardly more than an alehouse, and which welcomed navvies as long as they had money to spend; and The Bell, a superior establishment opposite the church, which boasted a coffee-room as well as a taproom, and, while it was not quite a post-house, hired out job horses and a variety of small vehicles. Benedict visited both establishments that evening, but it was to The First and Last he went to begin with, for he had promised to meet Dandy Dick there, to give him news of his sister.

Benedict did not see the boy at first, but Fand, running ahead, picked him out in the shadow of the porch and ran to thrust her muzzle up at him. Benedict could not detach Dandy from the concealing shadows, even to go inside and talk in comfort.

'No sir, I couldn't,' he said, deeply embarrassed. 'T'wouldn't be fitting.'

'Let me be the judge of that. Come, I'll buy you some ale and plate of faggots. I dare say you're hungry.'

Dandy licked his lips involuntarily, but still he shook his head. 'No, sir, no, sir. I couldn't. I'm too dirty to be seen with you. On'y tell me about Liza, sir. Is she all right?'

'The doctor says she will be perfectly well by and by. She's tired and weak, but nothing worse.'

The boy nodded, too overcome to speak. Benedict searched his face for a likeness to his sister. It was there, but what in Liza was a felicitous combination of features, in the boy looked merely mean and underbred. It was curious, Benedict thought, how the fraction of an inch here and there could make the difference between a pretty face and a plain one.

'What's to come of her now, sir?' Dandy asked at last.

'A home question,' Benedict said. 'I'm afraid I can't answer it yet.'

'I wisht I could take care of her,' Dandy whispered, 'but I'm not big enough. I couldn't fight them, the men in my shant. One of 'em 'ud take her off me, and then —'

Benedict knew exactly what he meant: it was one of the things he had been worrying about. Left to her own devices, the girl would be at the mercy of the first man she met, and in these parts, that was likely to be a navvy. Benedict was second to none in his admiration of their good qualities, but tenderness towards women was rarely one of them. There were navvies who, though rough and uncouth, were fond of their wives and looked after them, but there were far more who took their pleasures where and how they pleased, and looked upon women as a commodity.

It occurred to Benedict just then that to be female, pretty, and poor must be the worst of all combinations. Without a protector, such a person was simply prey, and would only survive by becoming as brutalised as her persecutors. He realised that he had taken up responsibility for Liza when he went with Dandy Dick to the shanty on the hill, and that he could not put the burden down until he had her safely settled somewhere. He had no idea where that somewhere would be, but two things he vowed inwardly: one, that she should not go back to her stepfather; and two, that she should not end up like Een-eye Peg.

When Dandy had slipped away into the darkness, Benedict decided to go into the hostelry and solace himself with a glass or two of something. The taproom was warm and smoky, but not too crowded at this end of the week. There were several villagers there, and two gangers from the workings talking to one of the contractors. As Benedict hesitated inside the door, wondering whether to join them, he heard his named called, and looking round saw Daniel Beavor, one of the assistant engineers, occupying a cosy booth on his own, with a bottle of brandy on the table in front of him.

'Come and join me,' he invited cheerfully. His face was a

little flushed and his neckcloth more than a little rumpled. 'Come and have a wet. It's my birthday, and a damned dull one too! Come and talk me out of the dismals.'

Benedict sat down opposite him. 'I'd be happy to join you, but I don't know that I'll make very cheerful company. I have rather a knotty problem to solve, and I must solve it tonight.'

Beavor waved a hand. 'Never mind,' he said. 'Tell me all about it, and I'll add my intellect to yours. Between us we ought to be able to come up with a solution.' A frown developed between his brows. 'Unless it's money, of course. Nothing to be done about that, I'm afraid. Tell me it ain't money?'

'I suppose it *is* money in a way,' Benedict said. 'At least, if I were a rich man I could do as I liked, and pay people not to mind it.'

'One of the sad truths of life,' Beavor said, staring into the depths of his glass as though it were a camera obscura on the whole world. 'Sad, sad truth. Sad,' he added, in case Bendy hadn't got the point.

'Yes,' said Benedict. They mused in silence for a while.

'So what it is?' Beavor asked at last.

'What's what?'

'This problem of yours.'

'Oh, that! Well, it's rather knotty.'

'So you said. Does it,' Beavor leaned forward and lowered his voice conspiratorially, 'involve a *female*?'

'How did you know?' Benedict asked, a little alarmed to think that his dilemma had already become public property.

But Beavor sighed. 'The knotty ones usually do,' he said wisely. 'Have a wet and tell me about it.'

A sympathetic ear was tempting, even if Beavor was unlikely to have any solutions for him. 'The girl in question, you see – she isn't well. Confined to her bed, can't take care of herself, and the sawbones thinks she'll be out of commission for a fortnight, and poorly for a month. But my landlady don't approve of her, and wants her out of the house tomorrow.'

'What sort of a girl?'

'Oh, just a girl. Of the lower orders, but very decent, only of course people like Mrs Brooksby always think the worst of

209

girls like that, especially if they're pretty.'

Beavor looked at him with considerable awe. 'She's in your lodgings?'

'Well, yes – in my room. In my bed, in fact, though it isn't —'

'You took this girl to Ma Brooksby's and installed her *in your own bed*?' Beavor gaped. 'By God, Morland, you're a cool one! And you look,' he added in puzzled tones, 'as though butter wouldn't melt in your mouth.'

'It isn't what you think,' Benedict said impatiently. 'I can't explain it now, but the thing is Mrs Brooksby wants the girl out —'

'I should just about think she does!'

'– and I don't know where to send her. She can't go back where she came from, and she's terrified of the workhouse —'

'Come, dear boy,' Beavor said, taken aback, 'you can't put her in the workhouse! Too shabby by half!'

'I know,' Benedict said shortly. 'But where can I put her, that's the question. Even if I could find lodgings where the landlady would take her in – and you know what they're like —'

'Oh quite. It wouldn't do at all. You must rent rooms for her, that's all,' Beavor said simply.

The idea had not occurred to Benedict. He examined it now from all angles. 'I don't know of any,' he said, as the first objection presented itself.

'Sanders Lodge,' Beavor said promptly. 'You know the big, grey house just past the turning that goes up to the squire's place? It's let out in rooms, and I happen to know there's a set vacant, because Arbel left 'em yesterday to move into my lodgings. Tired of finding for himself. I was thinking of swapping with him, but I'm comfortable enough where I am, and Ma Davidson cooks like an angel.'

Benedict raised the other immediate problem. 'But I couldn't afford to pay for rooms and my lodgings. I manage all right as I am, but I'm not well-blunted enough for both.'

Beavor shook his head rather owlishly. 'Why should you want both? Not that attached to Ma Brooksby, are you?'

'No, but —'

'Principal reason I didn't move out of my lodgings was that

if you live in rooms you need someone to cook and wash for you. Seems to me you're well covered there. Time you had your own establishment. Past time, by all accounts.'

'But the girl – you don't understand, Beavor. She's young and pretty and – well, but we're not – not married.'

'Didn't suppose you were, old boy.'

'But what would people say?'

Beavor goggled. '*You* ask that? The man who installed a girl in Ma Brooksby's best front bedroom without turning a hair?' He shook his head wonderingly. 'I'll tell you what they'll say. If anyone bothers to think anything, which they won't, they'll think it's the most natural thing in the world that a young man in the prime of life should have a little nest to be comfortable in, and a little bird of paradise in the nest to be comfortable with.'

Benedict thought suddenly of Annie and the apartment in Little Helen Yard. Someone had installed her there, in a 'little nest': he wondered who. Nicky believed it was him – or pretended to believe it – and believed he had treated the girl so badly she had been driven to take her own life. He shook the images away angrily. To be unjustly accused was one of the most enduring pains of life, he thought. Poor Liza, condemned by all for someone else's crime! Dr Hubert – Mrs Brooksby – every hand against her; every opinion against him, too, just for helping her! He would like to shrug them all off, wipe the dust of them from his feet, have nothing more to do with them ever!

Well, why not? The thought of independence, of being able to come and go as he pleased without anyone asking questions, was very tempting. And he'd be able to have Fand indoors with him, instead of tying her up in a yard. Liza would probably be glad to cook and clean for him in exchange for being kept safe. It would be just like being someone's housekeeper; and as she had pointed out, no-one else in this village would take her in as a servant now.

'I'll do it,' he said suddenly at the end of this long train of thought.

'Do what?' asked Beavor, whose mind had wandered to other subjects in the meanwhile.

'I'll take the rooms. Mrs Brooksby will be sorry she spoke to me like that.'

211

'She might be,' Beavor said doubtfully. 'But in my experience landladies are never sorry for anything. Landladies are always right, even when they're in the wrong.' This dazzling epigram so impressed him that he smiled and drained his glass in a silent toast to his own wit.

Benedict thought he'd better ask some questions before Beavor left the earthly plane together. 'Who do I see about the room, Beavor, do you know? I'd like to get it settled tonight if I can.'

'Landlord of The Bell owns the place – Simcock. D'you know him?'

'Not really. I've only been in there once or twice.'

'Don't blame you. Desperate dull place, The Bell. But I can point him out to you, if you like.'

'Now? Will you go with me now?'

'Certainly, old fellow. No time like the present. He hires out gigs and carts and so on as well, if you should have a lot of luggage to carry up there. You might bespeak one while you're at it.'

'Good idea,' Benedict said. 'Let's go then. What a good chap you are, Beavor, to solve my problems for me!'

'N'tall,' Beavor said politely. 'Always glad to be of service to a friend.'

Benedict returned to his lodgings that night to find Mrs Brooksby still up. She was hovering about the hall, evidently waiting for him, and he was glad to give her the meeting. He had hoped for the opportunity to spoil her night's rest for her.

'Oh, Mr Morland, there you are,' she began grimly, but he let her go no further.

'Here I am, Mrs Brooksby, and you'll be glad to know I have made my arrangements. I shall be removing the girl first thing tomorrow morning.'

'I'm glad to hear it, because I tell you, Mr Morland, I'm not —'

'I shall be leaving at the same time,' he interrupted her, 'so I shall have to cut short our delightful conversation now and go and pack.'

'Leaving?' she said, satisfyingly taken aback.

'For good, Mrs Brooksby.' He made a movement towards the stairs.

'Come now, Mr Morland,' she said, fluttering a hand towards him, 'there's no need for you to be going. I never asked for that, nor would I. You've been a good lodger – up until this unfortunate business – and I make no complaint.'

'Thank you. I am going, however.'

She bridled. 'Haven't I always made you comfortable, just as if you was my own son? And that's a nice room, the best in the house. There's none better nor cleaner in the village, and I'm more than generous in the matter of coals and candles – as you'll find out if you go elsewhere.'

Benedict smiled sweetly, enjoying himself very much. 'If you will excuse me, Mrs Brooksby, I have a great deal to do.'

'Oh, have you indeed?' she said, growing angry. 'You march in here at this time of night and tell me you're leaving, just like that, without a word of thanks for all I've done for you – and not even the courtesy of giving me notice. A week's notice is your terms, I'd like to remind you! And if you think you can take advantage of a poor, helpless widow —'

'I paid you yesterday for the coming week, so that will do instead of notice, I think. And if there's been any extra expenditure on account of the girl, I will settle it with you now.' He put his hand into his pocket and drew out his purse – horribly light now, since paying Simcock a week's advance for the rooms on top for what he had paid Mrs Brooksby yesterday.

The sight of the purse reminded Mrs Brooksby of what she was losing, and she swallowed down her anger with an effort. 'Now then, Mr Morland, there's no need for that, I'm sure. Why don't you go on up to bed and we'll talk about it in the morning. We don't want to be parting on account of a few words spoken in haste, do we? I'm sure I've always been very fond of you, and there's no-one I'd sooner have in my front bedroom. As for the girl – well, I admit I was rarely put out when you brought her here, but if she's going in the morning there's no harm done after all. I won't say there hasn't been a bit extra on food and washing on her account, but it's a small matter, and I'm willing enough to forget all about it.'

'Thank you, you're very kind,' Benedict said, putting his purse away.

Mrs Brooksby blinked. 'Not at all, not at all! You go on up, then, and tomorrow when the girl's gone I'll clean your room for you and it'll be as though all this never happened. And I might get in a nice bit of steak for your dinner tomorrow. My gentlemen always like a fried beefsteak, with onions.'

Benedict smiled serenely. 'Thank you, but I shan't be here for dinner. As I told you, I'm leaving tomorrow morning, first thing. But I'm sure your other lodgers will enjoy it.'

It was one of the best moments of his life so far, he thought, as he walked up the stairs leaving her speechless. She recovered her voice as he reached the turn.

'Where are you going to? You'll not get lodgings just like that!'

'I've made my arrangements, thank you,' he said airily.

'But what's your direction? Suppose anyone was to ask for you, or a letter come?' she said desperately.

'I can always be found at the works,' he said and walked on up the stairs, hoping that her unsatisfied curiosity would plague her all night.

It was still dark when Benedict reached Sanders Lodge the next morning, for he had to effect the move before he went to work, and the shift at the workings started early. It was probably not the best way to arrive at a new home. The place was not only dark, it was very cold, for there was no fire burning, of course, and Fand pressed close to his legs and kept her tail down as though disapproving of the lack of comfort. The furnishings were sparse and shabby, as might be expected; but the place was roomy enough, rather like a university set, with a living-room, bedroom, and a tiny scullery, and whatever it lacked in elegance, it made up for by being absolutely private. Benedict felt his spirits rise at the thought of such freedom, the first in his life. It was as if he had become a grown-up at last.

He had insisted on carrying Liza up the stairs, and now he set her down on her feet carefully and said, 'Wait, I'll light a candle. There now, what do you think of it?'

She looked around slowly. 'It's very nice,' she said doubtfully, after a moment. 'But who does it belong to?'

'Simcock, the publican at The Bell. He lets out the whole house in rooms. I've rented this set. You'll be quite safe here – and best of all, there'll be no-one to point the finger at you or say unkind things.'

She turned to look at him searchingly in the wavering light of the one candle. 'But you've had to leave your lodgings on my account.'

'Oh, don't worry about that,' Benedict said jubilantly. 'I really enjoyed wiping Ma Brooksby's eye! And these rooms are much cheaper, of course, so in the end it ought to work out about the same, even with two of us to feed.'

'You – you mean to keep me, then?' she said falteringly.

'Well I can't let you starve, can I?' he asked. She didn't seem as pleased as he had expected her to be. 'Naturally I hope that you'll oblige me by doing the cooking and cleaning and so on – but not until you're well, of course.' She didn't respond, and, puzzled, he added, 'You're welcome to stay here for as long as you like. Once you've got your strength back, you're perfectly free to leave if you want to go off somewhere else, but I thought – it seemed to me – what I mean is, I shan't turn you out, you know.'

Still she said nothing, only stood where he had placed her, looking round the room with eyes so devoid of expression it was impossible to tell what she might be thinking. But he reminded himself sharply that she was probably exhausted, considering all she had suffered recently. He was being selfish in wanting her to be pleased: he should think of her, not himself, at this point.

'There'll be plenty of time to look round later. For the moment I think you ought to go straight back to bed. The doctor said you weren't to get up for a fortnight, remember. The bedroom's through here. Can you walk, or shall I carry you?'

'I can walk,' she said; but she swayed so alarmingly that he put his arm round her and supported her into the next room.

'I'll have to get some sheets from somewhere,' he said, 'but at least there are plenty of blankets.' She sat down on the bed. 'Are you all right?' he asked.

'Just tired,' she said.

'You get yourself into bed, then, while I see if there's anything to kindle a fire with,' he said. 'Simcock swore there was wood and coal here somewhere, so it's only a matter of finding it. Then I'll have to go off to work. I'm sorry to have to leave you all alone, but I'll try to come back at dinner time to see that you're all right. And tonight I'll get everything sorted out, and make up a bed for myself on the sofa in there. It's a good, big one, luckily.'

She looked up at him with an arrested expression in her eyes. 'You're going to sleep on the sofa?' she asked in the thread of a voice.

'You're the one who isn't well,' he said. 'Don't you think you ought to have the bed?'

It seemed a long time before she spoke again. 'You should have the bed. You're the master.'

'You make me sound like a tyrant! But don't worry, I don't mean to use the sofa for ever. I'm quite sure I can buy a truckle bed for a few shillings, and when you're fit again we might swap rooms, if you think it would be better.'

'Yes,' she said. And then, her voice suddenly warming, 'You are very kind to me.'

A weight lifted from his spirits, and he smiled at her. 'That's all right. I know what it's like to be an outcast.'

Héloïse was sitting with Sophie in the morning room, while the rain streamed steadily down outside the window. They were about their usual morning occupation of fine sewing – Sophie working on a chemisette for Fanny, Héloïse on a shirt for Nicholas. In the evening, without the benefit of the light, Sophie supplied them both with work out of the poor-basket. Since Sophie would not yet receive general visitors, the monotony of their daily occupations was varied only by morning calls from Prudence or Agnes; their evenings by Jes and Rosamund. Then, while they sewed, Rosamund might play for them, or Jes read to them; and once, when Dr Hastings stepped round on his way home, there was a conversation about politics to which Héloïse listened with relief, and Sophie not at all.

Héloïse watched her daughter covertly while they sewed. The silence between them had not been broken for half an hour, and it was plain to Héloïse that Sophie's thoughts were far away, though her fingers stitched busily enough in the here and now. Héloïse was worried for her, and knew Dr Hastings was too. She had recovered sufficiently from her miscarriage no longer to be called ill, but she was pale and thin and too easily tired. She had no appetite, and struggled to eat only to save her mother from worrying. Héloïse was afraid she was slipping away from them.

It was early days yet, Héloïse chided herself. She of all people knew how long it took to accept the loss of a dear companion, the love of one's life. She did not think she would ever know again the gladness of being alive that she had felt while she was James's wife; and if death were to come for her tomorrow, she would not be sorry to lay down her burden. But she was an old woman; Sophie was not yet thirty-three, and Héloïse longed to see some sign in her of the return of her former calm good spirits. Sophie never smiled, rarely spoke, hardly ate; passed her hours in empty silence; seemed interested in nothing; and even when Fanny was brought down to visit them, Sophie only looked at her with sighs and tears.

The sound of a carriage drawing up outside roused Héloïse's interest, and she put down her needle to listen. Sophie did not pause in her stitching, seeming unaware of it. The sounds below proved they had a visitor, but Héloïse had to say, 'I wonder who that can be?' twice before Sophie even looked up.

And then she only said, 'I'm sure I do not know,' before going on with her work.

A few moments later the door opened and Rosamund came in like invading sunshine in her primrose gown and cashmere shawl, fine droplets of rain glinting like dew on the front curls of her red-gold hair; everything about her bright and alive as she came forward to kiss them both. Jes came in behind her, and apologised for the disturbance.

'I see you were both very seriously occupied, and about your proper, womanly duties. How is it, my love, that I never see you with a needle in your hand?'

'Perhaps you may yet, if you are patient enough,' Rosamund said, and sat down with her aunt and cousin. 'No, no, don't disturb yourselves. We are very happy to sit at the table while you go on working, for we have something to talk to you about. Come, Jes, sit here. You shall go first.'

Lord Batchworth took the chair opposite his wife, and Rosamund gave him a rueful look. She had begged them not to disturb themselves, but in Sophie's case it had hardly been necessary: she had gone straight back to her sewing, as though even the appearance of Lord Batchworth at this hour could not rouse her interest.

Héloïse came to their rescue. 'Is it a matter of business that you want to discuss with Sophie? I know you're usually about your mills at this time of day.'

'About my own mills, or about Hobsbawn Mills,' Jes said, taking his cue. Sophie looked up at last, and he hastened to secure her attention. 'I have been looking into your affairs, as you know, Sophie, and I've found them in a very good way. Your husband was careful and methodical, and everything goes on prosperously; but you must have a manager.'

'Must I?' Sophie said obediently.

'Indeed you must, unless you mean to turn yourself into a mill-master. You need a manager, or perhaps I might call him an agent. Someone to go between you and your employees, to explain each to the other, to see your wishes are carried out. It must be someone you trust – you will not want to go down to the mills yourself —'

'No,' she said suddenly. She looked at a memory and shuddered. 'I was there once. I never want to set foot in them again.'

'Then your agent must be someone you can receive here, in your house, and talk to comfortably. A gentleman, in fact.'

Sophie nodded slightly, but said nothing. It was Héloïse who spoke. 'Would a gentleman be willing to take on such a position?'

'One gentleman would.' Jes turned back to Sophie with a smile. 'I took the liberty of enquiring on your behalf of the one person who is ideal in every way. You are acquainted with him already. Indeed, he was your husband's close friend – and Jasper, I know, would have been as eager to help him as he is now to help you. I mean Henry Droylsden, of course.'

'Henry?' Sophie said. She didn't exactly smile, but her expression softened a little.

'Oh yes, Sophie, he is the very person,' Héloïse said. 'He was always so kind and pleasant. When you had your first Season here —'

'Yes,' said Sophie quickly, as though she did not want to be reminded.

'If you are in agreement,' Jes went on, 'I can undertake all the arrangements on your behalf, as to salary and terms. You might find it embarrassing, perhaps, to discuss such things with him?'

'Yes please, if you will,' Sophie said. 'The salary should be a handsome one,' she added thoughtfully. 'Poor Henry.'

'Very well,' Jes said. 'I will attend to it tomorrow, then, and arrange everything for you. Of course,' he went on carefully, 'he will want to call on you. May I tell him he may wait on you tomorrow evening?'

'Yes, of course,' Sophie said unemphatically. 'I shall always be glad to see Henry.'

'If we come too,' Rosamund said, with a triumphant glance at her husband, 'we might have a musical evening – don't you think, Sophie? If Mr Droylsden and I play, you could provide the voice, for none of us can sing like you.'

She put down her needle and turned her head away wearily. 'I can't sing any more,' she said. 'How can you ask me? I wish you would leave me alone.' And she got up from the table and walked from the room.

'Oh dear,' Héloïse said. 'And it was going so well.'

'Never mind,' Jes said. 'One step at a time. She has had such a very great shock, it will take a long time for her to get over it.'

'But I am afraid,' Héloïse said in a low voice, 'that she will never get over it.'

Rosamund looked from one to the other, and then she stood up too. 'I did not have the chance to tell her my half of the news. I shall go and do it now. Pray excuse me, Aunt.'

She hurried after Sophie. Héloïse looked at Jes. 'Is it something I might know?'

Jes sat down again. 'Most certainly. Rosamund has been putting off telling Sophie for fear it might upset her, but I think the time has come for benign shock to be attempted. The fact is that Rosmund is increasing. She is going to have our child.'

Héloïse looked at him in silence for a moment, and then put her hands up to her face as a wavering smile began, as if she thought it might need a little help to shape it.

Rosamund ran Sophie to earth in her bedchamber, where she found her sitting on the window-seat staring out into the grey veil of rain. She didn't look round as Rosamund came in, but when she came up behind her, Sophie said, 'Don't, please. Don't try to talk to me.' She wasn't crying, and Rosamund realised she had expected her to be; but the hopelessness of her voice was worse than tears.

'I have to, Sophie,' Rosamund said. 'You're the nearest thing I have to a sister. I have to try.'

'There's nothing you can do. I know everything you could say, but it doesn't make any difference. It doesn't bring him back, you see.'

Rosamund sat down on the window seat facing her, and waited. 'I don't want to go on living,' Sophie said at last, in a low voice. 'I wake in the morning, and I feel so tired. Everything's dark, and cold, and black. I don't understand why I can't just die.' She drew a long breath. 'I loved him so much.'

'Yes, I know.'

'Every day I have to realise all over again that he's dead. My life is pointless without him.'

'You have Fanny,' Rosamund said.

Sophie stared blindly at the rain. 'I can't feel anything for Fanny. I know I ought to love her, but all I can think of is Jasper. I want him so much it hurts me.' She folded her arms round her chest in an instinctive gesture. 'Why did they kill him? It hurts so much I want to die.'

'Sophie, I've got something to tell you,' Rosamund said. 'Yes, you must hear this – it's important. Please look at me.' Sophie turned her blank face from the window. Her dress of mourning crepe was too big for her – she had grown thinner even since it was made a month ago. Fear touched Rosamund, and made her angry. 'Are you listening to me now?' she demanded.

'Yes, I'm listening,' Sophie said wearily.

'Here is my news then. I'm going to have a baby.' No reaction. 'Do you hear me, Sophie? I'm going to have a baby.'

Then Sophie's arms uncurled themselves, her hands came out blindly like tendrils, she seized Rosamund's shoulders and gripped them hard, staring into her face with such an extraordinary expression that Rosamund was afraid she was going to have a fit. 'Is it true?'

'Yes, it's true. At the end of September – so you see, you can't die, because I'm scared to death about it, and I must have you with me. I'm so afraid something's going to go wrong, and Jes has to go back to London, and what will I do if you leave me?'

Sophie's hands did not relax their grip. She continued to stare into Rosamund's face, and after a while she drew in a long breath, like someone coming up from under water.

'I won't leave you, then,' she said.

Benedict ran up the stairs two at a time with Fand bounding behind him, and when he opened the door she thrust past him and ran forward to make excited circles round Liza, who was standing at the fireplace tending a pot. She turned, startled, and looked towards the door; then apprehension gave way to a shy smile. She lowered her gaze, but the corners of her mouth were curved.

'Did I make you jump? I'm sorry,' Benedict said. 'You're quite safe here, you know.'

'I know,' she said.

'But should you be out of bed?' he asked, examining what he could see of her face. 'You're looking flushed.'

'It's the heat of the fire, that's all,' she said. 'Go on away, dog,' she added in an undertone. 'You'll make me spill.' She resumed her stirring, which allowed her to hide her face even more thoroughly from him.

Benedict watched her for a moment in silence. There was no aversion in the averting of her face: she was merely shy. He could sense that she was happy – and see it, too, in the upright way she stood, and in the fact that she had taken the trouble to make herself presentable. Her hair was neatly pinned; she had removed the worst of the stains from her dress (he must get her something more to wear at the first opportunity!); and she had somehow contrived to wash her shawl – he withstood the temptation to finger it to make sure it was thoroughly dry. He felt very protective towards her, but with all the caveats he was satisfied with what had been achieved so far. His common sense told him that a woman on the brink of dying, or desperately unhappy and afraid, was unlikely to take so much trouble with her appearance.

'Something smells good,' he said at last. 'What are you cooking?'

'Soup,' she said. 'For your dinner, sir. There's not much meat to it – just a scrap of bacon – but it's good and hot. And there's a new loaf.'

'You've been out marketing? Are you sure you're strong enough? The doctor said you should stay in bed for a fortnight.'

'I'm well enough,' she said. 'Only a bit wambly sometimes on my legs.'

He thought about this. Now that the brief flush had left her face, she looked too pale and too thin. 'D'you know, I'm not sure that that doctor's advice was the best,' he said. 'All that fustian about a low diet: it seems to me that you need building up. Some good, red meat and half a pint of burgundy would serve you better than slops, in my opinion. As soon as I get beforehand with my wages again —'

She seemed embarrassed. 'Indeed, you mustn't worry about me, sir,' she said. 'I shall be quite all right. Are you ready for this soup now?'

'Just let me wash my face and hands, and I'll sit down with you,' he said, and went through into the scullery. A few minutes later he was sitting at the table with Liza placing a bowl of the soup in front of him, and a piece of bread to the side. He was so hungry after a morning on the workings that he had taken three mouthfuls before he realised she was not eating with him. 'Sit down here, and have your own,' he commanded, gesturing to the chair opposite.

'No sir, I couldn't,' she said, shocked. 'T'wouldn't be right.'

He pushed his chair back. 'Sit down and eat with me, or I

222

won't eat at all, and then this good soup will be wasted.' She looked at him doubtfully. 'I mean it,' he said, and remained standing implacably until she sighed and gave in, poured a second bowl of the soup, and brought it to the table. She sat, her cheeks flushed with consciousness, so he kindly turned his attention away from her and onto his plate, and resumed his dinner.

The soup was surprisingly good. As she had said, there was not much bacon in it, but there were onions and parsnips and pearl barley, and the whole was thickened with potatoes and flavoured with rosemary and thyme. 'How did you manage all this on the few pence I gave you?' he asked when the first pangs of hunger were dulled.

'I bought the bacon and onions and barley,' she said. 'Then I went for a walk up past the squire's house, and I found one of the gardeners turning out clamps, and he was throwing away the taters and parsnips that had gone mouldy. So I asked him and he let me have 'em, and I cut off the bad bits.'

He thought briefly of the kitchens at Morland Place and suppressed a smile. 'And the herbs?'

'I found them,' she said, her eyes down, veiled with curved, white lids like thick rose petals, and long dark lashes.

'Found them?' he said sternly.

'They was growing in a garden,' she said defensively, 'but I only took a bit that was sticking out through the palings into the street.'

'I hope nobody saw you,' he smiled.

'That's not stealing, is it, sir?' she asked. 'I thought if it was in the public highway —'

'I don't think you did any wrong, but I dare say the householders would think differently if they saw you. Better not do it again.'

'If I had a cutting or two, I could grow some herbs in pots on the window-sill. There's a nice, sunny one to this room. I need herbs to cook for you properly, sir.'

He felt touched and at the same time vaguely embarrassed by this, though he didn't quite know why. 'I wish you wouldn't call me sir,' he said at last, tackling the outward part of it.

The bright eyes were unveiled briefly. 'What am I to call you, then?'

'My name's Benedict.'

'I like that,' she said softly. 'It's a good name. Like a holy man.'

'There's nothing holy about me,' he laughed, but she didn't respond. He went on, 'Who taught you to cook, and about herbs and everything?'

'Mother did. *Her* mother was a farmer's wife, and taught her to do things tasty. Father – my own father – liked his grub too, and Mother made pies and puddings and stews and all. But my stepfather drank too much to know the difference. When a man's aled up he can't tell pig-swill from pea soup.'

'My father would never have believe women could cook at all.'

'Who fet his meals for him, then?' she wondered.

'Our cook was an old Frenchman – my uncle in the navy rescued him from France during the wars.

Her wide, bright gaze was fixed on him. 'Why, you must have been very rich folk, to have a French cook. Was your father a lord?'

'No, but my mother's a lady,' he said with a smile, and told her a little about Morland Place and his family.

'How sad you must be to have left it all,' she said.

'Yes, I miss it. It's a wonderful place.' He thought about Morland place often, especially in the drowsy moments before falling asleep at night; and he thought wistfully about his mother and Father Moineau. He avoided thinking about Nicky, for he was afraid of what resentment might betray him into supposing about his brother.

Oddly enough, he had hardly thought of Serena at all since the first few days on the road. She seemed remote now, a dream from another world, nothing to do with him any more – and impossible to imagine in the flesh when the reality which surrounded him was the mud and stone and metal, the sweating horses and navvies, the violent labour and harsh language of the railway workings. He felt bad that he had never written to her to tell her why he had left, but he hadn't known what to say, and he put it off day by day until it seemed pointless to write at all. She must have learnt from other sources by then why he had gone, and if he were not going to tell her the truth about it, it was better to leave well alone.

He had written to his mother to tell her that he was safe, but there had been no reply. He didn't know, of course, whether Nicky had allowed her to see the letter at all, or whether he had simply destroyed it; and when he wrote again, it was with that in mind. His letters had had to be circumspect to have any chance of reaching her, containing only the briefest outline of his life and his dutiful respects to her. But it was a thankless task, and aware of how even the most innocent of phrases could be misrepresented, he stopped after the third and did not write again.

Besides, what good would it do? He didn't suppose she really minded what had happened to him. When he had been at home, it had always been Nicky she loved; and in the last few months, since Papa died, she had hardly known he existed. It was better, he thought, to let sleeping dogs lie. He was making himself a new life away from Morland Place – a satisfying life – and there was no point in stirring up memories.

'I left under a cloud, as the saying is,' he said aloud at the conclusion of these thoughts. 'I wasn't wanted there, so it's best if I forget it all now.'

They finished their soup in silence. Fand came and sat beside him and put her head on his lap, and he stroked her ears absently while she beat a steady rhythm on the floor-boards with her muscular tail. Liza got up and cleared the table quietly, thinking he was absent in thought, but when she had finished he looked towards her and smiled and said, 'I was just wishing for some coffee. Never mind, next week we shall do better. We shall be beforehand with the world again.'

'Coffee?' she said wonderingly.

'Have you never come across it before?' he asked. 'Never mind, I can teach you how to prepare it.'

She hesitated, and then sat down again opposite him. He liked the straight way she sat, and the high way she held her head, which made her look almost queenly. There was a sort of fineness about her, he thought with a faintly surprised pleasure. There must be good stock in her bloodlines somewhere.

225

'Benedict,' she said, and his name spoken shyly by her made something inside him stir strangely. 'Can I ask you something?'

'Anything you like,' he said.

She took a moment or to assembly her words. 'Why are you doing all this for me?' she asked. 'I know Diccon fetched you out to me when I was sick, badgered you to come, most like – but why have you set me up here like this? Paying down good money to find me food and lodging. I don't understand. Why would you do it?'

He raised an eyebrow. 'That's a strange question.'

'No it's not,' she said. Her cheeks were flushed, but she went on determinedly, forcing herself to hold his gaze. 'You're a gentleman, and I'm just a common, ignorant girl. Why should you care about me? It seems to me that you're giving everything, and I've nothing to give you in return.'

'You've cooked this excellent soup,' he pointed out. 'And I can see you've swept the floor and made things nicer already.'

She shook her head, shaking away this suggestion. 'It's as if – as if I was a person like yourself, with the same right to be comfortable and decent and —' She put her hands to her cheeks. 'I'm not explaining it right, but you know what I mean. I owe my life to you, and now you're being so kind to me. Why?'

'To tell you the truth,' he said a little awkwardly, 'when I brought you to my lodgings I hadn't really thought what was to be done with you. I just had to get you inside, and it was the only place I could think of on the moment. But then everyone was so unkind to you, it made me angry. I knew what it was like to be unjustly condemned. It seems to me that we are like two strays cast out into the world. Why shouldn't we take care of each other, as friends do?'

Her embarrassment seemed to have faded. She looked at him steadily, and the slanting sunlight coming in through the window made her hazel eyes look almost gold. It reminded him suddenly of the fox he had seen in the moonlight all those years ago, which had looked up at him and exchanged a long gaze of recognition.

'Well,' she said slowly, 'I can cook and clean and wash. I

can be your friend. I can do that.'

He pushed Fand away and got up. 'I shall have to go back to work now, I'm afraid. But I think I know where I can lay my hands on couple of rabbits. If I bring them home tonight, can your roast them?'

'Aye,' she said, standing up too. 'That will make a grand supper, with roast onions and parsnips.'

'Yes,' he said, and suddenly thought how nice it would be to come back to a warm room and have his dinner cooked for him by Liza. How was it, he thought, that such simple things could suggest such pleasure? 'We could play cards afterwards. I have a pack amongst my things. Do you know how to play cribbage?'

'I only know Beggar Thy Neighbour,' she said with a shy smile.

'I'll teach you, then,' he said happily. 'I must go now. I'll see you tonight, then. Take care of yourself, Liza.'

'I will – Benedict,' she said.

'The benign shock seems to have worked very well,' Héloïse said to Lord Batchworth when he called at Hobsbawn House to return Fanny, whom he had taken out for a drive, in spite of the rain. Across the room Rosamund and Sophie were in conversation – or at least, Rosamund was talking while Sophie nodded encouragement from time to time.

'Do you think so?' Jes asked doubtfully.

'I see the difference,' Héloïse said. 'You must not expect too much too soon.'

'But she still looks so pale and uncomfortable. And still she never smiles, not even at my poor Fanny.'

'Not yet; but she is much better all the same. She is *here*, with us, not drifting far away; and every day she comes back a little more. I really think, now, that she will be well again one day. I was in doubt before.'

'I'm so glad,' Jes said. 'I'm very fond of Sophie.'

'I know; and I know how much you do for her,' Héloïse said.

'Not I any more: Henry Droylsden is taking over from me. He grasps everything so quickly! By the time I go back to London he will be in full charge; and I'm sorry to say I think

227

he will prove a better mill-master than ever I was! It's a good thing I have a new career in politics, or I should be hard put to it to keep my wife's respect.'

'When do you go back?'

'At the end of May.'

'Now that I see Sophie on the way to recovering, I begin to think I might go home too,' Héloïse said. 'There is so much to do there at this time of year, and my own work —'

At that point they were interrupted by Fenby, bringing a letter. 'For you, my lady,' he said, proffering it to Héloïse. She looked questioning. 'It came by a special messenger, my lady. He did not wait for a reply.'

Héloïse recognised Nicholas's hand on the cover, and excusing herself to the company, took it over to the table by the window and sat down to open it. Nicky's letter was brief.

Dearest Mama, the enclosed letter came for you today, and seeing from the handwriting that it is from my brother, I thought it best to send it to you directly, in case the matter should be urgent. I hope from my heart it does not contain bad news, or anything of a nature to upset you; but I would not for the world keep from you what is intended for your eyes. Everything here goes on well; I am taking care of everything and there is no need for you to hurry back. Ever your devoted, respectful son and servant, Nicholas.'

With trembling hands Héloïse lifted the letter which had been enclosed within the cover. It was directed to her, but there was no return direction: at the top it said only *Leicester, April 30th.* He did not mean to reveal his whereabouts, then. Disappointment, hurt, and a little thread of anger touched her. After so long, had he so little thought for her anxieties?

'*My dear Mother,*' said the letter, '*I write to you to let you know how I am going on, for little as I know you have ever cared for me, I suppose you will want to know that I am not disgracing the family name. I am glad to tell you that I have entered into the respectable apprenticeship of engineering, and hope to attain to such skills and knowledge as to be able soon to command the position of my choice. I have always been interested in railways, though I know you never understood my passion, and I am confident that there will be plenty of opportunities for me to advance myself in that field once I have finished my training. Then I shall command such salaries and dignities that I believe even you would not find contemptible, though you will think the sphere in which I earn them beneath you.*

'I have not written to you before because I knew you would be angry with me for leaving without your permission; and for the same reason I do not give my direction, in case you should try to force me to come back. I do not love Morland Place as my brother does. The country life is nothing to me. I could never have been content to be a squire, and happily leave all that to Nicky, who will do it very well. I mean to make my own way in my chosen profession, which I regard as infinitely superior to the condition of a mere landowner. I do not mean ever to come back to Morland Place. I shall become rich and famous, and you may hear of me one day in connection with some great undertaking or other; and then, through I was never dear to you, you may still be proud to speak of – Your son, Benedict Morland.'

The feelings with which she began to read were soon overcome by others – with pain, indignation, and bewilderment. He must be mad, was her thought on finishing the letter. How could he, if not mad, write such a letter – so arrogant, so cold, so careless of her feelings? It was not like him – it was not the Benedict she had known. But then, had she really known him? He had run away from home without a word to her, without even saying goodbye, and waited six months before even letting her know that he was alive and well. And this, all for the sake of becoming an engineer. How could that be so important to him – more important than mother, brother and home?

There was no word of regret in the letter, no word of love, only self-satisfaction, defiance, self-conceit. 'I do not love Morland Place' and 'mere landowner' and 'I do not mean ever to come back' and 'I shall become rich and famous'. Oh, this was no son of hers! He had been high-spirited, and got himself into pranks, and she had wondered sometimes that Father Moineau was not more worried about him. But she had never expected him to become such a stranger to her.

Suddenly she wanted to be home. She needed Morland Place, she needed her chaplain, she needed her dear son Nicky. Since James had died everything in her life seemed to be falling to pieces. She needed to get back to the one thing that stayed always the same: her home, her kingdom.

She looked up, seeing the others disposed about the room, politely ignoring her until she wanted their attention. She did not, most emphatically she did not, want to tell them what was in the letter! Benedict's shame was hers too, and she must bear it alone, for what he was, she had made him. Who else? No, she would tell no-one what was in that letter. She would tell them only that matters at Morland Place called her home, which was true. Sophie would be all right without her now, with Rosamund to take care of her. She wanted, with all the desperate ache of the bereaved, to go home.

CHAPTER THIRTEEN

It had been such a wet year – in some parts of Lancashire, 1831 was already the wettest in living memory – that a spell of hot, dry weather in August was doubly welcome. Grasscroft, the Earl of Batchworth's seat, was at its best, the park deeply green, dotted with handsome chestnuts and oaks in full leaf, the meadows gay with self-heal and shepherd's purse. An abundant harvest ripened in the sheltered upper fields, cut out from the shoulders of the moors; and the moors themselves basked in the sunshine under a blue sky just fretted with wisps of high cloud.

There was a place up on the moors, about eight miles from Grasscroft Hall, where a small hillock stood up from the rough sea of heather and bracken. It was covered in close emerald turf with a pile like velvet, and there was a grey rock outcrop at its crown. At its foot a brown stream cut deeply through the peat-layers, and fell over a stone lip with a pleasant small music, to make a pool where the sheep came down to drink.

Rosamund loved it up here, close to the sky, with no sound but the faint singing of the breeze against her ears. All around the bracken and heather stretched away in long folds of brown and rose-purple to the horizon. Far off to the north and east a smoke-blue smudge marked the line of the High Pennines; to the south and west every irregularity of the ground was marked out boldly with the indigo of its own shadow.

She was filled with a great, peaceful joy. The air was so clean it smelled of nothing at all; she breathed carefully, as though too much of it might kill her. The sunshine falling dazzlingly clean from the wide blue sky seemed to pass through her as though she were made of glass. When she tilted her head out of the stream of the wind for a moment, she could hear skylarks somewhere, faint with ecstasy as they pressed themselves up into the golden air. The baby lay quite still inside her for once, as if it were listening too, and she sent her thoughts to it: know this moment, remember it; for the whole of your life, know this place in your soul.

She seemed to have reached a fragile point of equilibrium. In six or seven weeks her difficult pregnancy would be over. For six months she had lived in fear, and as the moment of birth approached she would be afraid again. The labour had gone hard with her the first time, and there was no reason to suppose it would not be so again. She was afraid of the pain; afraid of dying; and Sophie's experience had shown that even at the last moment all might be lost. The baby might die. It might all be for nothing. But just for the moment it seemed that danger had turned its head and taken its eye off her. She leaned her back against the warm rock, her hands folded over the swell of the baby, and gazed out serenely at the world, revelling in the sense of ease.

Sophie sighed, and Rosamund turned her head slightly to look at her. Grasscroft had done Sophie good. She was looking a degree less weary and careworn; and the half-mourning of lilac muslin certainly suited her better than the dread black crape. Rosamund had bullied her gently into leaving it off, though it was a month early for the change. Sophie had been uneasy, but Rosamund had pressed it as being better for Fanny's spirits to see her mother's mourning lightened, and she had prevailed.

'How is it with you, Sophie?' she asked softly.

Sophie didn't answer for a moment. She went on staring out over the moors, and Rosamund went on looking at her. The deep lines of sorrow etched into her face made her look ten years older, though in fact she was a year the younger of the two. Her face was very thin, too, but there was a transparency about her which puzzled Rosamund. Some of the pain and discomfort of her bereavement had left her, certainly, but what had replaced it was not quite serenity, it was —'

'Better,' Sophie answered at last. 'I'm glad you persuaded me to come.'

'You should have come sooner,' Rosamund said. 'It wasn't good for you and Fanny to be shut up at Hobsbawn House all those months.'

'We weren't shut up,' Sophie said mildly. 'It's our home, just as it always was. We have to learn to live there without him, you know.'

'Do you still think about him often?'

'All the time,' Sophie said. She turned her head to look at Rosamund, and the sunshine, striking at her profile, made her eyes look transparent too. 'Did you think I didn't?'

'I don't know. It's so hard to know what other people feel, isn't it? However much I want to, I can't really know what you suffer.'

'No. I wouldn't want you to.' Sophie turned back to the moors. 'But then I can't know what it's like for you, to have a child you may never see.'

'Do you think this new baby will make it up to me?' Rosamund asked suddenly.

Sophie frowned. 'What an odd question. No. I don't know. I don't think it could, could it? Do you think it will?'

'No, but I think Jes does. He so very much wants me to be happy! And I think perhaps I *ought* to think that it will.'

'You're happy with him, aren't you?'

'Oh yes,' said Rosamund, and there could be no doubting it. 'I try to think how I would feel – if I lost him you know, as you —' She stopped, and then began again. 'I don't know how you bear it, Sophie.'

'I don't,' Sophie said. 'There is no bearing it. It just goes on.'

It wasn't what Rosamund wanted to hear, but she knew it was the truth. Grief was a fact, like pain, and there was nothing to be done about it. The best she could do was to distract the sufferer for a few months from time to time, until they either died or got better. But would Sophie get better? That transparency about her made Rosamund nervous. Could one recover from such a blow? But she had Fanny, Rosamund told herself; she must at least survive, for Fanny's sake.

Fanny was down below them now, at the foot of the hillock, playing with two of her cousins, Polly's third son Ashley, and

Roland's eldest, William who were both three years old. Rosamund had brought along a nurserymaid to take care of them, but it had not proved necessary. Fanny had taken complete charge of her small cousins. She had amused, instructed and entertained them with as much pleasure as if they had been her favourite playthings, and even now was gravely playing shop with them under the wheels of the phaeton, with stones for money and feathers, tufts of wool, flowers and moss for purchases. Their little darts of movement caught the eye now and then, and occasionally when the breeze dropped for a moment their high voices carried to the women sitting above them on the grassy mound.

'Fanny seems happier since she came here,' Rosamund said.

'I think she benefits from having the others to play with,' Sophie said. 'I'm afraid she has too little company at home.'

'I wonder that she didn't go with the others on the ride today, though. I'd have thought nothing would keep her from Jes's side.'

'I think perhaps she's feeling guilty,' Sophie said unemphatically. 'For being happy this last week or so. For beginning to forget her father.'

'It's natural she should. Five months is such a long time at her age.'

'Yes.' Down below in the play-shop, little Ashley Paston stood up too hastily and banged his head on the underside of the phaeton. His wails carried faintly up the hillock, but Fanny was bending over him before the maid could even rise from her place, and in a moment the grief subsided and he was trotting off to join his Cousin William in the search for moss-flowers. Nothing for her to do there. 'But she's a thoughtful child, and losing her father has changed her. I don't think she will ever be heedlessly merry again.'

'Everything's changed,' Rosamund said. 'And us most of all. I was listening to Thalia last night, chattering about her life in London, and it all seemed such a world away. Streets and hackney cabs and gas-lighting, theatres and balls and *ton* parties. Were we ever that young, Sophie?'

Sophie shook her head.

'Do you remember our coming-out ball?' Rosamund went

on. 'We knew nothing at all about what makes the world run, nothing about troubles and suffering. All we knew was that young men in red coats looked more handsome than in any other colour. How did we get from there to here?'

Sophie watched her daughter down below moving purposefully back and forth, organising the play, directing William to be the shopkeeper and Ashley the customer. The sun shone on her fair hair, for she had taken off her bonnet. Sophie felt a surge of love which was like sorrow. 'What will happen to her?' she said.

'To Fanny?'

'How will she grow up? The world is so full of troubles, and she's so very small.'

Rosamund wasn't sure what she was thinking. 'You'll take care of her, of course, as your mother did you. The world has always been a dangerous place.'

'Yes,' said Sophie. Then, 'If anything were to happen to me, you would look after her, wouldn't you?'

'Yes, of course,' Rosamund said, startled. 'But nothing is going to happen to you.'

Sophie turned to look at her seriously. 'All the same, there's only me now, and I have to think of it. If I were gone, I should want her to come to you. Promise me you'll take care of her.'

'Of course I promise,' Rosamund said. Sophie seemed satisfied, and turned away again, leaving Rosamund feeling unsettled, her contentment impaired, as though a shadow had passed over the sun. She shifted her position, feeling a little ache in her back. 'Do you know, all this fresh air is making me feel quite hungry. Shall we call the children, and see what's left in the picnic basket? They must have run themselves into an appetite by now.'

'Yes,' Sophie said obligingly, 'they ought to sit down and rest. Too much running about in the sunshine isn't good for them.'

Rosamund was sure the children would not agree with that, but she was also sure they would not object to being plied with patties and cold sausages and angel cake and raspberry tarts and junket from that capacious basket, in return for a little temporary restraint on their freedom.

The house party had been Jes's idea. The baby was to be born at Grasscroft, that was decided; and since Rosamund must be confined there not only for the birth but for some time beforehand, in order to be careful, Jes had made plans for her entertainment. Rosamund asked for Sophie and Fanny to be invited, but Jes had decided that all three of them needed company so as not to become mopish.

So by an exercise of personal charm close to alchemy he had somehow persuaded four extremely tonnish people to spend August hundreds of miles from any centre of fashion. True, he could offer superb shooting, interesting fishing, fine horses to ride, and a *chef de cuisine*, Monsieur Monsuchet, whose art was just coming into its peak of genius; but still Grasscroft was a great deal further north and east than any person of decided fashion was used to go.

Roland had not been so hard to persuade: after the birth of their third child in June – a boy they had called Titus – he was eager for Thalia to have country air and rest, even though to every eye but his she appeared bloomingly healthy and full of vigour. Thalia had conditioned that she would only go to such an out-of-the-way place if Cousin Polly would come too. Polly and her husband had already made their plans for Brighton; but the sudden death of Harvey, Marquess of Penrith, at the age of only forty-one, had not only saddened Polly, but had revived the scandal of his trial for murder and unpleasant gossip about his former relationship with her. It made it desirable to avoid any of the centres of fashion for the next few weeks, so a stay at Grasscroft, taking their four children to join Roland and Thalia's three, fulfilled all their requirements.

The means by which Polly's sister Africa and her husband had been persuaded to take their first holiday since their honeymoon eight years ago was to remain Lord Batchworth's secret, but they had added themselves and their boisterous twin boys to the party. They were all to stay for the whole month; and other guests from the country nearby were invited for shorter stays, or for dinner and evening parties, to vary the amusement.

Today the more active members of the house party had

gone out for a long ride over the moors to view a Roman fort and a waterfall – a twenty-mile point, with a picnic in the middle of the day, conveyed to a meeting place by grooms. Polly and Thalia had stayed at home with the babies; and so Rosamund and Sophie had driven up to the moors in the phaeton with Fanny, and the two little boys who were too young for a long ride.

In the evening, when the children had been swept off to the vast nurseries at the top of the house, the adults gathered in the drawing-room for their own enjoyments. Their numbers had been increased today by Henry Droylsden, and Prudence and Edwin Hastings, who had been invited down for a few days' rest from their toils.

Lord Batchworth brought a glass of champagne over to his wife. 'You missed a wonderful ride today, my poor girl,' he said. 'But your horse enjoyed it, which is something.'

'For shame! Don't torment her,' Africa said. 'It was very kind of you to let me ride Cedar, Rosamund. She went perfectly.'

'I'm glad to know she acquitted herself well. Parslow says she's too light in the hocks – calls her a park horse, if you please!'

'Parslow's right. She wouldn't do well over heavy ground, you know,' Jes said reasonably.

'Thank you, my love, but she suits me. We had a pleasant day too – and you notice that Fanny chose our company rather than yours! I think her passion for you is fading.'

'Just as well, I should have thought,' Africa said, taking a seat near Rosamund. 'With the new baby coming, she never would have kept the proud father's attention anyway.'

Rosamund chuckled. 'I wonder how long the new baby will keep his attention. He won't admit it, but he's on tenterhooks over whether it will get here before the Second Reform Bill goes up to the Lords.'

'It hasn't passed in the Commons yet,' George Paston pointed out. 'The vote will be taken in October, as I understand.'

'Oh, but it's bound to get past, don't you think?' Polly said. 'The Whigs have a bigger majority since the General Election.'

'Yes,' said Jes, 'and the Tories have had a clear warning from the country. Every single constituency that had a free vote in the General Election returned a reformist candidate, so they can hardly claim they don't know the mood of the people. I think there'll be enough Tory trimmers to shout down the die-hards. The Bill will get through the Commons, never fear. It's when it goes up to the Lords that the fun will begin.'

'Will it be a close-run thing, then, do you think?' Paston asked.

'On the contrary, I think will be soundly defeated. The bishops will all vote against it anyway, and as for the Tory lords —' He shook his head.

'Grey hardly modified the Bill at all, that's the trouble,' Rosamund said. 'There's been no real attempt to reconcile the opposition to it.'

'And what will happen if the Bill is defeated in the Lords?' Africa asked.

'There are only three possible courses of action,' Jes said. 'Either Grey will have to modify the Bill – which is what the King wants but Grey is dead set against; or Grey will have to resign and let the Tories put forward their own Bill – which is what Grey thinks must happen and the King is dead set against.'

'That's only two,' Polly objected.

'Yes, true,' Jes said with a smile, 'but the third possible course of action is something everyone is dead set against – in fact, they all declare it to be *im*possible, Whigs, Tories and the King.'

'But what is it? Don't be tiresome,' Africa demanded.

'The impossible possibility is for the King to create enough new peers of Whig persuasion to outweigh the natural Tory majority in the Lords.'

'Good God!' said Paston, looking shocked. 'He can't do that!'

'Surely you don't meant it?' Polly said. 'To humiliate the Lords like that? Surely the King would never agree?'

'Oh, the idea strikes such horror into everyone's hearts that Grey would never even ask it, still less the King grant it,' Jes said. 'That's why I left it out of the case.'

238

'It looks like another impasse, then,' Polly said. 'I don't see how you are ever going to get this Reform through.'

'Frankly, neither do I,' said Jes. 'But it must be done. We must find the way to do it.'

'There's comfort here for you, anyway, Rosamund,' Africa said. 'If the Bill is bound to be defeated in the Lords, it won't really matter whether Jes is there or not, will it?'

'There's my logical cousin!' Rosamund laughed. 'Now why didn't I think of that I must say I shall be glad if I can persuade him not to leave me. It's bad enough that you will all be going back to London for the Coronation next month, and I shall have to miss it.'

'From what I've heard, it won't be so very jolly,' Paston said. 'The King wants it done with as little fuss as possible, so there'll be no banquet or fireworks or anything of the sort – nothing like the sumptuousness of the last one.

Rosamund smiled. 'Mother said in her last letter that the entire expense is to be kept down to twenty thousand pounds, so perhaps Gunters will contract for the whole thing!'

'I should stay home if I were you, Batchworth,' said Paston.

'Oh, but it won't do to cut,' Africa said quickly. 'The poor King, it would hurt his feelings dreadfully! Some of the Tories are saying they won't attend – that horrid Robert Peel for one – and even Lord Wellington is being most ungracious.'

'Oh, don't worry, Jes wouldn't be so tawdry as to cut. Papa Danby would never forgive him if he let Billy down. He and Tom are both devoted to the King, because he's such a good old man.'

'He's not stupid, either,' Jes said. 'When Taylor told him about the Tories threatening to stay away, he cut them to size by saying that it would be quite convenient if they did – more room in the Cathedral, and less heat.'

'Well, he won't be inconvenienced by my presence, at any rate,' Rosamund said with a little sigh. 'But we shall have a celebration here for the tenants. One can't cheat them of one of their traditional opportunities to feast and get drunk.'

Prudence said, 'I know you don't mean it quite like that, but I wish you will not jest about drunkenness. It's the greatest evil that besets the lower orders.'

'My servants would not thank you for describing them so,' Rosamund said amusedly. 'And as for the tenants —'

'If you had seen the things Edwin and I see every day in Manchester – the desperate poverty, the children so dirty and neglected, the women so miserable – not to mention the violence and depravity – and all because the men will drink away all their wages, swilling themselves into insensibility every Saturday night.'

'That sort of thing has always existed,' Rosamund said. 'Even in the days before the factories. Sophie will tell you about the spinners and weavers who worked for her father in their own hones. They always liked to spend four days working their fingers to the bone so that they could spend three days drunk on the proceeds.'

'But drunkenness is getting worse,' Prudence insisted. 'With all these unlicensed beer shops that are springing up since the new act was passed – and the beer so dreadfully adulterated nine times out of ten! – there's temptation on every street corner, and no encouragement for any man to mend his ways and be prudent.'

'I thought the beer shops were a good idea,' Paston said mildly. 'Better for them than drinking gin all the time, isn't it? Beer's a very weak drink, after all, not like ale or spirits.'

'But it would be better for them not to drink alcohol at all,' Hastings said firmly. 'I'm afraid it's that which keeps them in poverty.'

'They can never get beforehand with the world when half or more of what they earn goes on drink,' Prudence said. 'I believe very firmly that Total Abstinence is the only way for them to better their condition. I addressed a meeting on the subject only last week, and the attendance was remarkable.'

Henry Droylsden joined in. 'I must say, that seems a bit hard on them, Pru,' he said lightly. 'The poor things have so little pleasure in their lives, I can't see why you want to rob them of the main one. And after all, they can't drink water, can they?'

'No,' Prudence said, 'and that's another worry, of course – the contaminated water supplies.'

'Well there's no need for us to worry about that now,' Rosamund said, tired of the trend of the conversation.

'We shall all have to worry about it soon,' Dr Hastings said gravely. 'I wonder none of you has mentioned the cholera yet, but you may take my word the newspapers will soon be full of it.'

'Cholera?' said Morpurgo. 'I heard that they had it in Asia, but surely that doesn't affect us?'

'We have no reason to be complacent,' said Hastings. 'It's spreading rapidly: Sicily, Sardinia, Corsica – they've had it in Marseilles since June, and there are cases as near as Brest and Rotterdam now.'

'I'd no idea it had come so close,' Henry remarked. 'I know Jasper was always saying we would have to worry about it one day, but —'

'Surely,' Rosamund said impatiently, 'we shall not have it in England?'

'We've had it before,' Henry pointed out. 'There was an outbreak in Manchester when I was a child. I think the Irish brought it in – or that's what was believed at the time.'

'It flourishes in the dirtiest and most overcrowded dwellings,' said Hastings, 'and the trouble is that there are always plenty of places like that in the great seaports. That's how it spreads: the sailors catch it, and carry it from country to country by ship. Then it spreads amongst the lower orders, especially the poorest.'

'Well there's still no reason to suppose it will come here, so I see no sense in being alarmed,' Rosamund said firmly.

'No-one wants to spread alarm, my dear Lady Batchworth,' said Hastings. 'In fact, with all the unrest in the country, it is most important not to upset the urban poor —'

'The urban poor?'

'Because it is very much their disease. We already have the rural poor rioting – no sense in inviting the urban poor to join them. But I will just mention, as we are all sensible people here, that the Government has had a Central Board of Health set up since June to decide what to do if the cholera does reach England. And it will be as well for us to have local plans ready against the eventuality, so that it does not take us by surprise. I need hardly remind you that Liverpool is a great seaport, and separated from Manchester by only a short distance.'

There was a silence at the end of this speech, which at last Rosamund broke.

'Well there's no need for us to think about it this very minute, is there? We have other plans to discuss of more immediacy – to wit, the possibility of having a dinner and ball next week. Jes and I have been fancying it. It will be moonlight all next week, and there are one or two families in the country that I should not be shamed to have you all meet. What do you think, Thalia? Polly? It would not be anything very great, but we are all pretty people, and we might sit down twenty to dinner and have ten or twelve couples to dance. What do you think to something quite informal and pleasant?'

The topic was taken up with interest, even by the Hastings. There were only two silent – Sophie, because she was thinking of other things, and Henry, because he was looking at Sophie.

The sunlight was cool and the morning dewy when Henry stepped outside. The sky was clear and pale, promising another hot day; the air smelled fresh; and the loudest sound was the call of a wood-pigeon from the dark, spread branches of a great cedar tree on the lawn. The only hint that it was almost September was an autumnal softness to the air; otherwise it might have been a midsummer morning.

Henry had had four days at Grasscroft this time. He was very grateful that Lord Batchworth invited him down so often, for otherwise he didn't know how he would have got through the time. He had got used, in the months since he had become her manager, to seeing Sophie almost every day, and he found that when he didn't see her, he grew anxious and restless. Being here at Grasscroft with her and Fanny had been a delight, albeit in some ways a painful one. Nothing could be kinder than the way the Batchworths treated him, but he could not but be aware of the awkwardness of his position.

A crunching of gravel announced the arrival of Lord Batchworth, coming round the house from the stables. He stopped before Henry, squinting into the sunlight. 'You're out early,' he said. 'It's a wonderful morning, isn't it?

Aylesbury and Paston and I are going to take guns out in the park today. Can I tempt you to join us?'

'I wish I might,' Henry said, 'but I'm rather afraid I must go back to Manchester.'

'You're leaving us?'

'I wish I were not,' he said, 'but I have been here so long already —'

'If it seems so very long, I won't argue with you,' Jes grinned. 'I'm sorry your time has been passed so tediously!'

'You know that to be impossible! I'm more grateful than I can say for your hospitality, and I'd gladly stay twice as long; but I ought to go back and see how things are at the mills. I must not neglect Mrs Hobsbawn's business, and there will be many small matters which need my attention.

'Well, I won't attempt to argue with you. You must know best. but I shall be sorry to see you go. We all will. Especially Mrs Hobbawn,' he added.

Henry was too old to blush, but he felt uncomfortable. 'I don't – why do you say so?'

Jes moved a little to get the sun out of his eyes, so that he could examine Henry's face. 'Have I spoken out of turn? I'm sorry. I thought I detected a distinct partiality for you in her manner.'

Henry examined the gravel. 'Mrs Hobsbawn is in mourning.'

'True. But mourning is not the same as insensibility.' Henry had nothing to say to that. 'You have taken over the running of the business and relieved her of all worries and responsibilities. I'm sure she is very grateful, and gratitude, you know —'

He was not allowed to finish what was hardly likely to have been a proper piece of logic. Henry looked up quickly. 'Gratitude can have no part in it. I am employed as her manager. She pays me a handsome salary for taking care of her business; and do you think I would do less than my best, whoever was paying my wages?'

'I didn't mean to offend you, my dear fellow,' Jes protested. 'Would I have asked you to take on the work and the worry if I didn't think you were the best man for the job?'

'I'm sorry. I'm absurdly touchy on the subject,' he

243

acknowledged. 'But it is the *devil* of a situation!' he burst out as if against his will.

Jes eyed him with sympathy, understanding a great deal more after these few exchanges. At last he said, 'Shall we understand each other? I do not mean to be impertinent, but I have a strong interest in the welfare of Sophie and Fanny; and I have a great liking and respect for you.'

'Thank you,' said Henry.

'And I know that you do a great deal more for Sophie than simply run Hobsbawn Mills. I have kept a weather eye on her affairs ever since Jasper died, and Sophie tells Rosamund more than perhaps she is aware of. You have advised her and helped her in so many ways, taking Jasper's place in the sense of —'

'I could never take his place,' Henry interrupted, looking rather glumly at his boots.

Jes tried again. 'Poor Jasper is more than six months' dead. I know that that is a very short time to be getting over the shock of his death, but for Fanny's sake as well as her own, Sophie must not shut herself up for ever.' Henry looked up. 'The difficult and delicate problem is that Sophie is a very wealthy woman. She is also extremely innocent and vulnerable.'

Henry looked indignant. 'If you think that I would ever dream —' he began hotly.

Jes held up a hand, smiling. It was exactly the reaction he had got from Jasper in the same situation. What was it about Sophie, he wondered, that provoked such old-fashioned chivalry in her admirers?

'Indeed, I hope you would dream!' he said. 'Sophie and Fanny need a man to take care of them and keep the wolves of this wicked world from eating them up, and frankly, Henry Droylsden, there is no-one I would sooner see them entrusted to than you. Much as I liked Jasper, I have to confess that he was sometimes too unworldly for his family's good. I think you would take better care of them than he did.'

Henry looked at him for a moment, and then sighed. 'May I speak to you frankly?'

'Please do. Shall we walk as we talk? The sun is growing hot.'

They turned and walked side by side along the paved walk and down the shaded side of the house, and Henry told Jes of his feelings.

'I think I must always have loved her, but of course she was another man's wife. I was allowed to run tame in their house, and she was kind to me, and laughed at my jokes, and treated me like a favourite brother, and I loved her, I thought, like a sister. But since Jasper died, I've seen her very differently. It's as though a veil has been lifted from my eyes. I would die to serve her. But it's hopeless. I talk of Jasper dying, but in her own eyes she's still a married woman. I don't think that will ever change.'

'It already has,' Jes said. 'I see a difference in her. Day by day she comes back a little from the brink. She needs you to make sure that she does come back completely. Sophie is not a woman to live happily without a husband; and I have seen the way she turns to you, not just for advice but in all the little, conversational ways a woman turns to her husband. You are halfway there, man. Patience will see it through – patience and perseverance.'

Henry was silent a moment. 'But what am I to do?' he asked at last.

'What are you to do? Why, court her, of course.'

'But how can I?'

'*How* must be according to your own taste. With song, with poetry, with flowers – with taste and delicacy, I'm sure – with passion I hope —'

'You know what I mean,' he said despairingly, and spread his arms. 'Look at me! I have nothing but the salary *she* pays me. I am her employee. I have nothing and she – as you have pointed out – is a wealthy woman.'

'You have everything she has not – worldly wisdom, strength, courage – and much she needs besides – tenderness, warmth, disinterested love. If you are such a muffin as to be put off by a difference in your fortunes, I despair of you!' He stopped and turned to face his companion seriously. 'Truly, I understand and honour your compunction, but I am very sure it is not appropriate in this case. Sophie and Fanny need you far more than you need them. A lesser man would be deterred by the consideration of Sophie's wealth, but I think

245

you have enough greatness of soul to put that aside, and endure the shame of having a rich wife, for the greater good of her happiness.'

'Do you think so?'

'I know so! Must you really go back to Manchester this morning?'

'I'm afraid I must,' Henry said, frowning.

'And when could you return?'

He smiled suddenly, lighting his rather thin face in a most attractive way. Jes could see no reason why Sophie should not fall victim to his charms. 'If there is nothing seriously amiss, I could do all I needed to in a day.'

'Excellent man. Then you might do the round trip, you know, tomorrow. It is not above fifteen miles – two hours on a good horse will do it. I will lend you a good road horse from my stables; and you may repeat the trip as often as you think it necessary.'

'You are very kind,' said Henry.

'Not at all. Sophie stays for a few weeks more, but the rest of the party will soon be going back to Town, as you know, so we shall be in particular need of your company.'

'I don't know why you should go to so much trouble to help me,' Henry said rather shyly.

'Oh, I'm a great romantic, that's all,' Jes said cheerfully. 'And besides, I really cannot go on worrying about Sophie and Fanny as well as my own wife and child. I look forward with keener pleasure than you can imagine to handing that responsibility over to you.'

246

CHAPTER FOURTEEN

Rosamund was standing in the middle of her bedchamber, her eyes dilated with fear, when Sophie, summoned by a breathless maid, hurried in.

'What is it?' she searched her cousin's face. 'Is it —?'

Moss spoke for her. 'It seems that way, ma'am. Started this morning as soon as my lady woke up.'

Rosamund found her voice suddenly. 'I thought it was just gripes, from the grouse last night. I did eat rather too much supper.' She grimaced, and Sophie didn't know whether it was with pain, or in self-reproach.

'It may be nothing,' Sophie said, wanting at all costs to comfort her. 'It might be gripes. Or there are such things as false pains, you know. Polly said she had them with little Ashley.'

Moss caught her eye and shook her head minutely. Rosamund had been staring ahead with a look of inner preoccupation, but now she turned to Sophie.

'It's too soon,' she said. Her voice was despairing. 'Oh Sophie, what shall I do?'

Sophie tried hard to be calm and practical, though her heart was fluttering with anxiety. Given her own recent experience, she was the last person to reassure with any confidence. Rosamund had always been the strong one, the one in command; but now she had turned to Sophie, and Sophie must not fail her.

'If you are sure the baby is coming, then the first thing to do is to get you into bed, and to send word for the midwife or the physician or whoever was to attend you.'

'Jes had it all arranged,' Rosamund said, her voice hardly

247

more than a whisper, as though she were afraid a loud voice might dislodge something. 'The accoucheur was to come at the end of September – Jes invited him to stay for the shooting, so that he would be on hand all the time. He won't come now. He'll have other cases to attend. And Mother was to come for a month, but she'll be at Wolvercote now – too far away to get here in time. Oh Sophie, all Jes's careful plans come to nothing! All my fault!'

'Now, my lady,' Moss said sternly. 'Don't you start fretting yourself into a state. That won't do the baby any good, will it?'

'No use to soothe me like a child. I know it's too early. I've failed him.'

'Moss is quite right,' Sophie said as firmly as she could. 'Failed him, indeed! That's silly talk. The Duke of Wellington never talked about defeat, did he? What would he think of you if he could hear you now?'

'The Duke? Oh Sophie!' Rosamund laughed – an unwilling, quavery sort of laugh, but better than tears at any rate.

'That's right. You let Moss put you to bed, and I'll find out who is the best person to send for. Don't worry, dear Rosamund! We have a house full of mothers, after all. You won't come to any harm.'

Rosamund seemed about to refute the last statement, but a pain took her, making her grunt and double up. Sophie hurried to her side, and she and Moss edged her to the bed and sat her down. A line of sweat had appeared along Rosamund's upper lip. Moss sought Sophie's eyes over her mistress's head.

'If you was to send word for old Nanny, ma'am, she and I can take care of my lady while you speak to his lordship about the midwife. And there's a suit of childbed-linen and various other things laid by, which the housekeeper knows about, if word could be passed to her to send them up with one of the nursery-floor housemaids.'

'Yes, of course,' Sophie said. 'I'll do that at once.' She glanced at her cousin, and Rosamund deliberately unlatched the hand that was clutching Sophie's and released her.

'Come back afterwards,' she said tersely.

'I'll send for Mrs Hobsbawn all right, when we've got you

settled, my lady,' Moss said firmly.

Sophie took her cue and hurried away. Once outside the bedchamber her worries felt licensed to run loose and torment her. It was the 31st of August, and the baby was coming four or five weeks early. That was not good, especially given Rosamund's previous history of miscarriage.

First her own baby, now Rosamund's! The darker part of her mind hunted at inexplicable patterns of sorrow; curses and black pursuing shadows. Had Marcus, in his agony, let them loose like bats to flutter down at last and punish his wife and her seducer, blight their house and their line? Sins were sometimes punished here on earth. Her mother would not have it so, but Sophie knew it was true.

She wished Maman were here now to help her; or Aunt Lucy. Someone to take the responsibility from her. She was so weak and helpless. She had always depended on Maman; and then afterwards on Jasper. Jasper! She suddenly wanted him so badly that she had to stand still and let the pain wash over her; wanted him so badly that she thought she saw him standing at the end of the passage. She put out her hands to him instinctively, tears rising to her eyes as the sense of loss came to her again, with the awful, untiring freshness that made her wonder if she could ever be free of it, no matter how long she lived.

But it was not Jasper, it was Henry Droylsden, pausing on his way downstairs as he saw her coming towards him: kind Henry, who took care of her business for her, and made difficult things sound simple; ordinary, familiar Henry, with his pale face and twisted leg, and his clever hands that could draw music out of a fiddle. They were strong hands, and they caught hers and seemed to bear her up as she swayed dizzily.

'Sophie, what is it? You're trembling!'

'Oh – oh please – don't stay me. I must find Lord Batchworth at once!' She felt guiltily glad of his support, longed, absurdly, to throw herself into his arms and let him take over all her burdens; but there were things she must do. People were relying on her.

'Yes, of course. We'll go downstairs and find him, but let me help you. I'm afraid you're ill.'

'No, not ill, only distressed.' She leaned gratefully on his arm and let him escort her down the stairs, for her legs felt strangely weak. 'The housekeeper, too – I must send a message to her. And Nanny. Oh, why is there no servant about?'

'We'll find one. Don't be afraid,' Henry said soothingly. 'But can't you tell me what's happened?'

'It's Rosamund – she's gone into labour,' Sophie blurted out, oblivious for the moment of Henry's status as an unmarried man – and not even a relative. 'It's too early! Oh Henry, the baby will die!' The tears spilled over, and she gasped, trying to catch herself back from the brink, because now was not the time to break down. As if by magic, Henry's handkerchief appeared in her hand as it rose uncertainly to her face, and she blotted her tears on it gratefully.

'Oh my darling, don't cry!' he said. 'Everything will be all right. Babies do come early, don't they? I'm sure it will be all right.'

But Sophie's momentary lapse of control was over. With a sense of new shock which she had not yet the leisure to account for, she finished drying her eyes and blew her nose briskly as they reached the bottom of the staircase; and there she saw with relief that Raby, the butler, was in the hall, arranging the newly-arrived letters and newspapers on a salver.

Sophie let go of Henry's arm and hurried forward. 'Oh Raby, where is Lord Batchworth?'

Raby turned with stately slowness. 'His lordship is not in the house, madam. He and Lord Aylesbury and Mr Paston took guns out into the park.'

'He must be sent for at once,' Sophie said decisively. 'Please send someone to bring him back, and tell him that her ladyship needs him urgently.'

'Yes, madam,' said Raby automatically, though his eyebrows were rising.

'And please also send word to Nanny to go immediately to her ladyship's bedroom; and tell the housekeeper that the special linen and other things are required at once. A housemaid is to take them up. She will know who to send.'

'Certainly, madam,' said Raby. His eyebrows were back in place, his face composed: he had put two and two together.

The only sign of his emotions was a tiny shake of the head as he went away, covering the ground briskly though he did not appear to be hurrying. He had been in the Farraline family's service for two generations and had been hoping devoutly to make it three. He had been deeply concerned when his lordship had married a lady not in the first flush of youth, and his concern had grown year on year as there was no sign of an heir. He did not want his lordship to be the last of his line; and he and the other older servants had been all but holding their breath ever since it became known that her ladyship was increasing at last.

And now, he thought bitterly, it seemed as though it would come to nothing after all. Her ladyship was thirty-four years old, and as far as childbearing was concerned that meant she was at her last prayers. He had grown attached to her in the last few years, but he could not help the thought passing through his mind that it would be no bad thing if she were to perish in childbed, leaving his lordship free to contract a new union.

Except, of course, he reminded himself even more bitterly, that his lordship was so devoted to her ladyship that he would probably refuse to marry again if she died. He'd become a recluse and shut up the house and probably go into a decline; so they had all better redouble their prayers for a happy outcome.

Jes burst into the house looking almost wild. He had outstripped both his guests and the servant who had been sent for him by several minutes. Raby was hovering in the hall, waiting for him.

'Raby, is it true? How is she? What has been done?'

'Well, my lord —'

But Raby had no chance to say more, for Polly came on the scene at that moment. 'There you are! Yes, I want to speak to you. Come upstairs!'

She thrust her arm through his and walked him away. In an impatient undertone he said, 'You needn't be at such pains to be discreet! Raby must know perfectly well by now what's going on – which is more than I do at this moment. For God's sake, Polly —!'

251

'Hush! Do try to be calm. You must have guessed that Rosamund has gone into labour, of course; but nothing has happened yet.'

'It's too early! Oh God, she may die! Please don't let her die! Polly, what's been done? Tell me at once!'

'Moss and Nanny have put her to bed,' Polly said quickly. 'And your housekeeper told us that there is a physician down in the village – a Doctor Fairford – who has attended here from time to time in the past, so we sent off a servant to fetch him.'

'Fairford? Yes, he came once when Kit had a fall; and my mother used him for the servants. But I made arrangements with an accoucheur. And a month-nurse was to come.'

'Yes, well the accoucheur is in London and the month-nurse is still with her previous case, according to what I understand, so they will be no help to us in the present case,' Polly said briskly. 'Raby tells me that Fairford has attended lots of births in the village and surrounding farms, so he is no tyro.'

'Farmer's wives, yes, and the publican's widowed sister, but —'

'Well, we're all made the same way when it comes down to it. Now Jes, do calm yourself, smooth your hair, and straighten your neckcloth. Your wife wants to see you as soon as you come in, and you won't do her a bit of good if you alarm her.'

'Very well,' he said, taking a deep breath. He turned to face Polly. 'Just tell me truthfully how bad it is.'

Polly tried to smile reassuringly, but didn't quite manage it. 'Jes, my dear, we don't know yet. It has begun like an ordinary labour, but it is early, you know that.'

'Five weeks too early; and no-one on hand to help her!'

'I wouldn't say that, precisely,' she said drily. 'There are four women in the house who have all given birth themselves; and Nanny has assisted at two – yours and your brother's. And Doctor Fairford will be here soon. Everything that can be done is in hand. Now go and comfort your wife, and be cheerful. She needs to feel that you are not afraid of the outcome.'

'Yes,' said Jes. 'I understand. But oh, Polly, if I should lose her —!'

'You won't,' Polly said firmly laying a hand on his arm. She was far from confident, but she could not do less for him than he must do for Rosamund.

He seemed to understand what she was about, for he straightened his shoulders with determination. 'Who is with her?'

'Moss and Nanny, as I said. And the housemaid, Hetty, for running messages. And Sophie, of course.'

'Sophie?'

Polly shrugged. 'I would willingly have taken her place, of course, but it was Sophie she wanted, so we thought it best to humour her.'

Jes hurried upstairs, pausing only before a looking-glass on the half-landing to straighten his appearance and compose his expression. At the top of the stairs he found Henry Droylsden sitting patiently on a small, hard chair, his hands clasped between his knees, staring at the carpet. He looked up as Jes reached him.

'Nothing seems to have happened yet,' he said in answer to Jes's unspoken question. He glanced down the passage towards the fatal door. 'I wish it didn't have to be Sophie, but I suppose she'd worry more if she weren't there.'

'You shouldn't be here,' Jes frowned. 'But I suppose *you'd* worry more if you weren't.' Henry made a helpless gesture, like a shrug, and Jes dismissed him from his mind and walked on. The baby he had likewise dismissed. Sad though it was, he had already parted with it before he even entered the house: it had never really existed for him, except as a distant hope, almost a dream. It was only his wife who concerned him now; and the deep, black terror existed in his mind that he was going into that room to say goodbye to her. It was not a conscious thought – he would not allow it to be – but it was there all the same, hidden, like a weak place which might at any moment give way under his foot and send him screaming down into a bottomless pit.

Sophie thought it would have been easier if Rosamund had made more noise. 'Don't try to be brave,' she said as she bent over her to wipe the sweat from her brow. 'Scream if you like.'

But Rosamund only shook her head. Nothing escaped her clenched teeth except an occasional groan. Sophie held one of her hands and Moss the other, and between those outposts of feeling she lay alone, cut off like a besieged city, isolated by her travail. Jes had been and gone. She had wanted him terribly at first, but now he seemed apart from her, not concerned with the struggle that absorbed her. She was glad to know that he was nearby: if the time came for her to die, he could be fetched in a moment.

Now it was just her and the pain, and the kind watchers who stood guard over her: Moss and Sophie; old Nanny in the background, hoping for a new baby for her nursery – hoping but not expecting; and the doctor. He was in the background too, there in case of need. Sometimes he came and laid his hands on her, spoke to her encouragingly, and then stepped back. She didn't mind having him there. She liked him – he had a kind, simple face – but she didn't think he could help. She knew without having the words said that they had all given up the baby. It would die – perhaps was dead already. The only question in the mind of the watchers was whether she would die too.

It was in her mind; and she had seen it reflected in Jes's eyes as he bent over her to kiss her. *Kissing me goodbye*, she had thought. I'm sorry Jes, I'm so sorry. I brought you nothing but sadness. No heir, no son – now not even a wife. He had gone away to wait somewhere until they brought him the news. At first she had been able to feel his presence, somewhere out there in the house; but now it had faded. Now there was only her.

Oh it was a bitter thing to die! And lonely – she was so lonely! Sophie and Moss were a thousand miles away on either side of the bed, cut off from her in the place of the living, where she now had not right to be. She was in an in-between place, a vestibule between life and death, waiting for the word to come which way she was to go: back into the sunlight, or on into the darkness. She could see it out of the corner of her eye, the darkness – though when she turned her head it was only the curtains and the bedpost. Her little baby had already gone into the darkness; poor little mite, she hoped it would not be afraid. I'm sorry, she whispered to it;

I tried to give you life, but I couldn't.

Harder to think of the others, all those others she had denied life to, condemned to the darkness without mercy. Oh, that had been wicked! It was why she was being punished – she understood that now.

'All the souls,' she said. She could see them gathered reproachfully in the darkness, little, shadowy, pathetic things; waiting for her to join them. 'My fault, all my fault.'

Sophie saw her lips moving, and bent closer. 'What is it, Ros? What do you want?'

'My fault. I denied them.'

'Denied who, dearest?'

'I'm being punished. Deserve it.' A dry tongue to moisten dry lips. 'All the babies —'

'Oh my lady,' Moss said, putting her hand to her mouth.

'I killed them. Denied them life. Oh, so wicked! Killed so many —'

Horror took hold of Sophie as she understood what was being said. It couldn't be true! Not Rosamund? Oh surely, surely – 'No, Ros,' she said, appalled. 'Don't tell me any more.'

But the dreary whisper went on. 'It's my punishment. A life for a life. All the babies —'

Sophie could only shake her head wordlessly. But the black, batwing curses flapped closer. She dared not look up in case she saw them, but she felt the oppression of them, gathering around the bed. Not sent from Marcus, then, but let loose by Rosamund herself! No, no, that was terrible thinking, wrong thinking – ungodly, pagan, forbidden. She felt the blackness filling her mouth and nose and eyes. No! It was not like that! There was a merciful God, a sunlit world, order, kindliness, forgiveness. Maman, pray for me! Pray for us! Sweet Jesu, sweet Mother Mary, keep the dark things at bay! *Give us light*!

The doctor's voice broke through her frenzied thoughts: calm matter-of-fact, supremely ordinary. 'Now then, what have we here? Well, well, I think things are happening at last. That's the way, now, mother! Soon have you more comfortable.'

Rosamund's eyes, dilated in her pale face, sought his.

'What is it?' she whispered. She had felt a change come over her, a loosening, as though the stuff of her were unravelling. Was it time then? 'Am I dying?'

'Dying, pooh pooh! What sort of talk is that? The baby's coming, that's all!'

'Coming now?' Rosamund repeated faintly.

'That's right, and I shall need all your efforts to help me, so just keep your mind on the job in hand, if you please, mother, and don't let it wander where it has no business. Come, nurse, we shall want you now.'

Sophie found herself pushed aside by the bustling doctor, and was glad to yield her place to him, feeling weak and shaken by the almost supernatural experience she had had. Rosamund moaned. On the other side of the bed, Nanny had supplanted Moss, her wrinkled old face tense with vicarious effort as she pushed and grunted along with her mistress. At the foot of the bed the commonplace little doctor with the calm, steady eyes might have been a farmer helping a ewe to yean. His words were few and comfortable. He made no distinction for Rosamund's rank, but that was comforting too.

Sophie prayed. She had closed her eyes, and she missed the moment: knew only that there was a strange cry from Rosamund, startled but unimportant as if she had tripped on something and almost fallen; and then a loud sigh from Nanny; and the doctor's voice saying, 'Well, now, well now.' And a while later, 'It's a boy after all. No, no, mother, you lie still. You shall see him by and by. You still have work to do.'

Sophie opened her eyes at last to see the doctor wrapping something in the cloth Moss had handed to him, and pain struck her to the heart as she realised the baby hadn't cried. Tears welled helplessly, burning her eyelids. Even though they had long expected that it would not survive, it was still a dreadful blow, and doubly agonising to her, who had lost her own just this way, at the last moment. Angry with herself, she pushed the pain aside: it was Rosamund who mattered now. Crying wouldn't help her.

'Is there anything I can do?' she asked. From the corner of her eye she saw Moss wrap the thing close and take it away, to deposit it tenderly on a chair in the corner of the room. It was nothing now, no more than a stillborn lamb, which had carried the hope and love of so many all these months.

'Just hold mother's hand,' the doctor replied, 'and jolly her along. We've a little bit to do, haven't we, mother? That's right, that's right.'

His voice was cheerful and his hands steady, but his eyes were grave, and looking across at Nanny, Sophie saw the old woman's lips trembling: no new baby for her nursery now, only all this pain for nothing, sadness, loss. She understood none of what followed, only that there was a fight to be won for Rosamund's life; that the shadows had not been satisfied with one little soul. There was a bigger prize yet, and they were hungry for it.

Rosamund opened her eyes and looked up at Sophie. 'Is the baby all right?' she whispered.

Sophie struggled for her voice. 'Yes,' she said.

'A boy,' Rosamund said wonderingly. Then, 'Am I going to die?'

'No, of course not,' Sophie said. And she pressed her friend's hand tightly, knowing that both answers were false, and that lies were all she had to offer her now.

Was it an hour later, or two, or more? The doctor finally straightened his back and wiped the back of his bloody hand across his brow. 'Well, well,' he said softly, 'we have her now, I think. She's back on our side of the river. It was a bonny fight she gave us, but we have her.'

Sophie looked at Nanny, who was crying, and Moss, who was sagging with weariness, and then back to the doctor. 'You mean – she'll live?'

He smiled suddenly, and Sophie wondered how she could have thought him commonplace. 'I think there's a very good chance of it. But we must watch her closely, or she may still give us the slip.'

'Thank you, doctor,' Sophie said at last. 'We all owe you more than we can say.'

'Why, bless you, I didn't do anything,' he said kindly. 'It was the mother herself. She made up her mind to come back, that's all.'

'It's a miracle,' Moss said in a dead voice.

257

'No, no, nothing but hard work,' said the doctor. 'Now shall we just get her tidied up, and then someone can go and tell the husband.'

'His lordship,' Moss said, turning stricken eyes on Sophie. 'I'd forgotten for the moment.' Who was going to tell him the news: his child dead, his wife still in danger?

'I'll do it,' Sophie said. She felt exhausted. She did not have to go and tell Jes that Rosamund was dead. No joy, only the absence of the worst grief. It was hard to feel anything as strong as gratitude for that. Almost without knowing what she was seeing, she watched Nanny walk across to the chair where the poor little bundle was lying and bend over it. She was too tired even to feel grief for Rosamund's dead child.

Then Nanny said, 'Doctor!' in a strange voice. She straightened up, bringing the white bundle to them. Sophie didn't want to look, but she was too tired to move her eyes away. Nanny came close to the doctor and drew aside the cloth, and Sophie's heart lurched painfully. Oh such a little baby, so small and pathetic, too small ever to have had a chance! Its marbled flesh was still daubed with the birth stains. Why did Nanny expose it so? Oh cover it up, lay it aside decently, treat it with a little pity!

'Look,' Nanny said – unnecessarily, since they were all looking. And then Sophie saw the tiny hands make a grasping movement, as though trying to find something to hold on to. She stared, her eyes stretching so wide she could feel the touch of air of them. The hands moved again. She hadn't imagined it. The baby was still alive!

The doctor's voice was as calm as ever. 'Now that *is* a miracle,' he said.

It was Sophie who laid the tiny thing in Jes's arms. Nanny had washed it and wrapped it warmly, and it was still clinging to life – but by what a frail grasp!

'My son,' he said. His lips tried to smile, but did not quite manage it. His first child, and perhaps his only child: little as he knew about such things, he did not need to be told how unlikely it was to live. Yet as he looked down into the strangely undistinctive features, he felt the little thing knotting itself tightly into his fabric, taking hold of him in a way that made him feel weak with terror and love. If it died – when it died – it would tear part of him away with it, and he was not sure he would be able to survive such a wound.

Seeing his face, Sophie offered to take the baby away for him, but he held it closer in an automatic gesture of defence. 'How is Rosamund?'

'Very weak and tired. She has lost a lot of blood. But the doctor is hopeful that she will be all right.'

'Has she seen the baby?'

'Not yet. She doesn't know how weak it is.'

'I'll show him to her,' Jes said.

The doctor, who had been washing his hands, joined them. 'You'll need a wet-nurse,' he said without preamble. 'The mother will be too weak to nurse her child. As it happens, there is a respectable woman in the village – a Mrs Stanton – whom I delivered last week, who ought to have enough milk for two. If you like I can ask her for you.'

'Yes, please,' Jes said. 'But I can't let him go away: she must come up here. Offer her whatever she asks for. She must come right away.'

'I'll see what I can do,' Fairford said.

Jes looked up. 'She must come,' he said fiercely. 'My baby *must* live.'

Fairford shook his head. 'You must not be too sanguine. I would not have you hope for too much. You must understand that there is still danger attending the mother, and as for the child —'

Jes gave a strange, grim smile. 'And you must understand that I can have nothing to do with your fears. I thank you from the bottom of my heart for what you have done, Fairford, but you must take it from me that they will both survive.'

Fairford smiled. 'Have it as you please. Faith can work miracles – and happiness can heal. Go and speak to your wife, sir, and put your heart into her!'

A screen had been placed round one side of the bed to keep the light and the draught from Rosamund. Jes handed the baby to Sophie, who followed him round the screen and stood a little back as Jes leaned over his wife. She seemed to be sleeping, and he was shocked at how white and exhausted she looked. The loss of blood had left her skin transparent;

the shadows under her eyes were like bruises. Her face was drawn into planes which were emphasised by the low and sidelong light, and he saw in that moment how she would look when she was old. He loved her absolutely. He did not need to be told how nearly he had lost her: he saw it in the weariness of her face, even in sleep.

He would have withdrawn without speaking but she opened her eyes just then, and looked at him. Her expression did not alter, but she looked at him. He stooped and kissed her pale, damp cheek. 'Hullo,' he said. 'Welcome back, my wife.'

'Jes,' she said. She seemed a little confused. 'What time is it?'

'Almost five.' The information did not appear to convey anything to her. He went on conversationally, giving her time to me back into herself. 'It's been a long day, and I'm unaccountably hungry. At the risk of shocking your Cousin Polly, I shall order dinner to be put forward to six. I'd like it now, but Monsuchet would probably leave me if I asked him. He's promised us Davenport chicken tonight, and turbot in a champagne sauce. I hope you have an appetite – you've worked hard enough for it.'

The shadow of a smile touched her mouth at last. 'Foolish,' she murmured. Then, 'Have you seen the baby?'

'Yes, my love. A boy. How remarkably clever of you to manage a boy first time!'

But her eyes were anxious. 'It didn't cry. I didn't hear it cry.' She wet her lips. 'The baby died, didn't it?'

The courage of the question made him feel absurdly tearful. 'No, my darling, he didn't die.'

'You can tell me,' she said. 'I know it was too soon. It had no chance.'

He bent to kiss her again while he regained command of his voice. 'The baby didn't die, my foolish love. I've brought him to see you, Look!' He turned and took the baby from Sophie, and laid it gently in Rosamund's arm, turning back the shawl from the tiny sleeping face so that she could see it. 'There. Our son.' He wanted to say more, to be reassuring, but the expression on Rosamund's face, so closely mirroring the love and pain and fear and joy which were crowding his own heart, made it impossible for him to speak.

At last she said, 'He's so small.'

'He'll grow,' said Jes.

She looked up into his eyes. '*Will* he?'

He couldn't lie to that look, any more than he could give voice to the truth. Instead he said, 'We must think of a name for him – a grand, noble name, suitable to the future twelfth Earl of Batchworth. Of course he takes my cadet title, so he's already Baron Blithfield, you know!'

A little laughter spurted out of her. 'Baron Blithfield!'

'It does seem absurd, doesn't it, for such a tiny scrap? Let me take him from you, darling. Sophie's aching to hold him.' She yielded up the baby and Sophie took him away. Jes possessed himself of her hands, noticing anxiously how cold they were. 'Now you must get back your strength quickly. I want to go riding with you again very soon.' She smiled faintly. 'Think of all the things you haven't been able to eat for the last eight months! Now you can have anything you want again. What will you order first, I wonder?'

'Anything in the world?' she said, playing the game to please him.

'Anything in the world.'

She pretended to think. 'Anchovy toast,' she said at last.

He wanted to laugh, but the muscles of his face wouldn't seem to obey him. He had so nearly lost her. He gripped her hands as though he were hanging over a cliff and she was all that was holding him up. 'I love you,' he said. 'I love you so much. Don't leave me.'

'I love you too,' she said. 'I won't.'

It would have been hard for the guests of the house to know whether to feel joyful or apprehensive that evening, had not Lord Batchworth decreed it was to be a celebration. Mother and child were both alive, and the *but only just* which naturally followed the thought was not to be expressed.

Rosamund insisted that Sophie must go down like every-one else to dinner – which, after all, was not brought forward, so Monsuchet's feelings were not obliged to be lacerated after all. Sophie had not been out of the room all day, and there had been no leisure to feel the want of food and drink; but after Jes went down to take the good news to the rest of the household, she had begun to feel a both hungry and thirsty.

When Jes returned, he brought with him a bottle of champagne.

'We have all raised a toast down below, and everyone sends their love and congratulations, Ros my dear. Now you must have a glass of champagne because Fairford specifically advises it for mothers; and Sophie must have a glass because she is pale from her exertions; and Nanny and Moss must have a glass to drink the baby's health.'

Though Sophie rarely drank wine, the champagne seemed just what she wanted, thirsty and tired as she was, and certainly she felt much more lively afterwards. There was just enough in the bottle for one glass each, and just time to drink it before the dressing-bell was heard.

'Go now, Sophie dear,' Jes said. 'You will be wanted all the more tonight. Roland takes my place: I am having a tray up here with Rosamund, so that I can make sure she eats something – and to let Nanny and Moss go for their own dinner, which is shockingly delayed. I only pray they won't give me notice after today.'

He was determinedly keeping the atmosphere light, Sophie realised, so she made some cheerful reply, put down her empty glass and went away to dress. She passed along the passage towards the staircase, and there found Henry Droylsden still at his vigil, sitting patiently where she had found him hours ago, when it had all just begun.

'Sophie!' He stood up with a glad look as she reached him.

'Henry, what are you still doing here? You can't have been here all day?'

'I'm waiting for you. It's all right, I've heard the news. Batchworth told me. I went downstairs with him to drink a toast with the others, but then I slipped away again. I wanted to see if you were all right. You look all-in. How is it with you, really?'

'I'm perfectly all right, just a little tired,' she said automatically. He looked at her steadily, and she blurted out, 'Oh Henry, I have been so worried for her!'

'Aye, I had it out of the doctor before he left – a good, plain fellow, that, and just as well, since Batchworth seems determined to paint everything in bright colours. Well, I don't blame him. I think I'd be superstitious myself, in such a circumstance. But you need not pretend to me, unless you want to. I know how bad things have been.'

Sophie shook her head. 'I don't know what will happen. Rosamund is very weak, though the doctor thinks she will recover, if there's no relapse and no infection. But the baby – I've never seen such a tiny thing. Five weeks early! Oh Henry, it is so very sad, but I don't think it will survive very long.'

She felt the tears of pity rising, and tried to fight them down, but she was too tired for the struggle. She trembled, and then suddenly her legs seemed to turn to water, and she swayed helplessly.

'It's – it's just the champagne,' she gasped faintly; but Henry's arms were round her, holding her up, his strong hand at her waist, clasping her to him for support. She was shocked – and yet not shocked. The lightheadedness from the champagne and her long famine that day made her feel oddly irresponsible, as if she could do anything she liked; and just then she liked being held in Henry's strong arms.

'Oh – pray – don't —' she said, completely without conviction; and suddenly she remembered something. When she had come out of the room the first time and met him here, he had called her 'darling'. She had forgotten it until this moment; but plainly that was why her present situation had not entirely shocked her.

Oh but she must not, she must not let him hold her like this! Anyone might come – a servant might see them – and she was a widow in mourning! It was quite improper! 'Henry,' she said, but it didn't come out at all like a protest. Shocked with herself she put her hands up to his shoulders to push him away. 'We must not —' she began; but his face was very close to hers, and before she could understand what was happening she was kissing him. The first touch of his lips was shocking – almost physically shocking, like a sting of electricity – but then instead of pulling away she was returning his kisses eagerly. It was like a kind of madness, but just then she wanted him, all of him, hungrily – wanted him as a man, a lover, strange and yet familiar – wanted to be carried away on this wild turbulent mill-race of feeling.

A moment later she was sane again, and when she struggled away from him he released her instantly. He looked dazed. His lips were red from the fury of their kissing, but his face was pale, as though he'd been struck on the head and was going to faint.

'Sophie —' he began.

But she felt herself flush as red as he was white, as the realisation and the shame flooded through her. 'Oh don't!' she said disjointedly. 'Don't speak! I didn't mean – I can't – oh, I'm so sorry! Oh *please* let me go!' His hands were still lightly resting on her arms, and she pushed at him wildly, almost knocking him off balance.

'Sophie, no, you don't understand,' he protested quickly. 'There's nothing to be afraid of. I love you!'

'No,' she said – almost moaned. 'You can't – you don't – it's all wrong! I don't know what came over me. Oh forgive me —!' And she hurried away from him and ran up the stairs towards her own bedchamber, her face burning and her eyes filled with tears. How could she have done such a thing, such a dreadful thing? Jasper only a few months dead – Jasper her husband, her one true love; herself still in mourning; little Fanny in the nursery upstairs, the innocent, orphaned child! How could she have felt such a tumult of longing for Henry's arms? How could she have kissed him like that? And how could she ever face him again? Impossible to go down to dinner, *impossible*! But if she did not go, what would he think?

In the privacy of her own room she walked up and down, clenching and unclenching her fists, trying to compose herself, trying to breathe steadily. A light tap on the door made her heart beat violently, thinking he had followed her, but it was only the housemaid who had been told off to attend her. The girl gave Sophie a sympathetic look, and said she had come to help her dress.

Her presence calmed Sophie, and her silent sympathy reminded her that any agitation she betrayed at dinner would be quite naturally put down to the strain of her long day's vigil. The others would not expect her to be cheerful and composed. And as for Henry – no, she couldn't think of Henry yet. It made her heart thump uncomfortably. What had happened was just a moment's madness, a combination of her relief that Rosamund was alive, and the treacherous champagne. He would understand that, in time.

And what he had said to her – he did not, could not mean it. It was simply his reaction to the same things. When they met, he would behave just as he always had – like a kind friend, almost a brother. But how would she ever be able to meet his eyes?

Fairford did such a good job of negotiation with the respectable woman in the village that early the following morning Mrs Stanton arrived at the house, looking a little bemused, but with her luggage and her baby, prepared to stay. She was installed in a private room in the nursery-wing, less for her own comfort than to keep her infant separated from the others of the house, and she was warned sternly by Nanny that when she was not nursing his little lordship, she would be expected to make herself useful with plain needlework or perhaps a little light housework. The understanding was that she would be given transport down to the village three times a week to see her husband and family – which Nanny thought was shockingly generous – and that when his little lordship did not need her any more she would be dismissed with a present of money, the sum depending on how long she had been in service.

Another early visitor necessitated Lord Batchworth's being up with the dawn, and when he returned from seeing the visitor off again, he found Henry Droylsden wandering about the hall looking miserable.

'Ah, yes, you were intending to go off to Manchester today, weren't you?' Jes said. 'I've just been saying goodbye to the rector, who has been so good as to come up here before his breakfast – true nobility, I call that. I asked him to stay and have it with us, but he said he must be elsewhere.'

'The rector?' Henry said vaguely, and then looked alarmed as the implications came home to him. 'I hope —'

'Nothing like that!' Jes said quickly. 'He came up to baptise the baby, just as a precaution. They are both still with us.'

'I'm glad, sir,' said Henry.

'Even though for the moment you had forgotten them both? No, no, I'm not offended. You look like a man with something on his mind. Do you want to tell me about it?'

With a little encouragement, he told him. 'I just don't know what possessed me to kiss her like that!'

'Don't you?'

'Oh, it isn't as though I haven't been longing to do so for weeks – but at such a moment, when she was tired and distressed —!'

'My dear man, I'm sure you're refining too much upon it. It was impetuous, perhaps, but by your account she does not seem to have been unwilling to be kissed.'

'That's no excuse. It was abominable behaviour on my part,' Henry moaned. 'I took advantage of her, and it's no wonder she wouldn't meet my eyes all through dinner last night, and excused herself immediately afterwards to go to bed. I must have ruined whatever small chance I ever had of winning her. She will never trust me now.'

'Don't fall into a despair,' Jes said heartily. 'I think in the long run it may have been no bad thing. It may teach her something about her own feelings.'

'Her feelings? But it was all the work of the champagne, and the stresses of the day! In her normal state of mind —'

Jes shook his head sadly. 'You must have your head stuffed with wool! Do you really mean to tell me that you believe if it had been me she encountered just then —'

'You're a married man,' Henry said stiffly.

'You argue like a lawyer! Very well then, do you think she would have kissed any other unmarried man at that moment, who happened to be there? Because if you do believe that, you certainly don't deserve her, and I may have to call you out into the bargain.'

Henry was silent for a moment. 'If you are right —'

'I know I am. And remember this: she will be far more embarrassed by her lapse of decorum than you by yours.'

'Do you think so? Poor Sophie!' he said warmly.

'If I were you, I would concentrate on trying to make her feel comfortable again. Behave as though nothing has happened; be just as you were to her before; and as soon as she is out of mourning —'

'So long!'

Jes grinned. 'Or perhaps a little before that. I leave it to your good sense to determine!'

CHAPTER FIFTEEN

When by the fifth day Rosamund had not suffered any complications or begun a fever, Fairford allowed himself to be cautiously optimistic, and said that he need no longer visit her every day.

'I shall come at once, of course, if anything should occur to alarm,' he said. 'But I think all she needs now is to get back her strength.'

Jes marvelled at the calm, commonsense pronouncements. His only previous experience of physicians was of those who had attended his mother over the years. She had enjoyed ill-health as much as her sons enjoyed robustness, and nothing was more delightful to her than to be discussing her case with Sir Somebody Something, and having him tell her he had never seen another case like it. Pronouncing on her spasms, fluttering, nervous fits, languors and faintings, these mighty men had been as grave as they were polysyllabic, shaking their heads and prognosticating vague but calamitous complications.

Now here was Fairford uttering whole sentences that Jes could understand, and which set his mind at ease.

'Plenty of nourishing food – let her eat what she likes. A little sound wine every day. And sunshine: carry her to the sofa by the window, and let the window be set open as long as there is no wind – the fresh air will do her good. Above all, let her to be kept in a cheerful, settled frame of mind. Don't let her worry or fret about anything.'

'And the baby?' Jes asked, almost reluctantly. He had no wish to divert the stream into less comfortable directions.

Fairford gave the impression of shrugging, though he

didn't actually move his shoulders. 'That, I'm afraid, must be a matter of luck,' he said. 'He's taking nourishment, but he's so small he will be susceptible to any disease which happens to find him. I recommend that as few people as possible come near him, to lessen the likelihood of infection. Keep him warm, let everything around him be kept scrupulously clean – and hope for the best.'

It seemed commonsense advice, and Jes was glad of it, though he thought wryly that it was not likely to make Fairford rich. Why would anyone wish to pay a large fee to a man who told them nothing more than they could have told themselves? He ordered a dozen of claret and a whole hind-quarter of pork to be sent down to Fairford's house as a gesture of his esteem.

He wished, though, that he had something more positive to tell Rosamund about the child. She was still very weak, but liked to have him sit by her and talk, though visits from the rest of the party had been limited to a few minutes each. She tired quickly of anyone but Jes and Sophie.

'So everyone's leaving today?' she said.

'They must, if they are to attend the Coronation.'

'Do you wish you could go?'

'Not at all. Do you?'

'I'd sooner stay quietly here with you. Polly will be able to tell Mother and Papa Danby how I am.'

'I've written a letter for her to take.'

'Oh, good. I shouldn't like Mother to worry. How quiet it will be without the children.'

'Yes. Poor Fanny will have no-one to play with.'

'She will be happy with only you.'

'If I can spare the time from you and my son.'

She chuckled. 'My son! How you like using those words!'

He kissed her hand. 'The best two in the world, except for *my wife*. Have I mentioned to you how glad I am you didn't die?'

'No more than a thousand times. I'm glad too.' A silence. 'I hope Sophie won't be moped to death with no-one but us for company.'

'Henry Droylsden will be coming and going.'

'Will he? I'm glad. I like him.'

'He's in love with Sophie.'

'Did he tell you so? Is that why you've been asking him so often?'

'Partly. Will you care if they marry?'

'He has no fortune at all.'

'Sophie has enough for both.'

'How liberal of you! Very well, they may have my blessing.'

'Don't tell Sophie that. She might be frightened off if she thinks you suspect her of inviting advances while she's in mourning.'

'It's only half-mourning. And Sophie thinks a great deal too much of the conventions,' Rosamund began, and then caught his eye and smiled. 'Yes, and I'm not so tactless as I used to be when I was young. You may trust me.'

He bent to kiss her. 'To me you will always be nineteen, just as you were when I first set eyes on you – and I was as penniless and obscure as Henry Droylsden. I little thought then that you would one day be my wife and the mother of my child.'

'You might have done a great deal better for yourself,' she said seriously.

'Not in any particular. And by the way, we must think of a name for our son. We can't go on calling him "the baby" for ever.'

'He won't be a baby for ever,' Rosamund said, and then felt a cold touch of fear on the back of her neck, that listening Fate might interpret the words differently. There is nothing so superstitious as the mother of a frail baby.

Jes saw the shadow in her eyes, and said cheerfully, 'Well, what shall it be? I must confess I've tried out all the usual names in my mind, and I can't work up any enthusiasm for the Charleses or Henrys or Edwards.'

'We might follow Thalia's pattern and call him Justinian or Tiberius. Or we might just name him after his father.'

'Heaven forfend! One Jesmond Farraline in a family is enough.'

'Well, you have other names. What do you say to Aubrey?'

'Why not go the whole hog and call him Cavendish?' Jes said facetiously.

But Rosamund inclined her head, testing the idea. 'Cavendish? Yes, I rather like that! It's dignified. Cavendish

Farraline – I think it sounds rather well.'

'My love, are you serious?'

'Perfectly. Don't you like it?'

Jes smiled. 'It shall be as you choose; but if he hates it when he reaches the age of reason, I shall be sure to tell him it was your idea!'

When Tom Weston had the news from his brother Aylesbury that Rosamund had been delivered of a son, he felt, as well as the pleasure and concern natural to the occasion, a rather sad sense of irony. He had been keeping to himself the information about Charlotte's whereabouts, so as not to upset his sister during her pregnancy. He had hoped to tell her once she was safely out of childbed; but now it seemed there was nothing to tell.

Only two days before he had had another visit from Sherrick.

'It ain't good news, captain. You remember last time, the Angus female said she was afraid something was up?' Sherrick had established contact with the cook, and met her once a month on her day off for a report on Charlotte's health and progress. 'Said Mr Fadden had been giving her dark looks?'

'Yes, I remember,' Tom said.

'It turns out that just after that, the child was forbidden to visit the kitchen any more.'

'You mean Mrs Angus been found out? I thought she was sensible enough, and fond enough of Charlotte, to manage the business secretly.'

'Maybe she was. I can't say what happened. But she was due to meet me on Wednesday and she didn't turn up.'

'Was there no message?' said Tom.

'Nothing. I was worried, o' course, so I went down to look at the house. Found it all shuttered up – enquired at the smithy – family all gone away, quite sudden, no-one knows where.'

Tom slammed his fist into his palm. 'Skipped, by God!'

'As you say. We was done in the eye, right and proper.'

'But perhaps they've only gone for a short time – a vacation, a sea visit or something of the sort? Mr M's health —?' Tom suggested hopefully.

'Blacksmith says they've given up the house entirely. Not coming back.'

'Damn it, now we have it all to do again! The Lord only knows where they will have gone!'

'I don't hold out much hope of finding them again,' Sharrick said. 'If they know they've been discovered once, they'll be doubly careful to cover their tracks from now on.'

'If you don't want the job, you only have to say so,' Tom snapped.

'T'aint a matter o' that. I'm not out to rob you, taking money for what I can't deliver. I wouldn't even know where to start, see? The carrier as moved the furniture weren't a local man; and while they was working, Fadden stood by the whole time to make sure no-one spoke to 'em.'

'That does suggest a degree of caution. But what about the servants?'

'The cook was dismissed a month ago, and put straight on the coach to Rayleigh, where she comes from. Even if I could find her, she won't know nothing. The rest was paid off by Fadden in lieu of notice on the last day, and no hint as to where the family was going.'

'And the little girl?'

'I spoke to one of the housemaids – wench with a squint, local girl. She says the little girl cried when the cook was dismissed, and after that none of them was allowed to talk to her. Hendorp or Fadden chivvied 'em around, and the little girl was never left on her own for a minute.'

'So the family did know – or suspect – something,' Tom mused.

'Maybe,' Sharrick shrugged roughly. Then he went on in a different voice. 'This housemaid said she was watching out the winder when the carriage went by early in the morning. Blinds were drawn – couldn't even wave goodbye to the little 'un. Makes you wonder what kind of folk they are.'

When he had time to think about it afterwards, Tom couldn't help feeling guilty. If he hadn't meddled, the family would not have felt driven to move again. And who could guess what degree of imprisonment they would impose on the child now? He had done it for a good reason, but he wondered now if it had been good enough.

271

But perhaps, if Marcus removed to an even more remote place, he might feel safe at last and allow Charlotte more freedom. Tom could only hope it would prove so. At all events, he had agreed with Sharrick that the pursuit must be given up. To begin again, searching without any clue, and for a quarry that was on its guard, would be a hopeless task. Tom paid the former runner his last fee, and bid him farewell.

Rosamund had another child now – another life. Charlotte was no longer part of it. Tom wondered what would happen to the child at last. When Marcus died, which could not be at any great distance in time, she would surely be returned to society. That was his first thought; but on second thoughts, he doubted. It seemed to him that Barbarina must be as determined as her brother to conceal the child, or she would not have gone along with the business so far. And that suggested a very unpleasant sort of madness, for she hadn't even Marcus's excuse, of having been crippled by a duelling-shot.

The day of the Coronation, September the 8th, was attended by celebrations in every town and village in the country, for however much or little people cared about politics, everyone loved an excuse to make merry; and on the whole King William was liked. He had the advantage of following the most unpopular monarch in history since King John: Reform Billy, as the people called him, was at all events a great improvement on his brother George IV.

The village where Benedict was living was no exception. The day itself was to be a general holiday, as was traditional, and Bendy as much as the navvies under him was looking forward to staying late abed, and then spending the day in idle pleasure, eating a great deal more than usual, and drinking, he hoped, a little more than was good for him.

The village was getting out all its bunting and ribbon, including the rosettes and favours made up for General Elections, and every house of any size was planning to fly the Union Flag from some vantage point. Gardens had been tidied, fences painted, the village green scythed to perfection; and The Bell had planted the beds under its front windows with a patriotic display of red, white and blue flowers. Even

The First and Last had washed its windows, both inside and out, to the bewilderment of some of the older regulars, who now felt so uncomfortably exposed at their simple pleasures that one of them had felt compelled to wash his neckerchief and brush his jacket for the first time since his sister's wedding. As his sister now had three children, the eldest of whom was eight years old, these unwarranted acts of vanity earned him the nickname of 'Beau' from his drinking-companions.

The public celebrations were to be lavish. There was to be a special service of thanksgiving at the church, after which the vicar was to lead a procession through the village street, headed by himself and his churchwardens carrying the church banners, the schoolchildren carrying posies, and the various elders and dignitaries of the village and neighbour-hood, carrying anything they saw fit. Behind them would come the leading villagers in their best clothes, and since everyone seemed to consider him or herself a leading villager, it was a puzzle to know who would be left to line the road and cheer.

When the parade reached the village green, the jollifica-tions would begin. There was to be a feast, including a whole ox donated by Farmer Roberts, a bushel of apples donated by the wealthy Mrs Treadgold, and ale for everyone donated by Squire. There was to be dancing, games for the children bowling for a pig (also donated by Farmer Roberts, acknowl-edgement of whose generosity was tempered by the fact that he was well known to be the skittles champion of West Leicestershire), a juggler, a bottle-balancer, various side-shows, and a series of tableaux got up by Mrs Treadgold and the ladies of the Society for the Promotion of Total Absti-nence Amongst the Labouring Poor, in costumes donated by Mrs Simcock of The Bell, and sewn by the nimble fingers of herself and her two barmaids.

The great day dawned, and Benedict, who had planned on sleeping until noon, found old habits too ingrained and woke annoyingly early. He could still enjoy the sensation of not getting up, however, and rolled over onto his back and listened to the early birds chorusing outside the window, with the pleasant knowledge that he was not going to be joining them this morning. He must have dozed off again, for the next time he woke it was to a stronger light, and the irresistible smell of bacon frying. Liza was up!

He sat up in bed and ran a hand over his chin, wondering whether he could get away with not shaving. Probably not, if he was to take Liza to the celebrations on the village green. It would be the first time they had been out in public together. She was eager to attend, though he had some slight apprehension in case anyone was unkind to her. But on such a day, when everyone was making merry and most people would be drunk, she might surely pass unnoticed in the crowds.

He could hear her moving about in the other room now. Once she had fully recovered her health, she had insisted that he had the bedroom while she slept in the living-room. As soon as he had had shillings to spare, he had bought a little truckle bed for her, which she trundled away tidily during the day behind the sofa. She had proved a very good manager with what he gave her for housekeeping, and was proud of the tasty dishes she cooked for him while actually saving him money. Even given that he had two of them to feed and clothe now, his living was still cheaper than when he had been at Ma Brooksby's, and he had nothing at all to regret in his quixotic action in rescuing her.

To the smell of bacon was now added the smell of coffee – a combination so rich and enticing that he felt the forces of life tingling all the way down to his toes. No possibility of staying in bed under that attack! He flung the bedclothes back and jumped up, and had only just time to dive back under them as the door opened, for he had not been wearing a nightshirt.

Fand shouldered in first and came pattering over to the bed, followed by Liza, who didn't seem to have noticed his flurry of movement. She was balancing a laden tray, and concentrating on keeping the tip of her tongue firmly pinned between her teeth.

'What's this?' Bendy said, fending off Fand's frantic morning joy. 'Breakfast in bed? What, are you making an invalid of me?'

'Oh no,' she said quickly, looking up and blushing. 'It's a special treat, for Coronation Day. I thought you would like to have it like the grand folks do, just as if you were back at your mother's house.'

He was amused, but was careful not to let it show. She could be easily hurt, where her ideas of his past life were mistaken.

'What a splendid notion,' he said. 'And I smell coffee, too! Extravagant girl!'

'I got you all the things you like,' she said, setting the tray down on the bed. 'Bacon and sausages and kidneys, new bread and honey, and I fried the eggs just the way you like them.'

'Good Lord, so you did! What have I done to deserve all this?'

'You work so hard every day,' she said seriously. 'And I don't see as you have much fun beyond it, so I thought today everything should be for you, and the way you like.'

He hardly knew whether to laugh to cry. She must have been planning this for days, he thought. 'Well, you must have some of this,' he said, lifting the tray onto his knees. 'There's too much for one.'

'Oh no,' she said quickly, and took an instinctive step backwards. 'There isn't a bit too much. You must be starved of hunger – it's well past the time you usually eat.'

He was, and there wasn't a doubt he could clear the tray without help from anyone. 'Very well, but I don't care to eat alone, so you will have some bread and honey at the very least, or I shall be forced to give it to Fand, and that would be a terrible waste, wouldn't it?'

She smiled slowly, and he noticed anew how very pretty she was when she smiled. His sense of faint surprise made him wonder if she had been smiling less of late, or whether he had just been too preoccupied to notice her.

'All right,' she said, and perched herself on the furthest end of the bed. 'Come here, Fand, don't be a bother,' she added, for Fand had caught the glorious smell of bacon and kidneys, and was in danger of forgetting her upbringing.

'That's better,' Bendy said, lavishly buttering a thick slice of bread. He smeared it with honey and, 'There, now!' held it out to Liza, who took it from him with her swift, glancing smile. 'I have something to tell you,' he went on, tackling the heavenly bacon (fried crisp, what a girl!) 'Some news – very exciting news.' He looked across to see how she was taking it. 'Am I whetting your appetite?'

She finished a mouthful and retrieved the crumbs from her lips with a finger. What pretty, pink lips she had – and a dainty, almost pointed finger.

'No, for what news can that be? You can't have heard it this morning, for you haven't been out.'

'I knew it yesterday, but I wanted to save it until today, when I could tell you at leisure.'

'It's good news then?'

'To be sure. The very best.' He demolished an entire egg and followed it with a kidney before continuing. 'You see before you, dear Liza, a young man who is no longer a lowly, common, despised 'prentice. You see before you a genuine, newly-promoted, warranted-by-Mr-Stephenson-himself, Assistant Engineer!'

She stared, her eyes shining. 'Oh Benedict, I'm so pleased for you! How did you hear it?'

'Mr Rankin told me. He brought me a letter from Mr Stephenson to say that my work has been so satisfactory and my contributions so valuable that I am promoted; and my salary goes up as of this very day by fifty pounds a year!'

Now she turned pale. 'Why, that's nearly a whole pound a week,' she whispered, and put her hands to her cheeks with a gesture almost like horror.

'Very true! I can't fault your arithmetic,' he grinned. 'These sausages are excellent, by the way! Biggs must have a new recipe – the last lot were all gristle.'

'They're from Mr Roberts's farm,' she said absently. 'There weren't any left at Biggs'.'

'All gone for the feast today, I suppose. But listen Liza, I haven't finished telling my news yet!'

'There's more?'

'More, and more exciting! I'm being transferred to Glenfield – what do you think of that?'

'Glenfield?' she said blankly.

'To the tunnel. They've hit some problems there – a bed of sand they weren't expecting – and they've got behind schedule. They want me to go and look at it, and stay on it

276

until it's finished. Don't you see,' he added when she did not react, 'what a compliment that is? It means Mr Stephenson thinks my ideas are worth having, that I can make a real contribution, not just by following instructions but by thinking out fresh ideas of my own.'

'Glenfield,' she said again, and her voice was dull with sorrow.

'Yes, Glenfield. Don't say it as though it were the vestibule to Hades!'

'It's a long way off, isn't it?'

'A fair way, yes.'

'Then – will it be too far to go from here each day?'

'Lord, yes! I shall have to be near at hand. There are plenty of lodgings in Glenfield itself, though. It's a larger place than this, and with the extra salary I ought to be able to rent somewhere halfway decent.' He put down his knife and fork and looked at her with exasperation. 'Liza, you're not crying? What on earth is wrong with you? I thought you'd be pleased.'

'I am pleased,' she said. The tears spilled over, and she gulped. 'I'm very pleased for you.'

'Then why are you crying?' he demanded. She put her face in her hands and her answer was too muffled to hear. 'What? Oh do tell me properly what's wrong, there's a dear girl,' he coaxed more gently. 'Look, you're upsetting Fand.'

She pushed away the dog, who was trying to lick her face for her, and pulled up her apron to wipe her eyes. A few more tears spurted, and she pushed them back determinedly with her fingers, took a deep breath, and said rather bravely, 'I am pleased for you, truly I am. Only – only you're going away and – and I don't mean to be a bother, but what will become of me?'

Benedict was too dumbfounded immediately to speak. Then he said, 'Is that what's troubling you? But of course I mean you to come too! Unless you don't like it, that is?'

'Like it!' she said breathlessly. Rain was followed by sunshine. She even looked pretty with the tip of her nose red, he thought.

'I don't know who else is going to take care of me, if you don't come,' he said. 'Fand is very willing, but she can't cook worth a groat.'

Now Liza was laughing. 'Oh no!' she protested. 'But she and me together can do everything for you.'

'Then it's settled? You'll come with me to Glenfield?'

'Oh yes, yes please!'

'Thank God for that! You really gave me quite a fright, Liza. I wish you won't do that again!' She blushed at the teasing warmth in his voice, and murmured something that might have been either thanks or apology. 'And now I know you aren't going to abandon me,' he went on. 'I have a present for you.'

'A present?'

'Look over there, on the chair, under my coat. Something wrapped in brown paper.'

She fetched it, brought it back, sat on the bed staring at it.

'You can't see through the paper,' he suggested kindly. 'Wouldn't it be better to open it?'

She looked up, and her expression was strange. He couldn't tell if she was pleased or not. 'You are a great deal too kind to me,' she said. 'I don't know why you are.'

He tried to inject a lighter note. 'My dear girl, it's so much less effort than being unkind!'

'No,' she said seriously. 'There's not a gentleman in ten thousand as would do what you've done without – I mean, just for nothing. I do thank you, Benedict.'

Now he felt embarrassed. 'Open the parcel,' he said. She looked at him a moment longer, and then bent her head and set about the string. In a moment she had unwrapped it, touched it wonderingly with her fingers, and then stood up to hold it out at arm's length. It was a gown of fawn chequered muslin, stamped with a floral pattern in pink, mauve, blue and green, with a gathered shawl bodice under a wide cape collar, a full skirt and the full 'imbecile' sleeves that were the fashion now.

'I hope it fits you,' he said. 'I described you to the woman in the shop and she said it should. I think the colour will become you very well.' Liza stared at the dress and said not a word. 'It isn't new, you understand,' he added anxiously, 'but it did belong to a lady. There's a button missing from the cuffs, I'm afraid, but I thought you're so quick with a needle you might manage to do something about that.' Still she said nothing. 'Don't you like it?' he asked at last, rather chastened.

She turned to him, crushing the dress against her breast with both hands. Her eyes were as bright as a little fox's, and there was a spot of red on each cheekbone. 'It's the most beautiful,' she said emphatically, '*beautiful* dress I ever saw! But it's much too fine for me. It's a lady's dress, and I'm not a lady. Oh, but it's lovely! I don't know how I shall bear not to wear it!'

'Now look here,' he said indignantly, 'I didn't buy it for you not to wear. I want to see you in it today, when we go to the fair. Hang it, my girl, I paid down good blunt for that gown in the sole anticipation of seeing you in it!'

'But what if people see me,' she breathed, half afraid, half elated.

'I mean them to see you!'

'They'll think I'm putting on airs above my station.'

'Oh, deuce fly away with them!' he said jumping up onto his knees. 'You shall wear what you please, and anyone who don't like your gown can take themselves off somewhere else where they needn't see it! Oh look here, Liza, you will wear it, won't you?'

She nodded, her lips tightly closed in an almost mischievous smile. Then suddenly she laughed aloud. 'Oh, we'll make them jump, the tabbies!' she said. 'Me in my finery, puffing off the airs of a squire's lady, and you in your —' She looked at him, put her hand over her mouth and turned her head away. 'You in your bare skin,' she finished.

He realised that his last impetuous movement had left him quite exposed. Blushing he pulled the sheet up to his waist again. His discomposure seemed somehow to reassure her.

'You finish your breakfast in peace now, Benedict. I must go in the other room and see what wants doing to this gown before I can wear it. Shout when you're ready, and I'll bring in your hot water. Shall I take Fand away? Is she in your way?'

'No, she's all right here.' She headed for the door. 'Liza?'
She paused and looked back.
'You are pleased with it?'
'It's *lovely*,' she said.

279

The afternoon was well advanced and the slanting sunshine was full of the smells of the fair, of hot bodies and roasted meat and toffee, of horse manure and bruised grass and sawdust. Voices echoed flatly on the warm air, shouts from the stall-holders, the sound of a hurdy-gurdy somewhere, the shrill squealing of a pig followed by a gust of laughter. Around the edge of the green, horses dozed between the shafts of waiting carts and gigs, while geese and hens pecked between their feet for grains spilled from their nosebags. The clump of fine elms at the far end reached up into the soft September sky, moving their highest leaves with a sound like whispered conversation; while maids at the upstairs windows of houses leaned their arms on the warm window-sills, giggling together and inspecting the crowds below for handsome young men.

Benedict strolled with Liza on his arm. She looked almost like a lady in her new dress with the big sleeves, and her plain straw bonnet, which she had contrived somehow, in the short time available to her that morning, to trim anew with a bit of pink material and some large daisies. She had been very nervous at first, as if fearing that someone like Mrs Treadgold might come up to her in outrage and tell her to take off that lady's gown; but everyone was having too good a time to worry about anyone else, and the only looks she received were from other young men, who evidently thought how pretty she looked, and other young women who wanted to see how she had done it.

'What would you like to do now?' Bendy asked. The shadows were lengthening and the sunlight was taking on a golden tone.

She smiled shyly. 'Whatever you want.'

'No, really – what would you like?'

She hesitated. It seemed to her that the whole day had been arranged for her benefit, from the new dress onwards. Benedict had consulted her wishes in everything, paused wherever she wanted to stop and stare. He had secured her a good place to watch the tableaux, bought her hot gingerbread, baked apples, and mutton pasties, and paid for a visit to the freak show and a turn at bowling for the pig. And as final proof of his nobility, when her brother had come up to them in the crowd, he had not acknowledged him, but had chaffed him pleasantly, let him stroke Fand, and finally given him a penny to buy tablet.

But perhaps for Liza the greatest pleasure was that he gave her his arm as they walked about, making her feel like a real lady. She had never before been amongst other people in his company, and it made her feel she might hold her head up and look anyone in the face. Next to that, any other entertainment was gilt on the gingerbread.

'Come,' he said, 'what haven't we done? I must say, I'm beginning to get devilish hungry, aren't you?'

Before she could answer, they were accosted by a cheerful greeting.

'Morland! There you are! We've been expecting to see you all day. Where've you been?'

It was Daniel Beavor, accompanied by his friend Arbel. Each of them had a young woman on his arm, pretty young women whose bold eyes and much-trimmed dresses suggested that they were not the young men's sisters. They smiled at Benedict, and looked at Liza with unconcealed curiosity, plainly wondering what she was.

'Have you just arrived?' Benedict said. 'You've missed everything.'

'No, no, we've been here for hours,' Beavor said. 'I suppose we've passed you in the crowd, one way or another. It's a first-rate show, ain't it? Arbel said it wouldn't be up to scratch, but he's forced to change his mind now – ain't you, old fellow?'

'Unbearably rustic,' Arbel drawled, and the two young women giggled. 'Can't see any pleasure in watching red-faced rurals at play.'

'You saw the fun all right when you thought you'd won the pig,' Beavor said irrepressibly. 'You should have seen him, Morland – the last pin was teetering about for ever, and old Arbel was roaring like a ganger in a high gale, begging it to fall.'

Arbel glowered at him. 'Nothing of the sort.'

'Don't worry,' Benedict laughed, 'we won't give away your secret. You shall remain the one man who didn't enjoy the Coronation fair.' Fand had stepped forward delicately to sniff

281

at the young women's skirts, and the nearest one drew back with a little squeal of alarm. 'Don't worry, ladies, her fearsome appearance is as false as Arbel's sophistication. She won't hurt you.'

Beavor seemed to think introductions were due. 'This is Bessie, and this is Sally, by the way. They're sisters – uncommonly good arrangement, don't you think?'

He looked at Liza, and Benedict, though feeling unaccountably reluctant to do so, was obliged to respond. 'Liza, you know my friends Beavor and Arbel, don't you?' he said. Beavor merely grinned at her, but Arbel, having taken a glance at Benedict's face, performed a slight bow in Liza's direction. The two young women giggled again.

'Well, look here,' Beavor went on, 'now we've found you at last, we can make steps for The Bell, Arbel's hired a private parlour from old Simcock, and he's ordered the neatest, tightest dinner in the world, which I can tell you I'm vastly in need of. And you must come too, Morland, for we've ordered enough for six, and we'll have to pay for it between us, to say nothing of the hire of the room, which will ruin us to split two ways instead of three.'

Benedict glanced at Liza, but her eyes were hidden from him, and her face was as composed as always, making it impossible to tell her wishes.

'Do come, Morland,' Arbel added, with a note of urgency in his sophisticated drawl. 'You can't condemn me to an evening of Beavor's undiluted conversation, now can you?'

Benedict grinned. 'I've always been known for my philanthropic heart,' he said. 'We'll come with pleasure. We were just agreeing how hungry we were – weren't we, Liza?'

But her reply was inaudible.

The neatest, tightest dinner in the world had been consumed, along with a considerable amount of Simcock's claret – which, while it might offend the discerning palate, was not likely actually to cause death except in the hopelessly frail – and the party stepped out again into the village street. A host of lanterns had been lit, and the crowds were gathering again on the green for dancing. Beavor and Arbel and their young women were all for joining the throng. Their eyes were bright, their faces flushed, and Beavor had his arm openly around his young woman's waist, while her sister clung to Arbel's arm as though she were about to be snatched away by a hurricane.

Liza, by contrast, was resting only the tips of her fingers on Benedict's arm, standing very erect and with her head poised at its most queenly angle. When Benedict turned to her to confirm her desire to join the dancing, she said unsmilingly, 'I don't think Fand ought to be taken into that crowd – someone will step on her. I will take her back to the house.'

'Oh, yes, very true. We'll take her home first, and then come back and join the others.'

She lowered her voice still more. 'If you please – I don't want to come back.'

'You don't want to dance?' Bendy said in surprise.

She shook her head. 'I'll take Fand home for you. Don't you come: you stay with your friends and enjoy yourself.'

Benedict stared at her for a moment, trying to understand her objection, and concluded, silently, that she must be tired. 'Of course I'll come with you. Don't be silly. Just wait a moment while I tell the others.'

They had walked on and he had to run after them. Liza stood with her hand on Fand's collar, watching him with a growing unhappiness which she desperately wanted to conceal from him. She saw them halt and turn back, saw Benedict speak, saw Beavor's broad grin and Arbel's sly smile, saw the young women look at each other and giggle, saw Beavor slap Benedict encouragingly on the shoulder before the group parted.

Benedict came back to her, and she lowered her eyes and turned her head away. Tactfully he did not speak, but offered his arm in silence. When they reached home, she took off her hat in silence and went at once to make up the fire, which she had left banked, filled a bowl with water for Fand, who was very thirsty, and moved around performing other little ordinary tasks. Benedict sat and watched her, puzzled. He knew she was upset about something, but hadn't yet fathomed what it could be.

When she asked at last. 'Will you want supper? There's cold bacon, or bread and cheese,' he caught her wrist as she passed him and stopped her. She looked startled.

283

'What's the matter?' he asked.

'Nothing. What should be?' she said quickly.

Benedict shook his head. 'No, no, that won't do.' He kept hold of her wrist, removed the cloth from her hand, and obliged her to sit beside him on the sofa. 'You were very quiet all through dinner. You hardly ate anything, and you certainly didn't speak. You didn't want to dance, and now you won't even meet my eyes.' He paused, but she didn't look up. 'So you had better tell me what's wrong. You were so happy today, at the fair. What spoiled it?' She didn't answer, and he added, gently but firmly, 'I mean to have an answer, Liza. This isn't fair to me. I meant you to enjoy yourself today, and if you have not, I must know why.'

That roused her. She looked up eagerly. 'Oh, I did! It was splendid!'

'Until my friends came along. Don't you like them?'

She lowered her eyes again, and her free hand played unhappily with the fringe of the sofa-cushion. 'It's just —'

'Yes? What is it just?'

'Those two girls. Bessie and Sally.'

'Lord, is that what's upsetting you? But why must you be so nice? Beavor and Arbel are young men in the prime of life, and it's the most natural thing in the world that they should —'

'I know! Of course I know! But I could see them looking at me, the girls, wondering what I was. *They* wondered, but your friends didn't. They knew. And that's what everyone thinks, Benedict. Everyone in the village thinks I'm —' She stopped abruptly, biting her lip.

'Haymarket ware?' he suggested expressionlessly. 'And that's what upsets you? Do you care what a crowd of gossiping fools think?'

'Yes, I care.' Her cheeks were red, and she avoided his eyes. 'You rescued me – saved from the worst of fates. I'm grateful to you – more grateful than I can say —'

'I don't ask for gratitude. You repay me by looking after me.'

'Oh!' She pulled her hand free, only to use it to make a helpless gesture, despairing of being able to express the feelings which were, even for her, nebulous. 'That's not it!'

'What is, then?' She didn't answer, and he watched her, perplexed. He half understood, in a wordless way, what it was she was asking; but he was puzzled how to answer her because he didn't know himself. He had rescued her in the beginning from the merest compassion, as he might have rescued a drowning kitten; and he had continued as her protector because his anger had been roused by the harshness an unjust world had been ready to heap on her. Since then he had become too comfortable to wonder about the situation. He worked hard all day, and when he came home there she was, making him comfortable, providing a warm, clean home and a tasty dinner, just as though she were his mother. But she wasn't his mother.

'I'm not your housekeeper, so what am I?' she asked at last.

'I thought we were friends,' he said lamely. 'You said you could be my friend.'

She flashed him one look, hot with some emotion – anger, exasperation, grief, he didn't know what – and jumped up and ran into the other room.

He sat for a moment, his lips tight. Fand came up to him and pressed her muzzle into his hands, sensing the atmosphere, and he pulled her ears gently as he worried at the situation. Liza had been brought up poor but decent, he thought; she had been brought low through no fault of her own. He had given her a home, but had ruined her reputation, as the reaction of Beavor and Arbel proved. Well, no, not ruined: in that village she had had no reputation to begin with; but he had not restored it to her.

Well, that could be remedied, he thought. He stood up and went through into the bedroom, where Liza was sitting on the bed, her hands in her lap, staring at the wall. There were tears on her cheeks, and the sight of them desolated him.

'Liza, I'm sorry. Don't cry. I do understand,' he said. 'I haven't behaved towards you as I ought.'

'You have, you have!' she protested. 'That's just the —' She stopped, unable to go on.

'No, listen to me,' he said. 'There's nothing to be done here, in this village. I realise that; but when we go to Glenfield we can make it all right again. I will find you a respectable

285

place, as a housemaid or something, and I will think of a way of explaining my part in it so that no-one thinks that you're – so that they know you're respectable.'

'Oh Benedict,' she said despairingly.

'I shall miss you,' he said. 'I can't think how I shall go on without you, but you're quite right. I've been very selfish, letting you sacrifice yourself for my comfort.' He crouched down in front of her and tenderly wiped the tears from her cheeks with the back of a finger. 'Now don't cry, there's a dear girl. I can't bear it if you cry. Everything will be all right, you'll see.'

Her lips trembled, and more tears seeped out to replace those he had removed. 'I don't want to leave you,' she said, very low. 'Not even to be respectable again.'

'But we could still be friends,' he said, though he knew he was talking nonsense. A respectable householder would never believe in the friendship between her housemaid and a young railway engineer like Benedict. A respectable householder would not allow her maids to have followers.

'I want to stay with you,' she said.

'But then,' he began, thoroughly perplexed, 'everyone will think—'

'I don't care,' she cried; and with a kind of desperate courage, she put her arms round his neck. 'They're going to think it anyway,' she said, 'so we might as well make it true.'

The unexpected contact hit him like a bolt of lightning in the pit of his stomach: her soft, white arms touched his neck, her face was very close to his, and the scent of her, faint, familiar and exotically female, made the hairs on the back of his neck rise. 'No,' he whispered. 'No, Liza, you haven't thought—'

'I've thought,' she said. 'I want to stay with you.'

Tremblingly, she kissed him. Her lips brushed his like the touch of a moth's wings, and he felt almost sick with excitement. He'd left Serena a long time ago, and he was nineteen years old. Yet he held back. He had meant to protect her, not ruin her; and still she seemed, in both her strength and her helplessness, so absolutely his that all his instincts of care and responsibility rose up like castle walls around her, which no-one not even he, might breach. If he did, the consequences would be indelible. He had saved her life, and that meant that he belonged to her for ever. She could leave him if she wanted to, but whatever happened, he could never put aside the responsibility for her that he had taken up.

He cupped her little pointed face in both his hands and held it back from his, looking searchingly into her eyes. They were bright with the recent tears, and the long dark lashes were wet, but there was no fear or apprehension of him or of what was to come – and he saw then that it *was* to come, that it had become inevitable. He quivered, and surrendered, lowered his head and kissed her very gently, accepting his fate.

He must be very gentle, he thought: she had not known kindness from a man before. He realised now what a debt he owed to Serena, who had taught him how to be tender. He felt strong, powerful – a man at last. For the first time the reins of his life seemed to be in his own hands; and that this was a paradox – that he was powerful only because he was powerless to choose to harm or abandon her – occurred to him even at that apocalyptic moment. But it occurred only very distantly, in the back of his mind. The rest of his consciousness was absorbed and dazzled with the over-whelming sensations of making love to her.

BOOK THREE

The Tunnel

Dark, deep and cold the current flows
Unto the sea where no wind blows,
Seeking the land which no-one knows.

Ebenezer Elliott: *Plaint*

CHAPTER SIXTEEN

Sophie stood at the window, staring out into the empty street. The day was mild, dark and wet, swathes of rain falling constantly from the low sky and being smacked by a gusty south-westerly wind against the window-panes. It would be a dismal journey tomorrow, she thought. She and Fanny were to go to Grasscroft for Christmas. The Batchworths had been invited to Wolvercote, but had refused: the baby, Cavendish, had struggled through the first four months of his life to a perilous equilibrium, but they could neither risk taking him so far nor bear to leave him behind. Sophie and Fanny, along with as many other friends as would be enticed during the hunting season to a house which could offer no hunting, were to keep the Batchworths from being moped to death at home.

Since her invitation had arrived, Sophie had hardly known how she felt about it. Part of her looked forward to friendly faces and warm conversation, to the lights and fires and cheerfulness of a Christmas party; but there was also a reluctance in her to go away from here. It would be her first Christmas without Jasper. This time last year she had been not only happily married, but confidently expecting a child. How could so little time make so much difference? The house was desolate without him, too big, too empty; her continued occupation of it seemed pointless; and yet it had been their home, and here, if anywhere, were the memories of him. How could she go away, at this time of year in particular, and leave them? Her greatest fear, now that he was gone, was that she would begin to forget him. She had an almost superstitious dread that having lost him, she would lose her memories of him too.

But it would be better for Fanny to have company. She had begun to think that there would come a time when she would have to send Fanny away to school: in Manchester she would have too few opportunities of meeting other young ladies of her own age and rank. And then there would be the problem of launching her into society. Sophie tried to imagine herself, a widow, taking Fanny to all the parties and balls of a Season, and her spirits failed her. And how could she give parties of her own for Fanny, with no man at her side to help her receive?

From that point her thoughts moved naturally – all too naturally – to Henry Droylsden. Since the overwrought moment when he had kissed her (or was it that she had kissed him? She was rather afraid it was the latter) he had behaved with the greatest propriety towards her, treating her just as he had when Jasper was alive, with a sort of brotherly warmth. It had made it possible for them to go on meeting without embarrassment, and she was grateful to him for his consideration.

But she couldn't help feeling that he did have a special tenderness for her. He did so much for her that was not within the bounds of his salaried position as her manager: smoothed her path through the world, provided a rock to shelter her and a wise head to advise her. Indeed, in many ways he had taken over the rôle of husband – but without asking for anything from her in return but to be allowed to serve her.

She was deeply grateful to him, both for his kindness in what he did, and for his delicacy and forbearance in what he did not do. But she was still puzzled to know her own feelings towards him. She had always liked him, and now that she was alone she welcomed the respite from loneliness that his company gave her. She relied on him more and more to advise and guide her; a day in which she did not see him seemed an empty one; and she could not help noticing that Fanny had begun to accept him as an automatic part of any plan that was made.

But was there more between them than that? She hardly dared examine her more private feelings, for fear of what she might find. When her first fiancé, René, had died, she had felt

292

she could never bear to be kissed by anyone else; yet she had married Jasper and found an unimagined bliss in his caresses. It had shocked her a little to discover that sensual self within her, but she had come to terms with it, explaining to herself that Jasper was her one true love, and so all things were possible with him. She didn't want to betray him; she didn't want to find that she could take pleasure in anyone else's arms. Whenever she dared give the most tentative, sidelong glance at the memory of kissing Henry that day at Grasscroft, she turned instantly hot and cold, and shied away from it in confusion. Was that only embarrassment over her inappropriate, even indelicate, action – or was it something else? She wasn't sure that she wanted to know the answer.

But things couldn't remain as they were for ever. In two months more she would be out of mourning, and she dreaded what would happen then. She had been receiving morning-visits for some time now, and in the course of returning them had necessarily overheard hints and suggestions about herself that distressed her. Her wealth made her eligible, and as soon as she put aside her black gloves, she knew she would find herself the object of solicitous attempts to pair her off with this or that elderly bachelor or wealthy widower. She might even find herself the object of impertinent fortune-hunters; and the persecution would only cease when she finally accepted someone and put herself out of reach.

Interestingly, she had not heard anyone pair her name with Henry's, and that was both a tribute to his circumspection, and a comment on his lack of fortune. He must be as aware as anyone that he would not be considered a match for her, and it was quite possible – likely, even – that as an honourable man, and a proud one, such a consideration would prevent him from addressing her. She didn't know whether she wanted him to or not. Could she bear to be married again, to someone who wasn't Jasper? Yet she was afraid of spending the rest of her life alone. Was it fair to Fanny to deprive her of the support and protection of a father? Could she in fairness marry Henry for no warmer reason than that? Did he love her? Did she – could she – love him? She trod round and round the same thoughts endlessly, wishing most of all that there were someone to make the decision for her and tell her what to do.

Her reverie was interrupted by the sound of someone arriving below. A few moments later familiar footsteps came to the door, and Henry limped in, smiling, and advanced to shake her hand. 'Fenby said you were alone. I had thought Agnes would be here.'

'No, I haven't seen her. Did she mean to call?'

'On her way back from Fountain Street. But I suppose she was delayed, or changed her mind.' He looked at her carefully. 'You seem pensive. I hope I haven't disturbed you?'

'No, not at all. I was just thinking.'

'Standing in front of the window, looking out at the rain? I'm afraid they weren't happy thoughts.'

'I was thinking about Jasper,' she said. 'It will be our first Christmas without him.'

'You must miss him very much.'

Sophie looked at him searchingly. 'Yes, I do,' she said at last. 'Did you only call to see Agnes, or can you stay for some tea?'

'Thank you,' he said, 'I would love some tea.'

She rang the bell. 'What did you want to see me about?'

'Must I have an excuse?' he smiled quizzically. She seemed disconcerted by the question, so he went on quickly, 'It isn't a matter of business. I just came to tell you that I have been invited to Grasscroft for Christmas, and since I know you are going too, I wondered if I might offer myself as your escort on the journey. I don't like to think of a lady travelling without a male attendant, even for so short a distance.'

She smiled, though she did not quite meet his eyes. 'Thank you. I should be glad of your protection. We go tomorrow, and there will be very good room in our carriage for you, for Miss Molton does not go. I've given her leave to visit her own family for Christmas.'

'Splendid. Then I shall attend you at whatever hour you appoint,' said Henry. He wished he could see some encouragement in her confusion, but he could not flatter himself. Well, Christmas, with all its memories, was not the time to be making new attachments. He must be patient. In the spring, when the awful first anniversary was behind her, he might make the first tentative steps towards wooing her. For the moment he must be a kind friend, nothing more.

'I mean to leave at about eleven o'clock. Won't you come and have breakfast with us?' Sophie began, but was interrupted by the door's opening again, to admit the butler. 'I rang for tea, Fenby.'

Fenby was looking anxious. 'I beg your pardon, madam,' he said, 'but there is a Person below who wishes to see you. In short, madam, it is Mr Olmondroyd.'

Henry stiffened and glanced at Sophie. She looked perplexed. She did not know of Henry's suspicions, but she remembered how unpleasant Olmondroyd had been to Jasper – and was a little afraid of him besides.

'Tell him I'm not at home, if you please,' she said.

'I did take the liberty of saying so already, madam, but he insists on speaking to you,' Fenby said. 'He declares he won't leave the house until he's seen you.'

'I can't see him. I won't,' Sophie said, alarmed. 'Cannot you make him go away?'

Fenby hesitated. He was a small, slight man, and Olmondroyd was large, powerful and immovable. It was also the upper footman's afternoon off, as Sophie recollected in the pause that followed.

'Should you wish me to send for the constable, madam?' Fenby asked at last.

Henry stepped in. 'Would you like me to see him for you?' he asked Sophie.

She turned to him with relief. 'Would you? I would be so grateful. I can't think what he wants.' She looked doubtfully from Henry to Fenby and back, and seeing that they were much the same build, added. 'But perhaps, if he is very angry, it might be better to send for the constable after all?'

Henry gave a grim sort of smile. 'I can be angrier than he bargains for. Don't worry, there won't be an unseemly brawl in your vestibule, I promise you. Fenby, shew me to him.'

Olmondroyd was pent up in the business-room like a brooding storm. He surged restlessly as Henry came in and he saw there was no-one else behind him.

'Oh, it's you is it?' he said uncordially. 'What do you want?'

'I've come to ask you to leave,' Henry said shortly. 'At once, if you please.'

295

'Mistaken the direction, have I?' Olmondroyd sneered. 'I took this for Mrs Hobsbawn's house.'

'Mrs Hobsbawn will not see you.'

'I'll hear that from her mouth, not from a shag-rag lameter like you! Go and tell her I've got business to discuss with her, and her only. Sharp now!'

Henry felt himself quivering all over with rage, but he controlled himself with a violent effort.

'I have promised Mrs Hobsbawn that there will be no brawling,' he began, but Olmondroyd cut himself off with a laugh.

'Oh, have you? As if I couldn't knock you down with one hand tied behind my back! Try and turn me out, you pale green boy, and I'll send you to sleep for a week!'

'You can't provoke me,' Henry said. 'I have the means to remove you from this house and I will use it.'

'What are you dangling about here for anyway?' Olmondroyd interrupted. 'After the widow's money, are you, like that counter-jumping mill-hand she married last time? And him not cold in his grave yet! You don't waste time, do you, cocky?'

'I am Mrs Hobsbawn's agent, empowered to act for her in all matters of business.'

'Oh, are you? Set a hungry dog to guard the larder, eh? Well, more fool her, if she's taken you on with nothing but the shirt on your back – and that most likely full of holes!'

'Will you get out of here, or have I to make you?' Henry said savagely.

'I've come to talk business, and I will do it,' Olmondroyd retorted. 'If you must be her go-between, hop to it and tell her I want to buy the mills from her – and I'll give her a fair price too. I haven't come to sponge off her like some people – straight business, that's what I'm after.'

It was something Henry hadn't expected, and he was taken off balance. 'You must have run mad! Why on earth should she sell the mills to you?'

'Because mills need a man's hand to guide them. She can't run them herself, and a manager will line his own pockets and ruin her. Either she sells to me now at a handsome price, or she'll sell to me anyway in five years' time for a handful of peas, when the business is on the rocks and she's under the hatches. I'm a businessman, and she can take my word for it. Go tell her that; and be quick about it, for I haven't all day.'

Henry took a step closer, his hands kept determinedly down by his sides. 'Listen to me, Olmondroyd,' he said with quiet menace, 'your presence here is an insult to this house, and if you think for a moment that you will ever be allowed to come within ten yards of Mrs Hobsbawn you are as stupid as you are vicious. I told you I could make you go, and it wasn't an idle boast.' His voice rose a little. 'You evil man, I know all about your connection with Maloney and his friend Ballater! Fine friends for a businessman! And Duxbury is your go-between, isn't he? I know he has made payments to those two on more than one occasion – payments for services rendered, eh?'

'What are you talking about?' Olmondroyd looked rattled at the mention of the names.

'I know that it was you that murdered Jasper Hobsbawn – oh, not with your own hands, of course, but you planned it and paid for it, and if I could prove it, I would see you hang for it. As it is, if you don't get out of here and stay away, I shall make sure that what I know, everyone knows. You're not much liked as it is, but if you come anywhere near Mrs Hobsbawn ever again, I'll see to it you're shunned by everyone in this town. You won't have a friend to bury you by the time I've finished.'

Olmondroyd's apprehension had passed. 'You yapping, three-legged cur dog!' he sneered. 'You know *nothing*! I suppose you've been talking to some of your low friends in The Pack Horse? You must be soft in the head if you believe what they tell you. People of that stamp would libel their own mothers for tuppence! Anything you think you know, you've bought and paid for – aye, and you're too green to know specie from lead!'

'Those closest to you have betrayed you,' Henry said gravely. 'You are finished, Olmondroyd!'

'Oh am I? And if that's so, why aren't you telling it all to the magistrate, instead of threatening me like a dog in the gutter? I'll tell you why – because you've nothing against me! You've not a shred of proof, and all you can do is bluster.'

This was sadly true, but Henry made as good a show of it as possible. 'Proof or not, I can and I will make sure everyone knows what you are.'

'If you spread one word of these lies about me, I shall have you taken up for slander so quick it'll make your head spin, and we'll see how you like cooling your heels in the New Bailey for ten years! Don't cross me, little man,' Olmondroyd went on, leaning over Henry menacingly. 'I've been patient with you so far, but I've a short fuse at the best of times, and I could ruin you and yours with a snap of my fingers! Now just you listen to me: I want Hobsbawn Mills, and I will have them. I'll pay the widow a fair price; but if you persuade her not to sell, I'll drive the business to ruin, and then buy it for nothing when she's desperate to sell. I can do it, and I will, I give you my oath on that. So think carefully how you advise her, or you'll be doing her no service.' He straightened up. 'I'll go now, but I'll be back in a fortnight for her answer. And you —' He stabbed a short, thick finger suddenly at Henry's face, making him flinch, much to his own annoyance. 'I warn you – keep your mouth shut, and your lies to yourself.'

With that he turned and left, striding out into the hall and almost falling over Fenby, who had evidently been listening at the door. Olmondroyd brushed past him and let himself out, leaving the front door contemptuously open. Fenby scuttled like a nervous crab to close it, while Henry walked slowly upstairs, his emotions in turmoil. He felt he had not acquitted himself as well as he ought; but on the other hand, he had got out of Olmondroyd what was tantamount to a confession. His reaction to Henry's accusation proved it: he *had* been involved with Jasper's death. If he had not, he would have shown surprise, bewilderment, furious indignation.

The snippets of information and gossip Henry had been gathering had all pointed that way, and he was now satisfied in his own mind. But Olmondroyd was right that he had no proof, nothing he could take to a magistrate. It was damnable! All the same, how could Olmondroyd have been so confident of that? There was surely something unbalanced about a man who had so little fear of the consequences of his crimes. He must, literally, be mad. And he was also danger-ous. Henry wondered now whether it had been such a good

298

idea to accuse him openly like that, to show his hand when he had nothing to back it up. He was suddenly aware of how little protection he had against such a man. Confident as he was that Henry could prove nothing, Olmondroyd might yet feel it was better to have him out of the way; and unimportant as he was in the world, Henry would be an easier target even than Jasper had proved.

More worrying still, now that Olmondroyd had set his mind on buying Hobsbawn Mills, he would not leave Sophie alone. He could do what he threatened – ruin the business – and in the end either Sophie would have to sell Jasper's beloved factories to his murderer, or she would refuse and she and Fanny would be made paupers.

It must not be! Henry could not allow either of those things to happen. A cold resolve was forming in his mind as he limped towards the drawing-room: something was going to have to be done, and the only person who could do it was Henry Droylsden. He could not leave Sophie and Fanny undefended. Whatever the consequences to himself, he must go ahead with it. There was no other way.

He entered the drawing-room and Sophie, seeing his expression, hurried forward. 'Is he gone? Oh, he did not hurt you? Say he did not!'

Henry forced a smile. 'No, no, I promised you there would be no brawl. I talked to him and he went away, that's all.'

'But what did he want?'

Henry hesitated. 'It was nothing but impudence. He wanted to buy the mills from you. I told him at once that you would not sell. I hope that was right?'

'Oh – yes – of course!' She looked at him anxiously. 'Is that really what he wanted?'

He was glad to be able to speak the truth; in her present state of anxiety she would discern a lie. 'Yes, I promise you, that's what he wanted. But he can't make you sell, you know.'

She let out her breath in a sigh. 'No, he can't, can he? Oh Henry, thank you for seeing him for me! I am so very grateful. I don't know how I would have managed without you.'

'Fenby would have seen him off,' he said.

'Fenby!' She shook her head, and smiled a little unevenly.

'I wonder, after all the excitement, if he will remember to bring the tea.'

'I must beg your pardon and forgo the pleasure of taking tea with you after all. I'm afraid I must leave straight away. There is a piece of business I have to attend to.'

Sophie looked up at him doubtfully. 'Is it something to do with that man?'

He looked down into her face, hoping that his own did not reveal too much. But he could not give her the lie direct. 'You mustn't worry,' he said instead. 'He can't hurt you, you know. I won't let him.'

'Thank you,' she said. She laid her hand on his arm. 'But you will be careful, won't you? You won't do anything that might – that might provoke him to harm you?'

He put his hand over hers. Her solicitude was for him, he noted, not for herself. Just then he'd have given a fortune, if he'd had one, to know how much she felt for him. 'I'm not going to provoke him,' he said. 'It's just that there's a piece of business I must finish before I go to Grasscroft tomorrow.'

She looked relieved. 'Oh, is that all it is? I'm so glad. I was afraid you meant to go after him and fight him.'

Henry laughed shakily. 'He's twice my size.'

'That's what I was afraid of,' she said seriously.

The maid, Bessie, who came to wake Sophie in the morning, brought the news, spilling it out excitedly as she put down the tray beside the bed.

'Oh madam, such a shocking thing!' she said, pleased to have something so momentous to tell. Her eyes were round with it, but there was no distress in her excitement. 'It's all over town as there's been a murder done, and the gentleman as was murdered had not long before left this very house!'

Sophie felt as though she had been struck a heavy blow in the chest. She whitened, and her hand fluttered up to her throat. 'What – what do you say?' she whispered.

Thrilled with the effect she was having, Bessie nodded portentously to her mistress. 'It's true, madam! Peter had it from the milk-girl, who had it straight from the constable. And Mr Fenby come into the kitchen just as I was fetching your tray, madam, and them was his very words: the poor gentleman'd not an hour before left this very house, Mr Fenby said, when he was struck down and murdered quite horrible!'

Sophie felt her consciousness slipping as a torrent of ghastly memories tumbled through her mind: shadowy shapes and violent movements, helplessness and horror. Jasper, oh Jasper! There was a surging red-blackness before her eyes and a roaring in her ears. Her lips were numb, and she could only whisper, 'Who? Who is murdered?'

'Why, that Mr Olmondroyd, madam, what had been here and Mr Fenby couldn't get rid of him. Found in Back Bridge Street Lane, he was, with his head knocked in, dead as a fish. No-one knows who could have done such a thing, for no-one saw it happen, and – why, madam, are you all right? You've turned such a funny colour —'

Sophie slipped away from the world for a while.

Nobody in the household thought it at all strange that the mistress should have fainted dead away on hearing the news. Bessie was so heartily and universally condemned for blurting it out in that way that she was good for nothing for the rest of the morning. She sat in a corner of the kitchen with her apron over her head, sobbing and declaring to anyone who would listen that she hadn't meant to remind the mistress of the poor master's shocking murder like that, and she wished her tongue had been cut out before she had said anything so wickedly cruel.

Restoratives were applied to Sophie, and after a while she was able to sip a little hot coffee and eat a morsel of bread. When her colour had returned and her hands had stopped shaking, she declared herself well enough to get out of bed. But she was both shocked and worried: she couldn't help remembering Henry's sudden departure and the grimness of his expression, and an awful dread had fastened itself on her heart which she could hardly bear to acknowledge. He couldn't, *surely* he couldn't, have done anything dreadful? He had left hurriedly after Olmondroyd, and Sophie had been nearly sure that he was going to confront the man, perhaps to warn him not to come near her again. She had been afraid that Olmondroyd, provoked, might attack Henry, knock him down: he was a violent man and twice Henry's size. But that Henry might – no, it was impossible.

But suppose Olmondroyd *had* attacked him, and Henry, in defending himself, had grown desperate and hit out rather harder than he meant to? That was possible; but then if that were the case, why had Henry not gone straight to the magistrate, or fetched a constable, or a physician? If it were an accident, or a plain measure of self-defence, there would be no reason for him not to tell someone.

If it *were* an accident.

Sophie flung the thoughts away from herself angrily, pacing up and down her room. What was the matter with her? It was a wicked, stupid thing to think, and she would not think it! Olmondroyd had made many enemies, any one of whom might have taken revenge on him. In any case, Back Bridge Street Lane was a dark alley in a rough part of town, where a man might be set upon for the sake of his purse. Was she really believing that gentle Henry Droylsden would kill a man simply for annoying her? Was she really so wickedly vain? No, no! Henry would be here soon, and when she saw his face again, she would see exactly how ridiculous the idea was. She only wondered how she would be able to look him in the eye, having thought such outrageous things about him, albeit when her mind was disordered by the shock.

She was sitting with Miss Molton waiting for Henry to arrive for breakfast when Fenby came in, bringing the letters which Peter, the footman, had fetched from the post office. Peter had also brought the latest news, gleaned on the way home, and Fenby saw fit to offer it to his mistress with the post: that Olmondroyd had apparently been struck down from behind with several grievous blows to the head; and that nothing had been taken from him, not purse nor watch nor ring nor pin.

'That is strange,' Miss Molton said. 'But perhaps the attacker was frightened away before he could rob the poor man.'

'Yes,' Sophie concurred blankly. 'Poor man. I did not like him, but I did not wish him dead.'

Miss Molton decided her employer's thoughts ought to be guided into a more pleasant channel, and said, 'I wonder, ma'am, if Fanny will really want quite such a number of frocks? Since it will be entirely a grown-up gathering, I hardly think she will want more than two or three party dresses.'

Fenby had just opened the door to leave them, and a knocking on the street door below was clearly heard.

'Ah, that will be Mr Droylsden,' Sophie said, between relief and apprehension. 'Shew him up, Fenby, and then bring breakfast straight away.'

'Yes, madam.'

'Miss Molton, will you go and fetch Fanny down?'

But Miss Molton wanted directions about Fanny's trunk, which Janet was in the process of packing upstairs, so she was still in the room when Fenby returned alone.

'Where is Mr Droylsden?' Sophie asked, apprehension rising again as she saw Fenby's grave expression. 'Why didn't you shew him up?'

'It was not Mr Droylsden, madam, but a boy with a message from him.'

Sophie took the letter from the tray and opened it.

'*My dear Mrs Hobsbawn*,' it said. '*I must ask your pardon for not waiting on you as we arranged, but I met with a slight accident last night. It is nothing alarming, I hasten to assure you, but with a broken head and a blackened eye, I am quite unfit to be seen in your company. I feel somewhat shaken up into the bargain, and must therefore beg you to excuse me from accompanying you this morning. I hope and trust no inconvenience to you will result from this change of plan. I shall make my own way to Grasscroft as soon as I feel more the thing. Might I trouble you to give my apologies to our hostess and tell her that I hope to be with you all tomorrow morning? Ever your grateful, obedient servant, H. Droylsden.*'

Sophie folded the letter again, and deliberately refused to speculate on this strange coincidence, or on the style of the letter, which was not quite Henry's usual. She noted also that it had been written on cheap paper with rusty ink and a deplorable pen, and the wafer was damp and did not stick properly. Where could he have been when he wrote it? The Droylsden household was not so deep in poverty that it could not afford decent notepaper and fresh ink. The date was at the top, but no direction.

'What boy was it brought this?' she asked Fenby.

'I do not know him, madam. Quite an urchin in his

appearance. He did not wait, madam, but if there is a reply, our own boy —'

'Thank you, Fenby,' she said. 'There is no reply.'

Sophie was about to go downstairs to join the party in the drawing-room of Grasscroft Hall when she noticed that one of her sleeve-buttons had come undone, and she paused at the top of the flight to attend to it. It was a tiny thing with a tiny loop, and she was still fiddling ineffectually when a voice said, 'Can I be of any assistance?'

She looked up with a startled glance to find Henry Droylsden standing beside her, having presumably come from his room down the other corridor. 'Mr Droylsden!' she gasped.

'Mrs Hobsbawn!' he replied in kind, giving her a quizzical smile. 'Yes, I know I appear rather raffish, but you need not stare at me as though I were a Corsican brigand!'

'I didn't know you were here,' Sophie said faintly.

'I arrived only half an hour ago. Everyone had gone up to dress, so I did the same.' She was still staring at him with something like apprehension, and he said playfully, 'Do you think I should not have shewn myself in this condition? Have I erred unforgivably? I thought I would still be recognisable to my friends, at least.'

There was a cut surrounded by a swelling bruise on his left temple, and a further bruise on his left cheekbone which made the eye look rather puffy; but though he would not have been deemed acceptable in a public place, his injuries were not so hideous as to preclude his joining a private party of friends. Sophie grappled for something normal to say.

'You – you startled me, that's all. H-how did it happen?' she stammered at last.

'Oh, I was keeping low company, I'm afraid. My own fault entirely. May I fasten your button for you, by the by?' He stepped close and gently took hold of her hand, and then looked up at her in concern. 'Why, Sophie, you're trembling. What is it? Is something wrong?'

The tender tone of his voice almost undid her. She shook her head, and controlled her hand with an effort. 'Go on about your – your accident. Who attacked you?'

Henry made a grimace. 'I wish I knew! I would seek him

out and give him his headache again – I've had enough of it.'
He bent his head to concentrate on the button. 'I went to a
low ale-house where I used to gather information for my
journal. I may have mentioned it to you.'

'The Pack Horse,' she said.

'That's right. I had some enquiries of my own to put in
motion there, but when I left, someone attacked me just as I
turned into Wood Street Lane – hit me on the side of the head
with some kind of club.' He lifted a finger tentatively to his
bruised temple. 'I was felled like an ox, so I didn't see who it
was.'

'But why would anyone attack you?'

'I've no idea. They didn't even take my purse to account
for it. Perhaps they thought they had killed me and ran off in
a fright.' He finished with the button. 'There. What mon-
strous tiny things they are, to be sure!' He looked up at her
again. 'You look quite pale. I dare not suppose it's from
concern on my account.'

'I – of course I am concerned for you.'

'Tender-hearted Mrs Hobsbawn! But I can assure you I'm
perfectly all right, apart from having my beauty spoiled for a
week or two. I have a thick skull, you know!'

She withdrew her hand from his and gave it to her other
hand to hold. 'Did you – have you heard the news about –
about —?' She simply could not say the name.

Henry looked grave. 'You mean about Olmondroyd? Yes, it
was shocking, wasn't it? But one is tempted to think it must
have been a judgement: there's no doubt he was involved in
some pretty shady business.'

The Pack Horse, Sophie knew from conversation, was in
Wood Street, which ran parallel to Bridge Street. Indeed,
Wood Street Lane and Back Bridge Street Lane (where
Olmondroyd had been attacked) both opened onto Bridge
Street just opposite each other. Had two men really been
bludgeoned on the same evening within yards of each other,
for no reason? And did Henry really make no connection
between the two incidents – for he had not voiced any
suspicion, though she had given him the opportunity. In an
instinctive desire to escape from her thoughts she turned
away from him and began to walk downstairs, and he had to

305

hurry a few steps to regain his position by her side.

'I'm not surprised you're upset,' he said, looking at her averted profile and pale lips. 'You had no cause to like Olmondroyd, but it was a shocking end for him to come to; and its coming so soon after his visit to your house must be very distressing for you. I am sincerely sorry for it, but I hope you will soon be able to put it from your mind. It may help you to know that while I was employed by the newspaper I discovered many things about him which proved him not at all a man to be regretted in the passing.'

She stopped abruptly and looked at him. 'The note you sent me,' she blurted. 'You were not at home when you wrote it.'

He looked surprised, and then a little perplexed. 'No. The person who found me in the street helped me back to The Pack Horse, and the landlord kindly insisted on giving up his own bed for the night, since I was too groggy to go further. It was from there I wrote the note, and the tap-boy took it round to you.'

'Yes,' said Sophie, looking at him searchingly. 'I see.' It explained everything, and it was perfectly reasonable, except for the extraordinary coincidence, and the fact that there seemed no motive for either attack. And there was the odd abruptness of his departure from her house: why had he suddenly recollected the urgent business which had to be completed before he left for Grasscroft? She felt her suspicions were ungenerous, almost dishonourable on her part; but they existed, and she could not look at him with the eyes of the day before yesterday.

It was not until late that evening that Henry had a chance to speak privately to Lord Batchworth, and by then his head was pounding again and it was an act of pure heroism to pretend that he wanted to sit up late and blow a cloud rather than seek comfortable oblivion in his chamber. But the rest of the party would be arriving tomorrow, and it would be much harder then to separate Batchworth from his other guests.

As he shut the smoking-room door behind them, Batchworth eyed Henry frankly and said, 'You look as sick as a horse, so I guess this must be a business-meeting rather than a passionate longing for my Havana cigars. Sit down, for

God's sake, before you fall, and let me get you a stiffener.'

'Thanks,' Henry said briefly, allowing the chair by the fireside to come up underneath him. Jes made some agreeable clinking noises over by the corner table, and returned with a large glass of brandy. Henry took a restoring draught and sat for a moment with his eyes closed, waiting for the spirits to act. When he opened his eyes, Jes was seated opposite him, watching him sympathetically.

'You look like a pirate,' he said. 'An unsuccessful pirate, I should add. What is your story?'

'You've heard that Olmondroyd's dead?' Henry asked.

'The news arrived in the usual indirect route: Sophie's footman told my coachman, who told my groom, who told my manservant, and my man told me. The details may have become confused in the process. I gather Olmondroyd called at Sophie's house?'

Henry told the story briefly. 'When he left, I realised I had probably been unwise to threaten him. By hinting what I knew, I was giving him the opportunity to cover his tracks.'

'What did you know, by the by? You never came to me with anything.'

'You have had other things on your mind,' Henry said with a taut smile. 'And besides, I had no proper proof. It was all just tavern talk.'

'Well, tell me now, at any rate.'

'The story was that it was Maloney and Ballater who attacked Jasper that night, and that it was on Olmondroyd's order. But they weren't meant to kill him: Olmondroyd had only paid them to knock him about enough to frighten him. Olmondroyd wanted to destroy Jasper little by little, you see, so he could enjoy the process. But Maloney had his own spleen against Jasper, because of the strike at Hobsbawn Mills, you remember?' Joe nodded. 'Anyway, Maloney's a mad devil, and he lost his temper and went too far. Olmondroyd was pretty furious about it, but Maloney couldn't be left to tell his story where he would, so Olmondroyd paid him off and got him out of the country and back to Ireland.'

'But you say you had no proof of all this?'

'No, but I had learnt recently, through a go-between, that Duxbury's head clerk, a man called Warren, admitted he had made two large payments to Maloney. One was a day or two before Jasper's death; the other, perhaps more significantly, was a much larger payment on the day between the murder and the disappearance of Maloney and Ballater. It still wasn't proof, but it was a significant indication that the three of them were up to something; and Warren, more to the point, is a decent, respectable man whose word would count for something in a court of law.'

'Yes, I see. You'd spoken to Warren yourself?'

'No, only to my go-between. But after Olmondroyd's visit to Hobsbawn House, it occurred to me that Warren was my only real witness. I thought I had better go straight away to The Pack Horse and get hold of my go-between, and arrange to meet Warren with a view to getting him to swear a statement before a magistrate – just in case anything happened to him, or to me. I'm afraid I rather worried Sophie by leaving so soon after Olmondroyd – she thought I meant to go and fight him, the dear, unworldly creature! – but I wanted to get to Warren before Olmondroyd did.'

'Wise decision. So what happened at The Pack Horse?'

'I met with my man and told him what I wanted. He agreed to try to bring Warren to me next day. Then I left.' Henry shrugged. 'What happened then I can only guess. As I cut through Wood Street Lane, I heard footsteps behind me. I began to turn, to see who it was, and was hit on the side of the head, and that's all I remember.'

Jes looked thoughtful. 'And the same night Olmondroyd was struck down in much the same way, so I understand.'

'No-one saw either attack, but it's certain that he was struck down from behind, and did not appear to have put up any struggle. His clothes were not disarranged and he had not been robbed – as I was not. But he had been dealt a number of furious blows, not just the one. His skull was broken to smash.' Henry shuddered and took another draught of brandy. 'Thank God my assailant did not pause to finish me off in the same way! I suppose he must have thought I was killed by the first blow.'

'Yes,' Batchworth mused. 'Or perhaps the attacker had more personal spleen against Olmondroyd than against you: you were merely a nuisance to be dealt with, but he was truly hated.'

'Does it seem that way to you? I have been wondering whether someone overheard my enquiries in The Pack Horse – it was very crowded, and it's so dark and full of smoke in there that one can never be sure who is behind one. If someone followed me for the purpose of getting rid of me; and then later got rid of Olmondroyd in the same way ... But the only person I can think of who might have had cause to do it was Maloney, and he's in Ireland.'

'He went to Ireland,' Jes said. 'But you don't know that he is still there. He may have come back.'

'Perhaps,' Henry said. He was looking pale and worn. 'Certainly when he was in Manchester before he used to frequent The Pack Horse, he and Ballater. That's how I got the information on him in the first place.'

'If he overheard you arranging to take evidence which would implicate him, he might well have thought you were a danger to him.'

'And Olmondroyd?'

'Olmondroyd was always a danger to him. But he may even have thought Olmondroyd was using you, meaning to pin the murder onto Maloney to save his own skin.'

'That would account for the fury of the attack on Olmondroyd, perhaps,' Henry agreed doubtfully.

'But it's a great many ifs and perhaps,' Jes said. 'Nothing is certain except that you have a sore head —'

'And Olmondroyd's dead.' Henry drained his glass. 'I can't say I'm sorry about the latter.'

There was a thoughtful silence. 'May I refill your glass?' Jes asked.

'No, but thank you. I shall sleep sounder for that.' He looked at Jes. 'What do you think we should do next?'

'About Olmondroyd? Nothing. He has come by his dues at last. It's time to shake off his foul memory and move on. But what about you? You may still be in danger from attack, since your assailant must know by now that he did not kill you after all.'

Henry shrugged. 'I told my informant the next day that I did not want to see Warren after all. If my attacker was who I think, I believe he will let me alone as long as he sees I mean to do the same by him. But I shall be careful not to walk alone down any dark alleys for the next few months, just in case. I shall do well enough.'

Batchworth hesitated before broaching a subject of delicacy. 'What about Sophie?'

Henry fingered his bruised temple tenderly. 'What about her indeed?'

'She doesn't know about your suspicions of Olmondroyd?' Henry shook his head. 'I think that's best,' Jes agreed. 'I think you should put the whole thing out of your head now, and concentrate on more important matters. She'll be out of mourning soon.' Henry was silent. 'You do mean to ask her?'

'I – I'm not sure. Oh, I want more than anything to marry her, but —'

'If she were to accept you, it would be a conclusion to satisfy everyone who had her interests at heart,' Jes said encouragingly.

Henry frowned. 'I have thought, especially recently, that she was not indifferent to me; but tonight – did you not notice a change tonight?'

'What change do you mean?'

'I met her on the stairs coming down before dinner, and she seemed – almost frightened of me. And all evening I haven't been able to get her to speak two words to me. She even seemed to be avoiding my eyes. When the tea was brought in she changed seats just as I was coming to sit beside her on the sofa.'

'I didn't notice any difference in her manner,' Jes said. 'But if she found your appearance shocking, that would be very natural in a tender-hearted female, wouldn't it? She might well find it hard to look at the injuries that almost snatched you from us.'

'I wish I could be sure that's all it was,' Henry said.

'What else could it be?' Jes asked sensibly.

'You don't think she believes that I —?' Then he shook his head, smiling faintly. 'No, that's nonsense! She couldn't believe that.'

'I'm sure that as soon as your bruises fade, you'll find she smiles on you just as before,' Jes said, and Henry nodded, but doubtfully.

CHAPTER SEVENTEEN

The Second Reform Bill had been defeated in the Lords on the 8th of October, 1831, by forty-one votes, after a debate of only five days. At the time, Lord Batchworth had been glad enough to be able to get back home so quickly to his wife and child; but it had not escaped him that the situation was becoming more and more serious.

The defeat had been followed by public demonstrations of disapproval. Two London papers announced the news with black mourning margins around their front pages. A large number of shops closed and remained closed the next day, either in protest or for fear of riots. A monster meeting in Regent's Park was called, and a huge procession marched through the streets to present Lord Melbourne with an address to the King.

Protests had followed in other parts of the country. In Birmingham a muffled peal was rung for the death of the Bill. Monster meetings were held in all the large towns, stones were thrown through the windows of prominent anti-Reformists, and the bishops' palaces were surrounded with hostile crowds, for the bishops were well known to be opponents of the Bill. Riots broke out in Derby, where the Borough Gaol was stormed, and in Nottingham where the castle was set on fire. And in Bristol a mob attacked the Mansion House and set fire to the bishop's palace, and three days of violent rioting followed in which several people were killed and a vast area of houses destroyed. Eventually the cavalry had had to be brought in to restore order.

As the country palpitated with horror at the thought of revolution, Grey again offered to resign, in order to allow at least a minimum measure of reform to be brought forward by the Tories; but again the King refused. The Whigs must remain in office, he said, and must fight on for the Reform Bill in its substantially unaltered form.

The Third Reform Bill had been presented to the Commons in December. It contained a few minor concessions, which were expected to win over those lords who were afraid that the continued Parliamentary struggle would lead to civil war, but who needed some changes to enable them to save face. But they were not enough to tip the balance in the Upper House, and thus matters had rested when the Christmas recess intervened: the Whigs holding to the essentials of their Bill, the Tory lords standing fast by their resistance, and the Waverers flapping like disturbed pigeons from one roost to the other; while the King in Brighton insisted that a modicum of reason and flexibility on either side would resolve the problem.

As the new Bill ground its way through the Commons in February 1832, Lord Batchworth was in London again, and naturally called on the Theakstons to give them the latest news of Rosamund and Cavendish.

'She sends you everything proper and hopes you will pay us a long visit in the summer,' Jes said. 'We mean to have the formal Christening then, and a grand celebration, if—' He hesitated.

'If the baby lives until then,' Lucy supplied with a downward curve of the mouth.

Jes met her eyes. 'There's no use in pretending otherwise, is there, ma'am? We know the chances are against him.'

She nodded, and then said bracingly, 'Well, you will have others. You are not too old yet, either of you.'

Lord Batchworth bowed.

'But you should not allow her to brood so much over this one,' Lucy went on. 'She can't help him by shutting herself up with him all the time. You should have brought her to London with you.'

'It was not in my power to persuade her. And indeed, I wouldn't have come myself if it weren't for the Reform Bill.'

'Oh, that wretched Bill,' Lucy said impatiently. 'However,

I suppose it will pass in the Commons again. What are you needed for?'

'To try what I can do to persuade some of the Tory lords to change their minds. We must all do our utmost in that respect, otherwise we shall see the same pattern as before: the Commons will pass the Bill, and the Lords will kill it.'

'This third Bill is hardly any different from the first,' Lord Theakston pointed out. 'I doubt if you will see much movement in the High Tories or the bishops.'

'Lord Wellington doesn't mean to change his mind, I suppose?' Jes said without much hope.

'Not a chance of it,' said Lucy. 'And why should he? You Whigs make no concessions. I'm sorry to say it, Batchworth, but I think you are very wrong to go on with the Bill when the Lords have turned it down twice. They must know best, after all. That's what they are there for.'

'But the people of England, ma'am, have shewn their feelings so clearly.'

'The people of England will do very well if they are left alone. Grey would do better to ban these political unions: it's they who incite the lower orders to riot. And now there's this shocking talk of creating new peers to force the Bill through the Upper House. I hope it is nothing but talk. It must not happen!'

'But if it's the only way?' Jes said apologetically. 'The present Government is properly, constitutionally elected, and the Commons have voted for the Bill. Why should the Lords be allowed to block it?'

'And if you overrule one house at the behest of the other,' Lucy retorted sternly, 'and refashion Parliament every time the ministry of the day wants a Bill passed, what becomes of democracy?'

'I do see that, ma'am, but this is a special case; and surely the ministry of the day must have a fair chance of getting its legislation accepted, or what becomes of progress?'

Lord Theakston intervened. 'There you have put your finger on the essential dilemma, my boy. How far is it ever justified to force legislation through? Today it happens to be legislation that you approve of; but what about tomorrow, when a well-meaning, wrong-headed group puts up something you don't like?'

313

'Neatly put, Danby,' Lucy said with satisfaction.

'Ah well, that's different, of course!' Jes smiled. 'Naturally I mean all new ideas to be put to me first for my approval. But seriously —'

'Seriously, then,' said Lord Theakston. 'The main purpose of the Reform Bill is to abolish nomination boroughs, is it not? Would it not be an absurdity, then, to force it through by the creation of nomination peers?'

'I hadn't thought of it that way,' Jes admitted. 'But in any case, I've been arguing devil's advocate, because I don't at all approve of the idea of a large new creation. I can't think it would be a good idea to dilute the House in that way.'

'I'm glad to hear it,' Lucy said.

'Perhaps the Bill may get past the Lords this time,' Jes said hopefully. 'I understand a number of the lords who voted against last time have promised at least to abstain. We must all do our best to persuade the rest.'

While Jes was still in London, the death was announced of Lord Greyshott, Thalia's father. One evening he dismissed his valet from his bedchamber as usual, sat down beside the fire in his dressing-gown for a last glass of brandy as was his habit, and quietly died. It was both unexpected and embarrassing, for Lord Greyshott was alone in the house at the time: Lady Greyshott was staying in the country with her lover, Captain Twombley, and Maurice, the heir, was still in Leicestershire with friends. An anguished message was despatched to them, and to Thalia and Roland, who had not yet come up to Town from Wolvercote.

Jes met Maurice a few days later in his club, and after expressing his condolences, he asked Maurice which title he would use from now. He had already inherited his uncle's viscountcy of Ballincrea; his father's title was also a viscountcy. 'Is there a rule about it? Is one senior to the other?'

'Oddly enough, they both date from the same year,' Maurice answered. 'I dare say the first viscounts must have known each other, for they were both creations of Charles II in exile. But the cadet title on the Ballincrea side is older: the barony of Rathkeale goes back into the mists of history, so I suppose that may make the Ballincrea title senior.'

'You mean to continue to call yourself Ballincrea, then?'

'I expect my mother would like it, the title coming from her side of the family,' Maurice said, 'but much as I liked my uncle Ballincrea, I feel my first loyalty must be to my father.'

'So you'll be Lord Greyshott,' Jes concluded.

Maurice concurred 'There's another consideration, too. If I don't produce an heir – and I have to tell you I don't care for the idea of getting married – the Ballincrea title goes to Thalia's children, because it can pass through the females of the family. But the Greyshott title can only pass through the males, and if I don't breed it will go to one of Papa's very odd cousins. So I feel I ought to sport it as long as possible, out of loyalty to the poor old Guv'nor.'

'It's a terrible waste, your having two titles,' Jes pondered. 'You'll still only have one vote in the Lords, and we need every abstention we can get. You did promise to abstain on the Reform Bill, you remember,' he added anxiously as he saw Maurice begin to frown.

'As Lord Ballincrea I could have abstained with a clear conscience,' Maurice said, 'but as Lord Greyshott I feel duty bound to vote as my father would have voted. I can't betray him so soon after his death. It would be like taking advantage of him.'

'You won't abstain?'

'You know Papa was violently against the Bill. I'm sorry, sir, but I'm afraid I must vote against you.'

'I'm sorry to hear that,' Jes said, 'but you must follow your conscience, of course.'

It was like a game of grandmother's steps, he thought afterwards. They seemed to have been struggling to get the Reform Bill through for ever, without getting any closer to their goal. But his natural cheerfulness soon reasserted itself, and he recollected that if Maurice was not now going to abstain as Lord Ballincrea, at least he was only going to vote against as Lord Greyshott. They were really no worse off than before.

Héloïse laid down her pen with a feeling almost of shock. The last word was written. She had finished it at last, her History of the French Revolution which she had begun more than

315

thirty years ago, and which James had so often teased her would never be completed. She had begun to write it during her forced separation from James, as a way to ease the pain of being without him; and now, without him again – this time for ever – she had taken it up again and written to distract herself. She had written frantically, as though possessed; and now it was finished, her first feeling was not of relief but of loss.

She lifted her head and stared blankly ahead of her, listening. The house seemed unnaturally quiet. Where was everyone? She had a sense of returning from a long journey: what would she find now she was back? What would be different? For months now she had had no attention to spare for anyone or anything, and it came to her that she had no idea what had been going on in the life of the house and its inmates. Even Father Moineau, previously her most constant companion, she had seen only twice a day at mass, and then she had exchanged no words with him but the words of the litany.

She had a sudden, atavistic dread that she was completely alone, that everyone had departed and the house was utterly empty. That primitive fear, of waking on a bare hillside to find a hundred years had passed and all one's companions were long dead, lurked in the back places of the mind, and when it surged up, it left one feeling shaken and disorientated. For a moment she couldn't remember where in time she was, how far through her life. What had happened so far? What would she see when she looked from the window: winter or summer; saplings or grown trees?

Her thoughts, seeking comfort, turned first to James, and had to be reminded he was dead; dead more than two years, her dearest companion, her life's love. He had gone away and left her to mourn him, faithless to her at last who had been faithless so often in his life. Since she was seventeen years old she had loved no-one but him, built her life around him, fashioned herself in the shape of his needs and desires. In her fifty-fifth year she was too old to change. She would love him now until she died.

Her questing thoughts moved on. Where were the children? Sophie, poor grieving Sophie: she had neglected her, that was the truth. Wounded herself, she had had nothing to give her daughter in her even greater need. But Sophie would survive, she thought. She had those same resources deep inside her as Héloïse herself had, and they would see her safely through.

Bendy? No, Bendy was gone, dead to her too, it seemed; went away without a word of farewell, and had never come back; never written, except for that one, dreadful letter. Had he cared so little for her, then? Her conscience pricked her, told her that she had always loved Nicky best, and Bendy knew it; that she had never concerned herself to discover what Bendy needed or wanted. But she had not wilfully neglected him, nor been unkind. If he had come to her and asked, would she have refused him his career? Did he trust her so little?

And where was Nicky? Out about his tasks, she supposed. He was a good boy, taking the weight of responsibility from her shoulders, running the estate so as to leave her free for her writing. In recent months she had not had to make a single decision about anything. He had even, it seemed, organised the household, so that no-one had troubled her about the least thing. She had a momentary qualm, remembering the business of the letters that he had intercepted and burnt; but he had done it only out of concern for her. He had wanted to spare her, and his ardour had led him, for a moment, astray. A wrong deed could be forgiven when it was prompted by love. Nicky loved her, there was no doubt; her good son – her only son now.

She moved, finding herself stiff and rather cold. The fire had burned low, and no-one had come in to make it up. Outside a fitful sunshine was breaking through the watery clouds which scudded across the thin April sky. April – spring! Time of hope and renewal, budding and new life. Oh, but she was tired, and old, and the cold of age seemed to have settled deep in her. She flexed her hands and pushed back her chair, got herself to her feet, feeling the creaking pains adjust themselves to the new posture. Ingratitude! she chided herself. God spared her still to live in His wonderful world, and she should be glad and rejoice in it. By way of penance she decided she would go out and gather whatever was brightest and best of the spring flowers for the chapel –

though perhaps that would be too much of a pleasure to be a true penance. Still, the Lady would be glad to have her altar decorated again. It had been rather neglected of late.

It would soon be Easter – her favourite of the festivals. It would be good to have some young people around her. She would invite John and Mathilde to dine, and have them bring their children – she hadn't seen them for such a long time. Perhaps they would let one of them stay with her for a few weeks. Little Jemima, her favourite – it would cheer her to have a bright, laughing child about the house. And she would invite Sophie and Fanny to stay, too. Now that Sophie was out of mourning, she surely would not refuse to come; and Fanny and Jemima were just the same age – it would be pleasant for them to get to know each other.

She listened again. It was so quiet: were the servants at dinner? She realised she had no idea what time it was. The sunlight outside suggested it was the middle of the day, but she had no watch, and the clock on the chimneypiece had stopped. She would not ring in case they were at dinner. Instead she would go straight down to the chapel by the private stair and say a prayer, thank God for her finished work, and ask for strength to be glad in her continued life, and for guidance as to what she was to do with it.

Sophie had not intended to go out shopping alone, but at the last moment a note had come from Rosamund excusing herself from accompanying her. Cavendish seemed a little unwell, she said, and she had sent for the physician, and could not stir out until she had seen him. Sophie had sent back a note of warm sympathy. Rosamund's life was one of constant alarms, and since the Third Reform Bill was at present going through the House of Lords (having passed the Commons in March) Lord Batchworth was again in London, and Rosamund had to face them alone.

Sophie dithered a little, before sending for the carriage. Her errands were not absolutely vital, but there were a number of them. She had planned to call in at the mantua-maker's to choose the trimming for her new gown for Rosamund's Easter ball: she had already put off twice, and Madame Simone, who was vastly popular, had hinted that

318

the pressure of her work was such that the gown might not be ready in time if Mrs Hobsbawn did not come soon. Then, too, she really wanted to match the ribbon for Fanny's frock today, so that it could be finished ready for her to go to the concert tomorrow.

So in the end she took up her list (gloves and stockings, a new writing-desk for Fanny, a stern visit to the butcher in the High Street about the turkey, a rather more wistful call on the greengrocer in Market Street about apples) put on her bonnet and pelisse, and went out. She went first to Madame Simone's in Fountain Street, and was lucky enough to walk into the shop just ahead of Mrs Richard Ardwick, who was a tremendous talker. If she had arrived after her, she would not have got out under the hour. As it was she came in for a great deal of unsolicited information about the health and prosperity of Mrs Ardwick's unmarried brother-in-law Robert, who, she was assured, would also be at the concert tomorrow and had a love of music second only to dear Mrs Hobsbawn's.

Escaping at last from this puzzling exposition, Sophie continued with her errands, and at last was dropped outside Charlton's, the stationers, on the corner of Market Street and Exchange Street. At her other calls, the carriage had waited for her, but this part of Market Street was always so congested with traffic (Jasper's widening scheme would have been such a boon, she thought. Oh Jasper!) that she had to send it away and bid her coachman call for her again in an hour's time.

When her business in Charlton's was done (the writing-desk would be sent up tomorrow) she crossed the road, not without difficulty, and entered the Exchange in search of ribbon, gloves and stockings. Here she really began to feel the lack of Rosamund's company. The Exchange was always crowded at this time of day, and since Sophie was a very small person, she found herself uncomfortably pushed and squeezed. Rosamund seemed magically to clear a passage for herself by the force of her presence, and with Moss behind her, and sometimes a footman as well, to carry the parcels, there was never any danger of her being jostled.

Sophie realised belatedly that she ought to have brought a servant with her. She had no lady's maid in the regular way, but she could have brought one of the housemaids, or Peter, the footman – though it would have been a shame to take them away from their work. They had quite enough to do at home, without jauntering about all over town with their mistress; but really it was very unpleasant to be so crowded by strangers, and some of them, she thought, not even very nice-looking strangers.

When she had had her foot trodden on and received a sharp jab in the ribs from someone's elbow, she decided to give up her shopping and go home. But forcing her way through to the exit proved as difficult as moving in any other direction. She could make no progress, was having the breath squeezed from her, and when her bonnet was knocked askew for the third time she began to feel distinctly nervous and wished she had never come.

And then suddenly there was a man beside her, tipping his hat and grinning at her.

'Why, Mrs Hobsbawn, what can you be doing here all alone? You *are* all alone, are you not? Not even a servant with you? Dear me, that will never do! What can you be thinking about?'

It was Cecil Cutler, a contemporary of Percy Droylsden's, who had been one of the many young men who had courted her in her first Manchester season, when she had been mistakenly supposed to have a large fortune. He had dropped his pursuit of her when the mistake was discovered, and had later married a rather pert young woman, the daughter of a grocer, who had seven thousand pounds. The marriage had not prospered, both wife and fortune were now gone, and Sophie had lately heard that he had considerable gambling debts and was looking for a wealthy second wife.

All this fled briefly through her mind, but it was his over-familiar manner which alarmed Sophie, especially as he followed it up by taking hold of her arm. In such a crush it would have been allowable as a precaution against her being knocked over, had they been friends; but from such a slight acquaintance it seemed to Sophie an impertinence.

'Pray, Mr Cutler,' she began stammeringly, trying to withdraw her arm, 'pray do not —'

'Have no fear, dear ma'am,' Cutler said, bending over her. As his florid face approached hers she thought she smelled

320

wine on his breath – at this hour of the day, too! 'I would not dream of leaving you!' he went on. 'You are quite safe with me, I promise you. Just tell me where you want to go, and I will undertake to escort you there. My dear, you should not come out without a servant; but in the event, it has proved most fortunate, has it not?'

He was trying to draw her hand through his arm now, and the familiarity of the *my dear* made her angry as well as upset.

'Pray let me go, Mr Cutler,' she gasped, though her light voice in such a noisy place only encouraged him to lean closer to catch her words. 'I do not wish you to help me. I am going home.'

'I will take you to your carriage, then,' he said, his ripe smile looming suffocatingly close to Sophie's face. 'You really must not move a step from here without my arm, you know. You cannot have an idea of the crowds! You would be bruised and battered, my dear, and your pretty gown torn for a certainty. You really need a man to take care of you, Mrs Hobsbawn. If you had a husband, he would not have allowed you to come to the Exchange alone like this. But a pretty woman like you should never be without a husband – oh dear, no! It makes me quite angry to think of it. Dear Mrs Hobsbawn —'

He had hold of one of her hands, and his other arm was slipping around her waist, ostensibly to help her to move forward through the crowd. The unwanted, too-familiar contact made Sophie both angry and afraid, and she struggled ineffectually to get away from him, unable to make herself heard or to release her hand from his grasp. She was completely helpless. If only Rosamund were here! Oh, if Jasper were still alive, Mr Cutler would not have dared to behave so impertinently! She felt keenly what it was to be a woman without male protection.

And then, just as she was despairing of rescue, it came. Henry Droylsden was suddenly before them, his face set with anger, his eyes blazing.

'What is going on here? Mrs Hobsbawn – are you all right?'

Cutler stopped, but did not release Sophie. He looked down at Henry – for he was considerably the taller – with contempt. 'Out of the way, Droylsden,' he said shortly. 'I have matters in hand.'

Sophie was half fainting by now. 'Mr Droylsden!' she gasped. 'I – he – oh please help me!' Her free hand fluttered out to him.

'Cutler, you will let her go, if you please,' Henry snapped.

'Nonsense,' Cutler said, red in the face. 'I am taking Mrs Hobsbawn to her carriage. Step aside, Droylsden. Can't you see that your mistress is fainting?'

Your mistress. Henry whitened under the blow, but he kept his temper and his countenance. 'Nevertheless,' he said quietly but forcefully, 'you will let her go, or you will answer to me. Mrs Hobsbawn does not want your assistance. Don't oblige me to make a figure of you in public – or, I should say, more of a figure than you are making of yourself.'

'Why, you —!' Cutler bristled, and made a threatening movement towards Henry, letting go of Sophie in the process so abruptly that she almost fell. Henry sidestepped Cutler quickly and reached her in time to support her, and paying no further heed to Cutler began to help her towards the exit.

'Oh, that's your game, is it?' Cutler said raucously. 'Why, you thruster, I was on it first!' He raised his voice to shout after them. 'Come away, damn'd impudence! It was my idea! The widow belongs to me!'

Heads turned; amused or disapproving glances were bestowed. Henry ignored everything and moved steadily through the crowd.

'Pay no heed to him, Sophie,' he whispered. 'I'm afraid he's drunk and doesn't know what he's saying. Hold on to me. We'll soon be away from here.'

Luckily, as they stepped out into the street, the Hobsbawn carriage was just approaching on one of its slow passes, and Henry was able to catch the coachman's attention. It pulled up to the kerb; Henry helped Sophie in, climbed up beside her, and a moment later they were moving off, heading for home. Sophie, trembling with distress, could at first only lean back against the squabs and try to compose herself; but after a few moments she roused herself to thank her rescuer.

'I can't tell you how relieved I was to see you appear. Oh,

it was quite dreadful! I couldn't make him let me go. I'm so ashamed!'

'There's nothing for you to be ashamed of. No-one could think you did anything to encourage him. Cutler is an impudent scoundrel and everyone knows he is not the thing. I don't think he would have harmed you, but he needs a sharp lesson in manners.'

'I think he was in drink,' Sophie said. 'I could smell it on his breath.'

'That is the worst of excuses. To force his attentions on you in such a way!' Henry said indignantly. 'He ought to be horsewhipped!'

'It was dreadful,' Sophie said with a shudder.

'Well, you're safe now. Try to put it out of your mind,' Henry said comfortingly. They continued in silence for a while, and then, looking at her curiously, Henry could not help saying, 'I do wonder, though, that you went to the Exchange quite on your own. Please don't think me impertinent, but you ought to have had a servant with you. It isn't fitting for you to struggle with a crowd all alone.'

'I was to have gone with Rosamund, but she cried off at the last minute.'

'But still —'

'Yes, I ought not to have gone alone. I'm sorry.'

He turned to her impetuously. 'It isn't for you to apologise to me. But I can't help worrying about you. You ought to have a protector. You ought —' He broke off, biting his lip.

Sophie looked down, embarrassed. '*He* said that – Mr Cutler. He said I ought to have a husband to tell me what to do.'

'Damn his impudence,' Henry muttered. Then, 'He's right, though. Now that you're out of mourning, I'm very afraid that this sort of nuisance will happen again.'

Sophie thought of Mrs Ardwick's strange conversation with sudden enlightenment.

'Oh, I hope that no-one else will so far forget his manners,' Henry went on, 'but I'm afraid you may receive unwelcome attentions. If only —' He paused.

'If only what?' Sophie asked. Her pulse, which she thought had slowed to its normal speed, seemed to have quickened again.

Henry was struggling with some emotion. 'If only I were able to protect you,' he said at last. 'But I cannot always be on hand. As your manager —' He stopped. 'The mills require that I —' He stopped again.

'Yes,' Sophie said breathlessly. Her hand was in his, and she couldn't remember how it came to be there, or for how long.

He seemed to come to a decision. 'I must speak. Mrs Hobsbawn – Sophie – forgive me if I seem impetuous, or if this doesn't seem the right moment. One word from you will stop me. But I have been trying for so long to find the courage. I'm afraid you may be astonished – think me impertinent —' He shook his head at the inadequacy of his address. 'We have been friends for a long time —'

'A very long time,' Sophie agreed.

'I think I have loved you for as long as I've known you,' he said quietly, suddenly in command of his words. 'I have never been in a position to address you. Indeed, I am not now. You know well enough what my circumstances are – no-one could know them better. But I think you must also know how sincerely I love you.'

There, the words were out. Sophie raised her eyes to his and looked into his face for the first time as her avowed lover. It made her feel hollow, perilously excited. However long she may or may not have suspected it, it was quite different to hear it spoken aloud.

'It has seemed to me, especially recently, that you have become comfortable with me,' he went on gently. 'Have I been wrong and absurd to think that you cared for me, too?' She was unable to answer. 'I want to be able to protect you, serve you, keep you from being annoyed by idiots like Cutler.'

'You do so much for me,' Sophie managed to say. 'Not just at the mills. I know how many difficulties you sweep out of my way.'

'I want to do much more. I want to make you happy. Dear, dearest Sophie, may I hope? I know that in my position I ought not to address you, but I love you truly. If my devotion, service and protection can mean anything to you, I will live only for you. Will you marry me?'

Sophie was silent, trying to screw up enough courage to ask a question. Henry watched her face, hope dying as he saw nothing but doubt in her expression.

'Don't be afraid of telling me the truth,' he said at last. 'If it must be no, it will not change my devotion to you. I would do anything to serve you.'

'I wonder – would you?' Sophie said. Henry looked surprised. She seemed very embarrassed, was hardly able to meet his gaze. At last she said, 'I do care for you – very much. And it would be foolish to pretend I hadn't suspected you might ask me.'

'You don't think me impertinent?' Henry said anxiously. 'I have no fortune, no establishment —'

'Those things don't matter,' she said, waving them away with her free hand.

'Then – what does?' he asked, examining her expression. 'I see that something is troubling you.'

'It seems such a dreadful thing to think. I don't know that I do think it, really, but —' She bit her lip. 'I must ask you, or I shall never have peace of mind. That day that Mr Olmondroyd came to my house, and you sent him away for me – and then you went away so suddenly, without waiting for tea —'

'Yes?' he said expressionlessly.

She looked at him earnestly. 'You and he were attacked in the same part of town, quite mysteriously. Mr Olmondroyd died. It seemed such a strange coincidence, that I couldn't help wondering —'

'Sophie, what are you asking me?' She was silent. 'Can you really believe that *I murdered Olmondroyd*?'

The word shocked her into speech. 'No! That is – oh, I don't know!' she cried in distress. 'You said that you would do anything to serve me —'

'Including murder?'

She flushed. 'Not murder. Of course not that. But he had been troubling me – I was afraid of him – and you went after him so suddenly. I thought – I was afraid there had been a fight and that you —' She slowed and stopped in the face of his expression.

'If I had killed him accidentally in a fair fight, would I not have gone straight to the magistrate? Would I have left him

325

lying in the kennel and said nothing to anyone? Sophie, what have you been thinking?'

'I'm sorry,' she said in a small voice. He was not holding her hand now, and she could not remember at what point he had let it go. They went on in silence until the carriage pulled into the sweep of Hobsbawn House. The door was opened and the step let down, and Henry made to climb past her to get out first and help her down, but she stopped him.

'I'm sorry,' she said again. 'It was a stupid thing to suggest. Please forgive me.'

'There's nothing to forgive,' he said, trying again to pass her.

'You're angry with me. I'm not surprised,' she said, dropping her hand. In a low voice, as if to herself, she added, 'It was unforgivable.'

He sat down again, and gave her a shaky smile. 'I ought to be flattered, I suppose, that you think me such a Corsair that I would rush out and kill for the woman I love! Have I that piratical look, Sophie?'

She didn't smile. 'I've spoiled everything, haven't I?' she said mournfully. 'We won't be able to be comfortable again, as we were.'

'I think we will be,' he said. 'You haven't given me your answer yet. I know you must have time to think about it; but I hope that you will give me the chance to make you more than comfortable.'

'You still want to marry me?'

'Can you doubt it?'

'Though I almost called you a murderer?'

'You weren't so far wrong. I did want to kill him,' Henry said seriously. 'But it would have had to be face to face. I hope it is not in me to strike a man down from behind; and that was how Olmondroyd was killed.'

'I didn't know that,' she said in a small voice.

'Now you know it, I hope you will put it from your mind. I would not have you dwell on such things.'

She looked at him searchingly, and then nodded. 'Will you come in and take some tea?'

'No, thank you. Shall I call on you tomorrow?'

'Yes,' she said. 'Will you come early, and take breakfast

with me?' He hesitated, and she added diffidently, 'I have your answer for you.'

'Now?' He looked nervous. 'There's no need to rush. Don't you want to think about it?'

'I have thought. I have thought what it would be like not to be comfortable with you any more. I don't think I could bear that. The answer is yes. I will marry you, Henry, if you please.'

The footman holding open the carriage door all this time could not hear what they were saying, but since Henry was turned towards him he could see his face, and he could never have guessed from his expression what it was the mistress had just said to him. Stunned, was how the footman would have described Mr Droylsden at that moment; or perhaps, waxing extravagant, even poll-axed.

The Third Reform Bill scraped through in the House of Lords on April 14th by nine votes. The frantic efforts of Lord Grey and the Cabinet, the King, and interested people like Lord Batchworth, had paid off at last, for thirty-nine hostile peers changed their vote, either supporting the Bill or at least abstaining. Joy was unconfined; but after the Easter recess, the Bill would enter the committee stage in the Lords, and Lord Grey feared more trouble. He expected the clauses to be mauled, and a struggle to be put up over every word. But for the moment the progress was satisfactory, the House rose, and Lord Batchworth hastened north to spend two blissful weeks with his wife and child before duty called him back to London.

Héloïse had secured her plan of having her granddaughter Jemima for a long stay at Morland Place, and drove her over to Skelwith Lodge one day to collect her and her luggage.

Mathilde, looking prosperous and matronly in a very elaborate cap, and a handsome muslin and lace pelerine with its long ends tucked through her belt, came hurrying to meet her in the vestibule. They exchanged a warm embrace, but then Héloïse stepped back and looked about her, wrinkling her nose.

'My dear Mathilde, what is that strange smell?'

Mathilde laughed nervously, '"Strange" is a very polite

word for it, dear Madame. I would say abominable. Won't you come through into the garden room? I'm afraid one can't escape the smell on this side of the house, though John assures me it will go away.' She led the way through the staircase hall towards the back of the house.

'But what is it, *ma chère*?' Héloïse asked again, following her.

'Oh, it's just the improvements,' Mathilde said. 'There are a dozen men digging holes all round that side of the house. John has an idea for putting in a new kind of water-pump, you see, so that the servants will have water inside the kitchen, but that means bringing it in from the river, and laying pipes all across the meadow.'

'But you have the well, and you have always said it is a very good well.'

'Yes, it has never failed; but it's too far from the house for convenience – right over by the church wall. In fact, some people say that it was inside the churchyard at one time, and that the wall was moved years ago to put it into our land. There was a dispute over it when John first bought the land, but John won it, of course, and it is definitely our well now. It's tiresome, though – he's had to strengthen the wall just there, because the villagers keep breaking it down by climbing over to use the well. We can't seem to stop them, even though they've got their own pump no more than a hundred yards down the road. So all in all, it will be a boon to have our own water straight from the river to the kitchen; and it will save the servants so much time.'

'But the smell, *chérie*?' Héloïse reminded her.

'Oh! Yes, that was rather an accident. When the men were digging at the side of the house one of them broke through the drain from John's special closet upstairs. So now as well as laying the water-pipes, there has to be a new drain put in, and John thinks that while they are doing it, he might as well put in a water-closet for me, too, next to my dressing-room.' Mathilde looked doubtful. 'It is very kind of him, of course, and he is very clever, but it is making an awful lot of work and mess, and disrupting the servants dreadfully. There seems to be some sort of difficulty about laying the drain, too. John says that the ground here is not quite right, because of being so close to the river; but he is working on a new kind of pipe that he says will be better, so everything will be all right at last.'

Héloïse thought it sounded like a great deal of fuss and difficulty for little benefit, but John was always trying out new ideas, as she knew, and Mathilde was very proud of him, so she said, 'I'm sure it will. He is very clever.'

'He's the best husband in the world,' Mathilde said stoutly. She led the way into the garden room. This was a new addition to Skelwith Lodge, a sitting-room thrown out at the back with windows on three sides looking over the pleasure-grounds. The rest of the house, having a great deal of oak panelling and stained glass windows, tended to be rather dark, so the garden room made a pleasant contrast, and at the moment was full of sunshine.

Héloïse took a seat on a sofa near the window, and Mathilde hovered about her, making her comfortable. 'Sarah will bring the children down in a moment,' she said.

'Is she settling in well?' Héloïse asked.

'Yes, very well. It was good of you to let me have her.'

Héloïse shrugged. 'She had nothing to do at Morland Place now, poor woman, except white sewing, and she was pining for some children to care for. It was a kindness for you to take her.'

'Well she has proved a blessing for us, with Miss Rosedale leaving so suddenly.'

'Poor Rosy! Have you heard from her?'

'Just a note to say that she had arrived safely in Scarborough and had comfortable lodgings,' said Mathilde. 'I can give you her direction if you want it. I must write to her soon. I feel rather guilty about her. I'm afraid our girls proved too much for her in the end. Perhaps it was rather much to expect her to care for all five.'

'She is not a young woman,' Héloïse said. 'One tends to forget – but she was not so very young when she first came to us. You will have to find a new governess now, of course?'

'Yes, of course, but there's no immediate hurry. With Mary and Harriet visiting friends in York, and Jemima going to you, Sarah and I can manage the other three children very well. I'm very grateful to you for taking Jemima. She's just at the age to need a great deal of attention, which I haven't the time to give her.'

'It is entirely my pleasure to take her,' said Héloïse. 'She will be company for me, and give me something to interest me now that my History is done.'

Mathilde smiled. 'Ah yes, the History! We never thought it would ever be finished, you know! But what is to happen to it? When John saw Nicholas in York the other day he said you did not mean to have it published. Surely you will not just put it away in a drawer, after so much work?'

'That was my first thought,' Héloïse admitted. 'It seemed to me to have served its purpose. But I gave it to Father Moineau to read, and he thinks it ought to be made available to others, so he has undertaken to carry it to London and find a publisher for me. He knows someone he thinks can advise where to place it. So perhaps I may see it published before I die, after all!'

'It will be a tremendous success, I'm sure,' Mathilde said. 'Everyone will subscribe to it here in York: you have so many friends. And Lady Theakston will make sure it is bought in London, and Lady Batchworth in Manchester. You will be quite famous, Madame! Everyone will want to meet you.'

'You foolish girl, what nonsense,' Héloïse laughed. 'Change the subject, if you please.'

'Very well,' said Mathilde obligingly. 'Have you any more news from Sohpie?'

'Nothing more, except that she and Henry and Fanny are gone to Grasscroft with Rosamund. Their plans are still the same, to marry in the summer.'

'I wonder they should wait,' Mathilde said. 'If she loves him as I loved my John —'

'But Lord Batchworth is obliged to be in London for the Reform Bill, so they mean to wait for the summer recess when he can be at home. Sophie wants everything done in form. There has been enough unkind talk already about Henry's lack of fortune.'

'I see. Is that why they have gone to Grasscroft?'

'No, that is because they have the cholera in Manchester now, and Rosamund will not take any chances with the baby;

330

so she has taken him to Grasscroft, and begged Sophie to come too, for company.'

'It's a dreadful thing, the cholera,' Mathilde said. 'John says they have it very badly in Hull. You don't think we shall get it in York, do you?'

No, I don't think so. It has never come here before, after all. Manchester has had other outbreaks in the past, you know.'

'But they've never had it in Nottingham and Sheffield before, and John says they have it there now. And there are cases in Leeds, too. That's only twenty miles away.'

'But those are factory towns. York is not a factory town,' Héloïse pointed out.

'That's true,' Mathilde said, taking comfort. 'And it is only the poor who catch it. Ah, here's Sarah with the children at last!'

Jemima, almost eleven now, came running in, beaming with delight to see her grandmama again, bubbling over with excitement about her forthcoming visit, and wanting to know exactly what they would be doing every day for the next month. Lydia, aged nine, and Melpomone, who had just had her eighth birthday, followed more sedately, holding hands as usual – they were inseparable, and strangers sometimes took them for twins. Lydia was the dreamy one of the family, always spinning stories in her mind which she told to no-one but her 'twin'. Melly, rather plain and solemn, idolised Lydia, and was very protective of her, keeping her out of harm, and finishing her undone tasks for her so that she should not get into trouble.

And bringing up the rear of the procession was the nursery-maid Sarah, rejuvenated by her new charges, and leading four-year-old Joshua by the hand. The heir of the house was a chubby, healthy, rosy-cheeked boy, his parents' joy and pride, and lamentably spoiled by his five sisters, and by every servant in the household now that Miss Rosedale was not there to prevent it. He had come now to bestow his gracious attention on his grandmama, and to sing to her the one verse of 'Polly Put the Kettle On' which he had mastered. Since in his generosity he was prepared to repeat it endlessly for his audience's delight, there was no chance of any further rational conversation while he was in the room.

CHAPTER EIGHTEEN

Relations between Harry Anstey and Nicholas Morland had cooled since the affair of the gloves, to the extent that they never met now except by accident. Harry supposed it was a feeling of awkwardness on Nicky's part – embarrassment at what he knew Harry knew about his family – and he had not attempted to force matters. When they met, they were civil, casually friendly, and it was enough: though Harry had sometimes regretted the loss of intimacy, his own life had been too full to spare much thought for Morland Place and the Morlands.

Harry was now advancing rapidly in his profession. Much more important work was being entrusted to him at Greaves and Russell, with the hint in the air that he might be taken into partnership at last. There were satisfactions outside of work, too: he had been courting Celia Laxton, Ceddie's sister, for six months, and was only wanting the opportunity to speak to her father. With the prospect of a respectable career only a year away, it seemed likely that Sir Percy would not withhold his consent.

That the business affairs of Mrs Makepeace were in the hands of Greaves and Russell was not something that had ever impinged on Harry, for it was always Mr Russell himself who dealt with the widow. But when one day Mr Russell was ill and Mr Greaves otherwise engaged, Harry was told to go and see her at her house in Nunnery Lane to receive instructions on a business matter she wanted put in hand. It was only when he had pulled the bell and was waiting to be admitted that he suddenly remembered the uncomfortable business of the gloves, which of course had been bought at

Makepeace's shop; and he wondered sadly whatever had happened to Benedict, and where he was now.

The elderly butler who opened the door seemed to look on Harry with no great favour, which flustered him. 'To see Mrs Makepeace on a business matter – from Greaves and Russell,' he said, trying to be grand but sounding even to his own ears like a very junior clerk. He felt that Avis was looking through him and finding him wanting.

'Your name, sir?'

Harry presented his card, and added for good measure, 'Mrs Makepeace has some instructions for my principals, I believe.'

Avis looked as though he doubted it, but shewed Harry into the book-room and went away, saying that he would see if madam was at liberty.

Harry paced about the room, looked at the spines of the rather dull tomes and concluded they had been bought at least a generation ago, and for self-improvement rather than pleasure; glanced at himself in the looking-glass above the fireplace and hastily smoothed down his hair and adjusted his neck-cloth; found a rough fingernail and fretted at it absently as he stared about him. He had never met Mrs Makepeace, knew nothing about her except that she was the wealthy relict of the well-known leather merchant. He expected to find nothing particularly interesting about an elderly cit's widow, and was not prepared, therefore, for what he saw when the soft click of the door opening and the rustle of silken skirts made him turn.

'I am Mrs Makepeace,' said the vision in a soft voice. 'What is it you want with me?'

Harry tried frantically to regain control of his jaw. That mass of red-gold hair, that creamy skin, those velvet brown eyes ...! Though not in the first flush of youth, she was a handsome woman by any standard, and also had the rare quality of radiating sensational heat while appearing perfectly cool herself.

'I – I – I beg your pardon, ma'am,' he managed to say at last, rather huskily. 'I was given to understand you had instructions for me.'

She crossed the room to stand in front of him, regarding

333

him with an unexpectedly searching look. 'Mr Russell does not send his articled clerks to me on matters of business. Who sent you? What is it you want?'

He was puzzled by her evident suspicion; but then thought that perhaps his initial surprise had been too openly shewn, and had offended her. 'Mr Russell is unfortunately indisposed, ma'am,' he explained. 'He offers his sincere regrets that he has been obliged to send me in his place; but perhaps if the matter is not one of urgency, you would prefer to wait until Mr Russell is able to attend to it himself?'

She looked at him a moment longer, and then gestured towards the sofa. 'Sit down,' she said abruptly. He sat, surprised, and after a moment she sat too, facing him, at the other end of the sofa. 'Mr Anstey,' she said at last, 'can I trust you?'

Harry groped for the right words. 'I am Mr Russell's most senior clerk, ma'am. He would not have sent me to such a valued customer as yourself if he did not have confidence in me. I assure you that —'

'I do not question your competence,' she interrupted him in that same abrupt manner. 'I am asking about your discretion. Can I speak to you in confidence?'

An extraordinary idea came to him, and made him blush; but a second glance at her beautiful but grave face dispelled the beguiling notion. She was troubled; she wanted to confide in him. His chivalry reared its head. He said seriously, 'I assure you, ma'am, that anything you do me the honour of telling me will not be disclosed to anyone without your instructions.'

She gave him a faint smile. 'Thank you. I believe you.' A pause followed. Evidently she was marshalling her thoughts – or perhaps her courage. Her hands were lightly clasped, and she turned the large diamond ring on her wedding-finger round and round as she pondered. At last she said, 'Mr Anstey, you were a friend of Benedict Morland's, I believe?'

'Why – yes, ma'am,' he said. The question took him unprepared. 'I grew up with him and his brother – spent much of my time at Morland Place.'

'Yes, he told me so,' she nodded. 'He liked you – trusted you. He said you were a good person.'

Harry could not help staring. 'You – I beg your pardon, ma'am, but – you knew Bendy?' It seemed so unlikely, given the differences both in age and station.

Her mouth was nervous, but her eyes held his steadily. 'We were lovers,' she said. 'You see now why I wanted to be assured of your discretion.'

Harry was only twenty-four, and had undergone no experience in his life which helped at all with this situation. The frankness of her confession – the pictures it conjured up —! His mind reeled as he felt the blood rush to his cheeks. *Bendy? My God! The lucky dog! She's superb – but, poor woman, does she know what he really was?* But he must not stare at her. She needed reassurance. Hastily he gathered his scattered thoughts together and said hoarsely, 'I swear to you – I promise – I shan't say a word. But —'

She nodded. 'What I want from you is to know where Bendy is, and what has happened to him. The last time I saw him he was in his normal spirits: happy, affectionate, cheerful just as usual. The following day I received a hasty, scribbled note from him, and I have never seen him or heard from him since. I know, from what I have overheard in the shop and elsewhere, that he has left Morland Place, but I cannot find out why, or where he has gone. All I hear is garbled nonsense. I have striven to put him out of my mind, but when you came here today, I recognised your name: I know you were his friend. Please, can you tell me what has become of him?'

'I don't know where he is,' Harry began slowly.

'But you know why he left,' she said, watching his face. 'I see that you do. I beg you to tell me. I loved him, you see, and I worry about him.'

'I don't think you would like what I could tell you,' Harry said anxiously. He could not believe she had been party to Bendy's depravity; he did not want to be the one to destroy her idea of him. 'Please – it is better to leave well alone. Bendy's gone now. What he did —'

'Ah,' she cried, 'but what *did* he do? You cannot leave me in ignorance, indeed you can't! Think what it means to me, and have pity on me, Mr Anstey. I swear no-one will ever know it was you who told me.'

In the end, of course, he told her. He was not proof against

335

her continued pleas. He told her everything he knew, and she listened in silence; but as the tale unfolded, she did not, as he expected, grow more grave, solemn, disgusted. At first she seemed only puzzled; later, disbelieving, almost amused.

'But this is all nonsense!' she said at last. 'He was not like that at all! It was not possible that he could have behaved in such a way.'

'Perhaps, ma'am, you did not know him as well as you thought.'

She laughed, and it was a pleasant sound, breaking the tension. 'No, Mr Anstey, I knew him very well, better than anyone else could! Better than his mother or his brother – better, it's plain, than you did! Consider, he confided in me in a way that was not possible with anyone else. I promise you, he was gentle and kind and good. He would never have harmed a soul.'

'But – but the gloves, ma'am – the evidence of the gloves!'

'If that is all your evidence, it is nothing at all. Listen to me! He was with me on the day he lost his gloves – that's what he wrote in the note I received the next day. He had thought they were in his greatcoat pocket, but as he was riding home it began to snow —'

'Yes, the snow did begin that day. I remember,' Harry said.

'Very well – and when he felt in his pocket, the gloves were not there. He did not know where he had lost them, and asked me, if I found them in my house, to keep them for him. But he was with me that day, the day he lost his gloves. Do you understand? He was with me *all that day*.'

'With you? You mean —'

'Yes! I could have proved his innocence, but plainly the foolish, chivalrous boy would not name me. I could have told you that it was not him who killed that old man. And as to the other matter, the girl – what was her name?'

'Annie?'

'Annie. He told me about her. Yes, don't look so surprised! I told you he confided in me. She had been his first – adventure, shall we say – when he was a boy, but it was all over long ago, before he met me. He had seen her once or twice about the city, and concluded that she had gone into someone's keeping. He told me everything, you see. It was

336

not him who was visiting her, Mr Anstey, not him at all.'

Harry was silent, thinking back to that unhappy time. Why had he been so sure Bendy was guilty? Not just the gloves – though they had seemed important at the time. No, it was because Nicky had told him – Nicky had known all about it. Nicky had not been surprised at the news of Bendy's crimes. He had known about them already.

'But – but his brother told me,' he stammered, the horrid thought struggling for birth in his unwilling mind. 'Nicky told me – he knew all along about Bendy and the girl. He was there that day. He saw him!'

'No, Mr Anstey,' said Mrs Makepeace. 'If Nicholas was there at all, it was not Bendy he saw, because Bendy was with me.'

'Oh, Nicky was certainly there,' Harry began eagerly. 'I know that, because I saw him coming from the lane —'

He stopped abruptly. He stared blankly ahead, while Serena watched him, not without sympathy, waiting for him to reach his own conclusions. 'I don't believe it,' he said at last, flatly.

'Don't you?'

'Nicky wouldn't do that. You don't know him! To do those things, and then put them off onto his brother? His own brother? He wouldn't.'

'I accuse him of nothing,' she said evenly. 'Perhaps he was genuinely mistaken. I can only tell you I *know* that Benedict is innocent. For the rest, I care nothing.'

There was an uncomfortable silence, and then at last Harry roused himself to say, 'What do you want to do?'

'I don't know. What is there to do? You say you don't know where Bendy is.'

'No. But perhaps Nicky – or his mother —'

'Yes, his mother – that's a point. Nicholas wanted to protect her from the shock, you say. How frail is Lady Morland?'

He shrugged. 'She has hardly left Morland Place for months now. She is elderly – a widow – I can't tell you more.'

She thought for a moment. 'Who else knows what you've told me? Apart from Nicholas?'

'Only my brother Jack. There was never any formal

337

accusation, you know. No criminal charge.'

'But it hangs over him still, like a sword. Until his innocence is established, he must remain in exile.' She tapped her fingers agitatedly. 'It is unfinished business, Mr Anstey – and I am a businesswoman.'

He said slowly, 'You might swear an affidavit that Bendy was with you all afternoon. That could be managed discreetly, I'm sure: indeed I could undertake it, if you wished. Then it could be lodged with my brother Jack, who is a magistrate, as you know, in case it should ever be needed.'

'Yes, that ought to be done, in case anything should happen to me. But for the rest – how to get word to Bendy that it has been done? And how to clear his name with his mother?'

'His mother knows nothing of it. She thinks he has run away to seek his fortune, nothing more. Nicky told her that, to protect her.'

Mrs Makepeace nodded thoughtfully. 'She would have to be told of the supposed crime before she could be told he was innocent of it. And if she is truly frail —'

Harry said hesitantly, 'She is a very pious woman, ma'am. Everyone knows that. Very strict and virtuous.'

'And just?' Harry didn't answer. 'I must feel my way carefully,' she said, as though to herself. 'I must test the ground every inch of the way. Well,' she grew brisk, standing up to indicate that the interview was over, 'you may leave everything to me. Do nothing, say nothing, if you please.'

Harry stood too. 'Just as you say ma'am. But —'

'Yes, Mr Anstey?'

'Will you let me know what happens? Bendy was my friend, and if he has been unjustly accused —'

'I will send you word, if anything happens.' She rang the bell, and Harry remembered that he had been sent here on business, and asked her tentatively if she wanted to discuss it. 'No, no, it was not urgent. This is much more important. Tell your principal that I have changed my mind, if you please.' He bowed, concealing a worried frown, but she looked at him with a sudden smile. 'I won't let them think I was not satisfied with you, Mr Anstey. When I next have business with your company, I shall ask specifically for you.'

'Thank you very much, ma'am,' Harry said from the heart.

He was not in the least surprised that Bendy had fallen in love with her: she was so very sympathetic.

The crisis over the Reform Bill flared up in May as soon as it entered the committee stage. Lord Lyndhurst proposed that Schedules A and B – the lists of boroughs to be disenfranchised – should not be discussed until everything else had been gone over. Since the Schedules were the most controversial part of the Bill, Lord Grey interpreted this proposal as a warning that the Tory peers intended to destroy the Bill altogether. He went straight to the King at Windsor with an ultimatum: either the King must agree to create sufficient peers to pass the Bill unamended, or the Whig Government would resign forthwith.

On the 9th of May, the King, in tears, regretted that he did not find it compatible with his duty to create the peers asked for, and bid his Cabinet farewell. The news of Grey's resignation set off a new surge of unrest around the country. A large group of businessmen refused to pay their taxes in protest. In London there was a run on gold, organised by the radicals, and financial disaster was only averted by prompt action by the Rothschilds and the Barings. Monster meetings were held in all the large towns, and there was renewed fear of mob violence. An incident in Birmingham was even more alarming to those in authority: a detachment of the Scots Greys who had been turned out to stop a march refused to do so. They told their officers that they would prevent attacks on property, but would not impede a peaceful protest with which they were in complete sympathy.

For a week all was confused, rumours flew about like disturbed bats, the King's carriage was stoned, and solid citizens believed that England was trembling on the brink of revolution.

Tom Weston, encountering Lord Batchworth walking across the Park, asked him what was going on.

'I've heard the most ludicrous story this morning,' he said, falling in beside his brother-in-law, 'that the King has made secret plans to slip away to Hanover and raise a French army to invade England and restore his authority.' Jes snorted with contemptuous laughter, and Tom added, 'Yes, of course it's pernicious nonsense, but there are enough who are in the mood to believe that sort of thing. Facts seem hard to come by at the moment. What is happening, sir? Is it true that Lord Wellington is to form a government?'

'That is the King's idea,' Jes admitted. 'He wants to put together a Tory ministry that will sponsor the Bill as it stands, in the hope that the opposition peers will trust a Tory cabinet's judgement and give in.'

'It seems a crazy idea,' Tom said. 'The Tories have opposed the Bill all along as being fundamentally wrong. They can't now say it's right simply because it's being sponsored by its enemies.'

'The King would do anything rather than create new peers,' Jes said, 'so hopeless cause or not, he sent Lyndhurst round to sound out the Duke. There really isn't anyone else with the stature to pull it off; but I doubt whether even Wellington will find anyone to support him.'

'What about Peel?' Tom asked.

'He refused to have anything to do with it. He told Lyndhurst at once that to adopt the Bill after opposing it for so long would be dishonourable.'

Tom shook his head. 'If Peel feels that, how can the Duke believe he ought to go on with it?'

'I don't know. I suppose he sees it as his duty. He always was a whale on duty, you know! But even if he's willing to cut his own throat, he won't find anyone to join him.'

'Not anyone that he'd be willing to serve with, at least.'

'He asked your step-papa, did you know that?'

'What?' Tom exploded.

Jes smiled. 'I think the King had primed him, hoping Lord Theakston might do it for love of him.'

'Papa Danby hasn't a dishonourable bone in his body,' Tom said firmly.

'Quite. He said he would support the Bill, but not a Tory ministry that said one thing and did another. And your mama told the Beau that if he went on with this shabby business, she would never speak to him again.'

'That's like her!' Tom laughed, but then grew serious. 'But if the Beau can't do it, what's to be done? One reads such things in the newspapers! The country's a slow match burning towards a powder keg. I've heard that the radicals – people like Place and Hunt – believe they can start a revolution whenever they want.'

Jes shook his head. 'I'm not so sure. One can always incite a mob in the heat of the moment, but sustaining it is another matter. And the basic nature of our people is not violent.'

'All the same,' said Tom, 'we've very few trained troops around the country to keep order; and after Birmingham, there's no knowing whether they'd obey their orders anyway.'

'It's a dangerous situation,' Jes conceded. 'We must go on trying to persuade the anti-Reform peers to change their minds, before the mob does it for them.'

On the 17th of May Lord Batchworth went looking for the new Lord Greyshott, and ran him to earth at last at Crockford's. It was not a club Jes often used, but it was popular with the younger set: the food there was very good, and the play was very deep. Maurice seemed pleased to see him, and at once gave up his place at the hazard table.

'Hullo! Looking for me? You came just in time to rescue me. To say the truth, I was getting in damned deep.'

'Getting through your father's fortune in a hurry?' Jes said.

Maurice shrugged. 'It passes the time. And once one starts in at that sort of thing, you know, it looks paltry to break off before the others.'

'So if the others won't break off either, you all lose your fortunes?'

'Can't all lose – stands to reason,' Maurice pointed out. 'Someone must win.'

'You young fool,' Jes said kindly, 'haven't you learned the first rule of gaming, that it's only the house that wins?'

'Oh well,' Maurice said with a crooked smile, 'one must do something.'

'You should get married,' Jes said firmly.

Maurice sighed. 'I'm beginning to think I may have to. It was all very well when the Guv'nor was alive, but I have a damned weight of responsibility on my shoulders now. There's that barracks of a house in Hanover Square – couldn't let it out if I wanted to – and the place in

Lincolnshire that no-one's ever visited, to say nothing of my uncle's estate up on the Borders. And then there's the seat in the House. The Guv'nor wouldn't like it all to come to nothing. But I must say getting riveted ain't my idea of fun.'

'You might find you like it,' Jes said.

'Well, lots of people do it, that's a fact.' He brightened. 'Did you hear that Mama's going to marry her lover? Captain and Mrs Twombley! What a joke!'

'I'm glad to hear it,' Jes said warmly. 'I hope you don't mind it?'

'Lord, no! Twombley's a trump card – one of the best. I'm glad she'll be happy at last. They're going to take a house in Conduit Street – which reminds me, I must remember to tell Tom Weston that Twombley's rooms are going to be vacant. He's wanted to move into Albany for years.'

The mention of Tom reminded Jes of what he had come to say. 'Let's go and find a quiet corner – if such a thing exists in this pantomime palace!' he said, and Maurice obligingly led him through into the library. They settled into a quiet corner, and Jes said, 'You've heard, I expect, that the Duke of Wellington has given up the attempt to form a government.'

'No, has he? Well, I'm glad of it. It didn't seem right to me.'

'I spoke to him this morning in the Park. He doesn't like it, but he thinks the battle against Reform is all but over. The mood of the country makes it dangerous to resist any longer. Now it's a matter of getting the best terms for surrender, he says.'

'The Duke, surrender? I don't believe it.'

'He knows the alternative,' Jes said. 'A revolution in the 1830 French style. That's why I've come to you. I want you to give me your promise to abstain from the vote.'

'I've told you, Batchworth, I have to vote as Papa would have.'

'Quite. And your Papa at this point would have seen that the alternative is worse. The Duke sees it: a large creation of peers would damage not only the House, but the whole country.'

'The King would never do it,' Maurice argued. 'He's said he won't.'

'He will say he won't until there really is no alternative; but in the end he knows there must be Reform, and he will create peers if he's forced to. I want to see that he isn't brought to that point. Now that Wellington has withdrawn, if you and one or two others declare that you won't vote against the Bill, it may be enough.'

Maurice sighed. 'You drive me hard, Batchworth. I don't know.' He pondered for a moment. 'Well, if the others promise too, I'll promise. But I'm not going out on a limb, even for you. How many have you asked?'

'Between us – Taylor and Holland and Anglesey and a few others – we've asked about a dozen. You'll see at the debate this evening. You will be there, won't you?'

'Oh certainly, if you think it's important.'

'It's of the greatest possible importance,' said Jes.

But at the debate that evening, the Tory peers did not promise to drop their opposition. After a heated debate, they walked out of the chamber in a body, and Maurice, with a glance and an apologetic shrug in Jes's direction, got up and strolled out after them.

On the following day, May the 18th, Lord Theakston came out from St James's Palace and walked straight up St James's Street to Brooks's, where Lord Batchworth was waiting for him.

'Well, sir?'

'It's all over,' Theakston said. 'Have them bring me some brandy, there's a good fellow. It has been rather an upsetting morning.'

Jes contained his impatience, sent the waiter for brandy and glasses, and waited until his father-in-law had taken a stiffish draught before renewing his enquiry. 'Can you tell me what has happened?'

'Grey and Brougham arrived about an hour ago, asking for audience, but the King was expecting them already. They asked for an unconditional promise to create as many peers as necessary – carte blanche. The King was very much affected.'

'I can imagine he was,' Jes said. 'But he must realise there's no other way to get the Bill through.'

'Doesn't make it any more palatable,' Theakston reflected. 'Brougham said to me afterwards that he hadn't expected the

King to suffer so much. He said it was the only audience he'd ever had in which the King remained seated – normally he paces around in his quarterdeck way, you know. But he looked really old and ill. I was sorry to see it – very sorry.'

'But he did consent?' Jes said anxiously.

'Yes. He consented.' Theakston sipped his brandy. 'That was not the worst part, though. The King said, "Very well, since it must be so, I consent," – and then Brougham asked to have it in writing!'

'My God!'

Theakston nodded. 'Billy was very angry, and affronted, and asked if they doubted his word. But Grey went along with Brougham – though he looked shocked too – and in the end the King sent for paper and pen.'

'His predecessor would have sent them to the Tower,' Jes said with grim humour.

'Prinny would have started a revolution by now,' said Lord Theakston. 'But as I said to Billy afterwards, the fact that the promise is in writing may well be his salvation – and ours.'

'Because there's no going back on it?'

'Because now that they know he must do it if asked, the Tory lords will want to make sure he never *is* asked. There won't be any more resistance now, I promise you. There isn't more than a small handful of them who don't fear the mass creation of new peers more than they fear the Reform.'

'I hope you're right, sir,' said Jes.

'I know I am,' Theakston said. 'The Bill will go through now, and we shall have no revolution. But it's been a near thing, my boy. Perhaps we shall never know how near.' He gave a small shudder and drained his glass. 'And now,' he said with a wry smile, 'I have only to persuade my dear wife to be glad of it. I think she may prove a tougher opponent than the King.'

Nicholas was at first disapproving of Jemima's presence at Morland Place, especially when he discovered she was to make a long stay.

'It will tire you out, Mama,' he said. 'Looking after a child of that age, all energy and questions – the strain will be too much for you. The irritation to the nerves – your health —'

'I am perfectly well, my dear,' Héloïse said in some

344

surprise. 'You paint a picture of me as an invalid, but I am very well and strong, and I have never suffered from nervous complaints.'

'All the same, Mama, you are no longer young, and I do not think you remember how tiring it can be to be shut up in a house with a boisterous child.'

Héloïse laughed. 'I do remember, which is more than you can, my Nicky, since it has never happened to you. I love to have little children about me, and I shan't be shut up in the house, I assure you. I mean to be out of doors as often as I can with Jemima. If the weather is fine, we shall hardly ever be in the house, I promise you.'

That seemed to comfort Nicholas. 'Well, if it is what you want —' he said generously. 'You have been too much confined in the last few months. Spend all your days in the fresh air, then. I will take care of everything, in the house and around the estate.'

'When Jemima's visit is over, I will take up the reins of the household again,' Héloïse promised him.

'Oh, but I don't want you to,' he said quickly. 'There is nothing to do that need trouble you. The servants all know their jobs very well, and when they need orders, I can give them. I want you to have a holiday from care.'

'What a good son you are,' Héloïse said. 'No mother ever had a better.'

So she took Nicky at his word, and gave herself up to enjoyment and to making Jemima's stay a pleasant one. The household did seem to run itself, and though there were things not done quite as she would like them done, she resolved not to think about that until Jemima had gone home. Then, whatever Nicky said, she would give up her holiday, take charge again, and bring everything back to its best.

One fine May day she walked with Jemima down to the village, where one of the Morland pensioners was unwell. It was a good opportunity, she thought, to demonstrate to Jemima the duties of the mistress of a house. 'When you are married, *ma mie*, you may find yourself with tenants and pensioners, and I would not have you forget that they are as much your responsibility as your own children.'

Her intention to pay the visit, announced at breakfast, had

caused a slight disagreement between her and Nicholas.

'What can you be thinking about, Mama?' he said crossly. 'Don't you know there is cholera in York? This is not the time to be going amongst the poor – especially the sick poor.'

In spite of Héloïse's assurances to Mathilde, the first case of cholera had been reported in the city a few days ago: a man called Hughes, who lived in Beedham's Court and earned his living ferrying people across the river. He was a pauper and a drunkard, and lived in one of the most squalid parts of the city, but the nature of his employment worried the newly set-up Board of Health, for he came in contact with so many people. By the 17th of May, there were ten cases in Beedham's Court, and the disease had spread to relatives in First Water Lane on the other side of the river. Given the ravages already seen in Leeds and Selby, York was bracing itself for trouble.

Héloïse said mildly, 'Huby is not sick with the cholera, my dear. Do you think I would take Jemima there if he were?'

'But he's poor, and it's amongst the poor that the disease spreads. You must not risk yourself.'

'Now Nicky, you must not condemn all of the poor because of those in Beedham's Court. You know what those lanes down by the river are like – dirty and foul-smelling and full of ordure. The houses in the village are not like that. Even the poorest of them is not foul. Jemima and I shall be perfectly all right.' Seeing that Nicholas was disposed to go on arguing, she added, 'I am more worried about you, *mon fils*, going into the city so often as you do.'

He looked at her sharply. 'But I do not go into those low places. Why should you think it? Who has been talking to you?'

'No-one,' Héloïse began, startled.

'I go to the decent, respectable places – the club and the shops and the pleasant streets, nowhere else. I don't come into contact with low people.'

'I am very glad to hear it,' Héloïse said, a little puzzled at his vehemence. 'I was only afraid that without thinking you might take a short-cut through one of those lanes —'

'Never!' said Nicholas firmly. 'I have never done such a thing.'

'Very well, my dear,' Héloïse said mildly. 'Then I shall not worry about you – and you shall not worry about me either.'

He opened his mouth to retort, and then closed it again, looked at her sharply for a moment, and then went on with his breakfast. Héloïse, going on with hers, studied him covertly. He looked very pale, and there were dark shadows under his eyes, but that was not unusual in him. He seemed no less well than usual, except that his complexion was perhaps rather muddy, and he had a spot or two. He seemed a little irritable, and she noticed that he did not eat very much breakfast, but that, sadly, was also not unusual. No, she concluded, there was nothing out of the ordinary to alarm her. She had worried about his health all his life, but here he was, after all – twenty-four years old and still with them.

She hoped it would not become necessary to reveal to him that Father Moineau was giving his assistance to those attending the cholera victims in the city. He had felt it was his duty, especially as he had so little to do at Morland Place these days, and she would not by any means stand in his way. He knew how to take care of himself, and Morland Place was too clean and well-ventilated to admit the disease anyway, but since Nicky was disposed to worry about it, it was best if he did not ask where Moineau was.

The last part of the walk to the village was a favourite with Héloïse, for some long-past Morland had planted along the track a short avenue of lime trees, and the glorious smell of lime flowers reminded her poignantly of her childhood in France. The day was marvellously fair, the sun pouring down like honey through the lime leaves, green-gold against a sky of unblemished blue. Beyond the shade of the avenue, the meadows basked in the sunlight, the grass thick and green and spangled here and there with newly-minted buttercups.

The air seemed to shimmer with birdsong, a background to the light, pleasant voice of the child beside her. Héloïse loved to hear her talk, to share her interests and answer her questions; loved most of all her innocent happiness. It made her feel as though life were a holiday after all, and age and sorrow merely a garment it was possible to slip off and discard. She wanted to catch Jemima's hand and run all the way to the end of the avenue, and though she walked on steadily, the happiness of the moment bubbled and chuckled through her like a stream, felt and heard, if unseen.

'What is it, Grandmama?' Jemima asked suddenly, breaking off in the middle of her chatter.

'What is what, child?'

'Why were you laughing?'

'I wasn't laughing,' Héloïse said.

Jemima was puzzled. 'I thought you were,' she said at last.

Héloïse understood that Jemima had sensed her mood, and was touched. 'I was laughing inside, perhaps,' she admitted. 'The sunshine – the lime flowers – you being here. It is a holiday. I am very happy.'

Jemima smiled up at her, glad of the fact without needing to understand it. 'I like it here,' she said. 'I wish I needn't go home.'

'But you would miss Mama and your sisters,' Héloïse pointed out.

'Yes, and little Josh, and Papa,' Jemima agreed. 'I'd forgotten that.'

'You can come again you know,' Héloïse said. 'You can visit as often as you like. I shall always be glad to have you here.'

Jemima nodded, satisfied with the best of both worlds. They came out of the avenue into the village, and turned along the street. A little further on they came to the village green, where a group of children were playing a game of kit-cat. Jemima stopped involuntarily, and watched for a moment until a wild stroke sent the cat flying to her feet. She picked it up, glanced apologetically at Héloïse, and tossed it back to the boy who had come running up to retrieve it. He was a nice-looking, fair-haired boy about her own age, and having eyed Jemima critically, he said, 'Want to play?'

Jemima looked so longingly that Héloïse, remembering that the bow must not be always bent, smiled and nodded.

'For ten minutes, then.'

Jemima grinned widely and ran off, and in a moment had taken up one of the sticks and was standing by her hole determined to prove herself or die in the attempt. Héloïse stood at the edge of the green and watched, enjoying the sunshine and the feeling of holiday which had not yet subsided. Here was continuity: the voices of the children in

348

their energetic play. There had always been children running about here, and though the individuals grew and changed and failed and died, the stream of life flowed on unstoppable. Death came, through accident, through disease, through old age, but it could not prevail as long as there were children.

She must speak to Nicky soon about finding himself a wife, she thought: a nice, suitable girl who would bear him sons and learn how to be mistress of Morland Place. Héloïse wanted a daughter-in-law to teach before she grew too old. She wondered if Aglaea Anstey would do. She was the right age, and from a good family: the Anstey girls were brought up in the old-fashioned way that Héloïse approved of. And the Ansteys had always been good breeding stock: the late Lord Anstey had been one of seven, and the present Lord was one of eight . . .

The road which ran through the village joined up further on with the Wetherby road, so there was always traffic passing along it. Héloïse did not notice the open barouche coming along the street until it drew up almost beside her, and then she naturally glanced round. It was an elegant vehicle, drawn by a pair of smart greys (not Morland horses, she noticed automatically) and driven by a liveried coachman with a footman beside him. The single passenger was a fashionably-dressed woman, veiled against the dust. To Héloïse's surprise she lifted back her veil, revealing a face that was vaguely familiar, and addressed her.

'Lady Morland – pray forgive me,' she said, seeming rather agitated. 'I must beg you to allow me to speak to you for a few moments.'

'Do I know you?' Héloïse asked in surprise.

'You have seen me before, though I don't suppose you would remember it. Your ladyship has done me the honour many times of entering my shop.'

'I know you now,' Héloïse said. 'You are Mrs Makepeace. How do you do? What may I do for you?'

Though glad to find Héloïse so affable, Serena could not flatter herself that what she had to say would be easy to impart. 'You are very kind, your ladyship,' she said nervously. 'I have an urgent need to talk to you on a matter of great delicacy. I beg you won't think me impertinent,' she added quickly, seeing Héloïse draw back a little in surprise, 'but I have been wondering for some time how I could contrive it, and seeing you standing here alone, I could not let the opportunity pass. Oh pray, ma'am, let me speak to you! It is very important.'

Héloïse studied the woman's face for a moment, and saw that she was quite serious, and very troubled. 'I cannot imagine what you can have to say to me,' she said, 'but I see you are in earnest. You may call at my house —'

'Oh, pray, ma'am, let me speak to you now,' Serena interrupted urgently. 'I cannot come to Morland Place. Pray be so very good as to step up into my carriage for a moment. I will not keep you long.'

It was the most extraordinary request, but since Héloïse could not believe the leather merchant's widow meant to abduct her in broad daylight, she bowed her head in assent. The footman had already gone to hold the horses' heads, and at a word from Serena, the coachman wound the reins and got down to help Héloïse in. He then went to join his colleague, so Serena was able to talk to Héloïse without danger of being overheard.

She spoke, hesitantly at first, and apologetically, but with increasing confidence as her tale unfolded. Héloïse listened, at first with astonishment and then with indignation. At one point she made as though to get up and leave the carriage, but Serena put out a beseeching hand, and she resumed her seat unwillingly; and gradually she grew thoughtful, and then unrelentingly grave. Jemima, looking round in a pause in the game, was not much surprised to see Grandmama sitting in another lady's carriage, but the expression on her face made a shiver pass through her, and for a moment the sun did not seem so warm, nor the game of kit-cat so pleasant as a moment before.

'Are we not to visit the sick person, Grandmama?' Jemima asked, as Héloïse walked with brisk steps back towards the lime avenue.

'That must wait until another day. We must go home now,' Héloïse said.

Jemima glanced up, and looked away again. She had never

seen Grandmama so grave. 'Is something wrong, Grandmama? Did someone die?'

Héloïse looked down at her in surprise. She had been so deep in her thoughts that she had hardly thought of Jemima for the last quarter hour. 'No, *ma mie*,' she said, trying to smile. 'It's nothing you need to worry about. There is something I must do, that's all – some questions I must ask. Don't talk any more now. I must think.'

They walked on in silence, and Héloïse wrestled with her unwelcome thoughts. It must all be a mistake, she told herself; there must, at least, be a simple explanation for everything. This was her dear son Nicholas she was thinking of! Whatever he did, he did only to protect her. But to have banished his own brother without giving him a chance to answer the accusation – and without consulting her – it was almost beyond belief that he could have thought that a proper way to behave! Did he really believe Benedict so immoral, simply on the evidence of a pair of gloves? No, but wait – he had told Harry Anstey that he had seen Benedict that day, when Mrs Makepeace said it was impossible.

She was lying, or mistaken, that was all. Nicky was telling the truth. He *had* seen Bendy there. But Benedict, her son, to be so depraved? Nicky keeping the true nature of her younger son from her? It was impossible! Bendy was not like that. In any case, it was not Nicky's business to come between her and Bendy, to take it on himself to send Bendy away. He had acted wrongly there, and if he could be so wrong in one thing —

She walked more quickly, with the restlessness of misery. What had been going on in her household? How could she have been so ignorant of it? She remembered, suddenly and unhappily, the letters from Manchester which Nicky had intercepted. He had behaved wrongly there, too; in such an underhand way. Was it possible —? *No!* Not Nicky. Better believe Bendy to be hopelessly corrupt than Nicky capable of deception. And there was that letter from Bendy – that terrible letter. She had it still, upstairs in her bedchamber, put away in her cedarwood box. She could not bring herself to throw it away. In a blind, superstitious way, she hoped that one day she might take it out to read it and find that it did not say what she thought it did. But she knew it word for word.

That letter proved the hardness of Bendy's heart. Nicky had known him false and had tried to protect her from the knowledge. Nicky was always so protective of her.

When she reached Morland Place she sent Jemima upstairs with a maid to take off her outdoor clothes, and without waiting to speak to anyone, hurried up to her bedchamber. She took her cedarwood box out of the drawer of her dressing-table and opened it. The letter from Benedict had been on the top, and it was not there. She stared a moment, and then in a forlorn hope turned everything out of the box, searching for the letter. It remained obstinately not there.

A cold dread settled in her heart, not a thing of reason, but the wordless dread that comes from an accumulation of impressions, some hardly perceived; a thing of shadows and whispers. She put the box away and went slowly downstairs. As she reached the foot of the stairs, Nicholas came into the hall from the direction of the steward's room.

'Oh, Mama, there you are. I thought I heard you come in. Did you have a pleasant walk?'

Héloïse did not answer. She looked searchingly at him for a moment, and then said bluntly, 'Benedict's letter – the one sent from Leicestershire – where is it?'

'I don't understand you,' Nicky said, but his eyes flinched, giving him away.

'I think you do,' Héloïse said. 'The letter was in my cedarwood box, where I keep all my little treasures. Now it is gone. You took it, Nicky. What did you do with it?'

His mouth moved silently, floundering for words. 'I got rid of it,' he said at last, with sulky defiance. Her face was so grim he could not look at her. 'I didn't want it upsetting you —'

'You went to my room, and opened my box, and took away a letter addressed to me?'

He attacked, as the best method of defence. 'He was always a bad son to you! He had no right to write things like that! Upsetting you – blaming you for his own faults – I couldn't bear to think of you reading those words over and over again and being hurt every time —!'

'You knew what the letter said?'

'Well, of course I —' He stopped, staring at her wide-eyed.

Héloïse's expression was peculiar. 'You sent the letter to

me, sealed, while I was in Manchester. I brought it back here and put it away without shewing it to you. How did you know what it said?'

Nicholas only stared, his mind revolving uselessly like a wheel out of gear, his throat so dry that even if he could have thought of something to say, he could not have said it. And at that moment, to his profound relief, they were interrupted. Ottershaw came into the hall, paused, and coughed discreetly.

'A letter has just come for you, my lady, from Skelwith Lodge,' he said. Héloïse turned from Nicky and took the letter from the tray, opened it, and read it without understanding a word. From Skelwith Lodge? Something about Jemima going back to visit her parents on Sunday. She forced herself to concentrate on the unwelcome interruption.

'My dear Madame,' it said. 'I write to tell you that we have sickness here, and though John does not wish you to be alarmed, he thinks it best if Jemima does not come to visit this Sunday as planned, in case it should be infectious. One of the nursery-maids went down with a fever yesterday, which we thought was only a heavy cold, but now Melly and Joshua are both ailing too. Tamworth has been in, and thinks we must take precautions, though he does not apprehend putrid fever – my worst fear, as you can imagine. Everything is being done, so you must not worry, but I do wish you were here to comfort me. However, Tamworth says we must not have any visitors until we are sure it is not the measles. I will write again so soon as there is anything to tell. Your affec. daughter, Mathilde.'

Héloïse looked up from the second reading. Ottershaw was still there, waiting to be dismissed; Nicky was watching her, his expression guarded. Two of Mathilde's children ailing – one of them the precious son-and-heir. There was no doubt in Héloïse's mind where her duty lay. To the butler she said, 'Have the carriage sent round at once, if you please. I am going to Skelwith Lodge.' Ottershaw bowed and turned away, and Héloïse handed the letter to Nicky. 'This you *may* read,' she said. 'On the other matter, I will speak to you later.' And without another word she left him and went back upstairs to put on her bonnet and gather the things she might need for the nursing of the sick.

CHAPTER NINETEEN

'It is certainly not the measles,' Héloïse said. 'The symptoms are not at all like. What can Tamworth be thinking of?'

'He did say he hoped it was not the measles,' said Mathilde.

'It is more like some kind of poisoning,' Héloïse said, frowning. 'What have the children been eating? Is it possible they could have been eating berries?'

'Oh, I'm sure not! They are watched very carefully when they play in the garden. Joshua in particular is never out of Sarah's sight.'

'Nevertheless, with diarrhoea and stomach cramps, it looks like poisoning,' Héloïse said. 'I had better speak to Sarah.'

But Sarah could not throw any light on the subject. 'I'm sure they haven't been picking anything up, my lady,' she said listlessly. 'I wouldn't be likely to let anything like that happen to my little boy. And besides, what about Charley – the maid, my lady? Even if the children were to fancy a nice red berry from the hedge, a full-grown housemaid would know better.'

'True,' said Héloïse. 'Then we must —' She stopped as a spasm crossed Sarah's face. 'What is it, Sarah?'

The nursery maid lifted anxious eyes to her former mistress's face. 'I think I have it too, my lady. If you'll excuse me, I must —' And she turned and left without ceremony.

Tamworth was sent for again, and by the time he arrived Sarah had taken to her bed, and Lydia and Harriet were both poorly. He examined them, and then faced Lady Morland with some trepidation. He had a fine reputation amongst the fashionable people in York, and they hung upon his every word with flattering attention, but there was something about this small, dark woman which he found intimidating.

'Well, ma'am – my lady – I don't quite know what to say to you.'

'You know very well what to say. This is not measles or scarlet fever or anything else of that nature,' said Héloïse impatiently. 'It is plainly something they have eaten.'

'Ah, one might suppose so, but there's the rub, ma'am – they have not all eaten the same things. The nursery has very different meals from the servants' hall. No, I incline to the theory that it is nervous gout —'

'It is *what*?' Héloïse interrupted incredulously.

Tamworth smiled condescendingly, surer of his ground now. 'Nervous gout, ma'am, is a new disease – quite a new disease – and confined to the very best families. I have treated Colonel Fitzwilliam for it in the last week, and Lady Parfitt is quite a martyr to it! I have no doubt that I am seeing an occurrence of it here. The children and the servants all went to church last Sunday, I believe?'

'Yes, of course,' Mathilde said nervously. 'We always attend – the whole household.'

'Precisely so! There you have the source of it, I am persuaded. A delicate, sensitive individual, with all the susceptibility of the refined nature, exposed to the nervous strain of a lengthy church service – with unheated pews, perhaps, and a stone floor underfoot – will easily fall prey to an inflammation of the delicate organs. It is only a wonder it does not happen more often.'

'But I thought gout affected the feet?' Mathilde said, bewildered.

'In some cases, it does. But gout has the ability to fly about the body, as perhaps you know. King George III suffered dreadfully from flying gout which settled in his brain, causing him to go mad; and our late King George IV was variously affected in the head, the stomach and the legs at different times.'

Mathilde had turned pale. 'But – but can it be cured? What will happen to my poor children?'

'I cannot conceal from you, ma'am, that it is not a trivial affliction; but fortunately it does respond to treatment if placed in the right hands – and mine, if I may be so bold as to praise myself, are the most experienced in all of York. You could not have done better than to call me in. I have no doubt that I can be of the greatest use in the present case.'

She began to thank him, but Héloïse interrupted impatiently. 'If this nervous gout of yours only affects the gentry, why have two of the servants contracted it?'

Tamworth gave her the superior look of one who has anticipated this question. 'Employment in the house of the refined, my lady, cannot fail to have a salutary effect on the nature of well-trained servants. The fact that they have contracted this unfortunate malady proves that they have indeed become more refined by constant contact with their betters.'

While Héloïse was still struggling with this circular argument, Tamworth bowed and excused himself. 'If you will excuse me, I must go and look at the new patient.'

When he had left them, Mathilde turned a relieved face to Héloïse. 'How sensibly he talks! One can see that Sarah would be susceptible, having been your servant for so many years. And Charley is a very good sort of girl indeed, which is why I chose her for the nursery. Tamworth gives one so much confidence. How glad I am that we have him!'

'Ma chère, he is talking nonsense, I am sure of it,' Héloïse said urgently. 'I never heard of this disease before.'

'He said it was new,' Mathilde pointed out.

'There are no new diseases, only new names. What is he giving the children? Is this it? Dover's powder, yes; and barley water, you say? Well, they cannot do any harm. But henbane? I do not think that can be right; it is much too strong for small stomachs. I think you ought to send for someone else, Mathilde, truly I do.'

'But Tamworth is the best in York. Everyone speaks very highly of him,' Mathilde said, a mulish look coming over her. 'I don't think John would like me to send for anyone else.'

She proved immovable on the point; but by the evening she had begun to feel ill herself, Lydia and Harriet were suffering from diarrhoea, and both Charley and baby Joshua had deteriorated rapidly into a state of severe collapse, with cramps in the stomach and legs. When Melpomone started to vomit, Héloïse lost patience, and without referring to

356

Mathilde or Tamworth she sent a servant with a message to Dr Bayliss (brother of the newspaper proprietor), and another to John Skelwith, who was out on business, bidding him come home.

Bayliss arrived first. Mathilde had retired to her room, and Héloïse met him and told him about Tamworth's diagnosis. Bayliss shook his head.

'My dear Lady Morland, I would do anything to serve you, but in the present case it would be most improper of me to comment on Tamworth's diagnosis or his treatment. If he has been called in by Mrs Skelwith, I cannot intervene. The care is his, unless Mrs Skelwith dismisses him.'

Héloïse looked stubborn. 'You are my physician, are you not? Then you can give me your diagnosis. I don't believe there is such a thing as nervous gout. I will describe the symptoms to you.'

'My dear ma'am, I must not hear you,' he began to protest, but she held up her hand.

'I am consulting you about myself,' she said firmly. 'These are *my* symptoms.' And she described the progress of Charley's illness.

Bayliss began by listening with a look of reluctance and half-concealed impatience; but as she spoke, his expression gradually changed to one of great gravity.

When she had finished, he said quickly, 'The stools – what is the appearance of the patients' stools?'

Héloïse looked surprised. 'I have no idea. You cannot suppose —'

'I beg your pardon! Which servant has been attending the sick rooms? Who empties the chamberpots in the sick rooms?'

'I have seen one of the maids come and go – Rachel, I believe, is her name.'

'I must go and speak to her. It is a matter of the greatest importance,' he said, and hurried out.

Héloïse waited, perplexed and anxious. While Bayliss was gone, Tamworth came in to report to her. 'Ah, Lady Morland. I am happy to tell you that I have sent for my assistant to bring round a draught which I have no doubt will be of the greatest benefit to the patients. It is made upon a recipe of my own – quite exclusive, you understand – and the ingredients, known only to me and my assistant, are very rare and precious, so you may be sure it will be efficacious. The petals of a certain orchid, for instance, which grows only in the farthest —'

Bayliss burst in looking agitated. 'Well, ma'am, I – oh, there you are, Tamworth. What have you been about, man?'

Tamworth bridled. 'May I ask, Lady Morland, what Bayliss is doing here?' he demanded stiffly.

Bayliss waved him aside with an impatient hand. 'I'm afraid I have some disturbing information for you, Lady Morland. I must ask you to brace yourself for a shock.'

'Perhaps you are not aware, Bayliss, that this is my case,' Tamworth interrupted angrily. 'Perhaps you do not know —'

Bayliss turned on him. 'I have no time for your etiquette now. You fool, why have you wasted time with your flying gout, or whatever it was? It is cholera, man, Asiatic cholera!'

'Dear God!' Héloïse felt the shock like a blow, knocking the breath from her. 'Are you sure?' she managed to say.

'I'm afraid so. There is no possible doubt. I have been dealing with the cases in the city, as you may know, and I recognise the symptoms.'

Tamworth snorted. 'You may think you do, but I assure you there are many diseases which appear —'

Bayliss turned on him. 'The stools,' he said. 'For God's sake, did you not examine them?'

'I hardly think,' Tamworth said affronted, 'that in front of her ladyship —'

'They have a characteristic appearance which is unmistakable,' Bayliss said to Héloïse. 'There is no doubt it is the cholera.'

'But I thought only the poor contracted it,' she said.

'That is usually the case,' Bayliss said. 'Cholera is generated by the waste heaps, night soil and other detritus which lie about the dwellings of the very poor.'

'Then I cannot understand how the Skelwith children have contracted it,' Héloïse said, frowning.

'It puzzles me too. Cholera spreads through the air in the miasma created by ordure and waste: victims inhale the infection in the miasma, and we believe it can also be passed on the breath of those already infected. Now there are cases in the village here, some only just across the street from here, but I cannot find that anyone with the disease has been to the house or had contact with any of the servants.'

'That is all beside the point, Bayliss,' Tamworth interrupted. 'This is my case. Mrs Skelwith called me in, and it is most improper of you to interfere in this way. You have no right —'

'I'm afraid it has now become a public health matter, Tamworth,' Bayliss said, keeping his temper. 'As an appointed member of the Board of Health, I have powers and duties which outweigh normal professional considerations. You can either stay and help me, or you can go, but my authority here is absolute.'

'Then I will go,' Tamworth said, his eyes flashing, 'but do not think you have heard the last of this. Lady Morland, your servant, ma'am.'

Héloïse hardly noticed his leaving. 'The miasma – I wonder —?' she said thoughtfully. Bayliss made an interrogative sound, and she told him about her visit three weeks ago, and the smell which had driven them to take refuge in the garden room. 'Is it possible that that could be the source of infection?'

Bayliss looked doubtful. 'I think it unlikely. The disease makes itself known usually within two or three days of infection – five at the outside. And there is no smell in the house now.'

'No, the drains and pipes are all finished,' Héloïse said. 'It is a mystery, then.'

'There is a great deal we don't know about cholera; but the fact remains that that's what it is.'

'What is your prognosis?' Héloïse asked fearfully. 'Will they recover?'

He hesitated, and then said, 'I have good hopes, ma'am. With careful nursing, the strong can survive – and these patients are well-nourished and well-housed. Those who die are usually paupers, whose bodies are already weakened by hunger and disease.'

'Yes,' said Héloïse blankly, 'it always was the disease of the poor.'

359

When John Skelwith arrived home, pale and tight-lipped with anxiety, he said much the same thing, and questioned Bayliss pretty sharply about his diagnosis.

'If the disease is generated by waste matter, this is the last house which ought to have suffered,' he said more than once. 'We have water-closets, and a special system of drains devised by myself to carry waste away. And with a new water supply I have laid on right to the house from the river, everything can be kept scrupulously clean. To be sure,' he said with a frown, 'the tiresome servants still insist on drawing water from the well for themselves – they seem to prefer it – but that's nothing to the point,' he pulled himself up. 'You are sure, Bayliss, that you know what this is?'

'It is cholera,' Bayliss said, 'I wish I understood why it has come to this house; but there is no time to worry about that now. We must concentrate on treating the sick.'

'I will do whatever you tell me,' Héloïse said.

He gave her a faint smile. 'I hope so, because I am going to tell you to go home.'

'But I must stay and nurse them. John cannot manage all alone.'

'I shan't be all alone,' John said quickly. 'I have a house full of servants.'

'That is not the same thing. Servants are not nurses.'

'I will send up a parish nurse if Mr Skelwith requires,' said Bayliss. 'I am your physician, ma'am, and I cannot allow you to expose yourself to infection. Your health will not stand it.'

Héloïse fixed him with a stern eye. 'If you think I will leave my ward and my grandchildren at a time like this —'

'Bayliss is right,' John interrupted. 'I can supervise the nursing very well myself. You have been here all day, and I can see for myself that you are exhausted. You must go home and rest.'

'And eat,' Bayliss said. 'A good dinner after your exertions is essential.'

'I cannot fight you both,' Héloïse said. 'But I will return tomorrow.'

The two men exchanged an enquiring look.

'Very well, if you must,' Bayliss said. 'I can see that you would fret if you were kept away entirely. But I must insist that you do not over exert yourself. Do not spend all day in the sick-room – take a turn in the garden to refresh yourself from time to time. And go home at night and have your proper rest.'

'I agree,' John said. Seeing Héloïse was still not convinced, he added, 'If you will not abide by Bayliss's rules, ma'am, I shall tell the servants not to admit you.' Héloïse bowed her head in surrender.

'When you get home,' Bayliss went on, 'I want you to fumigate the clothes you are wearing, gargle with salt water, and take the draught I shall have sent round. These are just precautionary measures, you understand. You would not wish to put your own household in danger, I know.'

Nicholas met her in the hall, his pale face set with a determination to have things out. 'Mama, I must talk to you,' he began.

'No, Nicky. Not now,' she said with finality. She felt exhausted, far beyond coping with anything of an emotional nature. She gathered her words for the briefest possible exposition. 'There is cholera at Skelwith Lodge. I do not wish Jemima to know about it. All may yet be well, and she should not be worried before the event. No, don't come near me! These clothes must be fumigated – and the carriage too, Ottershaw: have that seen to, if you please.'

Ottershaw bowed, his sharp eyes scanning his mistress urgently.

'But Mama,' Nicholas began, frowning, 'how can it be cholera?'

'I am going to my room now,' Héloïse said to both of them impartially. 'If any news comes from Skelwith Lodge, have it brought up to me at once. Otherwise, I don't wish to be disturbed until dinner.'

She walked away, leaving Nicholas deflated – and worried. He had thought of a number of convincing and affecting things to say about the missing letter, which he hadn't had a chance to impart to her. He also wanted to find out by discreet questioning who the strange lady was that she had spoken to in the village. He had had *that* out of Jemima, but the child wasn't able to tell him who it was, only that

Grandmama had talked with her for a long time, looking very serious, and then had changed her mind about visiting the pensioner and come straight home. It did not take much on Nicky's side to conjecture that the strange woman had imparted some unwelcome information; but was it about him? How much trouble was he in, and on what score? He felt a sense of impending disaster, and it made him both nervous and angry. He could do nothing practical to better his situation as long as his mother shut herself away, and the feeling of helplessness was frustrating.

News came from John Skelwith that evening: the usual measures were being taken, and Héloïse felt an undercurrent in his language which proved he found them humiliating. All the linen and cooking-utensils in the house were being washed at once – the benefit of his new water-system was thus established, and he could not help, even at such a moment, mentioning it with pride; the rooms were being fumigated, the servants' quarters whitewashed, and one or two of the junior servants were being sent home temporarily, to be out of the way. He himself was feeling well, but had cancelled all his activities for the immediate future: he would stay at home and supervise the nursing.

As to the sufferers, the news was not good. All had deteriorated. The servant Charley seemed close to death; Joshua and Melpomone were very weak; and Mathilde was suffering from cramps in the stomach and legs. The disease seemed to be following the same course with each of them, and the course was rapid.

Héloïse spent a miserable night, unable to do anything but worry and pray. Sleep was out of the question, though she felt tired to death. She heard all the clocks of the house strike the hours to three, and before four struck she got up and drew back the curtains at her window to see the pearl grey of approaching dawn. A thrush somewhere near had begun to sing, and she opened the casement to hear it better, letting in the cool, dew-scented air of morning. She wanted to go down to the chapel and pray, but she could not bear to leave the light and freshness here at the window; so she knelt on the window-seat and folded her hands on the sill.

Dear God, is this what you have spared me for: not to be useful, but to know myself helpless? I have tried to keep your laws. If there is work for me still, shew me what it is.

Duty: it was what she had lived for. She thought of Morland Place, left to her by her aunt, the other Jemima, instead of to either of her sons, Edward or James. *Left to me because she thought I would be the better guardian.* But had she been? It was not she who had run the estate, planted the crops and tended the flocks. First Edward, then James, and lately Nicholas had done the actual work; so what was she for? She remembered suddenly the summer's day when she had walked with her aunt about the gardens at Shawes, and Jemima had spoken to her of the duties of being mistress of Morland Place.

'I wanted to leave it to you,' she had said, 'because I knew that you would not only take care of it during your lifetime, but understand the necessity of choosing your heir as carefully.'

That was why Morland Place had never been entailed – so that each mistress or master could choose the best guardian to follow them. Héloïse had chosen Nicholas. There had never been any doubt that he would follow her, and she felt she had chosen well: a virtuous man, bred and educated to his position, dedicated to her and to Morland Place, and already, in her lifetime, well accustomed to running the estate. There was only one weak spot: that Nicholas was not married. Of course, he was only twenty-four, but if she were to die now, would she not be leaving her duty part undone? Was that why she felt uneasy and dissatisfied? She felt the spirits of her predecessors watching her, saw their shadows moving restlessly in the dark corners of the rooms, heard their whispers of concern in the sibilance of the wind in the chimney.

Nicky, my good son, my dearest. The rightful heir, the right person to guard the spirit of Morland Place.

But what about the letters from Manchester? And why did he take Benedict's letter from her room? How did he know what it said? Why did he send Benedict away without consulting her? Did he really believe him guilty or was it —?

No, no, Benedict had proved his unworthiness. Mrs Makepeace had been his lover – that was shocking enough; and then he had written that cruel, resentful letter. (But why did Nicky destroy it?) Nicky was her good son, kind, thoughtful, dutiful. (Then why did she feel so restless?)

She found her hands sweating, and unfolded them to turn the palms outwards to the cooling air. The thrush's song was unbearably beautiful. Its liquid tones sank into her heated mind and unlocked the well of sorrow there, so that the pure, cold spring of grief gushed up; and she wept. She was an old woman, but kneeling at the window in her white bed-gown, her long hair loose about her, with her small figure she might almost have been a child; and she wept like a child for all the losses of her life: her mother, her father, her brothers, her home and friends in France, her dear husband – her son Benedict, whom she had borne with such love – and now for something else, too. She had lost the sense of belonging, of closeness and oneness with her world. She was restless and afraid, and she didn't know why; and God seemed far away, His face turned from her.

Since his unfortunate experience last year, which had led him to the mercy of Dr Havergill, Nicholas had been very cautious about what he did and with whom, and he had often regretted the freedom he had enjoyed with Annie. He thought about her sometimes, managing never to allow the memory of his last sight of her to intrude. He had woven himself a fiction that she had gone away to another town of her own free will, and sometimes sighed sentimentally over the pleasant times they had had together.

The house in Straker's Passage, run by the accommodating and discreet Mrs Jeffreys, provided for his amusements pretty well, and though it was expensive, it was cheaper than keeping a girl in an apartment. After all, a kept girl was a waste of money for all the time one was not using her: better to hire when one wanted, and let someone else worry about the cost of food and lodgings. For five shillings he could rent one of Mrs Jeffreys' best rooms for an hour or two, with red curtains, looking-glasses, wax candles, clean linen, a chair, a large bed, and a cheval glass big enough to reflect everything. The girl cost extra on top of that, but ten shillings secured as nice a one as he needed – unless he wanted something unusual, in which case the charge was negotiable. Sometimes

Nicholas went there in a group with friends, usually Roger Mattock and his companions, or Carlton Husthwaite and his set. Then they might share a room and a couple of girls; but on those nights the drink they consumed – and sometimes opium too – meant that it didn't really work out any cheaper.

Fifteen shillings a time was a large outlay from his allowance, especially with other pleasures – eating, drinking, and gaming – to be paid for, to say nothing of the cost of his clothes, his club fees, and various incidental expenses. And then there was the money he had borrowed from the people in Low Petergate that Ferrars had introduced him to. The interest on the debt was so frightening he had not gone there a second time, and though they had been very accommodating about adding the interest to the capital when he found himself short in the pocket, he was aware that the reckoning would come sooner or later. Just lately he had not dared even to enquire how much the debt had risen to – he left negotiations with Ferrars' 'friends' to Ferrars himself.

All in all, Nicholas was only glad that he did not have to pay for his horses too. He spent quite a few frugal evenings at home, locked in his room with his ever-growing collection of curious books, trying to save money. A man couldn't stay at home every day, however, especially when his mother was in a disagreeable frame of mind. On the day after she had discovered that the letter was missing, he was only too glad to absent himself to give her time to forget all about it.

He went out early, to avoid having to have breakfast with her, and spent the morning at Twelvetrees working with some young horses. He was beginning to think a tilbury was rather a juvenile conveyance for a man of his stature, and intended asking his mother for a curricle as soon as he had a team chosen and trained to his satisfaction. After that he drove into York in the despised tilbury, had a bottle of claret at the club while he read the newspapers, partook of an early dinner, and then walked, feeling mellow, to Straker's Passage in search of a little amusement.

Mrs Jeffreys seemed very glad to see him. 'We are very quiet today, sir,' she said, ushering him into the coffee-room. 'A lot of gentlemen are staying away from the city because of the cholera.'

Nicholas was surprised. 'Oh, is that what it is? I thought the club seemed rather empty. But why on earth should they worry about the cholera?'

'My thoughts exactly, sir,' Mrs Jeffreys sniffed. 'Foolish, I call it! Everyone knows it only affects the lowest sort – the Irish, the paupers, and that sort of person – and you won't find anyone like that in my house. I warrant you!'

'I'm sure I won't,' Nicholas said politely.

'That's right, Mr Morland,' she said approvingly. 'Insulting to me, that's what it is, to stay away for such a reason – and insulting to my other gentlemen too. But I would ha' known I should not be disappointed in you, sir, and here you are indeed! Will you take a glass of something with me, Mr Morland – on the house?'

The man brought Madeira, and when she had sipped, Mrs Jeffreys grew confidential. 'The cowardice, not to say bad manners, of some, may prove to be the advantage of others,' she began mysteriously. 'I have something rather special in the house, Mr M, which I was saving for another gentleman of mine; but since he has chosen to stay away for no better reason than a spot of fever down by the river, I think I have every right to offer you the pleasure.'

Nicholas raised an eyebrow. 'Other people's leftovers, Mrs Jeffreys? What pleasure could there be in that?'

She smiled triumphantly. 'Ah, that's the whole point, Mr M, and the very reason a careful gentleman like yourself will snap at it, or my name ain't Polly Jeffreys. T'won't come cheaply, of course,' she added thoughtfully, 'but worth every penny, I think you'll find. It's a maidenhead, Mr Morland – a nice little, clean, untouched virgin.'

Nicholas, startled, said nothing; but nodded to her over his glass with sufficient encouragement for her to continue.

'My other gentleman, which I was talking about, has me look out for them for him. I procure him two or three every year. He won't hardly touch any other sort – declares the pleasure of it is beyond anything; to say nothing of the convenience, for what has never been broached, you know, can conceal no hidden dangers.'

'I do see that,' Nicholas said thoughtfully. 'But how do you know it is a virgin?'

'Why, bless you, sir, I know my suppliers! The child's mother is in the business herself, and has bred and trained her for it, and kept her a maid for that very reason. A maidenhead commands a pretty price wherever you go. She knows her business – and so, you may be sure, do I.'

'A child, you say? How old?'

Mrs Jeffreys looked solemn. 'Why, thirteen, sir, to be sure. Younger than that it would be illegal, for thirteen's the age of consent, as you well know, Mr M.'

'So young!' Nicholas said. In spite of himself, he felt somewhat shocked. That was barely older than little Jemima back at Morland Place – and she played with toys and sang nursery rhymes. 'How can her mother sanction it when she's so young?'

'Why as to that,' Mrs Jeffreys shrugged, 'the girl must take the first step some time, and until she do, she won't earn a penny for her mother or herself. If it is not done here, a coster lad will have it for nothing before many more months are out, and it would be a poor thing not to make the most of what can only happen once.'

Nicholas contemplated this philosophy for a moment, and found it sufficiently soothing. As to the thing itself – it was rather exciting, he thought. He had never had a maid before. It would be something new, as well as being as safe as it could be, which was very much an object with him. 'How much?' he asked at last.

'A hundred pounds,' Mrs Jeffreys said promptly. Nicholas gaped, but before he could protest, she went on, 'I would have charged Colonel F – the other gentleman, I should say – a hundred and fifty, but he has let me down. I like you, Mr M, and you are a good, regular customer. I will give you a preferential rate on this occasion, to introduce you to the sport. Once you have tried it, I promise you will prefer it to all other.'

'A hundred pounds! It's a great deal of money,' Nicholas said.

'A maidenhead's a very rare commodity,' Mrs Jeffreys said. 'And rare commodities cost dear. Consider, once it is gone, it's gone for ever; and this is a very fine, pretty girl, one of the nicest I've seen in a long while. Why, in London her mother could get two hundred pound for it, very likely more – but she does not wish to have the bother of travelling. So will you have it, sir, or shall I keep it for another gentleman I have in mind?' As he hesitated, she looked away with apparent indifference. 'I shall charge *him* a hundred and fifty, you may be sure, so you may please yourself.'

The thought of its being such a bargain clinched the matter with Nicholas. He imagined himself saying airily to Husthwaite and the others, 'Oh, Mrs J keeps an eye open for maidenheads for me. She knows I prefer 'em.' And if they took it up too, he would still have been first, and would be paying less than any of them for it!

Even so, he still had a bargain to drive. 'For that sort of money,' he said loftily, 'I shall expect to keep the room all evening.'

Mrs Jeffreys stood up, her plump hands making an involuntary grasping movement as they always did when she was pleased. 'Aye, and all night too, if you wish,' she said agreeably. 'Everything of the best! If you will give me a moment, sir, I will set up the room for you.'

It was the best room in the house. Mrs Jeffreys escorted Nicholas there, opened the door, and stood back to usher him in, saying, 'Here is Becky, sir, and I'm sure you will like her above anything. Stand up, Becky, and curtsey to the gentleman!'

The child, who had been sitting on the edge of the bed, stood up and curtsied quickly, and just for a moment Nicholas felt taken aback. She was so very small and young: she looked closer to ten than thirteen, a pretty little girl with the roundness of childhood still in her cheeks, fine, almost flaxen hair, and large solemn blue eyes, just now looking up at him with faint apprehension. For a fleet, unwilling moment, Nicholas thought of his mother, without exactly knowing why. It annoyed him to have her obtrude into his thoughts, and he dismissed her determinedly.

'Didn't I tell you she was a very fine girl?' Mrs Jeffreys said with satisfaction. 'I shall leave you now. Just ring if there's anything you require.'

'Thank you,' Nicholas said, and the door closed behind him.

Nicholas had never before stayed all night at Mrs Jeffreys' house, but the thought of the hundred pounds spurred him on to make the most of it; and his hostess plied him so well with brandy (that was expensive too – she charged far more than the club did, but one was hardly in a position to complain) that he grew too comfortable and sleepy to leave. When he woke in the morning the child was gone, and he was not sorry, for he had a thick head and a mouth like sand. One of the housemaids (squint-eyed and thin as a stick – Mrs J kept very ugly housemaids, presumably to differentiate them from her working girls) came in with hot water and coffee, and after a while he was able to get himself downstairs with some semblance of dignity.

Mrs Jeffreys came out to hand him his hat. 'I hope everything was to your satisfaction?' she said.

'Ah yes – yes, thank you,' Nicholas mumbled. He turned his hat round in his hands. 'What happens to her now?' he asked abruptly.

'For a month or two she'll be kept for my preferential clients,' she said, giving him a predatory look. 'I should be happy to number you amongst 'em, Mr Morland. The price is higher than usual, but a high price keeps off ill company, you know.'

The mention of price reminded Nicholas of that terrible hundred pounds. How ever was he going to find it? Plus the cost of all the brandy he drank – and there would be overnight stabling for his horse now, as well. His allowance would never stretch that far. Why did his mother keep him so damned short?

'Oh – er – I will let you know about that,' he said, avoiding Mrs Jeffreys' eyes.

She gave him a canny look. 'Just as you please, sir. And while we're on the subject, I have my bill here for you, if you would care to settle it before you leave. You know my terms, sir.'

Nicky grasped after some dignity. 'And you know that I always do settle, Mrs Jeffreys, but you cannot think I have a hundred pounds in my pocket just for the asking. Recollect that I did not come here last night expecting what I found.'

'To be sure, sir.' she said enigmatically. 'And when may I expect the honour of settlement?'

'As soon as it is convenient,' he said loftily. 'I cannot say more than that.'

'I leave it in your hands, then, sir,' Mrs Jeffreys smiled sweetly. 'It will be convenient to *me* to have the money within the week, if you please. But if you prefer, I can send the bill to Morland Place for settlement at the month's end.'

Nicky cleared his throat sternly. 'No, no, I would not put you to that trouble. Give it to me here – I will see you have your money by Saturday.'

He stepped out into the grey light of an overcast morning, squinting against the light, which even filtered by clouds was too bright for his headache. He saw a dark figure detach itself from the wall opposite and come towards him. 'Ferrars?' he said. 'What the devil are you doing here?'

'I came to find you, sir,' Ferrars said evenly. 'I thought I ought to warn you that you were missed last night, and again this morning. It might be as well to have some story ready against the catechism.'

'Don't be impertinent,' Nicky snapped. 'What do you mean, I was missed?'

'Your honoured parent, sir, has been sending all over the country for you,' Ferrars grinned, unabashed. 'I was despatched last night to see if your tilbury was in its usual place, and however reluctantly, I was forced to report that it was not there. So this morning, when I knew you hadn't come back, I guessed how it was, and slipped away to come into York and look for you. It didn't take me long to find you.'

'Damn your impertinence,' Nicholas said.

'Damn it as you please, sir,' Ferrars invited. 'I am at your command for whatever excuse you want to use, but I think you ought to have some explanation in mind. Your mother is in a rare taking.'

'Oh, deuce fly away with her,' Nicky muttered uncharitably. 'What is it now?'

'Bad news from Clifton, sir.'

'Clifton?'

'From Skelwith Lodge. The cholera.'

'Devil take it, I'd forgotten about that,' Nicky said.

'So your noble parent apprehended, sir, which has made her more than a little angry with you for staying away. Your place, she felt, was at her side in such a time of sorrow.'

'Time of sorrow? Don't tell me there are more of them sick?' Nicky said ungraciously. This was not the reception he wanted after a night of pleasure. It was quite taking the shine off it for him.

'Three of the children died yesterday,' Ferrars said with an air of enjoying Nicky's predicament, 'and Mrs Skelwith died during the night – word came first thing this morning. The other two children are very sick, and now Mr Skelwith has symptoms too. You may imagine your mother's state of mind.'

Nicholas could; so well that this time he did not even rebuke Ferrars for the freedom of his language. How was he supposed to have known that they would die? But that would not weigh, as he knew. 'God's teeth,' he groaned. 'Now I'm in a fix.'

'That you are, sir,' Ferrars agreed. He eyed his master speculatively. 'If I might suggest, sir – as the damage is done, it might be better to go and take a spot of something and some vittles somewhere while you think what's to do. You're not looking quite the thing.'

'I'm not feeling quite the thing,' Nicholas said plaintively. 'Too much damned brandy last night, and now you go and shock me like that. You know I'm not a robust man. You should have broken it gently.'

'A little breakfast will make you feel much better, sir,' Ferrars said. 'It's the best thing for the sanguineous affliction! Trust me. I know a nice little coffee-room not far away where no-one will know you, and we can talk in peace.'

Nicholas felt too done-up to argue with him, and fell in beside his man, unwillingly grateful to him for taking the decisions.

Ferrars was right: eating did make Nicky feel better. The coffee he had had at Mrs Jeffreys' had given him heartburn, but after several boiled eggs, a dish of mutton chops, and half a loaf of bread, washed down with a pint of small beer, he felt his affronted stomach and frayed nerves lie down to sleep,

371

and his headache dimmed to a distant rumble.

'Very well, you had better tell me what happened at home,' he said when he finally laid down his knife and fork.

'Her ladyship looked for you at breakfast yesterday – she'd had a disturbed night, according to what I heard, and was wanting to talk to you. Fortunately, one of the grooms knew that you had gone up to Twelvetrees, and her ladyship was pleased to think how hard you worked and resolved to speak to you when you came home to dinner.'

'Speak to me about what?' Nicky asked nervously.

'That I can't say, sir. She set off for Clifton after breakfast as she had planned. But then the news came just after noon that the little boy had died,' Ferrars said, resting his clasped hands calmly on the table top, 'and asking you to go to Skelwith Lodge to her ladyship. The message was sent to Twelvetrees, but by the time it arrived there, you had gone and no-one knew where. Her ladyship returned to Morland Place most reluctantly, on the physician's insistence, expecting to see you at dinner. But you didn't come to dinner, nor after it, and by then the message had come that the two youngest girls were dead, and Sarah too, and her ladyship was in a rare taking.'

Nicky groaned. 'Oh Lord, my poor mother! What did she do?'

'Well, she felt obliged to tell the little girl, Miss Jemima, and that was bad enough,' Ferrars said, staring neutrally at the wall behind Nicky's ear. 'Father Moineau was on hand, of course, and there was a tedious long – a long service in the chapel, I should say, which we were all obliged to go to. Having just come in, I couldn't get out of it.'

'You have my sympathy.'

'Thank you, sir. Well, then there was a vigil all night, and her ladyship wanted you to help with it and expected you from hour to hour, which was how it came about that she knew you hadn't been home at all, because there were servants up and about, and every one primed to look out for you. Then this morning the news came up about Mrs Skelwith, and that broke her ladyship's heart. Dr Bayliss came himself to tell her, and she was raging to go there, thinking if she could have nursed Mrs Skelwith through the night she might not have died. But the doctor wouldn't let her go up there, saying the disease is raging in the house and her ladyship worn out with caring. So I came out to look for you, leaving her ladyship talking about writing some letters —'

Nicholas's attention sharpened. 'Letters? To whom?'

'To Mrs Hobsbawn, I believe, sir – and to Mr Pobgee,' Ferrars said expressionlessly.

Nicholas paled. 'Pobgee,' he said.

'She looked quite grave when she said it, sir. Said she was going to ask him to come to the house to advise her on something.'

'For God's sake, on what?' Nicholas demanded violently.

'Who can say, sir? Some legal matter, obviously, since he's her man of business.'

Nicholas stared sightlessly ahead. 'I know what it is,' he whispered. 'She's going to change her Will.' He put his head into his hands and groaned. 'She's angry with me for going missing and she's going to change her Will and leave everything to Sophie.'

'It is one possible interpretation of the facts, sir,' Ferrars agreed.

'She can't do it, she mustn't!' he moaned.

'It would be unfortunate in the extreme,' Ferrars remarked, 'especially considering the money you have raised on the expectation. It would be difficult to explain that to our friends in Low Petergate.'

'I won't let her do it!' Nicholas cried. 'Morland Place is mine, it's always been mine, and Sophie shan't have it! I won't let Mama give it to her!'

Ferrars said nothing to this outburst, and after a while Nicholas lifted his face from his hands and stared ahead, his red-rimmed eyes widening, his pale face seeming to grow even a shade paler. A thought had evidently come to him, a thought which seemed, from his expression, at first frightening, and then gradually more appealing.

Ferrars watched him dispassionately. 'You have a plan, sir?' he asked after a moment.

'Perhaps,' Nicholas said. His lips curved in a ghastly smile. 'Perhaps it may not be necessary. It may be as well to be prepared, however.'

CHAPTER TWENTY

The candles twinkled in the thick darkness like pinpoint stars on a moonless night, seeming to light nothing but themselves. Benedict always thought they served only to make the darkness visible, as though it were a tangible thing, like black cloth filling the tunnel workings. The air was thick, foul and damp, and seemed hard to breathe – though it was not as bad today as it had been yesterday: then they had had to do some blasting, and the stink of gunpowder had filled their noses and made their throats raw.

Today they had hit the soft stuff, and the men were working with pickaxes and shovels. Almost invisible in the darkness, the pick-men tore away at the blank wall in front of them, a noise accompanying each blow which was half grunt, half groan. When one drew close enough to see, the candlelight touched a muscular shoulder here, a bent back there, naked and shiny with moisture; outlined a rough profile, the hair spiked with sweat and mud; glimmered on the water running down the walls and spreading out into a sheet underfoot. The shovel-men sloshed and slithered after the pick-men, swinging their brawny arms as they heaved the waste up into the barrows. It had been raining for two days now: everyone had got so used to being wet that they no longer noticed it. Benedict himself was soaked through: he could smell his coat if he thought about it – rank as a sheep; the water inside his boots had warmed to the comfortable temperature of invalid soup.

When the pick-men had cleared twelve feet, Benedict would call them to halt and the labourers would drag up the wooden shores, to hold the roof and sides until the bricklayers could do their part. Tunnelling was the worst part of making a railway, and sometimes the men would lose heart, toiling down here in the dark day after day like lost souls. It was the engineer's business to chivvy them on. Benedict was popular with the navvies, and they would do for him more than they would for some others, which was partly why he had been assigned to this job. The men worked a twelve-hour shift – twelve on and twelve off – but Benedict had been down here now for two days and the intervening night. They were not far off breaking through, and he could not bear not to be here when it happened.

A rumbling sound behind him was the soil truck coming back. He turned and stared through the darkness for the little bobbing glim. It was hard to tell distances with nothing to give perspective, and the faint outline of the moving horse and boy seemed still some yards off the instant before the horse's warm muzzle touched his hand and made him jump. The horse stopped; Benedict laid his palms on the animal's nose, and it moved its head up and down gratefully, using him to rub away an itch. The light swung upwards, and he saw Dandy Dick's face behind it, bending to rub his own nose on his upper sleeve.

'Is that you, Mr Morland, sir?' Dandy asked.

'Yes, Dandy. All well up above?'

'Raining fit to bust, sir.'

'I can tell,' Bendy said wryly. 'Go on down, the men are waiting for you.'

'Must be nearly through, eh, sir?' Dandy said conversationally.

'We shall do it this shift.'

'Liza will be glad. I saw her this morning. In quite a pucker that you didn't come up last night. I said I'd eat your supper for you, if she liked.'

'Go on with you, impudence,' Bendy said. His face was invisible to Dandy, but the boy heard the smile, and it warmed him. It had been more kind than he looked for in Mr Morland, to have brought him to Glenfield as well as his sister, and to have got him a good job as a horse-boy; but on top of that he had arranged with the parson's clerk to teach Dandy to read, two lessons a week in his off time, so that he could better himself. And though Liza didn't talk about it, he knew that Mr Morland was very good to her, never beat her or anything, and bought her nice things to eat and to wear. He had done a lucky thing, he reflected, asking Mr Morland for help, that day that Liza had come to him. They were set up for life, it seemed.

He slid his hand up the halter and gave a little tug. 'Come on, Smokey,' he said, and felt the horse bring its shoulders up into the collar, taking up the slack on the shafts and getting a foothold in the mud. He clicked encouragingly and led Smokey forward towards the lights of the pick-men.

And then there was a soft, deadly sound from above him – not quite a rumble, a looser, lighter sound than that – and someone close to him shouted 'Cave in!' Dandy turned his face up and felt a sharp patter of sand strike his cheek; turned his head instinctively towards his horse; and then the darkness collapsed on top of him, soft, heavy, Stygian, suffocating.

Benedict heard the shout and the roof collapse at the same instant, waited for one terrifying second for it to hit him, and then felt the earth bouncing in front of him, clods striking his shins. He crouched, putting his arms over his head. It was all one could do when there was a roof-fall – to protect the head, and keep the hands close to the body, so that one might have a chance of digging oneself out afterwards. An outflung arm might be trapped under a weight of earth, and be useless. The soft rumbling seemed to go on for a long time, but only a pattering of material was hitting him. He was at the edge of it, then – the real fall was going on in front of him.

At last the rushing and rumbling stopped. There was a moment's silence, and then shouts from behind him, and men were coming forward with lights. Thank God for that! Bendy thought, standing up slowly, brushing soil from his jacket, shaking it from his hair. He had lost his hat, but was more concerned that he had also lost his light. That was the worst thing in a collapse, for in utter darkness one very quickly lost all sense of direction, so that it was impossible to know which way to dig. The first man to reach him peered at his face and gave him his light, saying, 'Here, master. You all right, sir?'

'Yes, it missed me.' He raised his voice. 'Hold up your lights, lads, let's see how bad it is! Ho, shovels, there! And bring more props down!'

'It'll be the rain that's brought it down,' said the man beside him – Tom Daddy was his nickname, one of the older navvies, a man long on experience, and so short on teeth it was quite hard to understand what he said. 'We had a fall like this when we was diggin' under Crown Street, Liverpool. I hate wet-tunnelling. Give me rock an' blast any day, for all the danger!'

Bendy was examining the scene with his light held aloft. 'It doesn't look too bad,' he said with enormous relief. Already up ahead of him there was movement – men getting up, throwing the soft stuff off them. 'Let's get digging. Who's there? Ah Redhead, Spider – and you, Long Bob, get those props in over there, d'you see where it's sagging. We don't want the rest collapsing on us.'

'Must be thirty foot o'dirt come down,' Redhead said gloomily. 'Won't break through this shift now.'

'Gah! It'll be Beetle Billy'll do it after all,' said Spider, spitting sideways to register his disgust. 'He had twenty pun' on it wi' Walker's gang, that he'd see the break-through.'

'He's probbly been up atop, dancin' over our 'eads to bring it down,' Tom Daddy cackled.

'Less talk and more digging!' Benedict snapped. 'Let's get these men pulled out!' He was worried about Dandy Dick.

'Don't 'e fret, guv'nor,' said Long Bob. 'T'was all loose stuff – sand and moss and th'like. We'll have 'em all out in two shakes.'

Ah, there was the cart, tilted up at an angle; and the horse struggling to get to its feet, snorting with alarm and distress, hampered by the angle of the shafts. Benedict hurried round the side of it and reached over to undo the trace-clip, seeing Tom Daddy doing the same on the other side. And this heap of soil must be Dandy Dick. He put down his light and began clawing away with both hands. Why was he not moving? Everywhere men were shaking off the loose stuff, cursing, spitting, coughing, but Dandy wasn't helping himself. Bendy's hands encountered cloth. Another man was beside him, digging too. Between them they took hold of Dandy's coat and hauled him out, and Benedict leaned him against his knee, and passed his hand over the boy's face, cleaning it of soil. In the faint light he could see the eyes closed, no movement.

'Is he dead?' said the man beside him – another of the old hands, called Shag Daddy because of the tobacco he chewed. 'Clear his mouth out, master. Mebbe he had it open.'

Benedict prised open the mouth, hooked inside it with his fingers, found a little mud but not enough to have choked him. But where was his tongue? Had he bitten it off and swallowed it? There was nothing but slippery emptiness!

'He's got no tongue!' Benedict cried aloud in horror.

'Fallen back in his throat,' said Shag Daddy tersely. 'Pull that forward, sir, else he'll suffocate!'

Benedict reached further in, found the back of the tongue, worked his fingers round it (horrible feeling!) and pried it forward. As it came away from the back of the throat he felt a suck of air tear past his fingers and hastily withdrew them. The boy dragged in another hoarse breath and then began coughing violently. Bendy felt himself trembling with relief. He had seen accidents before – plenty of them – but this was Liza's brother. How would he ever have broken it to her?

'Thass right, sir. Give 'un to me now,' said Shag Daddy, pulling Dandy away from Benedict and turning him over onto his hands and knees with a dextrous strength which belied his age. Dandy was retching and crowing for breath. 'Goo you on, sir, where you're wanted. I'll take care o' the little 'un.'

'Get him topsides, then,' Benedict said tersely. 'He must see the doctor.' And then he turned to his other responsibilities. 'Tom Daddy, see to the horse. If he's sound, hitch him up – we'll need the truck. You two, over here with the shovels! There's a heap here that's not moving: see if there's anyone under it. Carefully, now! Ho, more props here —!'

When he came above ground at last, the rain had stopped, but a damp, cool evening was making an early end to the day. The air smelled of wet leaves, heavenly after the closeness of the tunnel, life-giving: Bendy stood still and sucked it in like a plant taking in water. His legs were trembling with weariness. The fall had claimed no lives, thank God – just

378

cuts and contusions, one broken arm, and Dandy Dick's concussion. He had been struck by something, probably a stone, but his head was not broken, and he was expected to be quite recovered after a good night's sleep.

Still, the collapse had been frightening at the time, and monstrously disheartening afterwards. It needed a great deal of work to clear it up, and to reinforce the roof for the bricklayers, and it looked likely that the break-through would fall to the honour of the next shift after all. Benedict would have liked to stay down and see it – it was always a thrilling moment when the men shook hands through the first hole in the last barrier – but he had gone over forty hours now without sleep, and knew it would be folly not to go up. Besides, there was a longing for hot water on him which could no longer be denied. Hot water, hot food, and a quart of good ale to assuage the underground thirst, which the men called Tunnel Drought – that's what he wanted now.

When he came out into the failing daylight he saw Liza. She was wearing a thick shawl and pattens, her gown pinned up out of the mud, her dark head bare to the damp air; and though there were several women waiting, all dressed much alike, she stood just a little apart from them. It seemed an unconscious thing and yet fitting, for she was not like them. While they folded their arms close about them and leaned their heads together, chatting, she stood very straight with her hands clasped in front of her, seeming only lightly poised on the earth as if she might rise gently off it at any moment. Her apartness came from inside her, he thought. The clouds were dark behind her head, but there was a thin rim of storm-light below them which etched her out, as though she were being distinguished even by nature from the rest of humanity.

Fand saw him and came forward, bowing and lashing her tail, flattening her ears out sideways and yawning in the extremity of her pleasure at seeing him again. He caressed her roughly and walked on towards Liza, the hound pressing against his legs and jabbing her muzzle at his hand.

'Well,' he said, reaching Liza, 'here's a welcome.'

'I heard there had been a roof-fall.' She scanned his face unsmilingly. 'You are not hurt?'

'Not at all,' he said.

Her eyes seemed to touch his face like tender fingers. 'There's blood on your cheek.'

'Is there?' He reached up and felt a cut, sore as he touched it, though he hadn't noticed it before. 'It's nothing.'

She had seen the wince. 'It is dirty. I will bathe it for you when we get home,' she said, turning towards the village.

He fell in beside her and Fand ran out ahead of them, joyfully sniffing at every clump of grass. 'Don't you want to know about your brother?'

'I saw him. I was here when they brought him up. The doctor said it is nothing but a concussion. He will be well tomorrow.'

'That's what I heard. But don't you want to go and see him?'

She walked on steadily, her face towards the storm-light set and unsmiling. 'They've carried him to his shanty. He'll be all right there. I had to wait for you.'

'I'm glad you did,' he said. He felt a little puzzled. There was something odd about her mood – something she was holding back from him. 'I'm glad, now, that I came up.'

She glanced at him sharply. 'You would not have stayed down another shift?'

'I did think of it,' he confessed. 'But I'm longing for a bath; and I kept thinking of your wonderful cooking. What's for supper?'

'I made a mutton pie yesterday,' she said absently. 'Or I've a brace of ducks ready to roast, and green peas.'

'I'm uncommonly hungry; I'll have both,' he said. 'That will be a meal fit for a king – worth almost getting killed for.'

She stopped abruptly and turned to face him. They had topped the rise; the village lay beneath them, a grey huddle in the fold of the land, no lights lit yet, though it was already twilight below the hill. A little damp breeze stirred the fine curls of hair at her temples; her face was pale, and she looked at him almost with a kind of desperation.

'Don't joke!' she said. 'When I heard the women run by, talking about the fall, my heart nearly stopped. I thought you must be dead.'

'I'm not so easy to kill,' he said lightly, embarrassed by her fervour.

'If you die, I don't want to go on living,' she said.

'Liza!' he said, gently protesting; and then he saw there were tears on her dark lashes. 'My dear, there's no need for all this. Here I am, you see, safe and sound.'

'You don't know what I went through,' she said, a statement of fact, not a demand for sympathy. She turned her face away, looking down, presenting him with her three-quarter profile and a curve of dark hair, like a subtle madonna. 'I think I am with child,' she said abruptly.

Benedict stood still. He wondered if he had heard rightly; then he wondered if she might be mistaken. But she had been pregnant before, he remembered, and the memory was sour. She ought to know the signs. She turned now to look at him sharply, and he realised he should not have been silent.

'You aren't pleased,' she said. 'But indeed it was not my fault.'

'No,' he said quickly. 'No, how should it be?'

Her lips trembled, escaping her iron control for a moment, and her fear rushed out in a little spurt. 'You won't abandon me?'

A surge of emotion pushed upwards through his tiredness like a mole breaking the earth to the air: sadness, tenderness, apprehension, guilt, dismay. 'No, I won't abandon you! What sort of question is that? I won't leave you.'

She looked at him a moment and then said, 'Thank you.' And then, a moment later, very quietly, 'I'm sorry.'

And all his selfish feelings sank, leaving only tenderness. She should not have to apologise for this. She should not have to fear his reaction. She was with child: it ought to be the occasion of rejoicing; and if it was not, that was his fault. He had not said the right things.

'I haven't really taken it in yet,' he said, and the honesty was so plain in his voice that she felt a tremor of hope. 'Are you sure?'

'I think so, I am, really.'

'And are you glad?'

'Are you?' She returned the question, watchfully.

Was he? A child – a baby. His child. Liza was carrying his child. Her belly would swell up like a ripening fruit, and one day out would pop his little likeness. Well, well. And what then? He tried to imagine a baby crawling about their house,

381

a toddler running with its arms outstretched for balance, a solemn boy learning to fish and tie knots and ride a horse. He shook his head. It was all too much. They were pale images, lacking substance. He was twenty years old, but he simply could not imagine himself a father, imagine a son of his own blood. A bastard son, of course, but a son all the same – like King Billy with his brood of Fitzclarences. Did a man feel differently about a legitimate son? He supposed he must. Well, he could be as good a father as King Billy, at any rate – and, he hoped, deal kindly by his mistress.

'I can't imagine what it will be like,' he said at last, honestly, looking into her eyes. He took hold of her hands, and went on, 'but when it comes, I expect I shall be very excited. I will never leave you, or let you down, Liza, I promise you that. I will always take care of you.' A little smile touched his lips. 'Both of you,' he added softly. 'I'm very fond of you, you know.'

She nodded, and her eyes were hidden from him. Fand came running back to see why they had stopped, circled them, touched their linked hands with her nose, and then sat looking up at them enquiringly.

'We'd best get on,' Liza said. She withdrew one hand from his, but it was only to slip it through his arm, turning again for home, and he turned with her, pressing her hand comfortingly against his ribs. Down in the valley the twilight had thickened like mist, and someone had lighted a lamp: a single yellow light glowing, more like a flower than a star.

It was a bad day for Nicky. When he got home, he found his mother had gone back to Skelwith Lodge, which in itself was a relief; but the steward's room door was locked, and when he asked Ottershaw for the key, the butler told him, with a carefully neutral face, that her ladyship had given instructions that no-one was to enter in her absence. Nicky felt his hands sweating. Now what had she discovered? he asked himself in terror. To have locked the steward's room seemed like an act of extreme anger. He toyed with the idea of breaking in through the window, but rejected it as impractical. He would have to break the glazing bars too, to get through, and someone would surely hear him and come and investigate.

While he was still standing outside the locked door, thinking, he heard a sound nearby and saw that the chapel door was slightly ajar. Father Moineau must be in there. He wondered if the priest knew anything about Mama's state of mind. It was difficult to tell how close Moineau's relationship was with her now. Since he had no children of the house to tutor, he spent much more time carrying out pastoral work amongst the Morland tenants, pensioners and dependents, and at St Edward's School, to which he was also chaplain. He met Héloïse twice or three times a day at mass, but otherwise was at home only to study in his own room; and increasingly he took his meals there, too, avoiding the family table.

Yet he was Mama's confessor, and had been for sixteen years, and in some ways it was a more intimate relationship than marriage. She might have told him what was on her mind. Nicholas went to the chapel door and pushed it, feeling how cold the heavy, age-darkened oak was against his palm, and the silent, weighty reluctance of it to swing open under his pressure. The single stone step down had been worn into a dish by generations of feet, which seemed somehow sinister to Nicholas. He put his foot into the dip, gingerly breathed at the chilly, perfumed air, and shuddered.

He hated the smell of the chapel, with its atmosphere of brooding stasis. It was as if the normal laws of nature did not operate in there. Time did not move on: each instant of *now* accumulated, thickening the air to soup. Stillborn piety decayed drily underfoot; sins of omission lay about unforgiven, stagnating in corners; boredom settled on every surface like dust, never to be disturbed, for the air never stirred in here. Nothing moved. Nicholas hated attending mass, and sought every excuse he could for absenting himself. Excuses he had to have: if he had told his mother how he felt about the place, she would have been profoundly shocked; but he felt as though he could not breathe. Even now the panic was mounting in him, tightening his chest as he walked reluctantly towards the altar, where the priest was kneeling in prayer.

Moineau heard, and turned his head, crossed himself and rose. Turning towards Nicholas, he raised his eyebrows enquiringly.

'Ah, Father, there you are,' Nicholas said weakly, trying to smile. 'Might I have a word with you?' Moineau inclined his head in acquiescence, and Nicholas gestured towards the door. In the muted light of the chapel, he thought his own white hand looked green, as though he were rotting. 'Outside,' he said in a hoarse whisper. Who knew what spirits of the house might be listening in this timeless soup that served for air? He turned and forced himself not to run, hearing the priest pad softly after him like nemesis. Past the pious portraits, past the dim memorials, past the stern saints, carved in wood and stone, stiffened into architectural reproof on their pedestals and in their niches. *When I am master, you will all be thrown out!* he swore inwardly. *My time will come. I will have the laugh of you!*

And when they were out into the vestibule, he reached past the priest and pulled the door closed, shutting the horrors in, and breathed more easily.

'I just wanted to ask you about my mother,' he said, trying for a conversational tone of voice. Moineau continued to look at him as though the question had not been completed. Goaded, Nicky went on, 'How is she? You saw her this morning, I believe?'

'She was very upset, of course,' Moineau said.

'Yes, of course she was. Shocking business! Poor Mathilde – practically a sister to me, you know. And those poor, dear little children!' He was babbling, he knew it, and took a breath. 'I wish she had not gone back to Skelwith Lodge. It can't be good for her to expose herself to sickness like that. To say nothing of the exertion. And at her age! I wonder you did not stop her.'

'It was not my place to stop her. Her ladyship knows her duty.'

And I don't know mine, I suppose? 'If I had been here, I would have stopped her.' Moineau gave an ironic bow. Nettled, Nicholas plunged where he had meant to tiptoe. 'What was she doing in the steward's room? I mean, surely you could have stopped her burdening herself with estate business, at a time like this?'

'Her ladyship went in there to write letters,' Moineau said, imparting this information with seeming enjoyment. 'You know that she prefers to write business letters in that room. While she was there she looked through some of the account books, and something seemed to strike her. She sent for me, and asked me why I no longer did the household accounts. I reminded her that she had instructed me, through you, to hand them over to your care eighteen months ago. She said that she had forgotten, thanked me, and sent me away.'

'Ah,' said Nicholas. It was like a short sigh of despair.

Moineau watched him a moment, with a regret as sharp as a blade pressing into his heart. He had brought up this child from the age of eight, had tried to shape him and guide him, and now could find nothing in him to love. He did not know what Nicky was thinking, but he could smell the darkness in him, the rank odour of sin, like stale sweat, which hung about him. The old saying came to him from his childhood memories: *Only poison fruit grows on a poison tree.* Something about Nicky made him afraid. He wanted to reach out and touch him, try to talk to him, try to draw him back from the dangers he felt he was on the brink of; but when he looked at that pale, brooding, somehow misshapen face, his courage failed.

'If there is nothing more you wish to know,' he said at last, 'I will go up to the day nursery. I promised to play backgammon with little Jemima.'

'Yes,' said Nicholas absently. 'That would be a charitable thing to do.' Moineau turned away. 'My mother wrote to Pobgee, I understand?'

Moineau paused. 'I believe her ladyship asked him to call here tomorrow,' he said, and when Nicholas said nothing more, went on up the stair and turned out of sight.

Nicholas went the other way, his brow furrowed with thought. As he crossed the staircase hall, he saw Ottershaw in the great hall. 'I am going to my room,' he said, 'I want to be told as soon as my mother returns.'

'Very good, sir.'

He need not have left that instruction, as it happened, for his mother sent for him as soon as she had changed her clothes. He was summoned to the steward's room, as before, and entered with trepidation: that locked door had unnerved him greatly.

'Mama,' he cried, hoping to get his impression over first. 'What news from Skelwith Lodge? Better news, I hope! I was so shocked when I heard: poor, poor Mathilde! Who could have believed it?'

'Nicky, where were you?' she said, cutting in. 'You were out all night. No-one knew where to find you.'

'I went over to Fulford to see John Fussell on a matter of business,' he said. He had thought this out, and it was a good one, unexceptionable. 'When I was preparing to leave, I discovered that my horse was slightly lame, so he and Louisa asked me to stay for dinner and the night. I sent a message home by one of their servants, but I understand the villainous man must have forgotten, or wandered off on some amusement of his own. I promise you he will smart for it – all the more for making you uneasy, dearest Mama!'

Héloïse watched his face while he spoke, and could detect nothing in it but shining honesty, and honest indignation. She sighed. 'I needed you here, very much,' she said. 'I felt it very much that you were not here to comfort me.'

'And I felt it very much when I came home and discovered what you had had to face without me,' he said. He felt tears spring to his eyes, and was impressed with himself. But it was true: she should not have had to bear her sorrow alone; and by now he had achieved his usual state of believing his own story. He had no recollection of Mrs Jeffreys' house: he saw himself examining the lame horse, sitting down to dinner with the Fussells, happy in the knowledge that a servant had taken the message to Mama.

That was all settled and good; but there was something else, wasn't there? He took a careful step into it.

'But you should not have worried yourself with estate matters at such a time,' he chided her gently. 'The good Father Moineau tells me you were looking through the account books yesterday, and you know you don't understand such things, poor Mama! You never could manage figures, could you? They must have muddled your poor head dreadfully. Remember what a quagmire you used to get yourself in when you tried to keep the books all those years ago? That's why —'

'Why did you tell Father Moineau that I wanted you to take

over the household books?' she asked abruptly, cutting him off.

He turned cold inside, but managed a sympathetic smile. 'Because it's the truth,' he said gently. 'Have you forgotten, Mama? We discussed it one day, a long time ago now, and you said that as I did the estate books, I might as well do the household accounts as well. Father Moineau had so much to do as it was; and we agreed that I needed to understand both parts of my inheritance. Surely you remember saying that?'

'No,' she said blankly. 'I don't remember it at all.'

'Well, I'm not surprised,' he said tenderly. 'You were so shocked with grief over Papa at that time that I don't suppose you remember much at all. That was why I told the good father what we decided, rather than letting you bother yourself with it. But you agreed I should, Mama. You can't think I would have given him such a message otherwise?'

'No,' she said. She seemed rather dazed. 'No, you would not, of course.' She stared blankly into the middle distance, her hands resting flat on an open page of the household accounts. Nicky tried, without appearing to, to see which page it was, but her hands were spread over too much of it. Now which of his little devices had she discovered? He had excuses for them all, but he would like to be prepared.

'Tell me,' she said suddenly – still staring sightlessly ahead of her, her voice light as though she was speaking from a great distance; 'tell me, why are you still entering wages week by week for people who have been turned off? There are two sewing maids, a housemaid and a gardener on the lists who no longer work for us.'

Oh, that one! He had forgotten that one! He had been drawing their wages to supplement his allowance for so long that he had forgotten he had ever turned them off. 'I expect it is a mistake,' he said, his mind whirring like a bobbin as he searched for a good excuse.

'A mistake?'

'You're sure they have been turned off?' Nicky said. 'After all, Mama, you no longer have your hand on the reins of the household —'

'It seems that I have left the reins down too long,' she said. 'Even so, I am quite well aware that the three maids are no longer here, and I have asked Ottershaw about the gardener. He says he left just after Christmas.'

Always extra expenses at Christmas. He had run up an enormous bill at the club, and there was the hunting season to get through. He had needed the money, so the gardener – what was the wretch's name? Tomkins? Timmins? – had had to go. He had not dared turn off another housemaid, in case Mrs Thomson complained to Mama. Mrs Thomson did not have a sufficient respect for Nicholas's authority. Mrs Thomson was a nosy, sharp-eyed, sharp-tongued old bitch, and would be the first to be turned off when he was master.

'Well, I'm sure Ottershaw's right,' he said genially. 'I expect I just forgot to cross him off the list, that's all.'

Now Héloïse looked at him, and her eyes were dark with what seemed uncannily like fear. What the deuce was she afraid of? Nicholas thought peevishly.

'But who have you been paying their wages to, Nicky? For the money goes out each week. I've seen the draughts on the bank. The money comes into the house, and goes somewhere. If it is not paid to them, who has it?'

He was floored, and suddenly found refuge in anger. 'Very well, then, I own it! I have taken it myself! But I needed it, every penny – and damn it all, I work hard enough, don't I? I do the work of four people around the estate! Every responsibility falls on my shoulders, day and night; everyone comes to me to have their problems solved, regardless of how I'm feeling – and my health has never been more than indifferent. But no-one thinks of me. I work my fingers to the bone to hold things together, and never a word of complaint has passed my lips, but all I get in return is a pitiful allowance a schoolboy couldn't manage on! You shouldn't keep me so short, that's the truth of it! A man don't like to be seen with his pockets to let, like a damned apprentice!'

She was shocked, taken aback by his tirade. 'But Nicky, you only had to ask. Have I ever denied you anything? All will be yours one day. You only had to ask me.'

'Ask you!' He snorted. Yes, ask her for money, and have her ask what he wanted it for! She never seemed to think a man needed a little privacy about his affairs! Everything was to be open with her, everything poked into, turned over, peered at.

So he was to make out a list of his gaming debts, was he? And his expenses at the cockpit and the dog-fight ring, the special books he acquired from London, his visits to Mrs Jeffreys – and yes, God damn it, he had that awful, awful bill to cover now! His rage rose up, hot and strong, poured scalding from his throat. 'Damn it, I shouldn't have to ask you! I should have what I want without that! I'm twenty-four years old, Mama – don't you think I'm entitled to a little dignity now? I do a man's job, and I want a man's respect! What do you think it makes me feel when I have to come crawling to your knees every time I want some money, like a dog begging for scraps?'

'Oh Nicky,' she said. She was crying, and for once he was glad of it. He felt triumphant, and strangely excited that he had made her cry. She had always held such power over him, like a sorceress, like a great goddess; but now he saw she was just a little old woman, soon to be dead. Then he would rule supreme!

'Oh Nicky, I never knew you felt like this!' she gasped through her tears.

'No, I don't suppose you did,' he said triumphantly.

'But I never would have wanted you to be dishonest. I could never have believed you would turn to that.'

'Dishonest? I like that! You've said yourself everything will be mine. How can I steal what is mine already?'

'Steal?' she said. Her voice was hardly more than a whisper. 'Oh Nicky!' She put her trembling hands up to her face, as though she needed to feel what it was doing. He reached automatically for his handkerchief and pushed it at her, and she took it and covered her face. His rage cooled, and he began to feel a little awkward.

'Well, well,' he said loudly. 'Look here, Mama, Don't be so upset. I'm sure there were faults on both sides. Please don't cry.' She did not emerge from behind the handkerchief. He looked at her hands and saw how old they were, how thin her wrists. One might snap them between a finger and thumb. She was an old woman. The words sank down into him and opened up the old wound of his fear again. His mother was an old woman, and old women die, don't they? No, don't think it! It mustn't be! Not his mother! His mother was strong, she could not fail! 'Mama, please don't cry,' he begged, pathetically now. 'Please don't!'

She emerged at last from the handkerchief, her eyes red but her cheeks dry now. She blew her nose briskly, straightened her back, folded her hands. 'I'm sorry,' she said. She smiled waveringly. 'My poor Nicky! It has been so hard for you, hasn't it? I did not realise. But I am going to change things. I have sent for Mr Pobgee. He will come tomorrow, and I will make some new arrangements.'

'What new arrangements?' he asked nervously.

She was still smiling, but the smile was stronger now. It made him feel rather strange. He had begged to have the goddess back, and here she was, but was it what he wanted after all?

'Better arrangements,' she said, maddeningly enigmatic. 'Leave me now, my dear son. I have much to do.'

He stood up automatically, for he never disobeyed that tone of voice; but he remained looking down at her for a moment, puzzled. She was turning the pages of the household book, studying them. 'Won't you leave that now, Mama?' he said. 'You are tired. You must not strain your eyes.'

'I have much still to do. I will see you at dinner. Leave me, *mon fils.*'

She spoke too firmly for him to resist longer. He turned and left, feeling that she had somehow regained the upper hand. She was in control again, and he was helpless, and he was filled with a weak rage, which battled inside him with his love for her and need of her. New arrangements, eh? Why would she not tell him *what* arrangements? Why should he be kept in the dark all the time, dependent on her, subservient to her, having to ask for every penny he spent? It was his money, after all – or would be soon. *What was she going to do?* He did not like that last smile of hers. It boded no good. Was she going to tie up the money in some way so that he could not draw on it? *Was she going to disinherit him?* No, that was too frightening to contemplate, worse even than the thought of her dying.

He walked like an automaton across the hall, up the stairs, down the passage to his room. Perhaps he had reached the end of the road. He could not go on and on like this, could he? Perhaps it was time he took his future into his own hands. He felt a sense of growing pressure, like the heaviness of the air before a thunderstorm. Something was going to happen, he thought – but what?

Héloïse went down the spiral stair, remembering involuntarily, as she so often did, how she had come down this stairs to her wedding almost twenty-six years ago. Kind John Anstey had been waiting for her at the bottom, to give her away – ah, and he was dead now, too! She pushed the heavy door and it swung silently open, releasing the familiar chapel smell of beeswax and incense and cold stone and a faint odour of dying flowers. On that day, her wedding day, it had been full of candles and sunlight and crowded with people, but she had had eyes for one only, the figure standing before the high altar, which she would have recognised at any distance. She walked forward now automatically, her mind so absorbed with her memories that it was only when she was halfway down the aisle that she realised there was someone there. The figure of a man, kneeling at the rail: the light of the candles on the altar illuminated him mysteriously, and for a moment her heart crowded up into her throat. Down superstition! It was not James – how could it be? A moment later he moved, blocking the radiance, and she realised it was Father Moineau. Well, indeed, and who else did she expect it to be?

Her soft slippers had made no sound on the stone flags, and she was almost upon him before he turned his head. Then he stood up quickly and turned to face her, looking at her searchingly. She smiled at him, seeing him suddenly with new eyes, as though she had not met with him in months. How long had he been so grey? she wondered. She didn't remember, either, that his hair had receded so far from his temples, or that his eyes had been so meshed with lines.

'Did I startle you?' she said. She heard that she had spoken in French, but he replied in English.

'A little. I did not hear you come in.' Still he scanned her face, as if searching for something he did not think she would

391

tell him. 'Is there something I can do for you?'

'You can give me your advice,' she said. 'I have come to a decision. You can tell me if it is the right one.'

'Better not,' he said. 'If it is your decision, better I should say nothing.'

She looked at him quizzically, tilting her head like a little bird. 'Do you know what it is, then?'

He made a movement of his shoulders, not quite a shrug. 'That it has to do with Nicholas, I guess. And Mr Pobgee is coming to visit you tomorrow.'

'You are very quick,' she said. 'Yes, it is about Nicky. I think I have not behaved well by him. He is not happy, and that is my fault.'

Moineau was silent. He thought of the strange, twisted, sin-smelling youth – he could not think of him as a grown man – who seemed to carry such wounds inside him, wounds which would not heal, and which cried out like hungry mouths to be satisfied. *Not happy?* How could such daylight terms be applied to something so dark? How was it that this woman saw only her beloved son, the baby and the child lightly clad in manhood? Perhaps she was right and he was wrong. He could not explain what he felt, nor even describe it in words; it was just that Nicholas frightened him.

'What is it you have decided?' he asked at last, because he loved her, and she wanted to tell him.

'You know that everything is meant for Nicky at last,' she said, looking up at him earnestly, her hands working together as though she were washing them – sign that she was nervous or uncertain. 'And it seems to me very hard that he should have to wait so long for the fruits of that when he already has the labour of it. He said to me earlier —' She paused, still flinching inwardly at the memory of his anger. 'He said he hated having to come to me to ask for every penny. That it was undignified. And indeed it is!' she cried in his defence. 'It should not be so. I have been unfair and thoughtless. So I have decided to ask Mr Pobgee to make a document for me, to give everything to Nicky now, rather than waiting until I am dead.' She looked at Moineau, who was silent. 'What do you think? Am I right?'

Are you right? His first reaction was chill, fear for her. To give him everything? To make herself powerless? It must not be! But then he took hold of himself, tried to be rational. What was he afraid of? This was her son, who loved her. She believed so, and she must know. Nicholas had always been meant to inherit, and it could make no difference whether he had it now or later, could it?

Except to me, of course, Moineau told himself wryly. He was Héloïse's chaplain and confessor, but if Nicholas became the paymaster, he would decide who was employed and who was not. But he wouldn't send away his own mother's priest, surely? Moineau didn't want to leave her. She was his home, the last little piece left of the old, ordered, peaceful world in which he had grown up. She was France before the revolution; she was mankind before the second fall. He needed her to keep his faith warm.

She was waiting – he had to answer her. Put aside selfishness. Was it a good thing to give Nicholas everything now? He had not been a bad master, as far as the estate was concerned; and his desire to own it was surely the earnest of his good intentions. Moineau knew no wrong of him: it was only an animal instinct in him that moved away when Nicky came near, an atavistic superstition that did not like to have Nicky's shadow touch him; and those things were unworthy and unChristian. He ought to put them aside. Besides, the responsibility might be the making of Nicky. And if he had everything, Héloïse would have nothing more to fear, he thought, without being sure what it was she might have to fear in other circumstances.

So he said at last, 'Yes, I think you are right. It is the right decision.'

For a long moment she said nothing, and then she made a sound like 'Ah!' – a half-articulated breath of relief. He reached out his hand, and she gave him both of hers. His hands were warm and dry, hers very cold, like the hands of a little marble statue.

'It will be time for dinner soon,' she said, 'and I must have some moments alone to compose myself. I have spent too much thought on this decision, and not enough on John Skelwith. I must pray for him, and his daughter Mary. They are so very sick, Father. How could it happen? How could my

393

poor Mathilde be taken, and all her children? if Mary dies, there will only be little Jemima left. And if John dies, she will be an orphan. Oh Father, how do we bear it? How do we understand it?'

'You know the answer to that – you who have taught it to me so often,' he said. They were speaking French now. The Faith seemed easier to articulate in the language of their birth. 'We do not understand – we accept. That is our part, as the child obeys the parent, not understanding his decisions, but trusting them.'

She gave a faint smile. 'It is something easy to tell someone else; harder to believe oneself.'

'Yes. Do you wish to take the sacrament now?'

'No, thank you. I will take it at my usual time. I want to pray alone now. I will go to the Lady-chapel.'

He bowed and released her hands, and she went alone to the little side chapel, built and dedicated by the first mistress of Morland Place, decorated by countless generations, made fine by Annunciata, Héloïse's great-great-grandmother, who had spent part of her life in France. Héloïse felt at home here. The wooden statue of the Lady was very old, any crudenesses of execution in the carving long since worn smooth by time and caressing hands. Her robes were painted blue and red, her hands and face gold after the old style. In previous generations she had been dressed, like a doll, in robes of real silk, but the practice had been discontinued before Héloïse ever came to Morland Place. The only relic of that time was her coronet of real gold and pearls, fitted around her golden painted brow.

Héloïse lit the candles and stood before the altar to pray. First for John and Mary; then for repose of the souls of Mathilde, daughter of her friend, whom she had rescued from France as a little child and brought up as her own; and for Mathilde's children, taken by this dreadful disease. And then her thoughts strayed to Nicholas again. It was right, what she was doing. She must have the good of Morland Place at heart, and whatever little faults Nicky had, they would disappear once he had control of his fortune and his destiny. He was the true successor, the rightful heir of the substance and the spirit of the Morland inheritance; and

394

coming into his inheritance would allow his nature to expand and his soul to flourish.

But though it was a happy thought, she still found her throat closing up with tears, for it was the end of the most important aspect of her life. She had been the guardian for so long, and she would miss the responsibility. It had not always been easy, but it was a sacred task, and she had undertaken it with a glad spirit. Now she must lay it down – but for the good of all, she reminded herself sternly.

But still the sadness welled up as though for the passing of something great and good, and tears filled her eyes, blurring her vision. *Sweet Mother Mary, guard the house, guide my son,* she prayed. *He will be the best master there has ever been.* A tear rolled free, and she caught it up with her finger, impatiently, trying to laugh at herself. Why such sorrow? It was a glad time! But still the tears would flow; and in the flickering candlelight, it looked to her as though the Lady was weeping too.

CHAPTER TWENTY-ONE

Nicky sat in his room, crouched near the fire, shivering, feeling a cold sweat run down under his armpits. What was wrong with him? Was he sick? He felt such a sense of apprehension, of approaching dread, that he could not even get up from his chair by the fire to go to bed. He was exhausted but he couldn't sleep. His nerves were all on edge. He felt afraid to turn his head from the flames, for fear of the darkness in the corners of the room. The house felt restless; it seemed to twitch like a sleeping dog, prey to nightmares. He could hear the bones of it creaking, as they did when there was a high wind; but there was no wind tonight. Outside, it was as still as death tonight.

What was Mama seeing Pobgee about tomorrow? That question kept popping its head up out of the water like an otter. He thrust it away. It didn't matter now. He wouldn't think about it. He wished his mind would not keep switching from thought to thought, flickering and jumping like shadows in candlelight. It was twitching like the house; and the house seemed full of whispers. Ever since he was a child, he had hated the fact that the Morlands were all buried in the crypt under the chapel. It was another reason for his hating the chapel – it seemed horrible to be walking about on the bones of your ancestors. And it wasn't just their bones, either. Their spirits seemed to hang about the house, always watching you over your shoulder to see what you were doing, and shaking their heads and sighing. You couldn't get away from them. They seemed to have soaked into the plaster and the woodwork like indelible stains. It was no wonder the servants thought the house was haunted.

He didn't believe in ghosts, of course. They always turned out to be something else. He and Harry Anstey once thought they saw a ghost on Hob Moor, when they were boys, but it had turned out to be a robber. Morland Place had had its share of violence in the past, and there were several stories of ghosts in the house. The hanged woman in the Great Bedchamber, for instance – horribly black in the face, and hanging from a huge hook in the main beam; and the headless priest who was sometimes seen wandering about the great hall and the servants' passage – he was the scourge of the servants' hall, much dreaded on moonlit nights, especially around Hallowe'en.

And the White Lady – she was the oldest of the ghosts, supposed to be some very early Morland who had drowned herself in the moat. She walked the upstairs corridors, dripping water and slime and rather pearly about the eyes, foretelling some great disaster to the house. Nicholas wondered, cynically, why if Morlands had such forewarnings of disasters they hadn't always managed to avert them. He didn't believe in ghosts. But the house felt so uneasy tonight, and he had such a strange feeling of foreboding . . .

Too much goose at dinner. Goose didn't really agree with him, even nicely roasted with saffron apples, one of Barnard's specialities. Mama had been very quiet at dinner. She had talked a little to Jemima, who had dined with them as a special treat, to take her mind off her sorrows. The maids were making up Jemima's black clothes, and she'd be wearing them tomorrow. He shuddered at the thought. A child in black always looked so horribly —

There was a particular creaking floorboard in the short passage outside his door which always gave him forewarning of someone's approach, and it creaked now. But everyone was in bed. Who could it be, creeping about out there at this time of night? He waited for the tap at the door, but nothing happened. The chill crept along his spine and made the hair lift on his scalp. Who was out there? He had heard no footfall, and no-one knocked. *What* was out there? Superstition took him by the back of the neck and he heard himself make a little whimpering noise. He stared at the door, his eyes stretched wide. Did the doorknob move? Was there a sound of hoarse breathing? But why no candlelight at the gap along the bottom? Whatever stood outside, it did not need to see its way.

He shook off the thought and tried to take a grip on himself. He did not believe in ghosts, and if there was someone in the passage, it was his duty to find out who it was. Some servant up to no good, probably. He distrusted them all. He stood up, finding his legs surprisingly weak, as though the bones had softened. I will not be frightened, like some half-witted kitchen-maid, he vowed. He made himself walk to the door, took hold of the handle, and after an agonising moment of hesitation, flung the door open.

It was the White Lady! The shock was like an iron bar driven through his heart. His chest and throat went rigid with terror. His mouth opened so wide his jaws hurt, but no sound escaped him: he was too terrified to scream. She stood there, at the end of the short passage, beyond the red-room door, clad in shapeless white to the floor, streaming green water like corruption; her face of awful pallor was grim as death, foretelling Hell's damnation for him – yes, for him! The pain in his chest was so terrible that he knew he was dying, but still he could not scream. A thread of saliva strung from his gaping mouth, and his brain fought for control as the blackness surged in on him from all sides – the blackness of oblivion.

'Oh Mr Nicholas, I was coming to fetch you. Oh please hurry, sir – it's the mistress.'

It was not the White Lady, it was Mrs Thomson, the housekeeper. Nicholas understood it only dimly through his paralysis; for he had forgotten how to breathe. He had to bring his hands up to his chest to press it in and out, and the first breath he managed to drag in was a searing agony. She was not streaming water of course – that had been a momentary illusion. She was wearing a dark green wrapper, hanging unfastened, over something voluminous and white – her bedgown, presumably. She was carrying a candle, but she had been too far from the door for it to shew its light.

All this observation had taken only the seconds it took her to speak. Nicholas, painfully gulping air, managed to croak, 'My mother? What's wrong with my mother?'

Mrs Thomson's face creased with desperate anxiety. 'Oh

Mr Nicholas, she's very sick – vomiting and voiding, and now the cramps in her legs have started. She didn't call anyone at first, thinking it was something she'd ate, but then she rang, and the maid fetched me. She's so very bad now, I think we ought to call the doctor. Will you come and see her?'

'Of course.' Nicholas said. Mrs Thomson had never spoken so supplicatingly to him and it was balm to his pride, made him feel masterful and strong. 'I'll go straight to her, but don't you delay any longer. Get one of the men up and send for Dr Bayliss right away.'

'Yes sir, I'll do that. But sir – you don't think —?'

Nicholas looked grave. 'I don't know. I'm not a medical man. But it does sound very like the cholera.'

'Oh mercy me!' Mrs Thomson cried out. 'I was afraid of it! And I warned her again and again not to go to Clifton. Oh my poor mistress! What will become of us?'

'Pull yourself together, Mrs Thomson. Your mistress needs you now. Go at once and have the message sent off to Bayliss. And then bring all the blankets you can find, and put some bricks in to heat. She must be kept warm.'

Glad to have something positive to do, Mrs Thomson hurried away, thinking that she had never liked Mr Nicholas so well as just now, when he spoke so sternly and decisively.

It was Havergill who came, for Bayliss was still at Skelwith Lodge. Havergill was as experienced a physician, but in spite of anything he could do, and in spite of Nicholas's careful nursing of the patient – for he never left her side, and gave her the draughts Havergill ordered with his own hands – Héloïse grew rapidly worse. The constant vomiting and diarrhoea were weakening her, and though Havergill gave her laudanum to calm the nerves of the stomach, she could take very little of it without bringing it up again. Her legs were troubled by a pins-and-needles sensation, and the cramping pains in her stomach grew more frequent. It was the most violent case Havergill had seen, and he was astonished that it had come on so rapidly. But cholera was not constant in its effects; it did vary greatly from person to person. The only thing he was sure of was that she was sinking fast.

No-one had thought, of course, to put off Mr Pobgee, and

he arrived at the time agreed to find the house in a state of prostration. Havergill was passing through the hall while the weeping footman was still explaining matters, and he sent the man away and drew Pobgee to one side. The two men were old friends, and could speak frankly.

'I come from Skelwith Lodge,' Pobgee said gravely. 'John Skelwith died an hour ago.'

'I knew he could not last long,' Havergill said. 'What a dreadful thing! You were with him at the last?'

'Yes, and he has placed his surviving child in the care of Lady Morland – he has no other relatives.'

'She is the natural choice of guardian,' Havergill said, worried, 'but she is so very sick herself —'

'How bad is it?'

'I don't think she will last the day,' said Havergill.

Pobgee was shocked. 'Good God! I had no idea – it is the cholera, I suppose?'

'I cannot think what else it can be. Bayliss warned her not to nurse the Skelwith children. She has exposed herself every day, against his advice, to the infection.'

'Her goodness – her adherence to duty —' Pobgee shook his head in grief. 'This is a dark day for Morland Place. For all of us. She is a very great lady.' His eyes were moist, and he paused to pass a handkerchief over his face. He had known Héloïse a very long time, and he had taken care of the Morland's business all his professional life. He felt like a father towards her. 'I did not think,' he said at last, 'to outlive her.'

'What will happen to the child now?' Havergill asked.

Pobgee shook his head. 'In the normal course of events, it would be for Lady Morland herself to —' He paused, thinking hard. 'I think I should see her. She asked me to come here today to undertake some business for her, but if she is in extremis, she may have other instructions for me.'

'Yes. And she ought to know about Skelwith,' Havergill agreed. 'If the guardianship has devolved on her, she must know, so as to pass it on to someone else.'

'Is she rational?' Pobgee asked gravely.

'Yes, her mind is quite clear, despite her bodily weakness. She is in pain and distress, but perfectly sensible.'

'Would it harm her to see me?'

Havergill had no time to answer, for Nicholas came running downstairs at that moment, looking for him.

'How long you have been, Havergill! Why do you not come upstairs? Oh, Mr Pobgee. Good day, sir. You are come to see my mother, I suppose, but —' Nicholas's mouth trembled too much for him to continue.

Pobgee stepped forward. 'My poor boy,' he said with great kindness. 'Havergill has explained it all to me. I am so very, very sorry!'

'Thank you, sir,' Nicholas said, his mouth a bow of misery. 'I know you have been her friend.' He choked and was silent.

'I hope so, indeed – and her faithful servant. Do you think I might see her for a few moments, my boy?'

Nicholas looked up sharply, his red-rimmed eyes narrowing. 'On no account in the world! What, bother her with business now, when she is so very ill? Havergill, tell him he cannot see her!'

'I can't say that, Nicholas,' Havergill said gently. 'Your mother is very ill, but her mind is quite clear. And there are matters of business which she ought to know about.'

'But she's *dying*!' Nicholas cried in agony. 'Don't you understand?'

Pobgee intercepted a glance from Havergill and said, 'All the more reason, then. I promise you I will not upset her – I am her old friend, as you have been so kind as to observe – and it will ease her mind to know all her business affairs are set in order. Remember she is not only your mother, my boy, but the mistress of a large estate. She will want to know that everything is settled.'

'I forbid it!' Nicholas said, his voice wavy with tears. 'I won't let you upset her!'

Havergill patted his shoulder. 'I tell you what we will do,' he said. 'I will just slip upstairs and very quietly ask her if she wants to see Pobgee, and we will abide by her decision.'

'No, if it must be, I will ask her,' Nicholas said, turning away; and exchanging a glance, Havergill and Pobgee followed.

The Great Bedchamber smelled of sickness and roses. In the vast bed where generations of Morlands had been born and died, Héloïse lay in pain, too involved with the convulsions of her physical self to be much aware that she was dying. Nicholas loomed up beside the bed, his face blotched with weeping and his eyes red-rimmed with lack of sleep.

'Pobgee's here, Mama, but you don't need to see him. I'll tell him to go away if you like.'

She focused on his face with difficulty. 'No,' she said, her voice a faint thread, like the last smoke from a dying fire. 'I must speak to him. Is Father Moineau here?'

'Yes. But Mama, you mustn't upset yourself,' Nicholas urged.

'Those two, alone. Leave me, Nicky. I will —' A spasm shook her. He clutched her hand until it passed. She seemed noticeably weaker after it. 'I will send for you again.'

He could do nothing but obey. At least he had the satisfaction of seeing Havergill turned out too. Outside he stood as close to the door as he could, but it was too heavy and massive for anything to be heard from inside. After some time the door opened, and Pobgee looked out. Nicholas saw with terror that he had a pen in his hand.

'No, not you, Nicholas. Havergill, will you have the goodness to step inside for a moment?'

Havergill moved forward. Nicky cried, 'Why not me? What's happening?'

'Hush,' said Pobgee, gently, as though to a child. 'Your turn will come. Wait, now.'

The door closed again. Nicky paced up and down, his hands clenching and unclenching. Once he saw little Jemima, with Matty, his own former wet-nurse, hand in hand watching him from the end of the corridor. He said something savage, and they went away.

The door opened again, and Havergill said, 'You may come in, now.' Nicky started eagerly towards him, and the physician caught his arm. 'Gently,' he said. 'She wants to say goodbye.'

The word tore through all Nicky's selfish fears to the heart, and stripped him naked and vulnerable, a little boy who was to lose his mother. He pushed past Havergill, briefly registered the fact that Pobgee was sitting at Mama's desk, writing, glared at the priest on the far side of the bed, and grabbed his mother's hand, sinking to his knees beside her.

'Mama! Oh Mama! Don't leave me! Please don't leave me here all alone!'

She looked ghastly, a caricature of herself. The skin was stretched taut over her face, wax-white, sheeny with death. Her dark eyes looked dull, like a fire going out. He held her hand so tightly that the bones grated, but it was cold and damp, no life there, no warmth, no mother.

'Nicky,' she whispered. 'My good boy.'

'Yes, Mama,' he said eagerly. 'Your good boy. You won't leave your good boy, will you?'

'*Mon cher, je dois* —' She gasped again, and seemed to sink into the bedclothes, as though the substance of her were evaporating. She barely disturbed the sheets now, she was so small and flat. She drew her lips back from her teeth and spoke again. 'Be true, Nicky. *Fidelitas*. Remember.'

'Yes, Mama! But you will get well again. You must get well!'

'I always loved you best,' she whispered. 'Kiss me goodbye.'

He bent over her and laid his dry lips against her cold, damp cheek. It was like kissing a corpse. He shuddered. 'Not goodbye, Mama. Not goodbye.'

'God bless you, Nicky. Leave me now,' she whispered when he straightened up. 'All of you but Father – Moineau —'

Now there was nothing left to do; no-one to demand anything of her but her priest. She felt puzzled, wondering why she had been so long spared, and then so rapidly taken. Had she done everything? Had she done what she had been kept for? She wanted to ask Moineau, but she hadn't the strength to form such a complicated question. She was so tired, and in so much pain, she wanted only to die now, and be at peace.

Moineau stood beside her, holding her hand. Above her the tester of the great bed. Nicky born in this bed. Good to die here. Good to be buried in the crypt with her own family around her. As an orphan child she had longed for family, had come all the way to England searching for it, found it here in wonderful plenty at Morland Place. Had been happy. Had

403

done her duty. Had sinned, too – oh, sinned!

'Forgiven?' she whispered.

Moneau couldn't speak for a moment; he nodded. She saw him swallow. Then he leaned his face near, and said, 'God loves you. He understands.' Holding her hand, he began to speak the words of the absolution softly into her ear, and she closed her eyes, feeling the familiar, sweet cadences of the Latin wash over her, washing her clean. She felt the soft touch of the oiled wool on her forehead, breast and hands, felt the pain and toil of the world's life slip away from her, leaving her like a newly-shelled chestnut, smooth, whole, unblemished – ready for the new life, which would be sweeter and stronger than she could yet imagine. When it was done, and he spoke no more, she opened her eyes, and saw that he was crying, his round face grey with trouble, his chins shaking as he tried not to sob. Then she remembered he would not be coming with her, and she was sad for him. He had to remain here and suffer. She tried to smile, to comfort him, and wasn't sure if she had managed it; then another spasm took her and she gripped his hand convulsively.

'No, my child,' he said. 'Don't struggle. Go to God now. *Il t'attend.*'

The spasm passed, her hand relaxed. He lifted it to his lips, held it against his cheek, and she felt his grey salt tears mingle with the holy oil. *Twice anointed*, she thought confusedly.

'Stay,' she whispered.

'To the end,' he promised. 'All is well.'

What was inside Nicholas had turned into a raging beast, and he was terrified even to open his mouth in case it sprang out and devoured everything. Rage and hatred and terror burned up inside him like a terrible bile. He wanted to smash everything within reach, tear and burn and destroy – himself most of all. And himself cowered small and far away, pale and little and spindly, a helpless tiny child naked on a rock in the middle of a howling sea. He was the helpless child and he was the raging beast, he was the storm and the black gulf and everything in between. He was everything and he was nothing at all. He paced up and down the drawing-room, waiting for the worst thing in the world to happen. He wanted his mother, and his mother was dying.

His mother was dead. Moineau came in, the tears still fresh on his face (how dare he cry for her? How dare he be the one who was with her at the end?) but he didn't need to say anything. Havergill nodded and went himself, for form's sake.

'She is with God now,' Moineau said, tried to speak more, shook his head and went away to sit at the table on the other side of the room, his back to them, his head in his hands.

Pobgee blew his nose briskly, and then straightened his shoulders and came over to pat Nicholas's shoulder.

'My poor boy, I know how much you must feel your loss.'

'No you don't!' cried Nicky in a high, childish voice. 'Nobody does. She was my mother!' And Nicholas the beast snarled inwardly and longed to tear Pobgee's arm from his body – *What have you done with my inheritance? What have you done, lawyer, black carrion crow?*

'Indeed she was,' Pobgee said soothingly, 'but you must try to be brave. Everything now falls upon your shoulders. You have a great responsibility to bear, and it will take all your courage to bear it as your mother would have wanted.'

'What are you talking about?' spat a Nicholas somewhere between child and monster. 'What responsibility?'

'Why, Morland Place, of course,' said Pobgee. Nicholas became very still. Indeed, he felt the furniture, the very walls hold their breath to listen.

'Morland Place?'

'Your mother left everything to you, you know. You are master of the whole Morland estate, and you must carry on where she left off, and uphold the honour of the family. You are very young, of course, but you have already put on the mantle, if I may put it so. And there is another responsibility you will not have anticipated: on his deathbed John Skelwith made your mother guardian to his last surviving child Jemima, and your mother wished the guardianship to pass to you. I see no reason in law why it should not. The poor child has no other kin —'

Nicholas was struggling to understand, and was not much interested in Jemima Skelwith one way or the other. 'What – what —' he stammered. 'You say my mother left everything to me?'

'Certainly,' said Pobgee. He looked askance. 'You were expecting it, I assume? I have always understood that you were to inherit, and that you knew it.'

Nicholas made a sound in his throat, which could have passed for assent. He swallowed, and said, 'What did—? I mean – she – my mother– sent for you yesterday. Do you know what – what for?'

Pobgee frowned. 'Poor lady, she must have had a premonition,' he said. 'Yes, I know why she sent for me.' He thought a moment, and then sighed. 'There seems no reason why you should not know now. It may serve to strengthen your resolve, when you know how much she loved and trusted you. Your mother sent for me to draw up a deed of transfer, to give the entire estate to you immediately. She did not wish you to have to wait until her death to be master of Morland Place. Well, in the unhappy event, it was not necessary of course – the terms of her Will being already—' He broke off, looking at Nicholas in consternation. 'My dear young man, what is it? Oh, calm yourself! This grief is excessive. You will harm yourself. You must try to be calm!'

He could not tell whether Nicholas was laughing or crying, but since laughter would have been so inappropriate, he assumed it must be uncontrollable, convulsive grief. At all events, it was not a safe indulgence for a man of Nicholas's frame. The sobs were interfering with his normal breathing, he was gradually turning purple, gasping and choking and whooping like a madman in an *extremis* of his own.

The Reform Bill rushed through the committee stage with extraordinary speed, and on June 4th was put to the vote in the Lords. The news of Brougham's piece of paper – the written agreement of the King to create as many new peers as was necessary to force the Bill through – had broken the Tory spirit. Wellington and Peel had withdrawn their opposition, the country was on the verge of revolution, and when it came to it, only twenty-two peers mustered to vote against it.

The country erupted in joy: there were gatherings, parades, speeches, banquets, illuminations, firework displays. The King was once more a hero – old sailor Bill, the Reformer-King, depicted in cartoons as cranky and eccentric, but loyally British, standing out against the machinations of his German wife and her circle who had wanted to destroy the country.

'I wonder how much the people, as we call them, really understand about this business?' Lord Batchworth said to Tom Weston as they shared a quiet celebration in Brooks's. Outside the streets were full of revellers, and now and then a louder than usual burst of cheering penetrated even those noble walls. 'It has been a titanic struggle in their name, but do they really know what it is they are celebrating?'

'A notable victory,' Tom said. 'A new beginning. The start of a new age.'

'All of those?' Jes said with a faint smile.

'Don't you believe it? Nothing will ever be the same again. Now we can really begin to build a new Jerusalem.'

'Yes. Yes, of course I believe it. I'm a little tired, that's all.' He straightened his shoulders. 'How did your mother take the news of our victory?'

'Very well, all things considered. She frowned a little, and then said, "Well, at least you can get on with some other business now."'

'A just comment,' Jes said. 'We've a great deal to do. There's Michael Sadler's new Factory Bill to shepherd through; there's the Poor Law in desperate need of reform – the Corn Laws – tithes – public health —'

'But at last we shall have a Parliament with the power to change things,' Tom said with satisfaction. 'We shall get things done!'

'Ah yes,' Batchworth said, 'always provided you retain your seat. Had you thought of that? No more nomination boroughs, my lad. You must stand on your own merits.'

Tom grinned. 'I'll chance it! What do you do now, by the way? Are you staying up?'

'No, I go to Grasscroft tomorrow. We're having a Reform Dinner for the county. Why don't you come down with me, and keep me company in the chaise?'

'Thank you, but I have things to do before the recess. I will see you next month in any case.'

'Ah, you hadn't forgotten, then?'

'Certainly not! I've never been a godfather before, and I'm

always interested in new experiences.'

'You should try marriage,' Jes said. 'Marriage, house-keeping and fatherhood – all new experiences just waiting for you to try them.'

'You tail-less foxes!' Tom laughed. 'Never satisfied!'

All over England the cholera raged, in towns large and small, from Newcastle to Exeter, from Hull to Bristol, from Liverpool to London; and while the newly-enfranchised middling sort rejoiced over the Reform Act and the opening of a New Age, the very poor in their festering tenements sickened and died, and were buried in the overflowing graveyards, sometimes covered by no more than six inches of earth. Graves were already so full that burying a new body often meant exposing someone else, and there were many grim stories of remains being tossed aside or working their way up and out: in St Martin-le-Grand a dog ran off with a meaty human femur; in Walmgate some children were found playing football with a human skull.

Boards of Health were set up everywhere, but there was little anyone could do. Infected houses were whitewashed, braziers of burning pitch and oakum were set up in courts to kill the miasma, sometimes middens were completely removed and kennels cleaned out. Pest houses were set up, and in some places new burial grounds set aside; and as it was found that the better fed amongst the poor had more resistance to the disease, there was some experiment with the issue of bread and beef tickets to paupers. Given money, they tended to spend it on drink rather than food.

At Grasscroft, Sophie was restless. Henry visited as often as he could spare the time from his duties, and the news he brought of the town always left her feeling guilty. In the past she had done work amongst the poor, and could imagine what they must be suffering now; but while Prudence Hastings was toiling alongside her husband to try to relieve those sufferings, Sophie was keeping herself safe and taking her ease in a rural idyll.

'It's different for Prudence,' Henry said on one of his visits, 'Since Hastings himself works in that field, it's natural for her to want to work alongside him. And she has no children: you have Fanny to think of. It would be wrong of you to risk bringing the infection home to her.'

'Do you think so?' Sophie said doubtfully. 'But cholera only affects the very poor.'

'There's always danger,' Henry reminded her. 'You can't have forgotten the letter from your Mama about the Skelwith children falling sick with it.'

'No,' said Sophie. 'I hadn't forgotten. You're right, of course. But I wish Maman would write again and tell me how they go on. Poor Mathilde! She is like a sister to me, Henry. Don't you think Mama would have written if they were getting better? Don't you think it must mean bad news that she hasn't written?'

He shook his head with much more certainty than he felt. 'I think she would have written at once if it were bad news. Probably they are all recovering, and she is having so much to do in nursing them all that she has forgotten she has not shared the relief with you.'

Sophie did not seem convinced. 'Well,' she said, 'but there, you see, Maman is nursing them, not taking refuge at Morland Place and cutting herself off from their suffering.'

'The Skelwiths are relatives; it's quite different. If you wanted to go and nurse a member of your family I would have nothing to say against it, but I see no point in your risking your health for complete strangers, when there's so little really that you can do for them. Better to be useful where you know you can be, take care of Fanny, and make sure that Rosamund does not fret herself to death.'

'Yes,' she said, and sighed. 'I do see your point.'

He watched her thoughtfully. 'Have you thought any more about naming a date for the wedding?' he asked after a pause.

She looked away, blushing a little in confusion. 'Oh – no – that is – I don't know.'

'Sophie, you *do* want to marry me? If you have changed your mind, don't be afraid to tell me. You can't believe that I would try to hold you to an engagement you had thought better of.'

'Oh no, Henry,' she protested, turning to look at him. 'You mustn't think —! It isn't that.'

'Then what is it?' She did not answer. 'I know I am not

409

what the world would consider a good match for you, but I do love you with all my heart —'

'Yes, I know,' she said. It wasn't quite what he had hoped to hear. He was afraid that she *had* changed her mind, but was too tender to tell him. He did not want her to pity him; yet, searching the depths of his own feelings, he was not sure that he would not still prefer to marry her, even if he only had her pity rather than her love. Pity might turn into love, given time; but nothing could come from nothing. If only she would name the date!

'Sophie —' he began tentatively, but she interrupted him.

'*Please*, Henry, don't press me! I will decide, I promise you; but not now. Not yet.'

Her doubts grew when she was alone, diminished when she had been with him for some time. When she was with him, he was the Henry she had known since she first came to Manchester, the friend of her husband, familiar, safe and unthreatening. But when she was alone and thought about marriage to him, she became afraid. Why could they not simply remain friends? Marriage meant physical intimacy, and she was afraid of it. She had shared it with Jasper, and had delighted in it, and it had seemed a thing which belonged exclusively to him. The notion that she might feel pleasure with another man seemed wrong and wicked, a betrayal, as bad as adultery. Yet the idea of the intimacy without the pleasure seemed even more wrong. She could not bear to contemplate that.

When she remembered the storm of feelings she had experienced in his arms on that one occasion, on the day Cavendish was born, it made her tremble. She had sometimes felt flickers of it since then – when he held her hand, smiled at her, looked at her in a certain way – and it frightened her. She did not want to feel like that; but equally she did not want to lose him. She cared for him very much, longed for his company when he was away, knew she depended on him too much to part with him. So she did the only thing she could think of, and delayed choosing a date for the wedding. She felt that she was being unfair to him, but she didn't know what else to do. She hoped that her feelings would resolve themselves one way or the other, and tried not to wonder what she would do if they did not.

Rosamund was too preoccupied to probe into Sophie's state of mind. They had always meant to have the Christening this summer, but now it was almost upon them, she was afraid that she was tempting fate. Cavendish had been well lately – the last upset had been in April when he had run a high fever which she had been convinced was going to carry him off, but which broke after thirty-six hours into an ordinary cold. But he was still very small for his age, carrying no spare flesh to lose when he got sick or went off his food, and she could never be off her guard. Every period of calm seemed to her no more than a lull in the continual storm.

During those lulls, she loved to be with him, singing to him, playing with him, watching with unending wonder how he learned and developed and changed a little every day. She was no remote mother, leaving her child with the nursery staff except for a ten-minute daily visit: he was with her for most of his waking hours. She would not allow herself to be aware that part of her reason for it was so that if he were taken, she would have plenty of memories.

She had learned the lesson with Charlotte. She thought about her often, but had nothing to remember, just those few weeks during which – how terrible it seemed now! – she had left her most of the time with her nurses. Fanny made her think of Charlotte. They were much of an age, and she liked to fancy that in Fanny she could see a little of how Charlotte would be looking at each stage of her development. But to be fair, all children reminded her of Charlotte. When Roland and Thalia arrived next month there would be William, Lucilla and Titus to remind her – and Thalia's burgeoning pregnancy, too. The new baby was due in September, and the name was chosen already: Hector, or Helen if it should be a girl. Thalia was certainly fulfilling her duty with admirable regularity. Perhaps if Jes were with her more – and now that the Reform Bill had gone through, she hoped he would be – she might conceive again. She would love to be able to present him with a numerous family. At this distance, she forgot how difficult her pregnancies and deliveries both were, and how afraid she had been of dying. At this distance she wanted only to fill Jes's nurseries, and make Cavendish less conspicuous to the eyes of the jealous gods.

On the day that Jes began his journey home from London, Rosamund and Sophie were alone together at the breakfast table. Rosamund had already had one breakfast, very early before her morning ride, but it seemed a distant memory now. This was the elegant breakfast at the fashionable hour of ten. Henry was expected later; Jes would be home tomorrow; the grand dinner was set for the day after; and this morning Rosamund had arranged to drive over to Leighton Park to visit Lady Wingate, her nearest neighbour.

'Are you sure you won't come with me?' she asked Sophie, not for the first time. 'I don't like to think of you sitting here all alone with nothing to do.'

'I never have "nothing to do",' Sophie replied. 'There is always sewing; and if I get tired of that, there are my paints. I still have the background to do on your portrait, which I ought to finish today if you want to have it framed for Jes's birthday.'

'True enough,' Rosamund conceded. 'Well, I shan't stand in your way, then. But you had better let me take Fanny off your hands. Lady Wingate likes children – and Fanny likes nothing better than showing off to strangers!'

Sophie was not obliged to reply to this calumny, for the footman, William, came in just then with the letters. Amongst them was one for her, which she took eagerly, hoping for news from her mother, and puzzled over.

'I don't recognise the writing at all,' she said, 'nor the seal.' Seeing that Rosamund was looking at her own letters, Sophie slipped the knife under it and unfolded the heavy paper. 'Why, it's from Mr Pobgee!' she exclaimed. 'Whatever can he —?'

After a few moments Rosamund, eagerly devouring Jes's latest letter, noticed the dense silence on the other side of the table, and looked up. Sophie's sallow face was so pale it seemed to have taken on a greenish tinge. She was gripping the sides of the letter so tightly that her knuckles were white, and her eyes moved back and forth across the lines as though she could not understand what she was reading.

'Sophie, what is it? You look so strange!'

Sophie made a sound, and her hands began to shake so

412

badly that she surely could not have read the paper she held. Rosamund jumped up, scattering letters, and went round the table. 'You're ill,' she said. 'You must lie down. Let me help you to the sofa. Have you your vinaigrette with you?'

'No, no,' Sophie managed to gasp. 'I'm not ill. It's – it's this letter. I don't understand it. Oh, pray, read it for me, tell me what it says! It must be a mistake.'

She found it hard to let go of the paper, and Rosamund had to ease it from her fingers.

'*My dear Mrs Hobsbawn,*' it said, '*may I first of all offer you my most sincere condolences on the loss of your honoured mother. It must have come as a great shock to you, as indeed it did to me. As you know I have been privileged to attend to her affairs of business these thirty years past, and counted myself her friend as well as her adviser. She will be sadly missed; none the less that her death accorded with the selfless dedication to duty which distinguished her life.*'

At this point Rosamund looked up. 'What can it mean?' she said.

Sophie met her eyes desperately. 'Does it – do I read it correctly? Does he say that my m-m-mother is dead?'

Rosamund nodded reluctantly. 'But I don't understand. If it were true, someone would have told you before. He writes as if he supposes you already know. It can't be true!'

Sophie gave a small shake of the head. She was thinking what Rosamund was thinking: Pobgee could not be mistaken about such a thing. But how? When? Why had Nicky not written? What had happened at Morland Place?

Rosamund read on. '*Your noble mother's Will is in my hands, and I do not think I am revealing anything you do not already know in telling you that the entire estate passes to your brother Nicholas. This estate of course includes the twenty-five per centum interest in the Hobsbawn factories which was retained at the time of your Marriage Settlement.*

'*Your late mother did request that certain small items of personal remembrance should be given to you on her death. This request was conveyed to me in a letter, of which a copy was kept with the Will and has now been passed to your brother. As the request is not actually part of the Will, it does not have the force of law, but I have no doubt that Mr Nicholas Morland will be glad to comply*

413

with his mother's wishes at whatever time it should suit you to apply to him for these keepsakes.

'*It remains only to add, in addition to my deepest sympathies for what must be your great affliction, that if there is anything that I can do for you at any time, either professionally or as an old family friend, I beg you will not hesitate to command me.*'

Rosamund finished reading and looked up. Sophie was sitting with her hands in her lap, staring at nothing, trembling.

'What does it mean, Ros?' she whispered. 'Maman dead? It can't be! I must be asleep and dreaming. Oh tell me I'm dreaming!'

'My poor Sophie,' Rosamund began helplessly.

It had the ring of truth to Sophie. She stood up suddenly, so quickly that she felt dizzy and had to catch at the edge of the table. 'I must go there. Now, at once! There is no time to waste.'

'Now? But Sophie —'

'No! Please, Ros, you must help me! I have to find out what has happened! Don't delay me – I cannot bear to delay!'

'Very well, I will help you, but sit down a moment until you are composed. I will ring for Hetty to pack for you. Moss shall help her. And you shall have the chaise, and my team for the first stage. Everything will be done as quickly as possible, I promise you. But you can't go alone. If you will only wait until Jes comes home, I will go with you. We could set off the day after tomorrow —'

'No! I can't wait. I must go now!'

'Then wait only until tomorrow morning, and let Henry go with you.'

'Please, Ros, try to understand! I must go straight away. Something terrible has happened, and I must know what it is. I can't rest until I know; I can't delay a single instant.'

Rosamund saw that she was determined, and argued no further. Besides, she would have felt the same way if she had received such a letter about *her* mother. 'Very well,' she said quietly. 'You shall have Moss to go with you, since I cannot.'

'Oh Ros, thank you! Are you sure you can manage without her?'

'Don't be silly. And my groom, Whittock, shall travel with

you too, to take care of the changes – you are in no state for the trouble. You had better go and prepare yourself. I will order the horses at the door in half an hour. Can you be ready by then?'

'Yes, oh yes!'

'The roads should be good. You can be at Morland Place before dark. And I pray to God you find —' She bit her lip. How could she wish Sophie might find it had been a mistake? Attorneys did not make mistakes of that kind. But what could have happened? It was a mystery – an abominable mystery.

Sophie pressed her hand in silent thanks and hurried to the door, and Rosamund rang the bell, running through in her mind the things that would have to be done. Moss warned – Hetty given instructions about packing – the horses ordered – Whittock told off to go along. Raby must give him money for the changes – she doubted whether Sophie had enough about her. A note sent off to Lady Wingate. Instructions to the boys about bringing her own horses back. They could get a change at Huddersfield – that would be a long stage, but the horses were fresh and Whittock would see the boys nursed them along. They could rest them well before bringing them home.

And all the time her mind gnawed and worried at the question of how her aunt had died, and why Sophie had not been told. Part of her was unreasonably afraid of learning the answer; and she hadn't yet had time to think about Aunt Héloïse. She could sense the shock of the news in the back of her mind, waiting for her to have the leisure to feel it. When Sophie was on her way in half an hour's time, then she would sit down and let it have its way with her.

415

Ottershaw met her at the door, looking gaunt and old. Though his appearance was as immaculate as ever, there was a haunted look to his eyes that shocked Sophie, for he had always been the model of imperturbability. The fact that he was in mourning livery gave the death-stroke to any hope she had cherished that the whole thing might be an incomprehensible mistake.

'Oh Miss Sophie!' he cried, revealing the depths of his emotion by forgetting her proper title, 'You here?'

'Ottershaw – my mother – what happened?'

'We didn't know if you knew, Miss Sophie – when you didn't come —'

'I didn't know. No-one told me, until I got a letter from Mr Pobgee this morning.'

Tears filled the old man's eyes. 'It's been that dreadful here, miss, and Mr Nicholas quite wild with grief. No-one can get near him, except his man, and as to asking him questions —' He shook his head and drew out a black-bordered handkerchief to dab his cheeks. 'I would have gladly undertaken to write to you myself, miss, if it was too much trouble for the master, but as to asking him, I wouldn't dare. It was Mr Ferrars arranged the funeral, but there was no-one but us there, the household I mean, miss, and —'

'She is buried already?' Sophie said blankly.

'In the crypt, alongside your father and Mr Edward, just as she would have wanted. Father Moineau conducted the service, of course, before he —'

'But, good God, when did she die? How long ago?'

'Two weeks ago, miss. And the funeral was last week.'

Sophie stared at him in stunned silence. Two weeks ago. She had not even been given the chance to come to the funeral. What was going on here? But before she could ask anything more, they were interrupted by a sharp voice from behind them.

'Visitors? Ottershaw, you were told there were to be no —' As Ottershaw turned, Sophie's slight form, which had been concealed by his bulk, was revealed to the newcomer, and he stopped abruptly. Sophie, looking past the butler, saw her brother's man, who had just come into the hall from the direction of the steward's room. Ferrars composed his face and bowed low. 'Mrs Hobsbawn – what a pleasant surprise, ma'am.'

Sophie looked at him coolly. She had never liked him, though she supposed it was unfair to be prejudiced against a man for his physical appearance. But his tone of greeting her seemed to be ironic. 'Where is my brother?'

'The master has gone to York, ma'am.'

'When will he return?'

'I am not at liberty to say.'

'Where is he gone? Do you expect him back tonight?' Sophie asked impatiently.

'I believe he has gone to his club,' Ferrars said stiffly. 'He gave me no instructions as to his return.'

'If he has gone to his club, he will come back tonight,' Sophie said to Ottershaw rather than Ferrars. 'Have my traps taken up to my old room, please, and ask Mrs Thomson to make my servants comfortable.'

Ottershaw bowed, but Sophie did not miss the quick flicker of his eyes towards Ferrars as he did so.

'Might I ask if the master is expecting you, ma'am?' Ferrars asked. It was spoken politely enough, but the very fact that he asked made her raise her eyebrows.

'I doubt it,' she said shortly, preparing to pass him. To her astonishment he stepped slightly to the side, effectively blocking her path.

'Do you mean to make a stay here, Mrs Hobsbawn?'

It was insolence even she could not ignore, though she had never stood on her dignity with her servants.

'Is that any business of yours?' she snapped.

Ferrars smiled – never a pleasant thing to witness. His teeth were uneven and coated with a greenish film, and when he put the muscles of his cheeks into movement, it seemed to give a horrid life to the spots, blackheads and blemishes which decorated his face. 'Since the late, tragic event, my master has been accustomed to issuing his orders for the household through me, and as he did not anticipate having the pleasure of your company here, he has left no instructions for your reception. Indeed he has said most definitely that he does not want any visitors at all at Morland Place.'

Sophie faced him squarely. 'Do you mean to deny me?'

He looked at her thoughtfully for a long time, and Sophie began to feel that he would indeed dare even that; but at last her level, cold look seemed to work on him and he looked away and bowed slightly.

'Of course not, ma'am. I was merely trying to carry out my master's orders.'

'Most punctilious of you,' she commented shortly. She turned to the butler, thereby turning her back on Ferrars. 'Ottershaw, see to my bags, will you? I think I had better speak to Mrs Thomson myself. Is she in her room?'

'Yes, ma'am. Should I tell her —?'

'No, don't bother. I'll go there myself,' she said quickly. She didn't want Ferrars interposing any more objections, or getting to Mrs Thomson before she did. She smiled reassuringly at Ottershaw, and without even waiting to take off her bonnet and pelisse, she walked quickly away from them both and down the kitchen passage.

The housekeeper's room was on the opposite side from the butler's room, part of what had been the pantry in mediaeval times. She tapped briskly on the door and without waiting for a reply walked in. Mrs Thomson was sitting at her table writing something. She looked up with quick apprehension when the door opened, then gave an incoherent cry, got up so quickly she almost knocked over her chair, and in two steps reached Sophie and put her arms round her.

'Oh Miss Sophie, you came, you came!' she cried; and in a moment more they were both enjoying the luxury of a really abandoned cry.

★

418

'It's been so dreadful, you can't imagine,' Mrs Thomson said, absently screwing her handkerchief into a tight, wet ball. It was some time later, and they were sitting on either side of her table, both a little blotchy as to the face and distinctly red about the eyes. Between them was the decanter of Madeira Mrs Thomson kept in her room against her occasional nervous spasms. A glass each had helped to calm them, and the second glass was now easing the flow of communication. 'Mr Nicholas has been like a wild beast, quite mad with grief, and nobody durst go near him, except that Ferrars.' She spat the name so viciously Sophie had no difficulty in guessing how she felt about him.

'Has he been encroaching?'

Mrs Thomson hesitated. 'It's hard to say that, really, since he only does what Mr Nicholas tells him; but I do think – and Ottershaw agrees with me – that he has too much influence over the master for anyone's good. He spends a lot of time shut up alone with him, and then comes out and says the master wants this or the master wants that – well, how do we know what Mr Nicholas really wants? Father Moineau said to me before he left —'

'He's gone?' Sophie said, taken aback. She had meant to go and talk with him when she left Mrs Thomson. 'Father Moineau is gone?'

'Yes, as soon as the funeral was over. He said that there was nothing here for him any more, and that he wasn't going to wait to be turned off like a bad servant. Mr Nicholas had quite taken against him in the last few months, you see; which was why the father kept out of the way as much as possible, working with the poor in the village, and taking his meals separate. But of course he wouldn't leave the mistress. Only when she went, and he'd said the mass for her, he collected his things together and walked off – just as he arrived in the first place all those years ago, on foot with a bundle on his shoulder, do you remember, miss?'

'Did he say where he was going?'

'Not officially, no, but Ottershaw said that he'd been talking about the railway workings – you know how he was always wild about the railways, miss – and how the navvies were in desperate need of the word of God from a man who

419

could understand their ways. I believe they are a very wild, godless lot, miss, from what I hear, and the father must have felt he had a sort of mission to them. Anyway, he went off the very day of the funeral; and Mr Barnard left the next morning.'

Sophie was stricken. 'Not Monsieur Barnard too? Oh surely not! I depended on seeing him!'

'If he'd known you were coming, I dare say he'd have waited. You always were a pet of his, miss. But he wouldn't serve anyone but the mistress. He was a strange one, miss, as you very well know! He looked upon his cooking in such a funny way, almost as if it was a holy service. Cook for anyone he didn't care for he would not, and seeing as he's an old man now in any case, and has his bit saved up, he decided to retire from his calling altogether.'

'Do you know where he went?'

'That I can tell you: you remember your mama's Abigail Marie, who married Kexby the carrier and settled in a little cottage over to Shipton?'

'Yes, of course, – dear Marie!'

'Well, she's widowed now, miss, as I expect you knew, and Kexby being a good man left her very handsomely provided for.'

'And Monsieur Barnard's gone to live with her?'

'Well, miss, I do believe they mean to sell up and go back to France together. Mr Barnard being an old man now, and having no relatives, he was talking about wanting to lay his bones in his own country.'

'But Maman always promised him he should be buried in the crypt with the family!' Sophie cried.

'Yes, miss, and if he had died before her, that's what would have happened, I'm sure. But now she's dead —' She stopped and unscrewed her handkerchief to apply it to her eyes again. 'Oh dear, oh dear! I can't get over it! I can't seem to get a hold of it at all. My poor mistress! Oh Miss Sophie, it was a cruel, cruel thing!'

'She never spared herself,' Sophie said. 'That was her way.'

'But Dr Bayliss warned her against nursing the family at Skelwith Lodge, and such a mystery as it was that the cholera

420

should ever have gone there – for you know, miss, that it's the dirty, low houses that get it as a rule – well, the doctor guessed, and told her plainly, that it must be something different about that particular house that was to blame, and that she was risking herself by spending every day there. But leave poor Miss Matilda alone – Mrs Skelwith, I should say – she would not; and then the poor children besides, and poor Mr John; and now they're all dead. Every one.'

'Except Jemima.'

'Who was living here the whole time,' Mrs Thomson said eagerly, 'so it proves it! And the strangest thing of all is that only the family and the nursery-maids got it. The other servants were all right, which made Dr Bayliss believe it must be something in the nursery-floor rooms that was breeding the miasma, as it's called. But he had them whitewashed and fumigated, and it didn't make any difference. My poor mistress still took the sickness, and she was taken off quicker than all the rest. She was all right at dinner-time, and died the next morning.'

Sophie nodded, and reached across and pressed her hand, unable to speak for a moment.

'What will happen to Jemima now?' she asked at last.

'The mistress made Mr Nicholas her guardian, on her deathbed, Miss Sophie.' Mrs Thomson shook her head and sighed tremulously. 'That poor child! I've never seen such a little lost soul. When I see her little pale face, all bewildered-like —' She shook her head again.

'Perhaps I could offer her a home,' Sophie said. 'She's the same age as Fanny. They would be company for each other.'

'Oh miss, if you could, what a blessing it would be for her! Morland Place is no place for a little girl now. Frankly, miss, I don't know what's going to become of us all. If Mr Nicholas doesn't come back to himself —'

'It's early days yet, Mrs Thomson,' Sophie said soothingly. 'We are all grieved and shocked, and it will take time for us to mend. But Nicky might be very glad to let me take her off his hands just now. He can hardly want the trouble of a little girl at a time like this, especially when there's no woman of the house to take charge of her. When he marries, he might wish to take her back, but for the time being . . .' She nodded to herself decisively. 'I'll ask him when he comes in.'

'Ah, when!' Mrs Thomson said. 'As to that, miss, you may have a long wait. When he goes in to York he stays very late – sometimes all night – and then he doesn't come home in a state fit to talk to.'

'Then I'll wait until I can speak to him,' Sophie said firmly. 'I must find out the state of his mind, and why he didn't tell me about my mother.'

'Just too upset, I should think, Miss Sophie,' said Mrs Thomson. 'Out of his senses with grief, and not able to think of anything but himself and his loss.'

'I'm sure you're right,' Sophie said. 'I hope I can comfort him a little, and perhaps set him on a more even path. Poor Nicky! He always was her favourite, so I suppose it's harder for him than me.' Mrs Thomson looked as though she meant to say something, but changed her mind. 'What about you, Mrs Thomson?' Sophie asked next. 'What will you do?'

'I shall stay, of course,' she said, a little uncertainly. 'As you say, the master will get back to his usual self in time,' she amplified, 'and then I shall be happy to serve him as I served the mistress. I've been here a long time, and I shouldn't like to pull up my roots now.'

'But? You sound as if there's a "but".'

'Well, miss, supposing things didn't get better – supposing that Ferrars was to go on giving the orders – I don't think I could stand that, not being told my job by an upstart foreigner like him. I'm Yorkshire born and bred, and he's only from Kent, miss, when all's said and done; and a very low sort of people *they* are down south, as I don't need to tell you. Well, if things did get bad – though I'm sure they won't – but if they did, Ottershaw and me has plans. We have our bit saved all right, and the mistress always promised us both a pension which I'm sure Mr Nicholas will honour, and so we mean to set up somewhere together. Married, of course!' she added quickly, in case she had given the wrong impression. 'And I thought we might open a little cake and pastry shop somewhere to keep ourselves busy. I'm quite a good baker when I'm allowed near an oven, which Mr Barnard never would let me in this house, of course – and Ottershaw could serve behind the counter, service being his line.'

'It sounds an excellent plan.'

'Thank you, miss. But it's only just in case. We wouldn't leave the master, not unless we were forced to.'

When she left Mrs Thomson, Sophie went up to the nursery to see Jemima. The house was very quiet, and already seemed to have a slight air of neglect. Mrs Thomson had told her that in the months before her death, the mistress had handed over the running of the house as well as the estate to Nicholas, and he had instituted a regime of economy by dismissing quite a few of the servants, which had left her short of the staff to keep things as she liked them kept.

Walking alone along the upstairs passages, Sophie was suddenly aware of a strong sense of her mother's presence. For twenty-six years Héloïse had been mistress here: her spirit, her ideas, her personality had filled the house and formed its ways. Her light step, her pleasant voice, her happy smile had been encountered round every corner; she had known the inside of every closet and the history and personal desires of every servant. No detail had been too small for her to interest herself in, and there was no inch of the house that did not breathe her influence.

Sophie stopped still, suddenly overcome by her sense of loss. The memories flooded in; her mother's face appeared in her mind, the bright eyes, the warm smile; she remembered the scent that always seemed to hang about her, faint and fresh like moss in a cool wood; she thought of the loving arms which had so often been folded around her, comforting, approving. Never again. A shadow had passed over the sun. How could she manage in a world which did not contain Maman? Who would there be to be her unchanging rock, her inspiration, her safe place? She felt for a moment so desolate that it was like sickness. She stood with bent head in the emptiness of the corridor and waited for it to pass.

And when it had passed, she thought of Jemima, and the thought braced her. Jemima had lost her mother, her father and all her family; and now her grandmama too. If Sophie was desolated by her loss, what must that poor little girl be feeling? She felt her mother's spirit watching her approvingly. Yes, Maman, I understand! I will take her with me, and be a mother to her, just as you would wish. I'll give her a home and love and comfort her. That's what you would have wanted me to do. I won't fail you, Maman. You can be easy.

She suddenly remembered Plaisir, the house where she had been born and where she had lived with Maman and Mathilde until she was eight years old. There had always been laughter in the house, it seemed; she associated her mother with laughter, with sunshine and pleasure. *Don't be sad, my Sophie. Remember me with gladness. Fill your life with laughter, for life is too short for mourning.* Sophie could almost hear her saying it.

And Maman would want her to marry Henry, she suddenly felt sure of it. She had been mourning Jasper, but all things had their season, and life was the most precious gift of all, not to be wasted. The thought of Henry revived her, and lit a little warmth in the sad coldness of her heart. He would be her rock, her safe place. How could she have hesitated so long? As soon as she got back she would tell him, name the day. It would have to be delayed until the mourning period was over of course —

But there were things to do here first. She straightened her shoulders and with a firmer step walked on towards the nursery.

Nicholas did not come home that night. Sophie would have felt a little awkward about sitting down all alone to a ceremonious dinner in the dining-room; but in the event, it was not required of her. Ottershaw came to her to say, with many apologies, that the cook – a replacement brought in when Barnard left and *not* proving satisfactory, miss – had gone out after getting the servants' dinner at noon and not come back. He was probably, Ottershaw added darkly, sitting in the taproom of The Hare and Heather, as drunk as a wheelbarrow by now.

'It doesn't matter,' Sophie said, to comfort the butler whose pride was wounded by having to do with inferior servants. 'But I am very hungry. Could something be put up for me? Anything will do – bread and cold meat.'

'If you would be so good as to find it satisfactory in the circumstances, Miss Sophie, Mrs Thomson could prepare a repast for you which, though not approaching Monsieur Barnard's standards, would at least be better than bread and cold meat.'

'Thank you. I'm sure it will be excellent. I should like to have it as soon as possible, if that's convenient?'

'Certainly, Miss Sophie. And we were wondering also if you might find it more comfortable to have it in your room, on the little table there, the dining-room being so large and unwelcoming for one person alone.'

'That is a kind thought. But I have a better idea – bring it up to me in the nursery, if you please, along with Jemima's supper. I'm sure she needs the company as much as I do.'

So while Jemima had her rice and milk and cinnamon cakes at one end of the table, Sophie dined at the other on potato soup, chicken cutlets, cold ham with salads, a savoury of toasted cheese and anchovies, and a large bowl of strawberries with cream, which for a meal put up on such short notice she thought excellent. And when they had finished eating, she played several games of spillikins with Jemima, helped Matty undress her and put her to bed, and then read her a story until she fell asleep – in a happier frame of mind, Sophie hoped, than she had found her.

And Sophie went to bed in the Blue Room less restless and unhappy than she had expected to be, only half listening out for Nicky's return, conscious of having done some good in the house, and very hopeful of doing more in the morning.

The news that met her when she went down to breakfast was that Nicholas had come in about an hour ago and that Ferrars had put him to bed. She would have to wait to speak to him, then; and she spent the morning with Jemima, talking to her, playing with her, and taking her for a walk around the gardens. At noon the child was called in for her dinner, which was prepared at the same time as the servants' dinner. Sophie sat in the rose garden and watched the birds and pursued her own thoughts until at half past one a maid she had not seen before came out to tell her that a nuncheon of cold ham, cakes and fruit had been laid for her in the long saloon.

It was while she was sampling this that Nicholas walked in. He looked dreadful – gaunt and red-eyed, his skin dull and blotched – and though he walked steadily, when he flopped into a chair at the table and reached out for a glass, Sophie saw that his hands were shaking badly.

'Nicky, what were you doing last night?' she cried in consternation.

He had not offered her any greeting, nor even looked at her. Now he said. 'Enjoying myself, if it is any business of yours, my dear sister.' He was concentrating hard on filling his glass with wine, and managed it at last with only one drop spilled.

The effort did not escape Sophie's notice. 'I'm sure you were drinking too much, at least. You ought not to have more now. And yes, it is my business! You are my brother —'

'I wasn't drinking too much, as it happens,' he interrupted in the same flat, dull voice. 'I had just enough brandy to give me some precious moments of happiness – which you, apparently, begrudge me.'

'Of course I don't begrudge you happiness,' Sophie said anxiously, 'but that sort of thing won't secure it. You mustn't give way like this, Nicky. You must make an effort to —'

'Have you come all this way just to lecture me?' he interrupted disagreeably. 'Because if you have, you can leave straight away. Yes,' he put the glass down clumsily and fixed his bloodshot eyes on her, 'and why the devil have you come? Ferrars tells me you were interrogating him like a felon yesterday – and my butler and housekeeper! I won't have you coming here interfering with *my* servants.'

'Your servants?' Sophie said, surprised by the hostility he injected into the possessive.

'Whose else?' he said with an unpleasant smile. 'It may have escaped your notice, sister dear, that Morland Place is mine, Morland Place and everything in it. I am master here.'

Sophie's eyes filled with tears. 'Nicky, why are you talking to me like that? And why didn't you write when Maman died? Why didn't you tell me about the funeral?'

'Why should I?' he retorted.

'Why? Because she's my mother too,' Sophie cried.

He looked a little put out by that, a little ashamed of himself. 'Yes, well, you have your own life now,' he said sullenly. 'What happens here is nothing to do with you any

426

more. You —' He slammed his hand down on the table in sudden anger. 'All right, I forgot to tell you, is that what you want to hear? I forgot, and that's that! Now leave me alone!'

Sophie stared at him, deeply concerned. He was not talking rationally, she thought. Was he still under the influence of last night's carouse, or was there something else at work in his mind? 'I suppose you haven't told Bendy either?' she said slowly.

'Bendy? Bendy's gone. He doesn't exist. My mother cast him off, and decreed that his name should never be spoken again. He was dead to her, and he remains dead to me.'

'Nicky, Bendy came to see me in Manchester after he left here. I *know* he didn't do those things you accused him of.'

'You know, do you? Because he told you?'

'Yes!'

'And you believed him. What a simpleton you are! Do you think he was going to admit his guilt to you?'

'He didn't lie to me, I'm sure of it. Bendy is a good person. He'd never harm a soul, any more than you would.' Nicky didn't answer, drinking deeply from his glass. 'He ought to be told, at any rate. He has that right.' No answer. 'Well, I shall tell him, then!'

'You don't know where he is,' Nicky said triumphantly.

'I know how to find him. He was going to work for Mr Stephenson and if I write to him, he will send the letter on to Bendy.'

Nicky looked shaken. 'What do you want to write to him for? There's nothing for him, you know! Everything came to me. And I won't have him here! You tell him that! If he tries to set foot on my land, I'll set the dogs on him! I'll shoot him for a poacher!'

'Nicky!'

'I know what you're after! I know why you've come here, poking and spying about. You think you can find a way to cheat me out of my inheritance – but you can't! Morland Place is mine!'

'I know it is. I never thought it wouldn't be. Nor did Bendy. We always knew Maman would leave it all to you,' Sophie said. 'Nicky, I don't understand – why are you so upset?'

'You ask me that?' He gave a short, harsh laugh. 'My

mother is dead! Isn't that enough reason.'

'I'm grieving for her too,' Sophie said, 'but it doesn't make me speak hatefully to you.'

Nicholas emptied the glass and put it down, and as he began to refill it, Sophie saw that the shaking of his hands was much less. He seemed to be thinking, and after a moment he said in a quieter tone, 'I'm sorry. I suppose you are sad to lose her. But you haven't been here. You went off and made your own life, and she and I stayed here together. Just the two of us. She was much more mine than yours. I have a better right to grieve. And I was here when she died – I saw her suffer! Her last illness —!' He put his face in his hands and made a harsh noise like a sob.

Sophie watched him for a moment, and then said gently, 'Poor Nicky. I know you loved her very much. But you should have told me, not let me learn it in that cruel way from Mr Pobgee —'

The face emerged suddenly from behind the hands, like the evil little jack-in-the-box that had so frightened her in the nursery when she was a small child. 'Pobgee? What was he writing to you for?'

'To offer his condolences. And to say that Maman wanted me to have some keepsakes, which she mentioned in a letter. He said he gave you the letter.'

'Oh, *that's* why you're here, is it?' Nicholas said with an air of enlightenment. 'You've come to collect your plunder?'

The word puzzled Sophie. She said, 'That's not why I came here. I came to find out why you hadn't told me that Maman was dead.'

'Well I've told you now that I forgot. I'm sorry. So you can go now, can't you?'

'Why do you want to get rid of me?'

'Why do you want to stay? There's nothing for you here. You've no rights here any more. Morland Place is mine, and I can turn anyone out that I want to.'

'Of course you can,' she said, mystified.

'Right! Then you can pack your things and go. I mean it, now! I want you out of here this afternoon.' He was working up a rage again. 'Go back to Manchester. That's where you belong now. Go back to your precious Henry Hobblefoot and

428

your grimy factory friends – and don't come here again, do you hear me?'

Sophie was angry with herself for allowing her eyes to fill with tears. She dashed them away, and tried to speak calmly. 'I hear you, Nicky, and I'll go if you want me to. But you know this isn't your real self speaking. You are mad with grief, I can see that. You will come back to your senses one day soon, and when you do, I'll come and see you again. I want you to know that I don't blame you, and whatever you say, I won't let it hurt me, because I know you don't really mean it.'

'Oh, get out of here, Miss Piety! You make me sick!'

She stood up to go, and then remembered the important thing. 'There is one thing more, though. Jemima.'

'What about her?' he said, looking up quickly, with what looked like apprehension.

'I can see that you are too grief-stricken to be able to take care of her, and I'm sure you won't want the trouble of it, along with everything else. So I will be happy to take her home with me, and look after her for the time being. She and Fanny will be company for each other, and it will be much better for —'

'Oh no you don't, my girl! I am Jemima's legal guardian now, and no-one's going to take her away. She stays here, sister Sophie, and that's my final word – and my word is law in everything to do with her. Ask your precious Mr Pobgee if you don't believe me. Oh, and while we're on that subject, you're not going to take anything else out of this house, either. That letter Pobgee gave me is all very fine, but it's not part of the Will, and I'm not letting you get your hands on anything.'

'You won't give me the keepsakes our mother wanted me have?' Sophie asked quietly.

'She didn't say anything to *me* about wanting you to have them, and I was with her right to the end. If she'd wanted to give you anything, she'd have put it in the Will. That letter means nothing. There's no knowing even if it was Mama who wrote it. For all I know, it could be something you wrote yourself and slipped in amongst her papers, just to get your hands on her things.'

'How can you talk like that? I don't even know what's in the

429

letter!' Sophie said indignantly, before realising that it was undignified to haggle with him like this, when he was obviously not himself. In a few weeks, or months, when his mind had settled onto a more even keel, she would see him again, and everything would then be different. Poor Nicky! She only hoped his frail physical health would not be as badly affected as his mind plainly was.

The post-horses arrived from The Hare and Heather at three o'clock, the baggage was strapped on, and Sophie, with as much dignity as she could muster, took her leave. Saying goodbye to Jemima had been heartbreaking: a last plea to Nicholas to let her take the little girl had been met with a stony refusal. Now she said goodbye to Ottershaw and Mrs Thomson with tears, taking the chance to whisper as she shook hands for the last time a plea that they would look after the little girl, and send Sophie word if things got worse.

Nicholas appeared briefly at the great door as she stepped to the carriage – to make sure she really went, she supposed – and looking back she was filled again with pity for him in his terrible affliction of grief. What worried her more was the glimpse she had, over Nicholas's shoulder, of Ferrars, standing in the background, watching her departure. She climbed up after Moss into the carriage, the yard groom put up the step and closed the door, and the chaise lurched forward.

Sophie looked out of the window as they turned onto the track, gazing at the ancient barbican and the glimpse beyond it of Morland Place itself, and wondered despondently if she would ever see it again. And then she shook herself and replaced despair with determination. She waited until they were out of sight of the house, and then bid Whittock, Ros's groom, lean out of the window and tell the post-boys to take the track towards York instead of turning towards Wetherby.

'I want to speak to Dr Havergill before I go home. Tell them to drive to the hospital first. If he isn't there, they may know where I can find him.'

'Oh ma'am,' Moss protested, 'do you think it's safe? They have the cholera in York – Mrs Thomson was telling me – and the hospital is bound to be full of it.'

'You can stay in the carriage if you're worried. But I must

430

speak to him.' She wanted to ask him if Nicky's mental state was unusual, how soon it would wear off, and whether anything could be done to help him. She wanted to ask him to keep an eye on him if he could – and on Jemima. And, hard as it would be, she wanted to ask him about her mother. He had been there to the end, and she needed some account of her mother's last illness in order to be able to accept properly the fact that she was dead.

It was several days before Liza was able to learn from Benedict what had been in the letter. It had been brought one evening by a servant from The Bell in Leicester, where Robert Stephenson was staying temporarily, and Liza had assumed – as had Benedict at first – that the letter was from Mr Robert himself. But as she watched him read it and saw his expression change, she knew that it was something very dreadful. When he had finished he folded the letter, put it in his pocket, and with a muttered excuse, left the house with Fand running anxiously at his heels. He had returned several hours later, exhausted and wet through from the rain, still unable to speak to her; and thus had begun several days of deep anxiety for her, as Benedict sank into a personal black hell where she could not reach or touch him.

He was very busy at that time – it lacked only a month to the official opening of the first section of railway from Leicester to Staunton Road, and there was a great deal of finishing off to do – and he plunged himself into his work with the evident desire of distracting himself. But the terrible blackness went with him, and it hurt Liza to witness how punctiliously he treated all those around him, as though he were dealing with beings from another world; how politely he thanked her for the meals she put in front of him, though it was plain he might as well have been eating straw for all he tasted it. She tried to talk to him, lightly, about normal, everyday things, and sometimes he answered her, and sometimes he plainly didn't hear her, staring blankly from the other side of the barrier that had come down between him and the world. Fand sat near him, watching him, distressed; and when occasionally she reached up and pawed at his knee, he would absently stroke her head or pull her ears, which satisfied neither of them.

431

Then at last it broke, one night when they were in bed together. He had been lying on his back, sleepless, staring at the tester; Liza lay beside him, equally unable to sleep, listening to him breathing. Suddenly he reached out a hand, encountered her shoulder, and turning over onto his side facing her, ran it down over her body. She kept quite still, trying to listen to his thoughts. He moved his hand lightly back and forth over the curve of her belly, which was just beginning to show now; and then drew a great, shuddering sigh which seemed to be torn up from the depths of his soul.

'What is it, Benedict?' she asked him tentatively.

'You're going to be a mother,' he said. And then suddenly he was crying. She gathered him into her arms and he sobbed, his head on her shoulder, his arms tightly round her as if only she could save him from the abyss; terrible racking sobs that hurt him to cry.

When at last the storm was over and he lay quietly, hitching his breath like a child, she stroked his head tenderly. 'It was the letter, wasn't it?' She felt him nod. 'Can you tell me what was in it?'

And after a while, he told her everything. 'I should have written,' he said at the end. 'I should have gone back there and told her the truth. Now she's dead, and she died thinking I didn't love her, that I cared more for my career than her.'

'You did what you thought right,' Liza said.

'Did I? Or did I do what was easiest? Did I give in to my wounded pride? Oh, but Liza, I never thought she would die! She wasn't so very old, really, not even sixty! I always thought there was time. And now she's dead, and I wasn't there, and I didn't even go to the funeral. I'll never see her again!'

He cried again. After a while she said, 'What will you do? About your brother, I mean. From what your sister says it sounds as if he's quite mad.'

'Oh no,' Benedict said, shocked, 'only terribly grieved! He and Mama were always close, and since Papa died, it's really just been the two of them. He will come to his senses at last – provided he has the right people around him, and the right attention.' He lapsed into thought.

Liza said. 'You're worried about him.'

'Yes. Well, this business of refusing all visitors – even

sending Sophie away – it can't be good for him to be shut up all alone with nothing but the servants for company. And Sophie doesn't like this man of his – thinks him encroaching. I wish Father Moineau hadn't left. I must say, I think that was heartless of him, to go off leaving Nicky all alone at such a time.'

'I'm thinking of that little girl,' Liza said tentatively. 'What must it be like for her?'

'Yes, that's a queer business,' Benedict said thoughtfully, but she could hear he was thinking about something else. Soon it came out. 'Liza, what would you think about leaving Leicestershire?'

'To go where?' she asked carefully. Was he going to send her away? It was a fear which lived in the corner of her mind all the time.

'Well, you know that we are nearly finished here. In July the first section will open —'

'But you said it will be another year before the rest of the line to Swannington is finished.'

'Oh yes, but this is only a little mineral line, pretty small beer really. There are great things afoot, Liza! Now that the Reform Act has gone through, we shall have much more sympathetic parliaments, and there are going to be new railways springing up everywhere. I expect you've heard talk about the scheme to extend the Liverpool and Manchester railway to Birmingham, as the first stage in taking it all the way to London?'

'Isn't there a dispute about it?' she asked. She was growing nervous. Grand plans might not have a place in them for small people like her.

'Yes, but only about the route – no-one disputes that the extension ought to be built! It will take a year or two, I imagine, before the works begin, and when they begin, I want to be part of them —' He paused, seeming to hesitate over what he was about to say.

'Well, I'm sure Mr Stephenson will want you to work for him,' she said helpfully. 'He always seems pleased with your work.'

'I'll always be grateful to Mr Stephenson,' Benedict said firmly, as if someone had challenged the idea, 'but there's no doubt there are disadvantages to working for him. The company is so badly run; and they try to save money by leaving important work to inexperienced apprentices, so that things go wrong and cost a great deal to untangle. And even with the extra I'm being given now I've qualified, the wages really aren't very good. Railway promoters all need good engineers: a man who knows what he's doing should be able to command a high salary.'

'You are a good engineer,' she said.

'I think I am,' he said modestly. 'And the point I'm coming to is this, Liza: the Leeds and Selby company is advertising for an engineer. It's going to be quite an important railway – double track! – and if I were to secure the position, it would be very good experience for me, as well as a much higher salary; and then I should be in a strong position to get a senior appointment when the Manchester and Birmingham railway comes to be built. *And*,' he went firmly on as Liza drew breath to say something, 'I would be only twenty miles or so from York. It would be much easier to keep an eye on Nicky, and on Morland Place for that matter.'

As he paused for breath Liza took the opportunity of saying what she had been trying to say for some time. 'You must apply for the position. I'm sure you are right, and that it's the best thing for you. And they'd be fools if they did not take you.'

'Do you think so?' In the darkness he sounded almost shy, like a boy.

'I know so,' she said firmly.

'And you wouldn't mind living in Yorkshire?'

'You really want me to come with you?'

'Of course. Why should you doubt it? But would you come?'

After a brief pause her voice came through the darkness with a lift of joy. 'I would go *anywhere* with you. And I would love to see where you come from.'

He put his arms round her and found her face for kissing, then settled with his head next to hers, and his hand over the curve of her belly. 'The salary they mention is very good. We could have a nice little house for our son to be born in. He'd be a little Yorkshire lad after all.'

434

'What if *he's* a little lass?' she challenged.

'Oh, I like Leicestershire lasses the best,' he said, and proceeded to demonstrate the point to the satisfaction of both.

Nicholas was riding back from Twelvetrees, deep in gloomy thought. Checkmate wanted his dinner, and since his ears were pointing homewards, he broke into a trot whenever he felt his rider's attention wander; Nicky would post for a few paces, then realise he had not given the office to trot and pull his horse down to a walk. A few minutes later his attention would wander and Checkmate would slip carefully into a trot again.

Ferrars, riding just behind, found this an exhausting procedure, and as soon as the track widened sufficiently he pushed Beau up alongside Checkmate. 'Walk or trot, one or the other. I wish you would make up your mind,' he said.

Nicholas turned slowly to look at him. 'What?' he said in surprise. 'Were you talking to me?'

'I said that it is the sign of a weak mind, to keep changing it.' Nicholas stared at him, baffled and wondering whether to be affronted. Ferrars smiled inwardly. 'It is also the sign of a weak mind to indulge in regrets.'

'What are you talking about? You're babbling, man.'

'Not at all, sir. I merely point out that having killed your mother to get what you want, it is the act of a simpleton to spoil your enjoyment by repining.'

Nicholas paled so rapidly that he seemed to turn almost green. His eyes were aghast. 'What – what are you talking about?' he whispered, his mouth dry. 'Killed my —? My mother died of cholera!'

'Very clever of you, I thought,' Ferrars said in a matter-of-fact voice. 'Even Havergill didn't suspect, though if he had examined the symptoms more carefully he might have wondered. But as he was expecting cholera, naturally cholera was what he saw.'

'It was cholera!' Nicholas cried in terror. 'What else could it have been?'

Ferrars shook his head with a reproachful smile. 'You don't need to keep up the pretence with me, sir. After all, I know the 'pothecary you got the stuff from. I saw you talking to him. Vomiting, diarrhoea and stomach and leg cramps: the

435

same symptoms as cholera. A cleverly chosen poison.'

'Poison?' Nicky repeated, almost wildly.

'And who filled your mother's glass each time during that last dinner? Who gave her her draughts with his own hands when she was helpless in bed during her last illness? Why, her loving son, who would not allow anyone else to come near her, so tenderly did he care for her in her suffering.'

'You're mad!' Nicky cried in a strangled voice. 'I wouldn't kill her! I loved her! You mustn't say such things! If you don't hold your tongue, I'll — I'll —'

'Kill me?' Ferrars suggested silkily.

'I'll dismiss you! I'll send you away!'

'Oh, I don't think so. How could you manage without me? And I know so many of your little secrets, don't I, sir? What happened that last time you went to see Annie, for instance – do you remember?' Nicky was staring at him with his eyes bulging in fear. He looked, Ferrars thought, quite mad. 'Perhaps you really don't remember. I've often wondered how far it is a voluntary thing, this way you have of forgetting unpleasant things. Very useful it must prove at times. But if I could remind you about that unhappy day —'

'No!'

' —or about your father, perhaps. Odd, wasn't it, how such an experienced horseman could break his neck in a simple little fall like that?'

'*No! No! No!*' Nicky's cries were high and thin – like a rabbit's in the teeth of a stoat, Ferrars thought. Nicky's eyes bulged darkly like a rabbit's, too. 'I didn't – I wasn't – *it wasn't me!*'

'Don't you worry, sir,' Ferrars said soothingly, catching Checkmate's rein as the hack, startled by Nicholas's cries, broke into a jumpy trot. 'I'll take care of you. You have nothing to fear as long as I'm here to keep you safe.'

'What —?' You —?'

'That's right, sir. I'll take care of everything. I always have, haven't I?'

Nicholas stared, trying to calm his mind enough to catch hold of a thought or a meaning. 'You'll take care of things?'

'Since you ask me to, yes, I will,' Ferrars said obligingly. 'Of course, it's a lot of work, but I don't mind that – for you, sir. Perhaps it would be better, though, if you gave me some proper position, with authority over the other servants. They might not take my orders if they don't understand that I am your plenipotentiary.' Nicholas only stared at him, helpless, and Ferrars, satisfied, said, 'I might be called your agent, don't you think? After all, I'm not really your groom or your valet any more, am I? I do much more important things for you. *Agent* sounds well, I think.'

'Steward,' Nicholas said suddenly. Ferrars looked enquiringly. 'There always used to be a steward at Morland Place. He took charge of everything, answerable to the master only. We haven't had one for a long time, though.'

'Time we revived the office, then, don't you think? Steward of Morland Place – yes, that sounds well. I suppose that's why you have the steward's room,' he added conversationally. 'I wondered about that. Well, since you press me so, Mr Nicholas, I will be your steward. And the first thing I must do as your steward is to sort out the lamentable state of the service in your house. You will need a valet, since I will be too busy with other responsibilities. I have a man in mind who ought to do very well. And the butler and housekeeper will have to go. They are much too old and quite incompetent, besides being grown dreadfully disrespectful lately. I will find suitable replacements for them, people loyal to me – which is to say, to you, sir, since I am to be your other self.'

He looked sharply at Nicky to see if he would object, but Nicholas only stared dazedly ahead, no longer really listening. 'Do as you please,' he said. He was sinking back into his unhappy thoughts. It would be good to have Ferrars take care of all the troublesome details of everyday life. A competent man, Ferrars – and Papa had not wanted to hire him in the first place! But Papa had no idea about servants. What would he do without Ferrars now, he wondered? The man was invaluable.

Ah, there was the house now, coming into sight round the bend in the track. His, Nicholas thought with a little spurt of warmth. All his! He had got it at last, after all the trials and tribulations, after all the plots against him, all the people who had tried to cheat him. Well, he had had the laugh of them! Morland Place was his, and he could do whatever he liked with it, more powerful in his small realm than the King of England. Checkmate broke into a trot again at the sight of home, and Nicholas let him this time, tapping him on with his heel and even letting him break into a few steps of a canter on the downhill slope. Home, and comfort, and dinner. He could have anything he liked for dinner, he thought with a small spurt of triumphant pleasure. The cook would have to make *his* favourite dishes from now on; and he would never have another dish of spinach on his table as long as he lived!

The grooms in the yard took the horses, and the two men trod up the steps and in through the great door, held open ceremoniously by Ottershaw. You'll be on your way soon, my lad, Nicholas thought, and gave him a small smile of such maliciousness that Ottershaw blenched, and looked instinctively at Ferrars, walking only half a pace behind his master. But Ferrars' face was unreadable.

As they crossed the hall, Matty came in from the inner courtyard, escorting Jemima back from her walk. The little girl was dressed from head to foot in crow black — bonnet, pelisse, mittens, everything — so that only her small white face was showing. She paused at the sight of Nicholas and shrank back a little to let him go through to the staircase hall first, and he bestowed one glance on her as he passed. One glance at the face, still bewildered with grief, pale and thin and shadowed about the eyes; and one thought for the fact that, though one would never guess it, the child was probably the richest eleven-year-old in Yorkshire, for she had of course inherited her father's entire fortune, together with his business and all its profits.

And of course she was entirely in his, Nicholas's, care. He passed on with Ferrars, leaving her behind, and thinking that it was a pity really that she *was* only eleven. Mama had wanted him to get married, and little as he liked the idea, he supposed it would be his duty sooner or later. When he married – *if* he married – it would of course have to be an heiress; but an eleven-year-old was really out of the question. Still, he might decide to marry her later on, he thought as he started up the stairs. She was in his care and under his complete control until she was twenty-one; she couldn't go anywhere. There was plenty of time.